Philip Massinger, Thomas Coxeter

The Dramatic Works of Philip Massinger

Compleat. in four volumes. Vol. 3

Philip Massinger, Thomas Coxeter

The Dramatic Works of Philip Massinger
Compleat. in four volumes. Vol. 3

ISBN/EAN: 9783337344948

Printed in Europe, USA, Canada, Australia, Japan

Cover: Foto ©Andreas Hilbeck / pixelio.de

More available books at **www.hansebooks.com**

WORKS

OF

PHILIP MASSINGER.

VOLUME the THIRD.

CONTAINING,

A NEW WAY TO PAY OLD DEBTS.
The GREAT DUKE of FLORENCE.
The UNNATURAL COMBAT.
The BASHFUL LOVER.

<hr>

LONDON:

Printed for T. DAVIES in *Ruffel-Street, Covent-Garden,*
MDCCLXI.

A NEW WAY

TO

PAY OLD DEBTS.

A

COMEDY.

As it hath been often acted at the *Phœnix* in *Drury-Lane*, by the Queen's Majesty's Servants. 1633.

WRITTEN

By PHILIP MASSINGER.

To the Right Honourable
ROBERT Earl of Carnarvan,
Master Falconer of England.

My Good Lord,

PARDON I beseech you my Boldness, in pre-suming to shelter this Comedy under the Wings of your Lordship's Favour and Protection. I am not ignorant (having never yet deserved you in my Service) that it cannot but meet with a severe Con-struction, if in the Clemency of your noble Disposition, you fashion not a better Defence for me, than I can fancy for myself. All I can allege is, that divers Italian Princes, and Lords of eminent Rank in England, have not dis-dained to receive, and read Poems of this Nature; nor am I wholly lost in my Hopes, but that your Honour (who have ever express'd yourself a Favourer, and Friend to the Muses) may vouchsafe, in your gracious Acceptance of this Trifle, to give me Encouragement to present you with some laboured Work, and of a higher Strain, hereafter. I was born a devoted Servant to the thrice noble Family of your incom-parable Lady, and am most ambitious, but with a becoming Distance, to be known to your Lordship, which, if you please to admit, I shall embrace it as a Bounty, that while I live shall oblige me to acknowledge you for my noble Patron, and profess myself to be,

Your Honour's true Servant,

PHILIP MASSINGER.

A 2

Dramatis

Dramatis Perſonæ.

Lovell, an *Engliſh* Lord.
Sir Giles Overreach, a cruel Extortioner.
Wellborn, a Prodigal.
Allworth, a young Gentleman, Page to Lord *Lovell*.
Greedy, a hungry Juſtice of Peace.
Marrall, a Term-driver; a Creature of Sir *Giles Overreach*'s.
Order,
Amble,
Furnace,
Watchall, } Servants to the Lady *Allworth*.
Well-do, a Parſon.
Tapwell, an Alehouſe-keeper.
Three Creditors.

The Lady Allworth. a rich Widow.
Margaret, *Overreach*'s Daughter.
Waiting Woman.
Chambermaid.
Froth, *Tapwell*'s Wife.

A

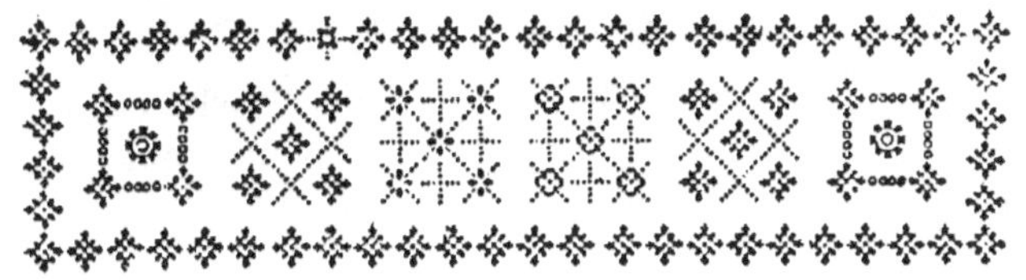

A NEW WAY
TO
PAY OLD DEBTS.

ACT I. SCENE I.

Wellborn, Tapwell, Froth.

Wellborn.

O Bouze? nor no Tobacco?
 Tapwell. Not a Suck, Sir;
Nor the Remainder of a single Cann
Left by a drunken Porter, all Night pall'd too.
Froth. Not the Dropping of the Tap for your Morn-
  ing's Draught, Sir:
'Tis Verity, I assure you.
 Wellborn. Verity, you Brach!
The Devil turn'd Precisian! Rogue, what am I?
 Tapwell. Troth! durst I trust you with a Looking-
  Glass,
To let you see your trim Shape, you would quit me,
And take the Name yourself.
 Wellborn. How! Dog?
 Tapwell. Even so, Sir.
And I must tell you, if you but advance
Your pile-worn Cloak, you shall be soon instructed
There dwells, and within Call (if it please your Worship)
A potent monarch call'd the Constable,

A 3

That

That does command a Citadel call'd the Stocks ;
Whose Guards are certain Files of lusty Billmen,
Such as with great Dexterity will hawl
Your tatter'd, louzy ——

    Wellborn. Rascal ! Slave !

    Froth. No Rage, Sir.

    Tapwell. At his own Peril ! Do not put yourself
In too much Heat, there being no Water near
To quench your Thirst ; and sure for other Liquor,
As mighty Ale, or Beer, they are Things, I take it,
You must no more remember ; not in a Dream, Sir.

      Wellborn. Why, thou unthankful Villain, dar'st thou
               talk thus ?
Is not thy House, and all thou hast, my Gift ?

    Tapwell. I find it not in Chalk ; and *Timothy Tapwell*
Does keep no other Register.

    Wellborn. Am not I He
Whose Riots fed and cloath'd thee ? Wert thou not
Born on my Father's Land, and proud to be
A Drudge in his House ?

    Tapwell. What I was, Sir, it skills not :
What you are, is apparent. Now for a Farewell :
Since you talk of Father, in my Hope it will torment
            you,
I'll briefly tell your Story. Your dead Father,
My *quondam* Master, was a Man of Worship ;
Old Sir *John Wellborn*, Justice of Peace and *Quorum* ;
And stood fair to be *Custos Rotulorum* ;
Bore the whole Sway of the Shire, kept a great House,
Reliev'd the Poor, and so forth : but he dying,
And the Twelve Hundred a Year coming to you,
Late Master *Francis*, but now forlorn *Wellborn* ——

    Welborn. Slave, stop ! or I shall lose myself.

    Froth. Very hardly ;
You cannot be out of your Way.

    Tapwell. But to my Story.
You were then a Lord of Acres, the prime Gallant,
And I your under Butler : Note the Change now :
You had a merry Time of't ; Hawks and Hounds,
                     With

With Choice of Running Horfes; Miftreffes
Of all Sorts and all Sizes, yet fo hot
As their Embraces made your Lordfhip melt;
Which your Uncle, Sir *Giles Overreach*, obferving,
Refolving not to lofe a Drop of 'em,——
On foolifh Mortgages, Statutes, and Bonds,
For a while fupply'd your Loofenefs, and then left you.
   Wellborn. Some Curate hath penn'd this invective,
      Mongrel,
And you have ftudy'd it.
   Tapwell. I have not done yet:
Your Land gone, and your Credit not worth a Token,
You grew the common Borrower, no Man 'fcap'd
Your Paper-pellets, from the Gentleman
To the Beggars on Highways, that fold you Switches
In your Gallantry.
   Wellborn. I fhall fwitch your Brains out.
   Tapwell. When poor *Tim Tapwell*, with a little Stock,
Some Forty Pounds or fo, bought a fmall Cottage;
Humbled myfelf to Marriage with my *Froth* here,
Gave Entertainment———
   Wellborn. Yes, to Whores, and Canters,
Clubbers by Night.
   Tapwell. True, but they brought in Profit,
And had a Gift to pay for what they call'd for;
And ftuck not like your Mafterfhip. The poor Income
I glean'd from them, hath made me in my Parifh
Thought worthy to Scavenger; and in Time
May rife to be Overfeer of the Poor;
Which if I do, on your Petition, *Wellborn*,
I may allow you Thirteen-pence a Quarter;
And you fhall thank my Worfhip.
   Wellborn. Thus, you Dog-bolt———
And thus———   [*Beats and kicks him.*
   Tapwell. Cry out for Help!
   Wellborn. Stir, and thou dieft:
Your potent Prince the Conftable fhall not fave you.
Hear me, ungrateful Hell-Hound! did not I
Make Purfes for you? Then you lick'd my Boots,
A 4

And

And thought your Holiday Cloak too coarfe to clean 'em.
'Twas I that, when I heard thee fwear, if ever
Thou could'ft arrive at Forty Pounds, thou would'ft
Live like an Emperor; 'twas I that gave it
In ready Gold.   Deny this, Wretch!
    Tapwell. I muft, Sir.
For from the Tavern to the Taphoufe, all,
On forfeiture of their Licences, ftand bound, [1]
Never to remember who their beft Guefts were,
If they grew poor like you.
    Wellborn. They are well rewarded
That beggar themfelves to make fuch Cuckolds rich.
Thou Viper, thanklefs Viper! impudent Bawd!
But fince you are grown forgetful, I will help
Your Memory, and tread thee into Mortar;
Not leave one Bone unbroken.
    Tapwell. Oh!
    Froth. Afk Mercy.

Enter Allworth.

    Wellborn. 'Twill not be granted.
    Allworth. Hold for my Sake, hold!
Deny me, *Frank?* They are not worth your Anger.
    Wellborn. For once thou haft redeem'd them from this
       Scepter.
But let 'em vanifh, creeping on their Knees;
And, if they grumble, I revoke my Pardon.
    Froth. This comes of your prating Hufband; you
       prefum'd
On your ambling Wit, and muft ufe your glib Tongue,
Though you are beaten lame for't.

---

[1] *On Forfeiture of their Licences ftand bound*
    Never to remember, &c.

  I have printed this after the old Copies.   Mr. *Dodfley* in his Collec-
tion reads,

      On Forfeiture of their *Licence* ftand bound
      Never to remember who *the* beft Guefts were, *&c.*

                      Tapwell.

Tapwell. Patience, *Froth* !
There's Law to cure our Bruiſes.
                [*They go off on their Hands and Knees.*
    Wellborn. Sent for to your Mother ?
    Allworth. My Lady, *Frank*, my Patroneſs ! my all !
She's ſuch a Mourner for my Father's Death,
And in her Love to him, ſo favours me,
That I cannot pay too much Obſervance to her :
There are few ſuch Step-dames.
    Wellborn. 'Tis a noble Widow,
And keeps her Reputation pure, and clear
From the leaſt Taint of Infamy : Her Life
With the Splendor of her Actions leaves no Tongue
To Envy, or Detraction.   Pry'thee tell me ;
Has ſhe no Suitors ?
    Allworth. Even the beſt of the Shire, *Frank*,
My Lord excepted : Such as ſue, and ſend,
And ſend, and ſue again ; but to no Purpoſe.
Their frequent Viſits have not gain'd her Preſence ;
Yet ſhe's ſo far from Sullenneſs and Pride,
That I dare undertake you ſhall meet from her
A liberal Entertainment.   I can give you
A Catalogue of her Suitors Names.
    Wellborn. Forbear it,
While I give you good Counſel.   I am bound to it ;
Thy Father was my Friend ; and that Affection
I bore to him, in Right deſcends to thee.
Thou art a handſome and a hopeful Youth,
Nor will I have the leaſt Affront ſtick on thee,
If I with any Danger can prevent it.
    Allworth. I thank your noble Care ; but, pray you, in
        what
Do I run the Hazard ?
    Wellborn. Art thou not in Love ?
Put it not off with Wonder.
    Allworth. In Love, at my Years ?

Welborn.

Wellborn. You think you walk in Clouds, but are
        tranfparent, [2]
I have heard all, and the Choice that you have made;
And, with my Finger, can point out the North Star,
By which the Loadftone of your Folly's guided:
And to confirm this true, what think you of
Fair *Margaret*, the only Child, and Heir
Of *Cormorant Overreach* ? Do'ft blufh and ftart,
To hear her only nam'd ? Blufh at your want
Of Wit and Reafon.

    Allworth. You are too bitter, Sir.

    Wellborn. Wounds of this Nature are not to be cur'd
With Balms, but Corrofives.   I muft be plain :
Art thou fcarce manumiz'd from the Porter's Lodge,
And yet fworn Servant to the Pantophle,
And dar'ft thou dream of Marriage ? I fear
'Twill be concluded for impoffible,
That there is now, nor ere fhall be hereafter,
A handfome Page, or Player's Boy of fourteen,
But either loves a Wench, or Drabs love him;
Court-waiters not exempted.

    Allworth. This is Madnefs.
How ere you have difcover'd my Intents,
You know my Aims are lawful; and if ever
The Queen of Flowers, the Glory of the Spring,
The fweeteft Comfort to our Smell, the Rofe
Sprung from an envious Briar, I may infer,
There's fuch Defparity in their Conditions,
Between the Goddefs of my Soul, the Daughter,
And the bafe Churl her Father.———

    Wellborn. Grant this true,
As I believe it; canft thou ever hope
To enjoy a quiet Bed with her, whofe Father
Ruin'd thy State ?

----

    [2] *You think you walk in Clouds, but are tranfparent.*
The old Reading was,

        You think you walk in Clouds, but are *tranfient,*
Which was certainly an Error of the Prefs.

                                Allworth.

Allworth. And your's too.

Wellborn. I confess it true.
I must tell you as a Friend, and freely,
That, where Impossibilities are apparent,
'Tis Indiscretion to nourish Hopes.
Canst thou imagine, (let not Self-love blind thee)
That Sir *Giles Overreach*, who to make her great
In swelling Titles, without touch of Conscience,
Will cut his Neighbour's Throat (and I hope his own too)
Will ere consent to make her thine? Give o'er,
And think of some Course suitable to thy Rank,
And prosper in it.

Allworth. You have well advis'd me.
But, in the mean Time, you that are so studious
Of my Affairs, wholly neglect your own:
Remember yourself, and in what Plight you are.

Wellborn. No matter, no matter.

Allworth. Yes, 'tis much material:
You know my Fortune, and my Means; yet something
I can spare from myself, to help your Wants.

Wellborn. How's this?

Allworth. Nay, be not angry.   There's eight Pieces
To put you in better Fashion.

Wellborn. Money from thee?
From a Boy? A Stipendary? One that lives
At the Devotion of a Stepmother,
And the uncertain Favour of a Lord?
I'll eat my Arms first.   Howsoe'er blind Fortune
Hath spent the utmost of her Malice on me;
Though I am vomited out of an Alehouse,
And thus accoutred; know not where to eat,
Or drink, or sleep, but underneath this Canopy;
Although I thank thee, I despise thy Offer.
And as I, in my Madness, broke my State,
Without th' Assistance of another's Brain,
In my right Wits I'll piece it; at the worst,
Die thus, and be forgotten.

Allworth. A strange Humour!   [*Exeunt.*

SCENE

S C E N E II.

Order, Amble, Furnace, Watchall.

Order. Set all Things right, or as my Name is *Order*,
And by this Staff of Office that commands you——
This Chain and double Ruff, Symbols of Power!
Whoever miſſes in his Function,
For one whole Week makes Forfeiture of his Breakfaſt,
And Privilege in the Wine-cellar.
   Amble. You are merry
Good Maſter Steward.
   Furnace. Let him; I'll be angry.
   Amble. Why, Fellow *Furnace*, 'tis not Twelve o'Clock
      yet,
Nor Dinner taking up; then 'tis allow'd
Cooks, by their Places, may be Cholerick.
   Furnace. You think you have ſpoke wiſely, Goodman
      Amble,
My Lady's Go-before!
   Order. Nay, nay, no wrangling.
   Furnace. 'Twit me with the Authority of the Kitchen?
At all Hours, and all Places, I'll be angry;
And thus provok'd, when I am at my Prayers
I will be angry.
   Amble. There was no Hurt meant.
   Furnace. I am Friends with thee, and yet I will be an-
      gry.
   Order. With whom?
   Furnace. No Matter whom: Yet, now I think on't,
I am angry with my Lady.
   Watchall. Heaven forbid, Man.
   Order. What Cauſe has ſhe given thee?
   Furnace. Cauſe enough, Maſter Steward:
I was entertain'd by her to pleaſe her Palate,
And, till ſhe forſwore eating, I perform'd it.
Now ſince our Maſter, noble *Allworth*, died,
Tho' I crack my Brains to find out tempting Sauces,

And

And raife Fortifications in the Paftry,
Such as might ferve for Models in the Low-Countries;
(Which, if they had been practis'd at *Breda*,
Spinola might have thrown his Cap at it, and ne'er took
    it)——
  Amble. But you had wanted Matter there to work on.
  Furnace. Matter! with fix Eggs, and a Strike of Rye
    Meal,
I had kept the Town till Doomfday; perhaps longer.
  Order. But what's this to your Pet againft my Lady?
  Furnace. What's this? Marry this, when I am three
    Parts roafted,
And the fourth Part parboil'd to prepare her Viands;
She keeps her Chamber, dines with a Panada,
Or Water-gruel, my Sweat never thought on.
  Order. But your Art is feen in the Dining-room.
  Furnace. By whom?
By fuch as pretend love her; but come
To feed upon her. Yet, of all the Harpies
That do devour her, I am out of Charity
With none fo much, as the thin gutted Squire
That's ftol'n into Commiffion.
  Order. Juftice Greedy?
  Furnace. The fame, the fame. Meat's caft away upon
    him;
It never thrives. He holds this Paradox,
Who eats not well, can ne'er do Juftice well.
His Stomach's as infatiate as the Grave,
Or Strumpets ravenous Appetites.
  Watchall. One knocks. [*Allworth knocks, and enters.*
  Order. Our late young Mafter.
  Amble. Welcome, Sir.
  Furnace. Your Hand:
If you have a Stomach, a cold Bake-meat's ready.
  Order. His Father's Picture in little.
  Furnace. We are all your Servants.
  Amble. In you he lives.
  Allworth. At once, my Thanks to all;
This is yet fome Comfort. Is my Lady ftirring?
Enter

Order. Her Prefence anfwers for us.
Lady. Sort thofe Silks Well.
I'll take the Air alone.

    [*Exeunt Waiting Woman and Chambermaid.*
Furnace. You air and air;
But will you never tafte but Spoon-meat more?
To what ufe ferve I?
 Lady. Prythee, be not angry;
I fhall er'e long; in the mean Time, there's Gold
To buy thee Aprons, and a Summer Suit.   [*Cool.*
 Furnace. I am appeas'd, [3] and *Furnace* now grows
 Lady. And, as I gave Directions, if this Morning
I am vifited by any, entertain 'em
As heretofore: But fay in my Excufe
I am indifpofed.
 Order. I fhall, Madam.
 Lady. Do, and leave me.
Nay, ftay you *Allworth.*

    [*Exeunt Order, Amble, Furnace, Watchall.*
 Allworth. I fhall gladly grow here,
To wait on your Commands.
 Lady. So foon turn'd Courtier.   [is Duty,
 Allworth. Stile not that Courtfhip, Madam, which
Purchas'd on your Part.
 Lady. Well, you fhall ov'rcome;
I'll not contend in Words. How is it with
Your noble Mafter?
 Allworth. Ever like himfelf;
No Scruple leffen'd in the full Weight of Honour:
He did Command me; (pardon my Prefumption)

---

  [3] *I am appeas'd, and Furnace now grows* Cooke.
Thus it ftands in the Old Editions. Mr. *Dodfley* reads,
   I am appeas'd, and Furnace now grows Cold.
But I think from the Senfe and Similitude it fhould be *Cool.*

          As

As his unworthy Deputy, to kiſs
Your Ladyſhip's fair Hands.
   Lady. I am honour'd in
His Favour to me. Does he hold his Purpoſe
For the Low-Countries ?
   Allworth. Conſtantly, good Madam :
But he will in Perſon, firſt preſent his Service.   [yet
   Lady. And how approve you of his Courſe ? you are
Like virgin Parchment, capable of any
Inſcription, vitious or honorable.
I will not force your Will, but leave you free
To your own Election.
   Allworth. Any Form you pleaſe,
I will put on ; but, might I make my Choice,
With humble Emulation I would follow
The Path my Lord marks to me.
   Lady. 'Tis well anſwer'd,
And I commend your Spirit : You had a Father,
(Bleſs'd be his Memory) that ſome few Hours
Before the Will of Heaven took him from me,
Who did commend you, by the deareſt Ties
Of perfect Love between us, to my Charge :
And therefore what I ſpeak, you are bound to hear
With ſuch Reſpect, as if he liv'd in me.
He was my Huſband, and how 'ere you are not
Son of my Womb, you may be of my Love,
Provided you deſerve it.
   Allworth. I have found you,
(Moſt honour'd Madam) the beſt Mother to me ;
And with my utmoſt Strength of Care and Service,
Will labour that you never may repent
Your Bounties ſhow'r'd upon me.
   Lady. I much hope it.
Theſe were your Father's Words. If ere my Son
Follow the War, tell him it is a School
Where all the Principles tending to Honour
Are taught, if truly followed : But for ſuch
As repair thither, as a Place in which
They do preſume they may with Licence practiſe
                         Their

Their Lusts and Riots; they shall never merit
The noble Name of Soldiers. To dare boldly
In a fair Cause, and for their Countries Safety
To run upon the Cannon's Mouth undaunted;
To obey their Leaders, and shun Mut'nies;
To bear with Patience the Winter's Cold,
And Summer's scorching Heat; and not to faint,
When Plenty of Provision fails, with Hunger;
Are the essential Parts make up a Soldier,
Not Swearing, Dice or Drinking.
  Allworth. There's no Syllable
You speak, but is to me an Oracle,
Which but to doubt were impious.
  Lady. To conclude,
Beware ill Company; for often Men
Are like to those with whom they do converse:
And, from one Man I warn'd you, and that's *Wellborn*:
Not 'cause he's poor, that rather claims your Pity;
But that he's in his Manners so debauch'd,
And hath to vicious Courses sold himself.
'Tis true your Father lov'd him, while he was
Worthy the loving; but if he had liv'd
To have seen him as he is, he had cast him off,
As you must do.
  Allworth. I shall obey in all Things. ◦
  Lady. Follow me to my Chamber, you shall have Gold
To furnish you like my Son, and still supply'd,
As I hear from you.
  Allworth. I am still your Creature.   [*Exeunt*.

S C E N E III.

Overreach, Greedy, Order, Amble, Furnace, Watchall.
Marrall.

  Greedy. Not to be seen?
  Overreach. Still cloistered up? Her Reason,
I hope, assures her, though she make herself
Close Prisoner ever for her Husband's Loss,

                                        'Twill

'Twill not recover him.

   Order. Sir, it is her Will;
Which we that are her Servants ought to serve,
And not dispute.   Howe'er, you are nobly Welcome;
And if you please to stay, that you may think so;
There came not six Days since from *Hull*, a Pipe
Of rich Canary, which shall spend itself
For my Lady's Honour.

   Greedy. Is it of the right Race?
   Order. Yes, Master *Greedy*
   Amble. How his Mouth runs o'er!   [Worship.
   Furnace. I'll make it run, and run: Save your good
   Greedy. Honest Master Cook, thy Hand, again! How
     I love thee.
Are the good Dishes still in being? Speak Boy.

   Furnace. If you have a Mind to feed, there is a Chine
Of Beef well seasoned.

   Greedy. Good!
   Furnace. A Pheasant larded.
   Greedy. That I might now give thanks for't!
   Furnace. Other *Kickshaws.*[4]
Besides there came last Night from the Forest of *Sherwood*,
The fattest Stag I ever cook'd.

   Greedy. A Stag, Man?
   Furnace. A Stag, Sir, Part of it prepar'd for Dinner,
And bak'd in Puff-paste

   Greedy. Puff-paste too, Sir, *Giles!*
A ponderous Chine of Beef! A Pheasant larded!
And red Deer too Sir *Giles*, and bak'd in Puff-paste!
All Business set aside; let us give thanks here.

   Furnace. How the lean Skeleton's rap'd!
   Over. You know we cannot.
   Mar. Your Worships are to sit on a Commission,
And if you fail to come, you lose the Cause.   [Dinner,

   Greedy. Cause me no Causes: I'll prove't, for such a
We may put off a Commission: You shall find it
Henrici decimo quarto.

       4 Other *Kukeshaws.*

  This is the Original, but Mr. *Dodsley* has *other quelques choses.* I
would preserve the *English Kickshaws.*

Over. Fie, Mafter *Greedy*,
Will you lofe me a thoufand Pounds for a Dinner?
No more for Shame! We muft forget the Belly,
When we think of Profit.
     Greedy. Well, you fhall o'errule me,
I could e'en cry now.   Do you hear, Mafter Cook?
Send but a Corner of that immortal Paftie;
And I, in Thankfulnefs, will by your Boy
Send you—a Brace of Three-pences.
     Furn. Will you be fo Prodigal?

Enter Wellborn.

Over. Remember me to your Lady.—Who have we
                              [here?

Wellborn. Don't you know me:
     Over. I did once, but now I will not;
Thou art no Blood of mine.   Avant, thou Beggar!
If ever thou prefume to own me more,
I'll have thee cag'd and whipp'd.
     Greedy. I'll grant the Warrant.
Think of *Pye-corner, Furnace!*
                    [*Exeunt Over. Greedy, Mar.*
     Watch. Will you out, Sir?
I wonder how you durft creep in.
     Order. This is Rudenefs
And faucy Impudence.
     Amble. Cannot you ftay
To be ferv'd among your Fellows from the Bafket,
But you muft prefs into the Hall?
     Furnace. Pry'thee vanifh
Into fome Outhoufe, though it be the Pigfty;
My Skullion fhall come to thee.

Enter Allworth.

Wellborn. This is rare:
Oh! here's *Tom Allworth, Tom!*
     Allworth. We muft be Strangers;

                                   Nor

Nor would I have you feen here for a Million.

> [*Exit Allworth.*

Wellborn. Better and better.   He contemns me too?

Enter Woman and Chambermaid.

Woman. Foh, what a Smell's here! What Thing's this?
Chamb. A Creature
Made out of the Privy. Let us hence for Love's Sake,
Or I fhall fwoon.
Woman. I begin to faint already.

> [*Exeunt Woman and Chambermaid.*

Watchall. Will you know your Way?
Amble. Or fhall we teach it you,
By the Head and Shoulders?
Wellborn. No, I will not ftir:
Do you mark, I will not. Let me fee the Wretch
That dares attempt to force me.   Why, you Slaves,
Created only to make Legs and Cringe;
To carry in a Difh, and fhift a Trencher;
That have not Souls only to hope a Blefling
Beyond black Jacks or Flagons; you that were born
Only to confume Meat and Drink, and batten
Upon Reverfions: Who advances? Who
Shews me the Way?
Order. My Lady.

Enter Lady, Woman *and* Chambermaid.

Chamb. Here's the Monfter.
Woman. Sweet Madam, keep your Glove to your Nofe.
Chamb. Or let me
Fetch fome Perfumes may be Predominant;
You wrong yourfelf elfe.
Wellborn. Madam, my Defigns
Bear me to you.
Lady. To me?
Wellborn. And though I have met with
But ragged Entertainment from your Grooms here;

B 2

I

I hope from you to receive that noble Usage,
As may become the true Friend of your Husband;
And then I shall forget these.——
      Lady. I am amaz'd,
To see, and hear this Rudeness. Dar'st thou think,
Though sworn, that it can ever find Belief,
That I, who to the best Men of this Country
Deny'd my Presence since my Husband's Death,
Can fall so low, as to change Words with thee?
Thou Son of Infamy, forbear my House!
And know, and keep the Distance that's between us:
Or, though it be against my gentler Temper,
I shall take Order, you no more shall be
An Eye-sore to me.
      Wellborn. Scorn me not, good Lady;
But as in Form you are Angelical,
Imitate the heavenly Natures, and vouchsafe
At the least awhile to hear me. You will grant
The Blood that runs in this Arm, is as noble
As that which fills your Veins; those costly Jewels,
And those Rich Clothes you wear, your Men's Observance,
And Women's Flattery, are in you no Virtues;
Nor these Rags, with my Poverty, in me Vices.
You have a fair Fame, and I know deserve it;
Yet, Lady, I must say, in nothing more,
Than in the pious Sorrow you have show'n
For your late noble Husband.
      Order. How she starts!
      Furnace. And hardly can keep finger from the Eye
To hear him nam'd.
      Lady. Have you ought else to say?   [Fortune
      Wellborn. That Husband, Madam, was once in his
Almost as low as I. Want, Debts and Quarrels
Lay heavy on him: Let it not be thought
A Boast in me, though I say, I reliev'd him.
'Twas I that gave him Fashion; mine the Sword
That did on all Occasions second his;
I brought him on and off with Honour, *Lady*:
And when in all Men's Judgments he was sunk,

                                        And

And in his own Hopes not to be buoy'd up;
I ſtep'd unto him, took him by the Hand,
And ſet him upright.

   Furnace. Are not we baſe Rogues
That could forget this?

   Wellborn. I confeſs you made him
Maſter of your Eſtate; nor could your Friends
Though he brought no Wealth with him, blame you for't;
For he had a Shape, and to that Shape a Mind
Made up of all Parts, either Great or Noble;
So winning a Behaviour, not to be
Reſiſted, Madam.

   Lady. 'Tis moſt true, he had.

   Wellborn. For his Sake then, in that I was his Friend,
Do not contemn me.

   Lad. For what's paſt, excuſe me,
I will redeem it. *Order*, give the Gentleman
A hundred Pounds.

   Wellborn. No, Madam, on no Terms:
I will not beg nor borrow Six-pence of you;
But be ſupplied elſewhere, or want thus ever.
Only one Suit I make, which you deny not
To Strangers: And 'tis this.   [*Whiſpers to her.*

   Lady. Fie, nothing elſe?   [Servants,

   Wellborn. Nothing, unleſs you pleaſe to charge your
To throw away a little Reſpect upon me.

   Lady. What you Demand is yours.

   Wellborn. I thank you, *Lady.*
Now what can be wrought out of ſuch a Suit,
Is yet in Suppoſition; I have ſaid all,
When you pleaſe you may Retire.——Nay, all's forgotten.
And for a lucky *Omen* to my Project,
Shake Hands, and end all Quarrels in the Cellar.

   Order. Agreed, Agreed.

   Furnace. Still Merry-maſter *Wellborn.*

       The End of the Firſt Act.

ACT II. SCENE I.

Overreach, Marrall.

Over. HE's gone, I warrant thee; this *Commiſſion*
    cruſh'd him.
  Mar. Your Worſhip has the Way on't, and ne'er miſs
To ſqueeze theſe Unthrifts into Air: And yet
The chap-fal'n *Juſtice* did his Part, returning
For your Advantage the *Certificate*,
Againſt his Conſcience and his Knowledge too;
(With your good Favour) to the utter Ruin
Of the poor Farmer.
    Over. 'Twas for theſe good Ends
I made him a *Juſtice.* He that bribes his Belly,
Is certain to command his Soul.
    Mar. I wonder
(Still with your Licence) why, your Worſhip having
The Power to put this thin-gut in Commiſſion,
You are not in't yourſelf?
    Over. Thou art a Fool:
In being out of Office, I am out of Danger;
Where, if I were a *Juſtice,* beſides the Trouble,
I might, or out of Wilfulneſs or Error,
Run myſelf finely into a *Premunire*;
And ſo become a Prey to the Informer.
No, I'll have none of't; 'tis enough I keep
Greedy at my Devotion; ſo he ſerve
My Purpoſes, let him Hang, or Damn, I care not.
Friendſhip is but a Word.
    Mar. You are all Wiſdom.
    Over. I would be Wordly Wiſe; for the other
    Wiſdom,
That does preſcribe us a well-govern'd Life,
And to do Right to others, as ourſelves,

I

I value not an Atom.

    Mar. What Courſe take you,
With your good Patience, to hedge in the Manor
Of your Neighbour Maſter *Frugall?* As 'tis ſaid,
He will not Sell, nor Borrow, nor Exchange;
And his Land lying in the midſt of your many Lord-
Is a foul Blemiſh.   [ſhips,

    Over. I have thought on't, *Marrall*;
And it ſhall take. I muſt have all Men Sellers,
And I the only Purchaſer.

    Mar. 'Tis moſt fit, Sir.

    Over. I'll therefore buy ſome Cottage near his Ma-
        nor;
Which done, I'll make my Men break ope his Fences;
Ride o'er his ſtanding Corn, and in the Night
Set Fire on his Barns, or break his Cattles Legs.
Theſe Treſpaſſes draw on Suits; and Suits, Expences:
Which I can ſpare, but will ſoon beggar him.
When I have harried him thus Two or Three Years,
Tho' he ſue *in forma pauperis*, in ſpite
Of all his Thrift and Care, he'll grow behind hand.

    Mar. The beſt I ever heard! I could adore you.

    Over. Then, with the Favour of my Man of Law,
I will pretend ſome Title: Want will force him
To put it to Arbitrement: Then if he ſell
For Half the Value, he ſhall have Ready Money,
And I poſſeſs his Land.

    Mar. 'Tis above Wonder!
Wellborn was apt to ſeil, and needed not
Theſe fine Arts, Sir, to hook him in.

    Over. Well thought on.
This Varlet, *Wellborn*, lives too long, to upbraid me
With my cloſe Cheat put upon him. Will not Cold
Nor Hunger kill him?

    Mar. I know not what to think on't.
I have us'd all Means; and the laſt Night I caus'd
His Hoſt the Tapſter to turn him out of Doors;
And have been ſince with all your Friends and Tenants,
And on the Forfeit of your Favour charg'd them,
B 4

Though

Though a Cruſt of mouldy Bread would keep him from
        ſtarving,
Yet they ſhould not relieve him.   This is done, Sir.
    Over. That was ſomething, *Marrall*, but thou muſt
        go farther ;
And ſuddenly, *Marrall.*
    Mar. Where, and when you pleaſe, Sir.
    Over. I would have thee ſeek him out : and, if thou
Perſuade him that 'tis better ſteal, than beg.   [canſt,
Then if I prove he has but robb'd a Henrooſt,
Not all the World ſhall ſave him from the Gallows.
Do any thing to work him to Deſpair,
And 'tis thy Maſterpiece.
    Mar. I will do my Beſt, Sir.
    Over. I am now on my main Work, with the Lord
        Lovell,
The Gallant-minded, Popular Lord *Lovell* ;
The Minion of the People's Love.   I hear
He's come into the Country ; and my Aims are
To inſinuate myſelf into his Knowledge,
And then invite him to my Houſe.
    Mar. I have you.
This points at my young Miſtreſs.
    Over. She muſt part with
That humble Title, and write Honourable,
Right Honourable, *Marrall !* My Right Honourable
        Daughter !
If all I have, or e'er ſhall get, will do it.
I will have her well attended ; there are Ladies
Of Errant Knights decay'd, and brought ſo low,
That for caſt Cloaths and Meat will gladly ſerve her.
And 'tis my Glory, though I come from the City
To have their Iſſue whom I have undone,
To kneel to mine, as Bond-Slaves.
    Mar. 'Tis fit State, Sir.
    Over. And therefore, I'll not have a Chambermaid
That ties her Shoes, or any meaner Office,
But ſuch whoſe Fathers were Right Worſhipful.
'Tis a rich Man's Pride ! there having ever been

More

More than a Fewd, a ſtrange Antipathy,
Between us and true Gentry.

Enter Wellborn.

Mar. See! who's here, Sir ? [5]
Over. Hence, Monſter Prodigy !
Wellborn. Sir, your Wife's Nephew ;
She and my Father tumbled in one Belly.
    Over. Avoid my Sight ! thy Breath's infectious,
      Rogue !
I ſhun thee as a Leproſy, or the Plague.
Come hither, *Marrall,* this is the Time to work him.
[Exit Overreach.

    Mar. I warrant you, Sir.
    Wellborn. By this Light, I think he's mad.
    Mar. Mad ! had you took Compaſſion on yourſelf,
You long ſince had been mad.
    Wellborn. You have took a Courſe,
Between you and my venerable Uncle,
To make me ſo.
    Mar. The more dull ſpirited you,
That would not be inſtructed. I ſwear deeply ——
    Wellborn. By what ?
    Mar. By my Religion.
    Wellborn. Thy Religion !
The Devil's Creed !—But what would you have done ?
    Mar. Had there been but one Tree in all the Shire,
Nor any Hope to compaſs a penny Halter,
Before, like you, I had outliv'd my Fortunes,
A With had ſerv'd my Turn to hang myſelf ;
And preſently, as you love your Credit.
    Wellborn. I thank you.

    5 *See! who's here, Sir ?*

    I cannot help thinking but ſomething is loſt here. *Marrall* ſays,
See! who's here, Sir ? Over. Hence, Monſter, Prodigy ! Wellborn
anſwers as if the other had ſaid, *Who,* or *what art thou ?* ——
Sir, your Wife's Nephew, She, and my Father, &c.
Mar.

Mar. Will you ſtay till you die in a Ditch, or Lice
    devour you ?
Or if you dare not do the Feat yourſelf,
But that you'll put the State to Charge and Trouble,
Is there no Purſe to be cut ? Houſe to be broken ?
Or Market-Women with Eggs that you may murder,
And ſo diſpatch the Buſineſs ?
    Wellborn. Here's Variety,
I muſt confeſs ; but I'll accept of none
Of all your gentle Offers, I aſſure you.
    Mar. Why, have you Hope ever to eat again ?
Or drink ? or be the Maſter of Three Farthings ?
If you like not Hanging, Drown yourſelf : Take ſome
    Courſe
For your Reputation.
    Wellborn. 'Twill not do, dear Tempter :
With all the Rhetorick the Fiend hath taught you.
I am as far as thou art from Deſpair,
Nay, I have Confidence, which is more than Hope,
To live, and ſuddenly, better than ever.
    Mar. Ha ! ha ! theſe Caſtles you build in the Air
Will not perſuade me, or to give, or lend
A Token to you.
    Wellborn. I'll be more kind to thee.
Come, thou ſhalt dine with me.
    Mar. With you ?
    Wellborn. Nay more, dine *gratis.*
    Mar. Under what Hedge, I pray you ? Or at whoſe
Coſt ? Are they Padders, or Abram-men, that are your
    Conforts ?
    Wellborn. Thou art incredulous, but thou ſhalt dine
Not alone at her Houſe, but with a gallant Lady ;
With me, and with a Lady,
    Mar. Lady ! what Lady ?
With the Lady of the Lake, or Queen of Fairies ?
For I know, it muſt be an enchanted Dinner.
    Wellborn. With the Lady *Allworth,* Knave.
    Mar. Nay, now there's Hope
Thy Brain is crack'd.

Wellborn.

Wellborn. Mark there, with what Refpect
I am entertain'd.
   Mar. With Choice no doubt of Dog-whips.
Why doft thou ever hope to pafs her Porter?
   Wellborn. 'Tis not far off, go with me: Truft thine
         own Eyes.
   Mar. Troth, in my Hope, or my Affurance, rather,
To fee thee curvet, and mount like a Dog in a Blanket,
If ever thou prefume to pafs her Threfhold,
I will endure thy Company.
   Wellborn. Come along then.   *[Exeunt.*

SCENE II.

Allworth, *Waiting-woman, Chambermaid,* Order, Am-
     ble, Furnace, Watchall.

   Woman. Could you not command your Leifure one
        Hour longer?
   Chamb. Or half an Hour?
   Allworth. I have told you what my Hafte is:
Befides, being now another's, not mine own,
Howe'er I much defire to enjoy you longer,
My Duty fuffers, if to pleafe myfelf
I fhould negleft my Lord.
   Woman. Pray you do me the Favour
To put thefe few Quince-Cakes into your Pocket,
They are of mine own preferving.
   Chamb. And this Marmulade;
'Tis comfortable for your Stomach.
   Woman. And, at parting,
Excufe me if I beg a Farewell from you.
   Chamb. You are ftill before me. I move the fame
        Suit, Sir.   -   *[Kiffes 'em feverally.*
   Furnace. How greedy thefe Chamberers are of a
        beardlefs Chin!
I think the Titts will ravifh him.
   Allworth. My Service
To both.
                              Woman.

Woman. Ours wait on you.
Chamb. And ſhall do ever.
Order. You are my Lady's Charge, be therefore
That you ſuſtain your Parts.   [careful
Woman. We can bear, I warrant you.
                    Exeunt Woman and Chambermaid.
Furnace. Here, drink it off; the Ingredients are
And this the true Elixir; it hath boil'd   [Cordial,
Since Midnight for you.   'Tis the Quinteſſence
Of five Cocks of the Game, ten Dozen of Sparrows,
Knuckles of Veal, Potatoe-roots, and Marrow;
Coral, and Ambergriſe: Were you two Years older,
And I had a Wife, or gameſome Miſtreſs,
I durſt truſt you with neither: You need not bait
After this, I warrant you; though your Journey's long,
You may ride on the Strength of this till To-morrow
          Morning.
Allworth. Your Courteſies overwhelm me: I much
          grieve
To part from ſuch true Friends, and yet I find Comfort;
My Attendance on my Honourable Lord,
(Whoſe Reſolution holds to viſit my Lady)
Will ſpeedily bring me back.
          [*Knocking at the Gate*; Marrall *and* Wellborn
               within.
Mar. Dar'ſt thou venture further?
Wellborn. Yes, yes, and knock again.
Order. 'Tis he; diſperſe.
Amble. Perform it bravely.
Furnace. I know my Cue; ne'er doubt me.
                    [*They go off ſeveral Ways.*
Watchall. Beaſt that I was to make you ſtay: Moſt
You were long ſince expected.   [welcome;
Wellborn. Say ſo much
To my Friend, I pray you.
Watchall. For your Sake, I will, Sir.
Mar. For his Sake!

                              Wellborn.

Wellborn. Mum ; this is nothing.

Mar. More than ever
I would have believ'd, though I had found it in my
    Primer.

Allworth. When I have given you Reasons for my
    late Harshness,
You'll pardon and excuse me : For, believe me,
Though now I part abruptly, in my Service
I will deserve it.

Mar. Service ! with a Vengeance !

Wellborn. I am satisfied : Farewell *Tom.*

Allworth. All Joy stay with you.   [*Exit* Allworth.

Enter Amble.

Amble. You are happily encounter'd : I never yet
Presented one so welcome, as I know
You will be to my Lady.

Mar. This is some Vision ;
Or sure these Men are mad, to worship a Dunghill ;
It cannot be a Truth.

Wellborn. Be still a Pagan,
An unbelieving Infidel ; be so, Miscreant !
And meditate on Blankets, and on Dog-Whips.

Enter Furnace.

Furnace. I am glad you are come ; untill I know your
    Pleasure
I know not how to serve up my Lady's Dinner.

Mar. His Pleasure ! is it possible ?

Wellborn. What's thy Will ?

Furnace. Marry, Sir, I have some Growse, and *Turky*
    Chicken,
Some Rails, and Quails, and my Lady will'd me t' ask
What kind of Sauces best affect your Palate,   [you
That I may use my utmost Skill to please it.

                             Mar.

Mar. The Devil's enter'd this Cook; Sauce for his
    Palate
That on my Knowledge, for almoſt this Twelvemonth,
Durſt wiſh but Cheeſeparings and brown Bread on *Sun-*
    days.
Wellborn. That Way I like 'em beſt.——
Furnace. It ſhall be done, Sir.   [*Exit* Furnace.
Wellborn. What think you of the Hedge we ſhall dine
    under ?
Shall we feed *gratis ?*
Mar. I know not what to think ;
Pray you make me not mad.

Enter Order.

Order. This Place becomes you not ;
Pray you walk, Sir, to the Dining Room.
Wellborn. I am well here,
'Till her Ladyſhip quits her Chamber.
Mar. Well here, ſay you ?
'Tis a rare Change ! but Yeſterday you thought
Yourſelf well in a Barn, wrapp'd up in Peaſe-ſtraw.

Enter Woman *and* Chambermaid.

Woman. O ! Sir, you are wiſh'd for.
Chambermaid. My Lady dream't, Sir, of you.
Woman. And the firſt Command ſhe gave, after ſhe
    roſe,
Was (her Devotions done) to give her Notice
When you approach'd here.
Chambermaid. Which is done, on my Virtue.
Mar. I ſhall be converted ; I begin to grow
Into a new Belief, which Saints, nor Angels,
Could have won me to have Faith in.
Woman. Sir, my Lady——

Enter

Enter Lady.

Lady. I come to meet you, and languish'd till I saw
  you.
This first Kiss is for me; I allow a second
To such a Friend.
  Mar. To such a Friend! Heav'n bless me!
  Wellborn. I am wholly yours; yet Madam, if you
  please
To grace this Gentleman with a Salute.
  Mar. Salute me at his Bidding!
  Wellborn. I shall receive it
As a most high Favour.
  Lady. Sir, you may command me.
  Wellborn. Run backward from a Lady! and such a
  Lady!
  Mar. To kiss her Foot is, to poor me, a Favour
I am unworthy of——   [*Offers to kiss her Foot.*
  Lady. Nay, pray you rise;
And since you are so humble, I'll exalt you:
You shall dine with me to Day, at mine own Table.
  Mar. Your Ladyship's Table! I am not good enough
To sit at your Steward's Board.
  Lady. You are too modest:
I will not be deny'd.

Enter Furnace.

Furnace. Will you still be babling,
Till your Meat freeze on the Table? The old Trick still:
My Art ne'er thought on!
  Lady, Your Arm, Master *Wellborn:*
Nay, keep us Company.
  Mar. I was never so grac'd.
  [*Exeunt* Wellborn, Lady, Amble, Marall, Woman.
  Order. So, we have play'd our Parts, and are come
  off well.

But

But if I know the Myſtery, why my Lady
Conſented to it, or why Maſter *Wellborn*
Deſir'd it, may I periſh.
    Furnace. Would I had
The roaſting of his Heart that cheated him,
And forces the poor Gentleman to theſe Shifts.
By Fire! (for Cooks are *Perſians*, and ſwear by it)
Of all the griping, and extorting Tyrants
I ever heard or read of, I ne'er met
A Match to Sir *Giles Overreach*.
    Watchall. What will you take
To tell him ſo, Fellow *Furnace?*
    Furnace. Juſt as much
As my Throat is worth, for that would be the Price on't.
To have a Uſurer that ſtarves himſelf,
And wears a Cloak of one and twenty Years,
Or a Suit of fourteen Groats, bought of the Hangman,
To grow rich, and then purchaſe, is too common :
But this Sir *Giles* feeds high, keeps many Servants,
Who muſt at his Command do any Outrage ;
Rich in his Habit, vaſt in his Expences,
Yet he to Admiration ſtill increaſes
In Wealth, and Lordſhips.
    Order. He frights Men out of their Eſtates,
And breaks through all Law-nets, made to curb ill Men,
As they were Cobwebs.   No Man dares reprove him.
Such a Spirit to dare, and Power to do, were never
Lodg'd ſo unluckily.

                Enter Amble.

    Amble. Ha, ha! I ſhall burſt.
    Order. Contain thyſelf Man.
    Furnace. Or make us Partakers
Of your ſudden Mirth.
    Amble. Ha, ha! my Lady has got
Such a Gueſt at her Table—this Term-driver *Marall*—
This Snip of an Attorney.
    Furnace. What of him, Man?
                                Amble.

Amble. The Knave thinks ftill he's at the Cook's Shop
    in *Ram alley*,
Where the Clerks divide, and the Elder is to choofe—
And feeds fo flovenly !
    Furnace. Is this all ?
    Amble. My Lady
Drank to him for fafhion Sake, or to pleafe Mafter
As I live, he rifes, and takes up a Difh,   [*Wellborn.*
In which there were fome Remnants of a boil'd Capon,
And Pledges her in Whitebroth.
    Furnace. Nay, 'tis like
The reft of his Tribe.
    Amble. And when I brought him Wine,
He leaves his Stool, and after a Leg or two
Moft humbly thanks my Worfhip.
    Order. Rifen already.
    Amble. I fhall be chid.

Enter Lady, Wellborn, Marall.

    Furnace. My Lady frowns.
    Lady. You wait well——
Let me have no more of this, I obferv'd your Jeering.
Sirrah, I'll have you know, whom I think worthy
To fit at my Table, be he ne'er fo mean;
When I am prefent, is not your Companion.
    Order. Nay, fhe'll preferve what's due to her. [*Afide.*
    Furnace. This refrefhing,
Follows your Flux of Laughter,
    Lady. You are Mafter   [To *Wellborn.*
Of your own Will. I know fo much of Manners,
As not to enquire your Purpofes; in a Word,
To me you are ever welcome, as to a Houfe
That is your own.
    Wellborn. Mark that.
    Mar. With Reverence, Sir,
And it like your Worfhip.
    Wellborn. Trouble yourfelf no farther,

Dear Madam ; my Heart's full of Zeal, and Service,
However in my Language I am sparing.
Come, Master *Marrall.*

   Mar. I attend your Worship.

[Exeunt Wellborn, Mar.

   Lady. I see in your Looks you are sorry, and you
      know me
An easy Mistress : Be merry ; I have forgot all.
Order and *Furnace* come with me.   I must give you
Further Directions.

   Order. What you please.

   Furnace. We are ready. [Exeunt.

S C E N E III.

Wellborn, Marrall.

   Wellborn. I think I am in a good Way.

   Mar. Good Sir ! the best Way ;
The certain best Way.

   Wellborn. There are Casualties
That Men are subject too.

   Mar. You are above 'em,
And as you are already Worshipful,
I hope e'er long you will increase in Worship,
And be Right Worshipful.

   Wellborn. Pry'thee do not flout me.
What I shall be, I shall be.   Is't for your Ease,
You keep your Hat off ?

   Mar. Ease, and it like your Worship ?
I hope *Jack Marrall* shall not live so long,
To prove himself such an unmannerly Beast,
Though it hail Hazel Nuts, as to be cover'd
When your Worship's present.

   Wellborn. Is not this a true Rogue ?   [*Aside.*
That out of meer Hope of a future Cos'nage
Can turn thus suddenly : 'Tis rank already.

   Mar. I know your Worship's wife, and needs no
[Counsel :
Yet

Yet if in my Defire to do you Service,
I humbly offer my Advice, (but ftill
Under Correction) I hope I fhall not
Incur your high Difpleafure.
   Wellborn. No ; fpeak freely.   [ment,
   Mar. Then in my Judgment, Sir, my fimple Judg-
(Still with your Worfhip's Favour) I could wifh you
A better Habit, for this cannot be
But much diftafteful to the noble Lady
(I fay no more) that loves you : For this Morning,
To me (and I am but a Swine to her) .
Before th' Affurance of her Wealth perfum'd you,
You favour'd not of Amber.
   Wellborn. I do now then ? [6]
   Mar. This your Battoon hath got a Touch of it.
                [*Kiffes the End of his Cudgel.*
Yet if you pleafe, for Change, I have Twenty Pounds
                          [here,
Which, out of my true Love, I prefently   [you
Lay down at your Worfhip's Feet : 'Twill ferve to buy
A Riding Suit.
   Wellborn. But where's the Horfe ?
   Mar. My Gelding
Is at your Service : Nay, you fhall ride me,
Before your Worfhip fhall be put to the Trouble
To walk a Foot.   Alas ! when you are Lord
Of this Lady's Manor (as I know you will be) .   [acre,
You may with the Leafe of Glebe Land, call'd *Knaves-*
(A Place I would manure) requite your Vaffal.
   Wellborn. I thank thy Love : But muft make no ufe
What's Twenty Pounds ?   [of it.
   Mar. 'Tis all that I can make, Sir.
   Wellborn. Doft thou think, though I want Clothes, I
       could not have 'em,

---

[6] *I do now then ?*

   Mr. *Dodfley* reads, *Do I now then ?*—The old Reading is right, for
Marral fays, *This Morning before the Affurance of her Wealth had perfum'd you—you favour'd not of Amber.* Wellborn replies, *I do now then,*
giving him at the fame Time his Cudgel to fmell to.

For one Word to my Lady?

Mar. As I know not that——   [thee.

Wellborn. Come, I'll tell thee a Secret, and so leave
I'll not give her the Advantage, though she be
A gallant minded Lady, after we are married
(There being no Woman, but is sometimes froward)
To hit me in the Teeth, and say she was forc'd
To buy my Wedding Clothes, and took me on,
With a plain Riding-suit, and an ambling Nag.
No, I'll be furnish'd something like myself.
And so farewell; for thy Suit touching Knaves-acre,
When it is mine, 'tis thine.   [*Exit* Wellborn.

Mar. I thank your Worship.
How was I cozen'd in the Calculation
Of this Man's Fortune! My Master cozen'd too,
Whose Pupil I am in the Art of undoing Men;
For that is our Profession. Well, well, Master *Wellborn*,
You are of a sweet Nature, and fit again to be cheated:
Which, if the Fates please, when you are possess'd
Of the Land and Lady, you *sans Question* shall be.
I'll presently think of the Means.   [*Walks by, musing.*

Enter Overreach *speaking to a Servant.*

Over. Sirrah! take my Horse.
I'll walk to get me an Appetite.   'Tis but a Mile;
And Exercise will keep me from being pursey.
Ha! *Marral!* is he conjuring? Perhaps
The Knave has wrought the Prodigal to do
Some Outrage on himself, and now he feels
Compunction in his Conscience for't: No matter
So it be done.   *Marrall!*
Mar. Sir.
Over. How succeed we
In our Plot on *Wellborn?*
Mar. Never better, Sir.
Over. Has he hang'd, or drown'd himself?
Mar. No, Sir, he lives;

Lives

Lives once more to be made a Prey to you:
A greater Prey than ever.
    Over. Art thou in thy Wits?
If thou art, reveal this Miracle, and briefly.
    Mar. A Lady, Sir, is fal'n in Love with him,
    Over. With him! what Lady?
    Mar. The rich Lady *Allworth.*
    Over. Thou Dolt; how dar'ft thou fpeak this?
    Mar. I fpeak Truth;
And I do fo but once a Year; unlefs
It be to you, Sir.   We din'd with her Ladyfhip:
I thank his Worfhip.
    Over. His Worfhip!
    Mar. As I live, Sir;
I din'd with him, at the great Lady's Table,
Simple as I ftand here; and faw when fhe kifs'd him;
And would at his Requeft, have kifs'd me too;
But I was not fo audacious, and fome Youths are, [7]
And dare do any Thing be it ne'er fo abfurd,
And fad after Performance.
    Over. Why, thou Rafcall,
To tell me thefe Impoffibilities:
Dine at her Table! and kifs him! or thee!
Impudent Varlet.   Have not I myfelf,
To whom great *Counteffes* Doors have oft flew open;
Ten Times attempted, fince her Hufband's Death,
In vain to fee her, though I came a Suitor:
And yet your good Sollicitor-fhip, and Rogue *Wellborn,*
Were brought into her Prefence, feafted with her.——
But that I know thee a Dog that cannot blufh,
This moft incredible Lye would call up one
On thy Buttermilk Cheeks.

----

    [7] *But I was not fo audacious,* &c.

Mr. *Dodfley* has this Paffage,

        But I was not fo audacious *as* fome Youths are,
        And dare do any Thing, *&c.*

I think the old Reading right—if not, it ought to read,
        Who dare, *&c.*
                C 3   *Mar.*

Mar. Shall I not truſt my Eyes, Sir ?
Or taſte ? I feel her good Cheer in my Belly.
    Over. You ſhall feel me, if you give not over Sirrah :
Recover your Brains again ; and be no more gull'd
With a Beggar's Plot, aſſiſted by the Aids
Of ſerving Men and Chambermaids ; for, beyond theſe,
Thou never ſaw'ſt a Woman ; or I'll quit you
From my Employments.
    Mar. Will you credit this yet.
On my Confidence of their Marriage, I offer'd *Wellborn*
(I would give a Crown now, I durſt ſay his Worſhip)
                                        [*Aſide.*

My Nag, and twenty Pounds.
    Over. Did you ſo Ideot ? [8]   [*Strikes him down.*
Was this the Way to work him to Deſpair
Or rather to croſs me ?
    Mar. Will your Worſhip kill me ?
    Over. No, no ; but drive the lying Spirit out of you.
    Mar. He's gone.
    Over. I have done then : Now forgetting
Your late imaginary Feaſt and Lady,
Know my Lord *Lovell* dines with me To-morrow :
Be careful nought be wanting to receive him ;
And bid my Daughter's Women trim her up
Though they paint her, ſo ſhe catch the Lord ; I'll thank
        'em,
There's a Piece for my late Blows.
    Mar. I muſt yet ſuffer :
But there may be a Time.   [*Aſide.*
    Over. Do you grumble ?
    Mar. No, Sir.   [*Exeunt.*

        [8] *Did you ſo I doe.*
    Thus it ſtood in the Original. Mr. *Dodſly* reads,
            Did you ſo ?
    Which Reading makes the Verſe bad ; I fancy it ſhould be—
            Did you ſo Ideot ? Or elſe, *Did you ſo Dog ?*
    Which reads ſtill better, and is not improbable.
        The End of the Second Act.

                                    A C T

A C T III. S C E N E I.

Lovell, Allworth, *Servants.*

Lovell. WALK the Horses down the Hill:
            something in private
I muſt impart to *Allworth*.   [*Exeunt Servant.*
   Allworth. O my Lord!
What Sacrifice of Reverence, Duty, Watching;
Altho' I could put off the Uſe of Sleep,
And ever wait on your Commands to ſerve 'em;
What Dangers, though in ne'er ſo horrid Shapes,
Nay Death itſelf, though I ſhould run to meet it,
Can I, and with a thankful Willingneſs, ſuffer;
But ſtill the Retribution will fall ſhort
Of your Bounties ſhower'd upon me.
   Lovell. Loving Youth;
Till what I purpoſe be put into act,
Do not o'er-prize it; ſince you have truſted me
With your Soul's neareſt, nay, her deareſt Secret,
Reſt confident, 'tis in a Cabinet lock'd,
Treachery ſhall never open. I have found you
(For ſo much to your Face I muſt profeſs,
Howe'er you guard your Modeſty with a Bluſh for't)
More zealous in your Love, and Service to me,
Than I have been in my Rewards.
   Allworth. Still great ones,
Above my Merit.
   Lovell. Such your Gratitude calls 'em:
Nor am I of that harſh and rugg'd Temper
As ſome Great Men are tax'd with, who imagine
They part from the Reſpect due to their Honours,
If they uſe not all ſuch as follow 'em,
Without Diſtinction of their Births, like Slaves.
I am not ſo condition'd: I can make
A fitting Difference between my Foot-boy,

C 4

And

And a Gentleman by Want compell'd to ferve me.

Allworth. 'Tis thankfully acknowledg'd; you have
More like a Father to me than a Mafter.   [been
Pray you, pardon the Comparifon.

Lovell. I allow it;
And to give you Affurance I am pleas'd in't,
My Carriage and Demeanour to your Miftrefs,
Fair *Margaret*, fhall truly witnefs for me,
I can command my Paffions.

Allworth. 'Tis a Conqueft
Few Lords can boaft of when they are tempted.—Oh!

Lovell. Why do you figh? Can you be doubtful of
By that fair Name, I in the Wars have purchas'd, [me?
And all my Actions, hitherto untainted!
I will not be more true to mine own Honour,
Than to my *Allworth.*

Allworth. As you are the brave Lord *Lovell*,
Your bare Word only given, is an Affurance
Of more Validity and Weight to me,
Than all the Oaths bound up with Imprecations,
Which, when they would deceive, moft Courtiers practice;
Yet being a Man (for fure to ftile you more
Would relifh of grofs Flattery) I am forc'd,
Againft my Confidence of your Worth and Virtues,
To doubt, nay more, to fear.

Lovell. So young, and jealous?

Allworth. Were you to encounter with a fingle Foe,
The Victory were certain: But to ftand
The Charge of two fuch potent Enemies,
At once affaulting you, as Wealth and Beauty,
And thofe too feconded with Power, is Odds
Too great for *Hercules.*

Lovell. Speak your Doubts and Fears,
Since you will nourifh 'em, in plainer Language,
That I may underftand 'em.

Allworth. What's your Will,
Though I lend Arms againft myfelf, (provided
They may advantage you) muft be obey'd.

My

My much lov'd Lord, were *Margaret* only fair,
The Cannon of her more than earthly Form,
Though mounted high, commanding all beneath it,
And ramm'd with Bullets of her sparkling Eyes,
Of all the Bulwarks that defend your Senses
Could batter more, but that which guards your Sight.
But when the well-tun'd Accents of her Tongue
Make Musick to you, and with numerous Sounds
Assault your Hearing, such as if *Ulysses*
Now liv'd again (howe'er he stood the Syrens)
Could not resist ; the Combat must grow doubtful
Between your Reason and rebellious Passions.
Add this too ; when you feel her touch, and breath
Like a soft western Wind, when it glides o'er
Arabia, creating Gums and Spices ;
And in the Van, the Nectar of her Lips
Which you must taste, bring the Battalia on,
Well arm'd, and strongly liv'd with her Discourse,
And knowing Manners, to give Entertainment ;
Hyppolitus himself would leave *Diana*,
To follow such a *Venus*.

    Lovell. Love hath made you
Poetical, *Allworth*.

    Allworth. Grant all these beat off,
(Which if it be in Man to do, you'll do it)
Mammon, in Sir *Giles Overreach*, steps in
With Heaps of ill got Gold, and so much Land,
To make her more remarkable, as would tire
A Falcon's Wings in one Day to fly over.
O my good Lord ! these powerful Aids, which would
Make a mishapen *Negro* beautiful,
(Yet are but Ornaments to give her Lustre,
That in herself is all Perfection) must
Prevail for her. I here release your Trust ;
'Tis Happiness, enough, for me to serve you ;
And sometimes, with chaste Eyes, to look upon her.

    Lovell. Why, shall I swear ?

    Allworth. O, by no means, my Lord !
And wrong not so your Judgment to the World,

As

As from your fond Indulgence to a Boy,
Your Page, your Servant, to refuse a Blessing
Divers great Men are Rivals for.

    Lovell. Suspend
Your Judgment 'till the Trial.   How far is it
T' *Overreach*'s House ?

    Allworth. At the most some half Hour's Riding ;
You'll soon be there.

    Lovell. And you the sooner freed
From your jealous Fears.

    Allworth. O that I durst but hope it !   [*Exeunt.*

S C E N E II.

Overreach, Greedy, Marrall.

    Over. Spare for no Cost ; let my Dressers crack with
Of curious Viands.   [the Weight

    Greedy. Store indeed's no Sore, Sir

    Over. That Proverb fits your Stomach, Master *Greedy.*
And let no Plate be seen but what's pure Gold,
Or such whose Workmanship exceeds the Matter
That it is made of : Lay my choicest Linnen,
Perfume the Room, and when we wash, the Water
With precious Powders mix, to please my Lord,
That he may with Envy wish to bathe so ever.

    Mar. 'Twill be very chargeable.

    Over. Avaunt, you Drudge :
Now all my labour'd Ends are at the Stake,
Is't a Time to think of Thrift ?   Call in my Daughter.
And, Master Justice, since you love choice Dishes,
And Plenty of 'em ——

    Greedy. As I do, indeed, Sir,
Almost as much as to give Thanks for 'em.

    Over. I do confer that Province, with my Power
Of absolute Command to have Abundance,
To your best Care.

    Greedy. I'll punctually discharge it,

And

And give the beft Directions.——Now am I
In mine own Conceit a Monarch, at the leaft,
Arch-prefident of the Boil'd, the Roaft, the Bak'd;
For which I will eat often, and give Thanks,
When my Belly's brac'd up like a Drum; and that's
      pure Juftice.
   Over. It muft be fo.—Should the foolifh Girl prove
      modeft,   [*Exit* Greedy.
She may fpoil all; fhe had it not from me,
But from her Mother: I was ever forward,
As fhe muft be, and therefore I'll prepare her

            Enter Margaret.

Alone — and let your Women wait without.
   Marg. Your Pleafure, Sir?
   Over. Ha! this is a neat Dreffing!
Thefe orient Pearls, and Diamonds well plac'd too!
The Gown affects me not; it fhould have been
Embroiderid o'er and o'er with Flowers of Gold;
But thefe rich Jewels and quaint Fafhion help it.
And, how below? fince oft the wanton Eye,
The Face obferv'd, defcends unto the Foot;
Which being well proportion'd, as yours is,
Invites as much as perfect White and Red,
Though without Art. How like you your new Woman,
The Lady *Downfaln?*
   Marg. Well, for a Companion;
Not as a Servant.
   Over. Is fhe humble, *Meg*;
And careful too; her Ladyfhip forgotten?
   Marg. I pity her Fortune.
   Over. Pity her. Trample on her.
I took her up in an old tatter'd Gown,
(Even ftarv'd for want of Two-penny Chops) to ferve
      thee:
And if I underftand, fhe but repines
To do thee any Duty, though ne'er fo fervile,
I'll pack her to her Knight, where I have lodg'd him,
                       In

In the Counter, and there let 'em howl together.

    Marg. You know your own Ways; but for me, I
                                   [blush,
When I command her, that was once attended
With Perfons, not inferior to myfelf
In Birth.

    Over. In Birth. Why art thou not my Daughter?
The bleft Child of my Induftry and Wealth?
Why, foolifh Girl; wa'ft not to make thee great,
That I have ran, and ftill purfue thofe Ways
That hale down Curfes on me, which I mind not?
Part with thefe humble Thoughts, and apt thyfelf
To the noble State I labour to advance thee;
Or, by my Hopes to fee thee Honourable,
I will adopt a Stranger to my Heir,
And throw thee from my Care; do not provoke me.

    Marg. I will not, Sir; mould me which way you
      pleafe.

    Over. How, interrupted?

Enter Greedy.

    Greedy. 'Tis matter of Importance.
The Cook, Sir, is felf-will'd, and will not learn
From my Experience. There's a Fawn brought in, Sir,
And, for my Life, I cannot make him roaft it,
With a *Norfolk* Dumpling in the Belly of it;
And, Sir, we wife Men know, without the Dumpling
'Tis not worth Three-pence.

    Over. Would it were whole in thy Belly,
To ftuff it out; Cook it any way, prythee, leave me.

    Greedy. Without Order for the Dumpling?

    Over. Let it be dumpl'd
Which way thou wilt; or tell him, I will fcall'd him
In his own Caldron.

    Greedy. I had loft my Stomach
Had I loft my Miftrefs's Dumpling, I'll give thanks for't.
                         [*Exit Greedy.*
                           Over.

Over. But to our Buſineſs *Meg.* You have heard who
[dines here ?

Marg. I have, Sir.
Over. 'Tis an honourable Man.
A Lord, *Meg,* and commands a Regiment
Of Soldiers ; and what's rare is one himſelf ;
A bold and underſtanding one ; and to be
A Lord, and a good Leader in one Volume,
Is granted unto few, but ſuch as riſe up
The Kingdom's Glory.

Enter Greedy.

Greedy. I'll reſign my Office,
If I be not better obey'd.
   Over. Slight, art thou frantick ?
   Greedy. Frantick, 'twould make me frantick, and
      ſtark Mad,
Were I not a *Juſtice of Peace* and *Quoram* too,
Which this rebellious Cook cares not a Straw for.
There are a Dozen of Woodcocks———
   Over. Make thyſelf
Thirteen : The Baker's Dozen.
   Greedy. I am contented,
So they may be dreſs'd to my mind ; he has found out
A new Device for Sauce, and will not diſh 'em
With Toaſts and Butter. My Father was a Taylor ;
And my Name, though a Juſtice, *Greedy Woodcock* ;
And, e'er I'll ſee my Lineage ſo abuſed,
I'll give up my Commiſſion.
   Over. Cook !—Rogue, obey him.
I have given the Word, pray you now remove yourſelf,
To a Coller of Brawn, trouble me no farther.
   Greedy. I will, and meditate what to Eat at Dinner.
                                        [*Exit Greedy.*
   Over. And as I ſaid, *Meg,* when this Gull diſturb'd us ;
This Honourable Lord, this Colonel,
I would have thy Huſband.
   Marg. There's too much Diſparity

                                        Between

Between his Quality and mine to hope it.

    Over. I more then hope, and doubt not to effect it,
Be thou no Enemy to thyself; my Wealth
Shall weigh his Titles down, and make you equals.
Now for the Means to assure him thine, observe me;
Remember he's a Courtier, and a Soldier,
And not to be trifled with, and therefore when
He comes to woo you, see you do not coy it.
This mincing Modesty hath spoil'd many a Match
By a first Refusal, in vain after hop'd for.

    Marg. You'll have me, Sir, preserve the Distance that
Confines a Virgin ?

    Over. Virgin me no Virgins.
I must have you lose that Name, or you lose me.
I will have you private—start not—I say private ;
If thou art my true Daughter, not a Bastard,
Thou wilt venture alone with one Man, though he came
Like *Jupiter* to *Semele*, and come off too :
And therefore when he kisses you, kiss close.

    Marg. I have heard this is the Strumpets Fashion, Sir,
Which I must never learn.

    Over. Learn any thing,
And from any Creature that may make thee Great ;
From the Devil himself.

    Marg. This is but Devellish Doctrine !   [*Aside*

    Over. Or if his Blood grow hot, suppose he offer
Beyond this; do not you stay 'till it cool,
But meet his Ardor ? if a Couch be near,
Sit down on't, and invite him.

    Marg. In your House,
Your own House, Sir ? for Heav'ns Sake ! what are
                            [you then ?
Or what shall I be, Sir ?

    Over. Stand not on Form ;
Words are no Substances.

    Marg. Though you could dispense
With your own Honour ; cast aside Religion
The Hopes of Heaven or fear of Hell—excuse me
In worldly policy ; this is not the Way

To

To make me his Wife, his Whore : I grant it may.
My maiden Honour fo foon yielded up,
Nay proftituted, cannot but affure him,
I that am Light to him will not hold Weight
When tempted by others : So in Judgment,
When to his Luft I have given up my Honour,
He muft, and will forfake me.

    Over. How ! forfake thee ?
Do I wear a Sword for Fafhion ? or is this Arm
Shrunk up or wither'd ? Does there live a Man
Of that large Lift I have encounter'd with,
Can truly fay I e'er gave Inch of Ground,
Nor purchas'd with his Blood that did oppofe me ?
Forfake thee when the Thing is done ? He dares not.
Give me but Proof, he has enjoy'd thy Perfon,
Though all his Captains (Eccho's to his Will,)
Stood arm'd by his Side to juftify the Wrong,
And he himfelf in the Head of his bold Troop,
Spite of his Lordfhip, and his Colonelfhip,
Or the Judge's Favour, I will make him render
A bloody and a ftrict Accompt, and force him,
By marrying thee, to cure thy wounded Honour;
I have faid it.

Enter Marrall.

    Mar. Sir, the Man of Honour's come,
Newly alighted.
    Over. In, without reply ;
And do as I Command, or thou art loft.   [*Exit Marg.*
Is the loud Mufick I gave order for,
Ready to receive him ?
    Mar. 'Tis, Sir.
    Over. Let 'em found
A princely welcome.   Roughnefs a while leave me ;
For fawning now, a Stranger to my Nature,
Muft make Way for me.   [*Loud Mufick.*

Enter

Enter Lovell, Greedy, Allworth, Marrall.

Lovell. Sir, you meet your Trouble.
Over. What you are pleas'd to ftile fo, is an Honour
Above my Worth and Fortunes.
Allworth. Strange! fo humble.
Over. A Juftice of Peace, my Lord.
[Prefents Greedy to him.
Lovell. Your Hand, good Sir.
Greedy. This is a Lord; and fome think this a Favour;
But I had rather have my Hand in my Dumpling.
[Afide.

Over. Room for my Lord.
Lovell. I mifs, Sir, your fair Daughter
To crown my Welcome.
Over. May it pleafe my Lord
To tafte a Glafs of Greek Wine firft, and fuddenly
She fhall attend, my Lord.
Lovell. You'll be obey'd, Sir.
[Exeunt all but Overreach.
Over. 'Tis to my Wifh! as foon as come, afk for her!

Enter Margaret.

Why, *Meg? Meg Overreach* — How! Tears in your
Ha! dry 'em quickly, or I'll dig 'em out.   [Eyes!
Is this a Time to whimper? Meet that Greatnefs
That flies into thy Bofom; think what 'tis
For me to fay, *My Honourable Daughter:*
And thou, when I ftand bare, to fay, put on;
Or, Father you forget yourfelf. No more,
But be inftructed, or expect —— He comes.

Enter Lovell, Greedy, Allworth, Marrall. They falute.

A black-brow'd Girl, my Lord.
Lovell. As I live, a rare one.
Allworth. He's took already: I am loft.
Over.

Over. That Kiſs
Came twanging off, I like it ; quit the Room.—
[The reſt go off.

A little baſhful, my good Lord, but you,
I hope, will teach her Boldneſs.
    Lovell. I am happy
In ſuch a Scholar : But ——
    Over. I am paſt learning,
And therefore leave you to yourſelves : Remember.
To his Daughter.
[Exit Overreach.

    Lovell. You ſee, fair Lady, your Father is ſollicitous
To have you change the barren Name of Virgin
Into a hopeful Wife.
    Marg. His Haſte, my Lord,
Holds no Power o'er my Will.
    Lovell. But o'er your Duty ——
    Marg. Which forc'd too much, may break.
    Lovell. Bend rather, Sweeteſt :
Think of your Years.
    Marg. Too few to match with yours :
And choiceſt Fruits too ſoon plucked, rot, and wither.
    Lovell. Do you think I am old ?
    Marg. I am ſure, I am too young.
    Lovell. I can advance you ——
    Marg. To a Hill of Sorrow ;
Where every Hour I may expect to fall,
But never hope firm Footing. You are noble ;
I of a low Deſcent, however rich ;
And Tiſſues match'd with Scarlet ſuit but ill.
O my good Lord, I could ſay more, but that
I dare not truſt theſe Walls.
    Lovell. Pray you truſt my Ear then.

Enter Overreach, liſtning.

    Over. Cloſe at it ! whiſpering ! this is excellent !
And by their Poſtures, a Conſent on both Parts.
    Vol. III.   D   *Enter*

Enter Greedy.

Greedy. Sir *Giles!* Sir *Giles!*

Over. The great Fiend ſtop that Clapper!   [Noon.

Greedy. It muſt ring out, Sir, when my Belly rings
The bak'd Meats are run out, the roaſt turn'd Powder.

Over. I ſhall powder you.

Greedy. Beat me to Duſt, I care not;
In ſuch a Cauſe as this, I'll die a Martyr.   [bles.

Over. Marry, and ſhall, you Barathrum of the Sham-
                                        [*Strikes him.*

Greedy. How! ſtrike a Juſtice of Peace? 'tis petty
            Treaſon,
Edwardi quinto! But that you are my Friend,
I could commit you without Bail or Mainprize.   [you

Over. Leave your Bawling, Sir, or I ſhall commit
Where you ſhall not dine To-day: Diſturb my Lord,
When he is in Diſcourſe?

Greedy. Is't a Time to talk
When we ſhould be munching?

Lovell. Ha! I heard ſome Noiſe.

Over. Mum, Villain; vaniſh: Shall we break a
            Bargain
Almoſt made up?   [*Thruſts* Greedy *off.*

Lovell. Lady, I underſtand you;
And reſt moſt happy in your Choice.   Believe it,
I'll be a careful Pilot to direct
Your yet uncertain Bark to a Port of Safety.

Marg. So ſhall your Honour ſave two Lives, and
Your Slaves for ever.   [bind us

Lovell. I am in the Act rewarded,
Since it is good; howe'er you muſt put on
An am'rous Carriage towards me, to delude
Your ſubtle Father.

Marg. I am prone to that.

Lovell. Now break we off our Conference.—Sir *Giles.*
Where is Sir *Giles?*

Enter

Enter Overreach, *and the rest.*

Over. My noble Lord; and how
Does your Lordship find her?
　Lovell. Apt, Sir *Giles*, and coming,
And I like her the better.
　Over. So do I too.
　Lovell. Yet should we take Forts at the first Assault,
'Twere poor in the Defendant. I must confirm her
With a Love-Letter or two, which I must have
Deliver'd by my Page, and you give Way to't,
　Over. With all my Soul——a towardly Gentleman!
Your Hand, good Master *Allworth*; know my House
Is ever open to you.
　Allworth. 'Twas shut 'till now.　　　　　　[*Aside.*
　Over. Well done, well done, my Honourable Daugh-
Thou'rt so already: Know this gentle Youth,　[ter:
And cherish him, my Honourable Daughter.
　Margaret. I shall, with my best Care.
　　　　　　　　　　[*Noise within as of a Coach.*

Over. A Coach!
Greedy. More Stops
Before we go to Dinner! O my Guts!

Enter Lady, and Wellborn.

Lady. If I find Welcome,
You share in it: If not, I'll back again,
Now I know your Ends; for I come arm'd for all
Can be objected.
　Lovell. How! the Lady *Allworth*!
　Over. And thus attended!
　Marg. No, I am a Dolt;　　　　　[Lovell *salutes*
　　　　　　　　the Lady, the Lady salutes Margaret.
The Spirit of Lies hath enter'd me.
　Over. Peace, Patch,
'Tis more than Wonder! an Astonishment
That does possess me wholly!
　　　　　　D 2　　　　　　　　　　　*Lovell.*

Lovell. Noble Lady,
This is a Favour to prevent my Vifit;
The Service of my Life can never equal.

 Lady. My Lord, I laid wait for you, and much hop'd
You would have made my poor Houfe your firft Inn :
And therefore doubting that you might forget me,
Or too long dwell here, having fuch ample Caufe,
In this unequal'd Beauty, for your Stay ;
And fearing to truft any but myfelf
With the Relation of my Service to you,
I borrow'd fo much from my long Reftraint,
And took the Air in Perfon to invite you.

 Lovell. Your Bounties are fo great, they rob me, Ma-
Of Words to give you Thanks.   . [dam,

 Lady. Good Sir *Giles Overreach.*   [*Salutes him.*
How doft thou, *Marrall ?* lik'd you my Meat fo ill,
You'll dine no more with me ?

 Greedy. I will when you pleafe,
And it like your Ladyfhip.

 Lady. When you pleafe, Mafter *Greedy* ;
If Meat can do it, you fhall be fatisfy'd.
And now, my Lord, pray take into your Knowledge
This Gentleman ; howe'er his Outfide's coarfe,

       [*Prefents* Wellborn.
His inward Linings are as fine and fair,
As any Man's : Wonder not, I fpeak at large :
And howfoe'er his Humour carries him
To be thus accoutred ; or what Taint foever
For his wild Life hath ftuck upon his Fame ;
He may ere long, with Boldnefs, rank himfelf
With fome that have contemn'd him. Sir *Giles Over-*
If I am welcome, bid him fo.   [*reach,*

 Over. My Nephew !
He has been too long a Stranger : Faith you have :
Pray let it be mended.

     [Lovell *conferring with* Wellborn.
 Mar. Why, Sir, what do you mean ?
This is Rogue *Wellborn*, Monfter, Prodigy,

         That

That fhould hang or drown himfelf, no Man of Wor-
Much lefs your Nephew.   [fhip,
   Over. Well, Sirrah! we fhall reckon
For this hereafter.
   Mar. I'll not lofe my Jeer,
Though I be beaten dead for't   [*Afide.*
   Wellborn. Let my Silence plead
In my Excufe, my Lord, 'till better Leifure
Offer itfelf to hear a full Relation
Of my poor Fortunes.
   Lovell. I would hear, and help 'em.
   Over. Your Dinner waits you.
   Lovell. Pray you lead, we follow.
   Lady. Nay, you are my Gueft; come, dear Mafter
      Wellborn.   [*Exeunt. Manet* Greedy.
   Greedy. Dear Mafter *Wellborn!* So fhe faid; Heav'n!
      Heav'n!
If my Belly would give me Leave, I could ruminate
All Day on this: I have granted twenty Warrants,
To have him committed, from all Prifons in the Shire,
To *Nottingham* Jail! and now, dear Mafter *Wellborn!*
And my good Nephew!—But I play the Fool
To ftand here prating, and forget my Dinner.

Enter Marrall.

Are they fet, *Marrall?*
   Mar. Long fince: Pray you a Word, Sir.
   Greedy. No Wording now.
   Mar. In troth, I muft; my Mafter
Knowing you are his good Friend, makes bold with you,
And does intreat you, more Guefts being come in
Than he expected, efpecially his Nephew,
The Table being full too, you would excufe him,
And fup with him on the cold Meat.
   Greedy. How! no Dinner
After all my Care?
   Mar. 'Tis but a Penance for
A Meal; befides, you broke your Faft.
       D 3   *Greedy,*

Greedy. That was
But a Bit to ſtay my Stomach: A Man in Commiſſion
Give Place to a Tatterdemallion!
   Mar. No bug Words, Sir;
Should his Worſhip hear you ——
   Greedy. Loſe my Dumpling too?
And butter'd Toaſts, and Woodcocks?
   Mar. Come, have Patience.
If you will diſpenſe a little with your Worſhip,
And ſit with the Waiting Women, you'll have Dumpling,
Woodcock, and butter'd Toaſts too.
   Greedy. This revives me:
I will gorge there ſufficiently.
   Mar. This is the Way, Sir.   [*Exeunt.*

S C E N E   III.

Overreach as from Dinner.

   Over. She's caught! O Woman! ſhe neglects my
           Lord,
And all her Compliments applied to *Wellborn!*
(The Garments of her Widowhood laid by,
She now appears as glorious as the Spring)
Her Eyes fix'd on him; in the Wine ſhe drinks,
He being her Pledge, ſhe ſends him burning Kiſſes,
And ſits on Thorns, till ſhe be private with him.
She leaves my Meat to feed upon his Looks;
And if in our Diſcourſe he be but nam'd,
From her a deep Sigh follows. But why grieve I
At this? It makes for me; if ſhe prove his,
All that is her's is mine, as I will work him.

Enter Marrall.

   Mar. Sir, the whole Board is troubled at your riſing.
   Over. No Matter, I'll excuſe it. Pr'ythee, *Marrall,*
Watch an Occaſion to invite my Nephew
To ſpeak with me in Private.
                                              Mar.

Mar. Who? the Rogue
The Lady fcorn'd to look on?
    Over. You are a Wag.

Enter Lady and Wellborn.

Mar. See, Sir, fhe's come, and cannot be without
        him.
    Lady. With your Favour, Sir, after a plenteous Dinner,
I fhall make bold to walk a Turn or two
In your rare Garden.
    Over. There's an Arbour too,
If your Ladyfhip pleafe to ufe it.
    Lady. Come, Mafter *Wellborn.*
                    [*Exeunt Lady and* Wellborn.
    Over. Groffer and Groffer! now I believe the Poet
Feign'd not, but was hiftorical, when he wrote
Pafiphae was enamour'd of a Bull:
This Lady's Luft's more monftrous. My good Lord,

Enter Lovell, Margaret, *and the reft.*

Excufe my Manners.
    Lovell. There needs none, Sir *Giles:*
I may ere long fay Father, when it pleafes
My deareft Miftrefs to give Warrant to it.
    Over. She fhall feal to it, my Lord, and make me
        happy.

Enter Wellborn *and the Lady.*

Marg. My Lady is return'd.
    Lady. Provide my Coach,
I'll inftantly away: My Thanks, Sir *Giles,*
For my Entertainment.
    Over. 'Tis your Noblenefs
To think it fuch.
    Lady. I muft do you a farther Wrong,
In taking away your honourable Gueft.

D 4

Lovell.

Lovell. I wait on you, Madam, farewell good Sir *Giles.*

Lady. Good Miſtreſs *Margaret!* nay, come Maſter
    Wellborn,
I muſt not leave you behind, in ſooth, I muſt not.

Over. Rob me not, Madam, of all Joys at once.
Let my Nephew ſtay behind : He ſhall have my Coach,
And, after ſome ſmall Conference between us
Soon overtake your Ladyſhip.

Lady. Stay not long, Sir.

Lovell. This parting Kiſs : You ſhall every Day hear
By my faithful Page.   [from me

Allworth. 'Tis a Service I am proud of.

    [*Exeunt* Lovell, Lady, Allworth, Margaret, Marrall.

Over. Daughter, to your Chamber.   You may won-
After ſo long an Enmity between us,   [der, Nephew,
I ſhould deſire your Friendſhip ?

Wellborn. So I do, Sir.
'Tis ſtrange to me.

Over. But I'll make it no Wonder,
And what is more, unfold my Nature to you.
We worldly Men, when we ſee Friends and Kinſmen,
Paſt Hope, ſunk in their Fortunes, lend no Hand
To lift 'em up, but rather ſet our Feet
Upon their Heads, to preſs 'em to the Bottom ;
As I muſt yield, with you I practis'd it :
But now I ſee you in a Way to riſe,
I can and will aſſiſt you.   This rich Lady
(And I am glad of't) is enamour'd of you ;
'Tis too apparent, Nephew.

Wellborn. No ſuch Thing :
Compaſſion rather, Sir.

Over. Well, in a Word,
Becauſe your Stay is ſhort, I'll have you ſeen
No more in this baſe Shape ; nor ſhall ſhe ſay,
She married you like a Beggar, or in Debt.

Wellborn. He'll run into the Nooſe, and ſave my La-
    bour.   [*Aſide.*

Over. You have a Trunk of rich Clothes, not far hence
                                 In

In pawn; I will redeem 'em : and, that no Clamour
May taint your Credit; for your petty Debts,
You shall have a thousand Pounds to cut 'em off,
And go a Freeman to the wealthy Lady.
 Wellborn. This done, Sir, out of Love, and no Ends
 Over. As it is, Nephew.   [else——
 Wellborn. Binds me still your Servant. [supp'd
 Over. No Compliments; you are stay'd for: e'er y've
You shall hear from me. My Coach, Knaves, for my
To-morrow I will visit you.   [Nephew:
 Wellborn. Here's an Uncle
In a Man's Extremes ! how much they do bely you
That say you are hard-hearted !
 Over. My Deeds, Nephew,
Shall speak my Love; what Men report, I weigh not.
          [*Exeunt.*

The End of the Third Act.

<hr>

ACT IV. SCENE I.

Lovell, Allworth.

Lovell. 'TIS well. Give me my Cloak : I now dis-
      charge you
From further Service. Mind your own Affairs;
I hope they will prove successful.
 Allworth. What is blest
With your good Wish, my Lord, cannot but prosper.
Let after-times report, and to your Honour,
How much I stand engag'd; for I want Language
To speak my Debt: yet if a Tear or two
Of joy, for your much Goodness, can supply
My Tongues Defects, I could——
 Lovell. Nay, do not melt:
           This

This ceremonial Thanks to me's superfluous. 9
   Over. within. Is my Lord stirring?
   Lovell. 'Tis he! oh, here's your Letter! let him in.

Enter Overreach, Greedy, Marrall.

   Over. A good Day to my Lord.
   Lovell. You are an early Riser,
Sir *Giles.*
   Over. And Reason, to attend your Lordship.
   Lovell. And you too, Master *Greedy*, up so soon?
   Greedy. In troth, my Lord, after the Sun is up
I cannot sleep; for I have a foolish Stomach
That croaks for Breakfast. With your Lordship's Favour,
I have a serious Question to demand
Of my worthy Friend Sir *Giles.*
   Lovell. Pray you use your Pleasure.
   Greedy. How far, Sir *Giles*, and pray you answer me
Upon your Credit, hold you it to be
From your Manor House, to this of my Lady *Allworth's?*
   Over. Why, some four Miles
   Greedy. How! four Miles good Sir *Giles*
Upon your Reputation, think better;
For if you do abate but one half quarter
Of five, you do yourself the greatest Wrong
That can be in the World: for four Miles riding
Could not have rais'd so huge an Appetite
As I feel gnawing on me.
   Mar. Whether you ride,
Or go a foot, you are that Way still provided,
And it please your Worship.
   Over. How now, Sirrah? Prating

---

   9 *This ceremonial Thanks to me's superfluous.*

This is the old Reading which I have followed. Mr. *Dodsley* reads,
    This ceremonial *of* Thanks, &c.
We might alter it yet, and read,
    These ceremonial, &c.
    This ceremonious Thanks to me's superfluous.

Before

Before my Lord? No Difference? Go to my Nephew,
See all his Debts difcharg'd, and help his Worfhip
To fit on his rich Suit.

Mar. I may fit you too;
Tofs'd like a Dog ftill.   [*Exit* Marrall.

Lovell. I have writ this Morning
A few Lines to my Miftrefs, your fair Daughter.

Over. 'Twill fire her, for fhe's wholly your's already:
Sweet Mafter *Allworth*, take my Ring; 'twill carry you
To her Prefence, I dare warrant you; and there plead
For my good Lord, if you fhall find Occafion.
That done, pray ride to *Nottingham*; get a Licence,
Still by this Token. I'll have it difpatch'd,
And fuddenly, my Lord; that I may fay
My Honourable, nay, Right Honourable Daughter.

Greedy. Take my Advice young Gentleman; get your
          Breakfaft.
'Tis unwholfome to ride fafting. I'll eat with you;
And eat to purpofe.

Over. Some Furies in that Gut:
Hungry again! did you not devour this Morning,
A Shield of Brawn, and a Barrel of *Colchefter* Oyfters?

Greedy. Why that was, Sir, only to fcour my Stomach,
A kind of a Preparative. Come, Gentleman, [10]
I will not have you feed like the Hangman of *Flufbing*
Alone, while I am here.

Lovell. Hafte your Return.

Allworth. I will not fail, my Lord.

Greedy. Nor I, to line
My *Chriftmas* Coffer.   [*Exeunt* Greedy *and* Allworth.

[10] *A kind of a Preparative. Come Gentleman,*
       I will not have, &c.

Mr. *Dodfley* alters this, and reads

       A kind of Preparative. Come Gentlemen,
       I will, &c.

But to me 'tis very plain that *Greedy* by his former Advice to *All-worth*, now directs himfelf to him only; and not to the whole Company; nor could they be faid to eat *alone*, if he had not kept them Company.

Over.

Over. To my Wifh, we are private.
I come not to make Offer with my Daughter
A certain Portion ; that were poor and trivial :
In one Word, I pronounce all that is mine,
In Lands, or Leafes, ready Coin, or Goods,
With her, my Lord, comes to you ; nor fhall you have
One Motive to induce you to believe,
I live too long, fince every Year I'll add
Something unto the Heap, which fhall be your's too.
    Lovell. You are a right kind Father.
    Over. You fhall have Reafon
To think me fuch. How do you like this Seat ?
It is well wooded, and well water'd, the Acres
Fertile and rich ; would it not ferve for change
To entertain your Friends in a Summer Progrefs ?
What thinks my noble Lord ?
    Lovell. 'Tis a wholfom Air,
And well built Pile ; and fhe that's Miftrefs of it
Worthy the large Revenue.
    Over. She the Miftrefs ?
It may be fo for a Time : But let my Lord,
Say only, that he likes it, and would have it,
I fay, e'er long 'tis his.
    Lovell. Impoffible.
    Over. You do conclude too faft, not knowing me ;
Nor the Engines that I work by. 'Tis not alone
The Lady *Allworth*'s Lands ; for thofe once *Wellborn*'s,
(As by her Dotage on him, I know they will be,)
Shall foon be mine, but point out any Man's
In all the Shire, and fay they lie convenient,
And ufeful for your Lordfhip, and once more,
I fay aloud, they are your's.
    Lovell. I dare not own
What's by unjuft and cruel Means extorted :
My Fame and Credit are more dear to me,
Than fo to expofe 'em to be cenfur'd by
The publick Voice.
    Over. You run, my Lord, no Hazard.
Your Reputation fhall ftand as fair

In

In all good Men's Opinions as now:
Nor can my Actions, though condemn'd for ill,
Caft any foul Afperfion upon your's.
For, though I do contemn Report myfelf,
As a meer Sound; I ftill will be fo tender
Of what concerns you, in all Points of Honour,
That the immaculate Whitenefs of your Fame,
Nor your unqueftion'd Integrity,
Shall e'er be fullied with one Taint or Spot,
That may take from your Innocence and Candor.
All my Ambition is to have my Daughter
Right Honourable; which my Lord can make her:
And might I live to dance upon my Knee
A young Lord *Lovell*, born by her unto you,
I write *nil ultra* to my proudeft Hopes.
As for Poffeffions, and annual Rents,
Equivalent to maintain you in the Port,
Your noble Birth and prefent State require,
I do remove that Burthen from your Shoulders,
And take it on mine own : For though I ruin
The Country to fupply your Riotous Wafte,
The Scourge of Prodigals, Want, fhall never find you.
    Lovell. Are you not frighted with the Imprecations
And Curfes of whole Families, made wretched
By your finifter Practifes?
    Over. Yes, as Rocks are,
When foamy Billows fplit themfelves againft
Their flinty Ribs; or as the Moon is mov'd,
When Wolves, with Hunger pin'd, howl at her Bright-
I am of a folid Temper, and like thefe,   [nefs.
Steer on a conftant Courfe. With mine own Sword
If call'd into the Field, I can make that right,
Which fearful Enemies murmur'd at as wrong.
Now, for thofe other pidling Complaints
Breath'd out in Bitternefs; as when they call me
Extortioner, Tyrant, Cormorant, or Intruder
On my poor Neighbours Right; or grand Inclofer
Of what was common, to my private Ufe;
Nay, when my Ears are pierced with Widows cries,
And

And undone Orphans wash with Tears my Threshold;
I only think what 'tis to have my Daughter
Right Honourable; and, 'tis a powerful Charm:
Makes me insensible of Remorse or Pity,
Or the least Sting of Conscience.
　　Lovell. I admire
The Toughness of your Nature.
　　Over. 'Tis for you,
My Lord, and for my Daughter, I am Marble;
Nay more, if you will have my Character
In little, I enjoy more true Delight
In my Arrival to my Wealth, these dark
And crooked Ways, than you shall e'er take Pleasure
In spending what my Industry hath compass'd.
My Haste commands me hence: In one Word therefore,
Is it a Match?
　　Lovell. I hope, that is past Doubt now.
　　Over. Then rest secure; not the Hate of all Mankind
Nor Fear of what can fall on me hereafter,
Shall make me study ought, but your Advancement
One Story higher. An Earl! if Gold can do it.
Dispute not my Religion, nor my Faith,
Though I am borne thus headlong by my Will;
You may make Choice of what Belief you please,
To me they are equal; so, my Lord, good-morrow.
　　　　　　　　　　　　　　　　　　　　[*Exit.*

　　Lovell. He's gone—I wonder how the Earth can bear "
Such a Portent! I, that have liv'd a Soldier,
And stood the Enemies violent Charge undaunted,
To hear this Blasphemous Beast, am bath'd all over
In a cold Sweat: Yet like a Mountain he
(Confirm'd in Atheistical Assertions)

　　　" *He's gone, I wonder how the Earth can bear*
　　　　Such a Portent, &c.

　　All the Characters of this Piece are finely drawn, but that of *Over-reach* is inimitable; nothing could give us such an Idea of a designing cruel Extortioner, as the foregoing Scene, it is a Master-piece in its kind, and worthy of Observation.—Lord *Lovell* is a beautiful Contrast, and the Reflections he makes on *Overreach* is equally worth our Attention.

　　　　　　　　　　　　　　　　　　　　　　　　　　Is

Is no more fhaken, than *Olimpus* is
When angry *Boreas* loads his double Head
With fudden Drifts of Snow.

Enter Lady, Woman, Amble.

Lady. Save you, my Lord.
Difturb I not your Privacy ?
Lovell. No, good Madam ;
For your own Sake I am glad you came no fooner.
Since this Bold, Bad Man, Sir *Giles Overreach*,
Made fuch a plain Difcovery of himfelf,
And read this Morning fuch a devillifh Matins,
That I fhould think it a Sin next to his ;
But to repeat it.
Lady. I ne'er prefs'd, my Lord,
On others Privacies; yet, againft my Will,
Walking, for Health Sake, in the Gallery
Adjoining to your Lodgings, I was made
(So vehement, and loud he was) Partaker
Of his tempting Offers.
Lovell. Pleafe you to command
Your Servants hence, and I fhall gladly hear
Your wifer Counfel.
Lady. 'Tis, my Lord a Woman's,
But True and Hearty ;—wait in the next Room,
But be within call : Yet not fo near to force me
To whifper my Intents.
Amble. We are taught better
By you good Madam.
Woman. And well know our Diftance.
Lady. Do fo, and talk not, 'twill become your Breed-
    ing.   [*Exeunt* Amble *and* Woman.
Now, my good Lord; if I may ufe my Freedom,
As to an honour'd Friend ?
Lovell. You leffen elfe
Your Favour to me.
Lady. I dare then fay thus ;
As you are Noble (howe'er common Men

Make

Make fordid Wealth the Object, and fole End
Of their induftrious Aims) 'twill not agree
With thofe of eminent Blood (who are engag'd
More to prefer their Honours, than to increafe
The State left to 'em by their Anceftors)
To ftudy large Additions to their Fortunes,
And quite neglect their Births : Though I muft grant,
Riches well got, to be a ufeful Servant,
But a bad Mafter.

   Lovell. Madam, 'tis confeffed ;
But what infer you from it ?

   Lady. This, my Lord ;
That as all Wrongs, though thruft into one Scale,
Slide of themfelves off, when Right fills the other,
And cannot 'bide the Trial : So all Wealth
(I mean if Ill acquir'd) cemented to Honour
By virtuous Ways atchiev'd and bravely purchas'd,
Is but as Rubbifh pour'd into a River,
(Howe'er intended to make good the Bank)
Rend'ring the Water that was pure before,
Polluted and unwholefome.   I allow
The Heir of Sir *Giles Overreach*, *Margaret*,
A Maid well qualified, and the Richeft Match
Our North Part can make boaft of, yet fhe cannot
With all that fhe brings with her, fill their Mouths,
That never will forget who was her Father ;
Or that my Hufband *Allworth*'s Lands, and *Wellborn*'s
(How wrung from both needs now no Repetition)
Were real Motives, that more work'd your Lordfhip
To join your Families, than her Form and Virtues.
You may conceive the reft.

   Lovell. I do fweet Madam ;
And long fince have confidered it.   I know,
The Sum of all that makes a Juft Man Happy,
Confifts in the well choofing of his Wife !
And there, well to difcharge it, does require
Equality of Years, of Birth, of Fortune :
For Beauty being poor, and not cried up
By Birth or Wealth, can truly mix with neither.

And

And Wealth, where there's such Difference in Years,
And fair Defcent, muft make the Yoke uneafy:
But I come nearer.
　　Lady. Pray you do, my Lord.　　　　　　　[Daughter
　　Lovell. Were *Overreach*'s 'States thrice centupl'd; his
Millions of Degrees, much Fairer than fhe is,
(Howe'er I might urge Prefidents to excufe me)
I would not fo adulterate my Blood
By marrying *Margaret*; and fo leave my Iffue
Made up of feveral Pieces, one part Scarlet
And the other *London* Blue.　In my own Tomb
I will inter my Name firft:
　　Lady. I am glad to hear this:　　　　　　　[*Afide*
Why then, my Lord, pretend your Marriage to her?
Diffimulation but ties falfe Knots
On that ftrait Line, by which you hitherto
Have meafur'd all your Actions?
　　Lovell. I make anfwer,
And aptly, with a Queftion.　Wherefore have you,
That fince your Hufband's Death, have liv'd a ftrict
And chafte *Nun*'s Life, on the Sudden given yourfelf
To Vifits and Entertainments? Think you, Madam,
'Tis not grown publick Conference? Or the Favours
Which you too prodigally have thrown on *Wellborn*
Being too Referv'd before, incur not Cenfure?
　　Lady. I am Innocent here, and on my Life I fwear
My Ends are good.
　　Lovell. On my Soul fo are mine
To *Margaret*; but leave both to the Event:
And fince this friendly Privacy does ferve
But as an offer'd Means unto ourfelves
To fearch each other farther; you having fhewn
Your Care of me, I, my Refpect to you;
Deny me not, but ftill in Chafte Words, Madam,
An Afternoon's Difcourfe.
　　Lady. So I fhall hear you.　　　　　　　[*Exeunt.*

　　　　　　　　E　　　　　　SCENE

S C E N E II.

Tapwell, Froth.

Tapwell. Undone, undone! This was your Counsel,
[*Froth.*

Froth. Mine! I defy thee: Did not Mafter *Marrall*
(He has marr'd all I am fure) ftrictly command us
(On Pain of Sir *Giles Overreach*'s Difpleafure)
To turn the Gentleman out of Doors?

Tapwell. 'Tis true;
But now he's his Uncle's Darling, and has got
Mafter *Juftice Greedy* (fince he fill'd his Belly)
At his Commandment, to do any thing;
Woe, woe to us.

Froth. He may prove merciful.

Tapwell. Troth, we do not deferve it at his Hands.
Though he knew all the Paffages of our Houfe;
As the receiving of ftolen Goods, and Bawdry,   [him
When he was Rogue *Wellborn* no Man would believe
And then his Information could not hurt us:
But now he is Right Worfhipful again,
Who dares but doubt his Teftimony? Me thinks
I fee thee, *Froth*, already in a Cart
For a clofe Bawd; thine Eyes even pelted out
With Dirt and rotten Eggs; and my Hand hiffing
(If I fcape the Halter) with the Letter *R*.
Printed upon it.

Froth. Would that were the worft!
That were but nine Days wonder: As for Credit
We have none to lofe; but we fhall lofe the Money
He owes us, and his Cuftom; there's the Hell on't.

Tapwell. He has fummon'd all his Creditors by the
[Drum,
And they fwarm about him like fo many Soldiers
On the Pay Day; and has found out fuch a New Way
To Pay his Old Debts, as, 'tis very likely,
He fhall be Chronicl'd for it.

Froth.

Froth. He deferves it
More than ten Pageants.   But are you fure his Worſhip
Comes this way to my Lady's ?
     [*A cry within, brave Maſter Wellborn.*
Tapwell. Yes, I hear him.
Froth. Be ready with your Petition, and prefent it
To his good Grace.

Enter Wellborn *in a Rich Habit,* Greedy, Order, Furnace, *three Creditors :* Tapwell *kneeling, delivers his
 Bill of Debt.*

Wellborn. How's this ! Petition'd too ?
But note what Miracles the Payment of
A little Traſh, and a Rich Suit of Clothes
Can work upon thefe Rafcals.   I ſhall be,
I think, Prince *Wellborn.*
 Mar. When your Worſhip's married
You may be—I know what I hope to fee you.
 Wellborn. Then look thou for Advancement.
 Mar. To be known
Your Worſhip's Bailiff is the Mark I ſhoot at.
 Wellborn. And thou ſhalt hit it.
 Mar. Pray you, Sir, difpatch
Thefe needy Followers, and for my Admittance
(Provided you'll defend me from Sir *Giles.*
[*This Interim,* Tapwell *and* Froth, *flattering and bribing
   Juſtice* Greedy.
Whofe Service I am weary of) I'll fay fomething
You ſhall give me thanks for.
 Wellborn. Fear not Sir *Giles*   [me
 Greedy. Who ? *Tapwell ?* I remember thy Wife brought
Laſt New Year's Tide, a Couple of fat Turkies.   [ſhip
 Tapwell. And ſhall do every Chriſtmas, let your Wor-
But ſtand my Friend now.
 Greedy. How ?—With Maſter *Wellborn ?*
I can do any thing with him on fuch Terms ;—
         See

See you this honeſt Couple? They are good Souls,
As ever drew out Foſſet, have they not
A Pair of honeſt Faces?
    Wellborn. I o're heard you,
And the Bribe he promis'd; you are coufen'd in 'em;
For of all the Scum that grew Rich by my Riots,
This for a moſt unthankful Knave, and this
For a baſe Bawd and Whore, have worſt deſerv'd,
And therefore ſpeak not for 'em. By your Place
You are rather to do me Juſtice; lend me your Ear—
Forget his Turkies, and call in his Licence,
And at the next Fair, I'll give you a Yoke of Oxen
Worth all his Poultry.——
    Greedy. I am chang'd on the ſudden
In my Opinion! Come near; nearer, Raſcal.
And now I view him better, did you e'er ſee
One look ſo like an Arch-knave? His very Countenance,
Should an underſtanding Judge but look upon him,
Would hang him, though he were Innocent.
    Tapwell and Froth. Worſhipful Sir.   [Turkies,
    Greedy. No, though the great Turk came inſtead of
To beg any Favour, I am inexorable:
Thou haſt an ill Name: Beſides thy muſty Ale
That hath deſtroy'd many of the King's leige People,
Thou never hadſt in thy Houſe to ſtay Mens Stomachs
A Piece of *Suffolk* Cheeſe, or Gammon of Bacon,
Or any Eſculent, as the Learned call it,
For their Emolument; but ſheer drink only.
For which groſs Fault, I here do damn thy Licence,
Forbidding thee ever to Tap or Draw.
For inſtantly, I will in mine own Perſon
Command the Conſtable to pull down thy Sign;
And do it before I Eat.
    Froth. No mercy?
    Greedy. Vaniſh.
If I ſhew any, may my promis'd Oxen gore me.
    Tapwell. Unthankful Knaves are ever ſo Rewarded
                    [*Exeunt* Greedy, Tapwell, Froth.
                                    Wellborn.

Wellborn. Speak; what are you?

1. *Cred.* A decay'd Vintner, Sir,   [me
That might have thrived, but that your Wiorſhip broke
With truſting you with Muſkadine and Eggs,
And Five Pound Suppers, with your after Drinkings,
When you lodged upon the *Bankſide.*

Wellborn. I Remember.   [you.

1. *Cred.* I have not been haſty, nor e'er laid to arreſt
And therefore, Sir——

Wellborn. Thou art an Honeſt Fellow:
I'll ſet thee up again; ſee his Bill paid.
What are you?

2. *Cred.* A Taylor once, but now meer Botcher.
I gave you Credit for a Suit of Clothes,
Which was all my Stock, but you failing in Payment,
I was remov'd from the Shop-board, and confin'd
Under a Stall.

Wellborn. See him paid; and botch no more.

2. *Cred.* I aſk no Intereſt, Sir.

Wellborn. Such Taylors need not;
If their Bills are paid in one and twenty Years
They are ſeldom Loſers.——O, I know thy Face,
Thou wert my Surgeon : You muſt tell no Tales,
Thoſe Days are done.   I will pay you in Private.

Ord. A Royal Gentleman!

Furnace. Royal as an Emperor!
He'll prove a brave Maſter : my good *Lady* knew
To chooſe a Man.

Wellborn. See all Men elſe diſcharg'd;
And ſince *Old Debts are clear'd by a New Way,*
A little Bounty will not miſbecome me;
There's ſomething, honeſt Cook, for thy good Breakfaſts,
And this for your Reſpect; take't, 'tis good Gold,
And I able to ſpare it.

Ord. You are too Munificent.

Furnace. He was ever ſo.

Wellborn. Pray you on before.

E 3

3. *Cred.*

3. Cred. Heaven blefs you.   [me
Mar. At Four o'Clock the Reft know where to meet
                              [*Exeunt Order, Furnace, Creditor.*
  Wellboon. Now, Mafter *Marrall*, what's the weighty
You promis'd to impart ?   [Secret
      Mar. Sir, Time nor Place
Allow me to relate each Circumftance ;
This only in a Word : I know Sir *Giles*
Will come upon you for Security
For his Thoufand Pounds; which you muft not confent to,
As he grows in Heat (as I am fure he will)
Be you but Rough, and fay he's in your Debt
Ten Times the Sum, upon Sale of your Land ;
I had a Hand in't (I fpeak it to my Shame)
When you were defeated of it.
      Wellborn. That's forgiven.
      Mar. I fhall deferve it then. Then urge him to produce
The Deed in which you pafs'd it over to him,
Which I know he'll have about him to deliver
To the Lord *Lovell*, with many other Writings,
And prefent Money's. I'll inftruct you further,
As I wait on your Worfhip : If I play not my Part
To your full Content, and your Uncle's much Vexation,
Hang up *Jack Marrall.*
      Wellborn. I rely upon thee.   *Exeunt.*

S C E N E   III.

Allworth, Margaret.

Allworth. Whether to yield the firft Praife to my
                    Lord's
Unequal'd Temperance, or your conftant Sweetnefs,
That I yet live, (my weak Hands faften'd on
Hope's Anchor, fpite of all Storms of Defpair)
I yet reft doubtful.
      Marg. Give it to Lord *Lovell.*

                                              For

For what in him was Bounty, in me's Duty.
I make but Payment of a Debt, to which
My Vows, in that high Office regifter'd,
Are faithful Witneffes.

Allworth. 'Tis true, my deareft; [12]
Yet, when I call to Mind how many Fair Ones
Make wilful Shipwreck of their Faiths and Oaths
To God and Man, to fill the Arms of Greatnefs;
And you rife no lefs than a glorious Star
To the Amazement of the World, that hold out
Againft the ftern Authority of a Father;
And fpurn at Honour when it comes to court you,
I am fo tender of your Good, that faintly
With your Wrong, I can wifh myfelf that Right
You yet are pleas'd to do me.

Margaret. Yet, and ever
To me what's Title, when Content is wanting?
Or Wealth, rak'd up together with much Care,
And to be kept with more, when the Heart pines,
In being difpoffefs'd of what it longs for
Beyond the *Indian* Mines; or the fmooth Brow
Of a pleas'd Sire, that flaves me to his Will?
And fo his ravenous Humour may be feafted
By my Obedience, and he fee me Great,
Leaves to my Soul, nor Faculties, nor Power
To make her own Election.

---

[12] *'Tis true, my deareft;*
Yet, when I call to Mind, how many Fair Ones
Make wilful Shipwreck of their Faiths and Oaths
To God and Man, to fill the Arms of Greatnefs;
And you rife no lefs than a glorious Star.

In the old Copies the laft line is,

And you, rife up lefs than a glorious Star.

This I think is falfe; therefore I ventured to alter it. ———
Mr. *Dodfley* reads,

And you, rife up no lefs than, &c.

Which makes the Line too long, and confequently harfh to the
Ear.

E 4

Allworth.

Allworth. But the Dangers
That follow the Repulse.

Margaret. To me they are nothing :
Let *Allworth* love, I cannot be unhappy.
Suppose the worst, that in his Rage he kill me,
A Tear or two, by you dropt on my Hearse
In Sorrow for my Fate, will call back Life
So far as but to say, that I die your's,
I then shall rest in Peace ; or should he prove
So cruel, as one Death would not suffice
His Thirst of Vengeance ; but with ling'ring Torments,
In Mind and Body, I must waste to Air,
In Poverty join'd with Banishment ; so you share
In my Afflictions, which I dare not wish you,
So high I prize you, I could undergo 'em -
With such a Patience as should look down
With Scorn on his worst Malice.

Allworth. Heaven avert
Such Trials of your true Affection to me,
Nor will it unto you, that are all Mercy,
Shew so much Rigor.   But since we must run
Such desperate Hazards, let us do our best
To steer between 'em.

Margaret. Your Lord's ours, and sure ;
And though but a young Actor, second me,
In doing to the Life what he has plotted,

Enter Overreach.

The End may yet prove happy : Now my *Allworth*.
Allworth. To your Letter, and put on a seeming
   Anger.
Margaret. I'll pay my Lord all Debts due to his Title.
And when with Terms, not taking from his Honour,
He does follicit me, I shall gladly hear him :
But, in this peremptory, nay, commanding Way,
T' appoint a Meeting, and without my Knowledge ;
A Priest to tie the Knot can ne'er be undone
'Till Death unloose it, is a Confidence

In

In his Lordship will deceive him.

Allworth. I hope better,
Good Lady.

Margaret. Hope, Sir, what you please : For me
I muſt take a ſafe and ſecure Courſe ; I have
A Father, and without his full Conſent,
Though all Lords of the Land kneel'd for my Favour,
I can grant nothing.

Over. I like this Obedience.
But whatſoever my Lord writes, muſt, and ſhall be
Accepted and embrac'd.   Sweet Maſter *Allworth*,
You ſhew yourſelf a true and faithful Servant
To your good Lord ; he has a Jewel of you.
How ! frowning, *Meg ?* Are theſe Looks to receive
A Meſſenger from my Lord ? What's this ? give me it.

Margaret. A Piece of arrogant Paper, like th' In-
          ſcriptions.   [*Overreach reads the Letter.*

Over. " Fair Miſtreſs, from your Servant learn, all
          Joys
That we can hope for, if deferr'd, prove Toys ;
Therefore this Inſtant, and in private meet
A Huſband, that will gladly at your Feet
Lay down his Honours, tend'ring them to you
With all Content, the Church being paid her due."
—Is this the arrogant Piece of Paper ? Fool !
Will you ſtill be one ? In the Name of Madneſs, what
Could his good Honour write more to content you ?
Is there aught elſe to be wiſh'd after theſe two,
That are already offer'd ? Marriage firſt,
And lawful Pleaſure after ; what would you more ?

Margaret. Why, Sir, I would be married like your
          Daughter ;
Not hurried away i' th' Night I know not whither,
Without all Ceremony : No Friends invited
To honour the Solemnity.

Allworth. An't pleaſe your Honour,
(For ſo before To-morrow I muſt ſtile you)
My Lord deſires this Privacy in reſpect
His Honourable Kinſmen are far off,

And

And his Defires to have it done, brook not
So long Delay as to expect their coming;
And yet he ftands refolv'd, with all due Pomp:
As running at the Ring, Plays, Mafques, and Tilting,
To have his Marriage at Court celebrated
When he has brought your Honour up to *London*.

    Over. He tells you true; 'tis the Fafhion, on my
            Knowledge:
Yet the good Lord, to pleafe your Peevifhnefs,
Muft put it off, forfooth! and lofe a Night,
In which perhaps he might get two Boys on thee.
Tempt me no farther, if you do, this Goad .
Shall prick you to him.

    Margaret. I could be contented,
Were you but by to do a Father's Part,
And give me in the Church.

    Over. So my Lord have you,
What do I care who gives you? fince my Lord
Does purpofe to be private, I'll not crofs him.
I know not, Mafter *Allworth*, how my Lord
May be provided, and therefore there's a Purfe
Of Gold: 'twill ferve this Night's Expence; To-morrow
I'll furnifh him with any Sums. In the mean Time,
Ufe my Ring to my Chaplain: he is benefic'd
At my Manor of *Gotam*, and call'd Parfon *Will-do:*
'Tis no Matter for a Licence, I'll bear him out in't.

    Margaret. With your Favour, Sir, what Warrant is
He may fuppofe I got that twenty Ways, [your Ring?
Without your Knowledge; and then to be refus'd,
Were fuch a Stain upon me — If you pleafe, Sir,
Your Prefence would do better.

    Over. Still perverfe?
I fay again, I will not crofs my Lord,
Yet I'll prevent you too.—Paper and Ink, there!

    Allworth. I can furnifh you.

    Over. I thank you, I can write then.

                      [Writes on his Book.
   Allworth. You may, if you pleafe, put out the Name
        of my Lord,

                          In

In Refpect he comes difguis'd, and only write,
Marry her to this Gentleman.
   Over. Well advis'd.   [Margaret *kneels.*
'Tis done: away.—My Blefling, Girl? Thou haft it.
Nay, no Reply.—Be gone, good Mafter *Allworth,*
This fhall be the beft Night's Work you ever made.
   Allworth. I hope fo, Sir.
            [*Exeunt* Allworth *and* Margaret.
   Over. Farewell.—Now all's cock-fure:
Methinks I hear already Knights and Ladies
Say, Sir *Giles Overreach,* how is it with
Your Honourable Daughter? Has her Honour
Slept well To-night? or, Will her Honour pleafe
To accept this Monkey, Dog, or Paroquet?
(This is State in Ladies) or my eldeft Son
To be her Page, and wait upon her Trencher?—
My Ends, my Ends are compafs'd!—Then for *Wellborn*
And the Lands; were he once married to the Widow—
I have him here—I can fcarce contain myfelf,
I am fo full of Joy; nay, Joy all over.   [*Exit.*

The End of the Fourth Act.

⁂⁂⁂⁂⁂⁂⁂⁂⁂⁂⁂⁂⁂⁂⁂⁂⁂⁂⁂⁂⁂⁂⁂⁂⁂

ACT V. SCENE I.

Lovell, *Lady,* Amble.

Lady. **B**Y this you know, how ftrong the Motives
                were
That did, my Lord, induce me to difpenfe
A little with my Gravity, to advance
(In perfonating fome few Favours to him)
The Plots and Projects of the down-trod *Wellborn.*
Nor fhall I e'er repent (although I fuffer
In fome few Men's Opinions for't) the Action.
For he that ventur'd all for my dear Hufband,
                Might

Might juſtly claim an Obligation from me,
To pay him ſuch a Courteſy ; which had I
Coyly, or over-curiouſly deny'd,
It might have argu'd me of little Love
To the deceas'd.

    Lovell. What you intended, Madam,
For the poor Gentleman, hath found good Succeſs :
For, as I underſtand, his Debts are paid,
And he once more furniſh'd for fair Employment :
But all the Arts that I have u'd to raiſe
The Fortunes of your Joy and mine, young *Allworth,*
Stand yet in Suppoſition, though I hope, well.
For the young Lovers are in Wit more pregnant,
Than their Years can promiſe ; and for their Deſires,
On my Knowledge, they are equal.

    Lady. Though my Wiſhes
Are with yours, my Lord : yet give me Leave to fear
The Building, though well-grounded.   To deceive
Sir *Giles* (that's both a Lyon and a Fox
In his Proceedings) were a Work beyond
The ſtrongeſt Undertakers ; not the Trial
Of two weak Innocents.

    Lovell. Deſpair not, Madam :
Hard Things are compaſs'd oft by eaſy Means ;
And Judgment, being a Gift deriv'd from Heaven,
Though ſometimes lodg'd i' th' Hearts of worldly Men,
(That ne'er conſider from whom they receive it)
Forſakes ſuch as abuſe the Giver of it.
Which is the Reaſon, that the politick
And cunning Stateſman, that believes he fathoms
The Counſels of all Kingdoms on the Earth,
Is by Simplicity oft over-reach'd.

    Lady. May he be ſo. —Yet, in his Name to expreſs it,
Is a good Omen.

    Lovell. May it to myſelf
Prove ſo, good Lady, in my Suit to you :
What think you of the Motion ?

    Lady. Troth, my Lord,
My own Unworthineſs may anſwer for me ;

For

For had you, when that I was in my Prime,
My Virgin Flower uncropp'd, prefented me
With this great Favour, looking on my Lownefs
Not in a Glafs of Self-love, but of Truth,
I could not but have thought it, as a Bleffing
Far, far beyond my Merit.

    Lovell. You are too modeft,
And undervalue that which is above
My Title, or whatever I call mine.
I grant, were I a *Spaniard*, to marry
A Widow might difparage me ; but being
A true-born *Englifhman*, I cannot find
How it can taint my Honour ; nay, what's more,
That which you think a Blemifh, is to me
The faireft Luftre. You already, Madam,
Have given fure Proofs how dearly you can cherifh
A Hufband that deferves you ; which confirms me,
That if I am not wanting in my Care
To do you Service, you'll be ftill the fame
That you were to your *Allworth*. In a Word,
Our Years, our States, our Births are not unequal ;
You being defcended nobly, and ally'd fo,
If then you may be won to make me happy,
But join your Lips to mine, and that fhall be
A folemn Contract.

    Lady. I were blind to my own Good,
Should I refufe it ; yet, my Lord, receive me
As fuch a one, the Study of whofe whole Life
Shall know no other Object but to pleafe you.

    Lovell. If I return not, with all Tendernefs,
Equal Refpect to you, may I die wretched.

    Lady. There needs no Proteftation, my Lord,
To her that cannot doubt.——You are welcome, Sir.

Enter Wellborn.

Now you look like yourfelf.
    Wellborn. And will continue
Such in my free Acknowledgment, that I am
Your

Your Creature, Madam, and will never hold
My Life mine own, when you pleafe to command it.

    Lovell. It is a Thankfulnefs that well becomes you;
You could not make Choice of a better Shape,
To drefs your Mind in.

    Lady. For me, I am happy
That my Endeavours profper'd.   Saw you of late
Sir *Giles*, your Uncle?

    Wellborn. I heard of him, Madam,   [fions
By his Minifter, *Marrall*; he's grown into ftrange Paf-
About his Daughter: This laft Night he look'd for
Your Lordfhip at his Houfe; but miffing you,
And fhe not yet appearing, his wife Head
Is much perplex'd and troubled.

    Lovell. It may be,
Sweetheart, my Project took.

Enter Overreach *with diftracted Looks, driving in* Marrall
before him.

    Lady. I ftrongly hope.

    Over. Ha! find her, Booby, thou huge Lump of
I'll bore thine Eyes out elfe.   [Nothing,

    Wellborn. May it pleafe your Lordfhip,
For fome Ends of mine own, but to withdraw
A little out of Sight, though not of Hearing,
You may perhaps have Sport.

    Lovell. You fhall direct me.   [*Steps afide.*

    Over. I fhall fol fa you Rogue.

    Mar. Sir, for what Caufe
Do you ufe me thus?

    Over. Caufe, Slave! why, I am angry,
And thou a Subject only fit for beating;
And fo to cool my Choler.   Look to the Writing;
Let but the Seal be broke upon the Box,
That has flept in my Cabinet thefe three Years.
I'll rack thy Soul for't.

    Mar. I may yet cry 'Quittance;
Though now I fuffer, and dare not refift.   [*Afide.*
                                            Over.

Over. Lady, by your Leave, did you fee my Daugh-
   ter Lady?
And the Lord her Hufband? Are they in your Houfe?
If they are, difcover, that I may bid 'em Joy;
And as an Entrance to her Place of Honour,
See your Ladyfhip on her left Hand, and make Court
When fhe nods on you; which you muft receive
As a fpecial Favour.
   Lady. When I know, Sir *Giles,*
Her State requires fuch Ceremony, I fhall pay it;
But in the mean Time, as I am myfelf,
I give you to underftand, I neither know
Nor care where her Honour is.
   Over. When you once fee her
Supported, and led by the Lord her Hufband,
You'll be taught better.——Nephew.
   Wellborn. Sir.
   Over. No more!
   Wellborn. 'Tis all I owe you.
   Over. Have your redeem'd Rags
Made you thus infolent!
   Wellborn. Infolent to you?   [*In Scorn.*
Why, what are you, Sir, unlefs in your Years,
At the beft, more than myfelf?
   Over. His Fortune fwells him:
'Tis Rank, he's married.
   Lady. This is excellent!
   Over. Sir, in calm Language, (tho' I feldom ufe it)
I am familiar with the Caufe, that makes you
Bear up thus bravely; there's a certain Buz   [riage:
Of a ftol'n Marriage; Do you hear? Of a ftol'n Mar-
In which 'tis faid there's fome body hath been couzen'd.
I name no Parties.
   Wellborn. Well, Sir, and what follows?   [ber,
   Over. Marry this! Since you are peremptory, remem-
Upon mere Hope of your great Match, I lent you
A Thoufand Pounds: Put me in good Security,
And fuddenly, by Mortgage, or by Statute
Of fome of your new Poffeffions, or I'll have you
                                        Drag'd

Drag'd in you Lavender Robes to the Gaol; you know
And therefore do not trifle.   [me,
     Wellborn. Can you be
So cruel to your Nephew, now he's in
The Way to rife? Was this the Courtefy
You did me in pure Love, and no Ends elfe?
     Over. End me no Ends; engage the whole Eftate,
And force your Spoufe to fign it; you fhall have
Three or four Thoufand more, to roar and fwagger,
And revel in bawdy Taverns.
     Wellborn. And beg after;
Mean you not fo?
     Over. My Thoughts are mine, and free.
Shall I have Security?
     Wellborn. No, indeed you fhall not;
Nor Bond, nor Bill, nor bare Acknowledgment;
Your great Looks fright not me.
     Over. But my Deeds fhall.——
Out-braved?   [*They both draw, the Servants Enter.*
     Lady. Help, Murder! Murder!
     Wellborn. Let him come on,
With all his Wrongs and Injuries about him,
Arm'd with his cut-throat Practifes to guard him;
The Right that I bring with me, will defend me,
And punifh his Extortion.
     Over. That I had thee
But fingle in the Field!
     Lady. You may; but make not
My Houfe your quarrelling Scene.
     Over. Were't in a Church,
By Heaven and Hell, I'll do't.
     Mar. Now put him to
The fhewing of the Deed.
     Wellborn. This rage is vain, Sir;
For Fighting fear not, you fhall have your Hands full
Upon the leaft Incitement; and whereas
You charge me with a Debt of a Thoufand Pounds;
If there be Law, (howe'er you have no Confcience)
Either reftore my Land, or I'll recover

A Debt, that's truly due to me from you,
In value ten Times more than what you challenge.
 Over. I in thy Debt! O Impudence! did I not pur-
              [chafe
The Land left by thy Father? That rich Land,
That had continued in *Wellborn*'s Name
Twenty Defcents; which, like a Riotous Fool
Thou didft make fale of? Is not here inclos'd
The Deed that does confirm it mine?
 Mar. Now, now:
 Wellborn. I do acknowledge none; I ne'er pafs'd o'er
Any fuch Land; I grant, for a Year or two,
You had it in Truft; which if you do difcharge;
Surrendering the Poffeffion, you fhall eafe
Yourfelf, and me, of chargeable Suits in Law;
Which, if you prove not Honeft (as I doubt it)
Muft of neceffity follow.
 Lady. In my Judgment
He does advife you well.
 Over. Good! Good! confpire
With your new Hufband, Lady; fecond him
In his difhoneft Practifes; but when
This Manor is extended to my Ufe,
You'll fpeak in an humbler Key, and fue for Favour.
 Lady. Never: do not hope it.
 Wellborn. Let Defpair firft fieze me.
 Over. Yet to fhut up thy Mouth, and make thee give
Thyfelf the Lie, the lowd Lie: I draw out
The precious Evidence; if thou canft forfwear
Thy Hand and Seal, and make a Forfeit of [*Opens the Box.*
Thy Ears to the Pillory: See, here's that will make
My Intereft clear—Ha!
 Lady. A fair Skin of Parchment!
 Wellborn. Indented, I confefs, and labels too;
But neither Wax nor Words. How! Thunder-ftruck?
Not a Syllable to infult with? My wife Uncle,
Is this your precious Evidence? Is this that makes
Your Intereft clear?
 VOL. III.   F   *Over.*

Over. I am o'erwhelm'd with Wonder!
What Prodigy is this? What subtle Devil
Hath raz'd out the Inscription? The Wax
Turn'd into Dust—The Rest of my Deeds whole,
As when they were deliver'd; and this only
Made nothing! do you deal with Witches Rascall?
There is a Statute for you, which will bring
Your Neck in a hempen Circle; yes, there is.
And now 'tis better thought; for, Cheater know
This juggling shall not save you.
　Wellborn. To save thee
Would begger the Stock of Mercy.
　Over. Marrall.
　Mar. Sir.
　Over. Though the Witnesses are Dead, your Testi-
　　　mony　　　　　　　　　　　　　　[*Flattering him.*
Help with an Oath or two; and for thy Master,
Thy liberal Master, my good Honest Servant,
I know, you will swear any thing to dash
This cunning Sleight: Besides, I know thou art
A publick Notary, and such stand in Law
For a dozen Witnesses; the Deed being drawn too
By thee, my careful *Marrall,* and deliver'd
When thou wert present, will make good my Title;
Wilt thou not swear this?
　Mar. I? No, I assure you.
I have a Conscience, not sear'd up like yours;
I know no Deeds.
　Over. Wilt thou betray me?
　Mar. Keep him
From using of his Hands, I'll use my Tongue
To his no little Torment.
　Over. Mine own Varlet
Rebel against me?
　Mar. Yes, and uncase you too.
The Ideot; the Patch; the Slave; the Booby;
The Property fit only to be beaten
For your Morning Exercise; your Foot-ball, or

The

The unprofitable Lump of Flesh; your Drudge;
Can now anatomize you, and lay open
All your black Plots, and level with the Earth
Your Hill of Pride; and with these Gabions guarded,
Unload my great Artillery, and shake,
Nay pulverize the Walls you think defend you.
    Lady. How he foams at the Mouth with Rage!
    Wellborn. To him again.
    Over. O that I had thee in my Gripe, I would tear
Joint after Joint!   [thee
    Mar. I know you are a Tearer.
But I'll have first your Fangs par'd off; and then
Come nearer to you; when I have discover'd,
And made it good before the Judge, what Ways
And devillish Practices you us'd too coozen
An Army of whole Families, who yet live;
And but enrol'd for Soldiers, were able
To take *Dunkirk.*
    Wellborn. All will come out.
    Lady. The better.
    Over. But that I will live, Rogue, to torture thee,
And make thee wish, and kneel in vain to die,
These Swords that keep thee from me, should fix here,
Although they made my Body but one Wound,
But I would reach thee.
    Lovell. Heav'ns Hand is in this,
One Ban-dog worry the other.   [*Aside.*
    Over. I play the Fool,
And make my Anger but ridiculous.
There will be a Time and Place, there will be Cowards,
When you shall feel what I dare do.
    Wellborn. I think so:
You dare do any Ill, yet want true Valour
To be Honest and Repent.
    Over. They are Words I know not,
Nor e'er will learn.   Patience the Beggars Virtue,

F 2   *Enter*

Enter Greedy *and* Parfon Well-do.

Shall find no Harbour here—after thefe Storms
At length a Calm appears.   Welcome, moft welcome:
There's Comfort in thy looks; is the Deed done?
Is my Daughter Married? Say but fo, my Chaplain,
And I am tame.

    Well-do. Married? Yes, I affure you.

    Over. Then vanifh all fad Thoughts; there's more
[Gold for thee.
My Doubts and Fears are in the Titles drown'd,
Of my Honorable, my Right Honorable Daughter.

    Greedy. Here will be Feafting; at leaft for a Month
I am provided: Empty Guts, croke no more,
You fhall be ftuffed like Bagpipes, not with Wind,
But bearing Difhes.

    Over. —Inftantly be here?   [*Whifpering to Well-do.*
To my Wifh.   Now you that Plot againft me,
And hop'd to trip my Heels up; that contemn me;
[*Loud Mufick.*
Think on't and Tremble. They come, I hear the Mufick.
A Lane there for my Lord.

    Wellborn. This fudden Heat
May yet be cool'd, Sir.

    Over. Make Way there for my Lord.

Enter Allworth *and* Margaret.

    Marg. Sir, firft your Pardon, then your Bleffing, with
Your full Allowance of the Choice I have made.
As ever you could make ufe of your Reafon,   [*Kneeling.*
Grow not in Paffion; fince you may as well
Call back the Day that's paft, as untie the Knot
Which is too ftrongly Faften'd.   Not to dwell
Too long on Words, this is my Hufband.

    Over. How!

    Allworth. So I affure you; all the Rites of Marriage
With every Circumftance are paft.   Alas! Sir,
Altho'

Altho' I am no Lord, but a Lord's Page,
Your Daughter and my lov'd Wife mourns not for it.
And for Right Honourable Son in Law! you may say
Your dutiful Daughter.

   Over. Devil! are they married?   [joy.
   Well-do. Do a Father's Part, and say, Heaven give 'em
   Over. Confusion and Ruin! speak, and speak quickly,
Or thou art dead.

   Well-do. They are married.

   Over. Thou had'st better
Have made a Contract with the King of Fiends
Than these.—My Brain turns!

   Well-do. Why this Rage to me?
Is not this your Letter, Sir? And these the Words?
Marry her to this Gentleman.

   Over. It cannot:
Nor will I e'er believe it: 'Sdeath I will not.
That I, that in all Passages I touch'd
At worldly Profit, have not left a Print
Where I have trod for the most curious Search
To trace my Footsteps, should be gull'd by Children!
Baffl'd and fool'd, and all my Hopes and Labours
Defeated, and made void.

   Wellborn. As it appears,
You are so, my grave Uncle

   Over. Village Nurses
Revenge their Wrongs with Curses; I'll not waste
A Syllable, but thus I take the Life
Which Wretch! I gave to thee. [*Offers to kill* Margaret.

   Lovell. Hold, for your own Sake!
Though Charity to your Daughter hath quite left you,
Will you do an Act, though in your Hopes lost here,
Can leave no Hope for Peace, or Rest hereafter?
Consider; at the best you're but a Man,
And cannot so create your Aims, but that
They may be crofs'd.

   Over. Lord! thus I spit at thee,
And at thy Counsel; and again desire thee,
And as thou art a Soldier, if thy Valour

F 3

Dares

Dares shew itself, where Multitude and Example
Lead not the Way, let's quit the House, and change
Six Words in private.

　　Lovell. I am ready.

　　Lady. Stay, Sir,
Con'est with one distracted?

　　Wellborn. You'll grow like him,
Should you answer his vain Challenge.

　　Over. Are you pale?
Borrow his Help, though *Hercules* call it odds,
I'll stand against both, as I am hem'd in thus.
Since, like a *Libyan* Lion in the Toil,
My Fury cannot reach the Coward Hunters,
And only spends itself, I'll quit the Place;
Alone I can do nothing: but I have Servants
And Friends to second me; and if I make not
This House a Heap of Ashes (by my Wrongs,
What I have spoke I will make good) or leave
One Throat uncut, if it be possible,
Hell add to my Afflictions!　　　　　*[Exit* Overreach.

　　Mar. Is't not brave Sport?

　　Greedy. Brave Sport? I am sure it has ta'en away my
I do not like the Sauce.　　　　　　　[Stomach;

　　Allworth. Nay, weep not, dearest:
Though it exprefs your Pity; what's decreed
Above, we cannot alter.

　　Lady. His Threats move me
No Scruple, Madam.

　　Mar. Was it not a rare Trick,
(And it pleafe your Worship) to make the Deed nothing?
I can do twenty neater, if you pleafe—
To purchafe and grow rich; for I will be
Such a Sollicitor, and Steward for you,
As never Worshipful had.

　　Wellborn. I do believe thee.
But first difcover the quaint Means you us'd
To raze out the Conveyance?　　　　　　　.

　　Mar. They are Mysteries
Not to be fpoke in publick: Certain Minerals

J

Incorporated

Incorporated in the Ink and Wax.
Befides, he gave me nothing, but ftill fed me
With Hopes and Blows; and that was the Inducement
To this Conundrum.   If it pleafe your Worfhip
To call to Memory, this mad Beaft once caus'd me
To urge you, or to drown, or hang yourfelf,
I'll do the like to him, if you command me.

  Wellborn. You are a Rafcall; he that dares be falfe
To a Mafter, though unjuft, will ne'er be true
To any other : Look not for Reward,
Or Favour from me; I will fhun thy Sight
As I would do a Bafilifk's.   Thank my Pity,
If thou keep thy Ears; howe'er I will take Order
Your Practice fhall be filenc'd.

  Greedy. I'll commit him,
If you'll have me, Sir?

  Wellborn. That were to little Purpofe;
His Confcience be his Prifon; not a Word,
But inftantly be gone.

  Order. Take this Kick with you.

  Amble. And this.

  Furnace. If that I had my Cleaver here,
I would divide your Knave's Head.

  Mar. This is the Haven,
Falfe Servants ftill arrive at.   [*Exit* Marrall.

Enter Overreach.

  Lady. Come again.

  Lovell. Fear not, I am your Guard.

  Wellborn. His Looks are ghaftly.   [Favours,

  Well-do. Some little Time I have fpent, under your
In Phyfical Studies, and, if my Judgment err not
He's mad beyond Recovery : But obferve him,
And look to yourfelves.

  Over. Why is not the whole World
Included in myfelf? To what Ufe then
Are Friends, and Servants ? Say there were a Squadron
Of Pikes, lined through with Shot, when I am mounted
F 4   Upon

Upon my Injuries, shall I fear to charge 'em?
No: I'll through the Battalia, and that routed,

> [*Flourishing his Sword in the Sheath.*

I'll fall to Execution.—Ha! I am feeble:
Some undone Widow sits upon mine Arm,
And takes away the Use of't; and my Sword
Glew'd to my Scabbard with wrong'd Orphans Tears
Will not be drawn. Ha! what are these? Sure Hangmen,
That come to bind my Hands, and then to drag me
Before the Judgment Seat.—Now they are new Shapes
And do appear like Furies, with steel Whips
To scourge my ulcerous Soul: Shall I then fall
Ingloriously, and yield? No; Spite of Fate
I will be forc'd to Hell like to myself;
Though you were Legions of accursed Spirits,
Thus would I fly among you,——
   Wellborn. There's no Help;
Disarm him first, then bind him.
   Greedy. Take a *Mittimus*
And carry him to *Bedlam.*
   Lovell. How he foams!
   Wellborn. And bites the Earth.
   Well-do. Carry him to some dark Room,
There try what Art can do for his Recovery.
   Marg. O my dear Father! [*They force* Overreach *off.*
   Allworth. You must be patient, Mistress.
   Lovell. Here is a President to teach wicked Men,
That when they leave Religion, and turn Atheists,
Their own Abilities leave 'em. Pray you take Comfort
I will endeavour you shall be his Guardian
In his Distractions: and for your Land, Master *Wellborn,*
Be it good, or ill in Law, I'll be an Umpire
Between you, and this, th' undoubted Heir
Of Sir *Giles Overreach*, for me, here's the Anchor
That I must fix on.
   Allworth. What you shall determine,
My Lord, I will allow of.
   Wellborn. 'Tis the Language ·
That I speak too; but there is something else

Beside

Beſide the Repoſſeſſion of my Land,
And Payment of my Debts, that I muſt practiſe.
I had a Reputation, but 'twas loſt
In my looſe Courſe; and 'till I redeem it
Some noble Way, I am but half made up.
It is a Time of Action; if your Lordſhip
Will pleaſe to confer a Company upon me
In your Command, I doubt not in my Service
To my King, and Country, but I ſhall do ſomething
That may make me right again.
   Lovell. Your Suit is granted,
And you lov'd for the Motion.
   Wellborn. Nothing wants then
But your Allowance.   [*Addreſſing himſelf to the Pit.*

F I N I S.

EPILOGUE.

EPILOGUE.

BUT your Allowance — and in that, our All
    Is comprehended ; it being known, nor we,
Nor he that wrote the Comedy, can be free
Without your *Mannumiſſion* ; which if you
Grant willingly, as a fair Favour due
To the Poet's, and our Labours, (as you may)
For we deſpair not, Gentlemen, of the Play:
We jointly ſhall profeſs your Grace hath Might
To teach us Action, and him how to write,

THE

THE GREAT DUKE

OF

FLORENCE.

A COMICAL HISTORY.

As it hath been often prefented, with good Allowance, by her Majefty's Servants, at the *Phœnix* in *Drury-Lane*. 1636.

WRITTEN

By PHILIP MASSINGER.

T O

The Truly Honoured, and my Noble Favourer,

Sir ROBERT WISEMAN, Knt.

Of *Thorrells-Hall*, in ESSEX.

S I R,

A S I dare not be ungrateful for the many Benefits you have heretofore confer'd upon me, so I have just Reason to fear that my attempting this way to make Satisfaction (in some Measure) for so due a Debt, will further ingage me. However Examples encourage me. The most able in my poor Quality have made use of Dedications in this Nature, to make the World take Notice (as far as in them lay) who, and what they were that gave Supportment, and Protection to their Studies, being more willing to publish the Doer, then receive a Benefit in a Corner. For myself, I will freely, and with a zealous Thankfulness acknowledge, that for many Years I had but faintly subsisted, if I had not often tasted of your Bounty. But it is above my Strength and Faculties, to celebrate to the Desert, your noble Inclination, (and that made actual) to raise up, or to speak more properly, to rebuild the Ruine of demolish'd Poesie. But that is a Work reserved, and will be, no doubt, undertaken, and finished, by one that can to the Life express it. Accept, I beseech you, the Tender of my Service, and in the List of those you have obliged to you, contemn not the Name of

Your true and faithful Honourer,

PHILIP MASSINGER.

A 2   Dramatis,

Dramatis Perſonæ.

COZIMA, Duke of *Florence*.
GIOVANNI, Nephew to the Duke.
LODOVICO SANAZARRO, the Duke's Favourite.
CAROLO CHAROMONTE, *Giovanni*'s Tutor.
CONTARINO, Secretary to the Duke.
ALPHONSO,
HIPPOLITO, } Counſellors of State.
HIERONIMO,
CALANDRINO, a merry Fellow, Servant to *Giovanni*.
BBRNARDO,
CAUPONI, } Servants to *Carolo Charomonte*.
PETRUCHIO,

FIORINDA, Dutcheſs of *Urbin*.
LYDIA, Daughter to *Carolo Charomonte*.
CALAMINTA, Servant to *Fiorinda*.
PETRONELLA, Servant to *Lydia*.

T H E

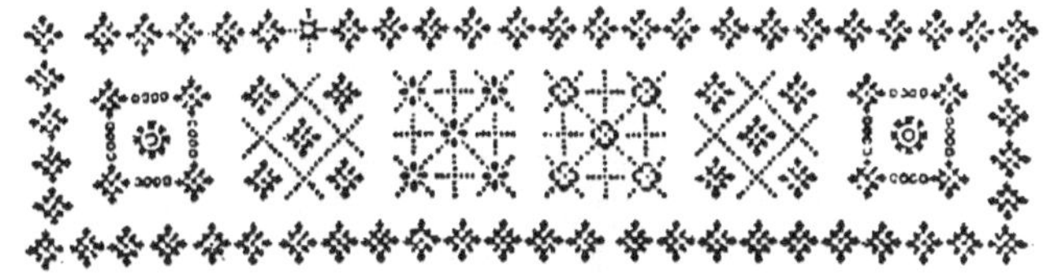

THE

GREAT DUKE

OF

FLORENCE.[1]

A COMICAL HISTORY.

ACT I. SCENE I.

Carolo Charomonte, Contarino.

Carolo.

YOU bring your Welcome with you.
    Contar. Sir, I find it.
In every Circumstance.
    Carolo. Again most welcome.
Yet, give me leave to wish (and pray you excuse me,
For I must use the Freedom I was born with)
The Great Duke's Pleasure had commanded you
To my poor House upon some other Service;
Not this you are design'd to : But his Will
Must be obey'd, howe'er it ravish from me
The happy Conversation of one
As dear to me as the Old *Romans* held
Their Houshold *Lars*, whom, they believ'd, had Power
To bless and guard their Families.
    Contar. 'Tis received so

[1] The Plot of this Play is taken from *Speed*, *Stow*, and other our *English* Chronicles, in the Reign of King *Edgar*.

On

On my Part, Signior ; nor can the Duke
But promife to himfelf as much as may
Be hop'd for from a Nephew.   And it were Weaknefs
In any Man to doubt, that *Giovanni*,
Train'd up by your Experience and Care
In all thofe Arts peculiar, and proper
To future Greatnefs of Neceffity
Muft in his Actions, being grown a Man,
Make good the Princely Education
Which he deriv'd from you.
　Carolo. I have difcharged,
To the utmoft of my Power, the Truft the Duke
Committed to me, and with Joy perceive
The Seed of my Endeavours was not fown
Upon the barren Sands, but fruitful Glebe,
Which yields a large Increafe ; my noble Charge,
By his fharp Wit, and pregnant Apprehenfion
Inftructing thofe that teach him ; making ufe,
Not in a vulgar and pedantick Form
Of what's read to him, but 'tis ftreight digefted
And truly made his own.   His grave Difcourfe,
In one no more indebted unto Years,
Amazes fuch as hear him.   Horfemanfhip
And Skill to ufe his Weapon are by Practice
Familiar to him : As for Knowledge in
Mufick, He needs it not, it being born with him ;
All that he fpeaks being with fuch Grace deliver'd
That it makes perfect Harmony.
　Contar. You defcribe
A Wonder to me.
　Carolo. Sir, he is no lefs ;
And, that there may be nothing wanting that
May render him compleat, the Sweetnefs of
His Difpofition fo wins on all
Appointed to attend him, that they are
Rivals ev'n in the coarfeft Office, who
Shall get Precedency to do him Service ;
Which they efteem a greater Happinefs
Then if they had been fafhion'd, and built up

To

To hold Command ov'r others.

   Contar. And what Place
Does he now bless with his Presence ?

   Carolo. He is now
Running at the Ring, at which he's excellent.
He does allot for every Exercise
A several Hour ; for Sloth, the Nurse of Vices
And Rust of Action, is a Stranger to him.
But I fear I am tedious, let us pass,
If you please, to some other Subject, though I cannot
Deliver him as he deserves.

   Contar. You have given him
A noble Character.[1]

   Carolo. And how, I pray you,
(For we that never look beyond our Villa's
Must be inquisitive) are State Affairs
Carried in Court ?

   Contar. There's little Alteration :
Some rise, and others fall ; as it stands with
The Pleasure of the Duke, their great Disposer.

   Carolo. Does *Lodovico Sanazarro* hold
Weight, and Grace with him ?

   Contar. Every day new Honours
Are showr'd upon him, and without the Envy
Of such as are good Men ; Since all confess
The Service done our Master, in his Wars
Against *Pisa* and *Sienna,* may with Justice
Claim what's confer'd upon him.

   Carolo. 'Tis said Nobly :
For Princes never more make known their Wisdom
Then whey they cherish Goodness, where they find it,
They being Men, and not Gods, *Contarino* ;
They can give Wealth and Titles, but no Virtues ;
That is without their Power.   When they advance
(Not out of Judgment, but deceiving Fancy)
An undeserving Man, howe'er set off

   [1] *Massinger* in this, and in many other of his Pieces, seems to have
copied *Shakespear* in the Manner of delineating his Characters.   See
the 1st Part of Henry IV. Act I.

VOL. III.   G   With

With all the Trim of Greatnefs, State and Power,
And of a Creature ev'n grown terrible
To him from whom he took his Giant Form,
This thing is ftill a Comet, no true Star;
And when the Bounties feeding his falfe Fire
Begin to fail, will of itfelf go out,
And what was dreadful, proves ridiculous.
But in our *Sanazarro* 'tis not fo:
He, being pure and try'd Gold, and any Stamp
Of Grace to make him current to the World
The Duke is pleas'd to give him, will add Honour
To th' great Beftower; for he, though allow'd
Companion to his Mafter, ftill preferves
His Majefty in full Luftre.
　　Contar. He, indeed,
At no part does take from it, but becomes
A Partner of his Cares, and eafes him,
With willing Shoulders of a Burthen, which
He fhould alone fuftain.
　　Carolo. Is he yet married?
　　Contar. No, Signior; ftill a Batchelor; howe'er
It is apparent, that the choiceft Virgin
For Beauty, Bravery, and Wealth in *Florence*,
Would with her Parents glad Confent, be won
(Were his Affection and Intent but known)
To be at his Devotion.
　　Carolo. So I think too.

　　　　Enter Giovanni *and* Calandrino.

But break we off.　Here comes my Princely Charge.
Make your Approaches boldly; you will find
A courteous Entertainment.
　　Giov. Pray you, forbear
My Hand, good Signior; 'Tis a Ceremony
Not due to me.　'Tis fit we fhould embrace
With mutual Arms.
　　Contar. It is a Favour, Sir,
I grieve to be deny'd.

Giov.

Giov. You shall overcome:
But 'tis your Pleasure, not my Pride, that grants it.
Nay, pray you, Guardian, and good Sir, put on:
How ill it shews to have that Reverend Head
Be uncover'd to a Boy?
    Carolo. Your Excellence
Must give me Liberty to observe the Distance
And Duty that I owe you.
    Giov. Owe me Duty?
I do profess (and when I do deny it
Good Fortune leave me.) You have been to me
A second Father, and may justly challenge,
For training up my Youth in Arts and Arms,
As much Respect and Service, as was due
To him that gave me Life. And did you know, Sir,
Or will believe from me, how many Sleeps
Good *Charomonte* hath broken, in his Care
To build me up a Man, you must confess
Chiron, the Tutor to the great *Achilles*,
Compar'd with him, deserves not to be nam'd.
And if my gracious Uncle, the great Duke,
Still holds me worthy his Consideration,
Or finds in me ought worthy to be lov'd,
That little Rivolet flow'd from this Spring;
And so from me to report him.
    Contar. Fame already
Hath fill'd his Highness's Ears with the true Story
Of what you are, and how much better'd by him.
And 'tis his Purpose to reward the Travail
Of this grave Sir, with a magnificent Hand.
For, though his Tenderness hardly could consent
To have you one Hour absent from his Sight,
For full three Years he did deny himself
The Pleasure he took in you, that you, here
From this great Master might arrive unto
The Theory of those high Mysteries
Which you by Action must make plain in Court.
'Tis, therefore, his Request (and that, from him,
Your Excellence must grant a strict Command)

G 2

That

That inftantly (it being not five Hours riding)
You fhould take Horfe, and vifit him. Thefe his Letters
Will yield you further Reafons.

   Caland. To the Court?
Farewel the Flower, then, of the Country's Garland!
This is our Sun, and, when He's fet, we muft not
Expect or Spring, or Summer; but refolve
For a perpetual Winter.

   Carolo. Pray you, obferve [Giovanni *reading the Letter.*
The frequent Changes in his Face.

   Contar. As if
His much Unwillingnefs to leave your Houfe
Contended with his Duty.

   Carolo. Now he appears
Collected and refolv'd.

   Giov. It is the Duke!
The Duke, upon whofe Favour all my Hopes
And Fortunes do depend.   Nor muft I check
At his Commands for any private Motives
That do invite my Stay here, though they are
Almoft not to be mafter'd.   My Obedience
In my departing fuddenly fhall confirm
I am his Highnefs's Creature.   Yet, I hope
A little Stay to take a folemn Farewell
For all thofe ravifhing Pleafures I have tafted
In this my fweet Retirement, from my Guardian,
And his incomparable Daughter, cannot meet
An ill Conftruction

   Contar. I will anfwer that;
Ufe your own Will.

   Giov. I would fpeak to you, Sir,
In fuch a Phrafe as might exprefs the Thanks
My Heart would gladly pay; But——

   Carolo. I conceive you:
And fomething I would fay; but I muft do it
In that dumb Rhetorick which you make ufe of;
For I do wifh you all.——I know not how,
My Toughnefs Melts, and, fpite of my Difcretion,
I muft turn Woman.

Contar.

Contar. What a Sympathy
There is between 'em.
   Caland. Were I on the Rack,
I could not fhed a Tear.—But I am mad,
And ten to one fhall hang myfelf for Sorrow
Before I fhift my Shirt.   But hear, you Sir,
I'll feparate you : When you are gone, what will
Become of me ?
   Giov. Why thou fhalt to Court with me.
   Caland. To fee you worried ?
   Contar. Worried, *Calandrino* ?   [Court,
   Caland. Yes, Sir. For, bring this fweet Face to the
There will be fuch a Longing 'mong the Madams,
Who fhall ingrofs it firft, nay, fight and fcratch for't,
That, if they be not ftop'd, for Entertainment
They'll kifs his Lips off.   Nay, if you'll fcape fo,
And not be tempted to a farther Danger,
Thefe *Succubæ* are fo fharp fet, that you muft
Give out you are an Eunuch.
   Contar. Have a better
Opinion of Court-Ladies, and take Care
Of your own Stake.
   Caland. For my Stake, 'tis paft caring ;
I would not have a Bird of unclean Feathers
Handfel his Lime-twig,—and fo much for him :
There's fomething elfe that troubles me.
   Contar. What's that ?   [tightly.
   Caland. Why, how to behave myfelf in Court, and
I have been told the very Place transforms Men,
And that not one of a thoufand, that before
Liv'd honeftly in the Country, on plain Sallads
But bring him thither, mark me that, and feed him
But a Month or two with Cuftards and Court Cake-bread,
And he turns Knave immediately.—I would be honeft ;
But I muft follow the Fafhion, or die a Beggar.
   Giov. And, if I ever reach my Hopes, believe it
We will fhare Fortunes.
   Carolo. This Acknowledgement

G 3

Enter

Enter Lydia.

Binds me your Debtor ever.——Here comes one
In whofe fad Looks you eafily may read
What her Heart fuffers, in that fhe is forc'd
To take her laft Leave of you.
   Contar. As I live,
A Beauty without Parallel.
   Lydia. Muft you go, then,
So fuddenly?
   Giov. There's no Evafion, *Lydia,*
To gain the laft Delay, though I would buy it
At any rate.   Greatnefs, with private Men
Efteem'd a Bleffing, is to me a Curfe;
And we, whom, for our high Births, they conclude
The only Freemen, are the only Slaves.
Happy the golden Mean! had I been born [3]
In a poor fordid Cottage, not nurs'd up
With Expectation to command a Court,
I might, like fuch of your Condition, fweeteft,
Have took a fafe and middle Courfe, and not,
As I am now againft my Choice compel'd
Or to lie grov'ling on the Earth, or rais'd
So high upon the Pinnacles of State,
That I muft either keep my Height with Danger,
Or fall with certain Ruin.
   Lydia. Your own Goodnefs
Will be your faithful Guard.
   Giov. O *Lydia!*
   Contar. So paffionate?

---

[3] *Happy the golden Mean! had I been born*
    In a poor fordid Cottage, &c.
Thus *Shakefpear* in *Henry* VIIIth.

    ——————— 'Tis better to be lowly born,
    And range with humble Livers in Content,
    Than to be perk'd up in a glitt'ring Grief,
    And wear a golden Sorrow.
Act 2. Scene 5.
Giov.

Giov. For, had I been your Equal
I might have feen and lik'd with mine own Eyes,
And not, as now, with other's; I might ftill,
And without Obfervation, or Envy,
As I have done, continued my Delights
With you, that are alone, in my Efteem,
The Abftract of Society: We might walk
In folitary Groves, or in choice Gardens;
From the Variety of curious Flowers
Contemplate Nature's Workmanfhip, and Wonders:
And then, for Change, near to the Murmur of
Some bubbling Fountain, I might hear you fing,
And from the well-tun'd Accents of your Tongue
In my Imagination conceive
With what melodious Harmony a Quire
Of Angels fing above, their Maker's Praifes.
And then with chafte Difcourfe, as we return'd,
Imp Feathers to the broken Wings of Time.
—And all this I muft part from.
    Contar. You forget
The Hafte impos'd upon us.
    Giov. One Word more,
And then I come.   And after this, when with
Continued Innocence of Love, and Service,
I had grown ripe for Hymeneal Joys,
Embracing you, but with a lawful Flame,
I might have been your Hufband.
    Lydia. Sir, I was,
And ever am, your Servant; but it was,
And 'tis far from me, in a Thought to cherifh
Such faucy Hopes.   If I had been the Heir
Of all the Globes and Scepters Mankind bows to,
At my beft you had deferv'd me; as I am,
Howe'er unworthy, in my Virgin Zeal
I wifh you, as a Partner of your Bed,
A Princefs equal to you; fuch a one
That may make it the Study of her Life,
With all th' Obedience of a Wife to pleafe you.
May you have happy Iffue, and I live

G 4

To

To be their humbleft Handmaid.
  Giov. I am dumb,
And can make no Reply.
  Contar. Your Excellence
Will be benighted.
  Giov. This Kifs bath'd in Tears
May learn you what I fhould fay.
  Lydia. Give me Leave
To wait on you to your Horfe.
  Carolo. And me to bring you
To the one half of your Journey.
  Giov. Your Love puts
Your Age to too much Trouble.
  Carolo. I grow young,
When moft I ferve you.
  Contar. Sir, the Duke fhall thank you.   [*Exeunt.*

S C E N E II.

Alphonfo, Hippolito, Hieronimo, *with a Petition.*

Alph. His Highnefs cannot take it ill.
  Hippol. However,
We with our Duties fhall exprefs our Care
For the Safety of his Dukedom.
  Hieron. And our Loves

Enter Cozimo, *the Duke.*

To his perfon.—Here he comes: Prefent it boldly.
  Coz. What needs this Form? We are not grown fo
As to difdain familiar Conference   [proud
With fuch as are to counfel, and direct us.
This kind of Adoration fhew'd not well
In the old *Roman* Emperors, who, forgetting
That they were Flefh and Blood, would be ftil'd Gods:
In us, to fuffer it were worfe. Pray you, rife.
Still the old Suit? With too much Curioufnefs [*Reads.*
You have too often fearch'd this Wound, which yields

                                      Security

Security and Reſt, not Trouble to me.
For here you grieve, that my firm Reſolution
Continues me a Widower; and that
My Want of Iſſue to ſucceed me in
My Government, when I am dead, may breed
Diſtraction in the State, and make the Name
And Family of the *Medicis*, now admir'd,
Contemptible.

   Hippol. And with ſtrong Reaſons, Sir.

   Alph. For, were you old, and paſt Hope to beget
The Model of yourſelf, we ſhould be ſilent.

   Hieron. But, being in your Height and Pride of Years,
As you are now, great Sir, and having too
In your Poſſeſſion the Daughter of
The deceas'd Duke of *Urbin*, and his Heir,
Whoſe Guardian you are made, were you but pleas'd
To think her worthy of you, beſides Children,
The Dukedom ſhe brings with her for a Dower,
Will yield a large Increaſe of Strength and Power
To thoſe fair Territories, which already
Acknowledge you their abſolute Lord.

   Coz. You preſs us
With ſolid Arguments, we grant; and, though
We ſtand not bound to yield Account to any
Why we do this or that (the full Conſent
Of our Subjects being included in our Will)
We, out of our free Bounties, will deliver
The Motives that divert us.   You well know
That three Years ſince, to our much Grief, we loſt
Our Dutcheſs; ſuch a Dutcheſs, that the World
In her whole Courſe of Life, yields not a Lady
That can with Imitation deſerve
To be her ſecond : In her Grave we buried
All Thoughts of Women : Let this ſatisfy
For any ſecond Marriage.   Now, whereas
You name the Heir of *Urbin*, as a Princeſs
Of great Revenues, 'tis confeſs'd ſhe is ſo :
But for ſome Cauſes, private to ourſelf,
We have diſpos'd her otherwiſe.   Yet deſpair not;

                              For

For you, ere long, with Joy shall understand,
That in our Princely Care we have provided
One worthy to succeed us.

   Hippol. We submit,
And hold the Counsels of great *Cozimo*
Oraculous.

Enter Lodovico, Sanazarro.

   Coz. My *Sanazarro* — Nay,
Forbear all Ceremony.   You look sprightly, Friend,
And promise in your clear Aspect some Novel
That may delight us.

   Sanaz. O Sir, I would not be
The Harbinger of aught that might distaste you.
And therefore know (for 'twere a Sin to torture
Your Highness' Expectation) your Vice-Admiral,
By my Directions, hath surpriz'd the Gallies
Appointed to transport the *Asian* Tribute
Of the *Great Turk* ; a richer Prize was never
Brought into *Florence.*

   Coz. Still my Nightingale,
That with sweet Accents do'st assure me, that
My Spring of Happiness comes fast upon me.
Embrace me boldly.   I pronounce that Wretch
An Enemy to brave and thriving Action,
That dares believe, but in a Thought, we are
Too prodigal in our Favours to this Man,
Whose Merits, though with him we should divide
Our Dukedom, still continue us his Debtor.

   Hippol. 'Tis far from me.

   Alph. We all applaud it.

   Coz. Nay, blush not, *Sanazarro* ; we are proud
Of what we build up in thee ; nor can our
Election be disparag'd, since we have not
Receiv'd into our Bosom and our Grace
A glorious lazy Drone, grown fat with feeding
On others Toil, but an industrious Bee
That crops the sweet Flowers of our Enemies,
And ev'ry happy Evening returns

Loaden

Loaden with Wax and Honey to our Hive.

Sanaz. My beſt Endeavours never can diſcharge
The Service I ſhould pay.

Coz. Thou art too modeſt;
But we will ſtudy how to give, and when,

Enter Giovanni *and* Contarino.

Before it be demanded.——*Giovanni!*
My Nephew! Let me eye thee better, Boy.
In thee, methinks, my Siſter lives again:
For her Love I will be a Father to thee,
For thou'rt my adopted Son.

Giov. Your Servant,
And humbleſt Subject.

Coz. Thy hard Travel, Nephew,
Requires ſoft Reſt, and therefore we forbear,
For the preſent, an Account how thou haſt ſpent
Thy abſent Hours. See, Signiors, ſee, our Care,
Without a ſecond Bed, provides you of
A hopeful Prince. Carry him to his Lodgings,
And, for his farther Honour, *Sanazarro,*
With the reſt, do you attend him.

Giov. All true Pleaſures
Circle your Highneſs.

Sanaz. As the riſing Sun,
We do receive you.

Giov. May this never ſet,
But ſhine upon you ever.
     [*Exeunt* Giovanni, Sanazarro, Hieronimo.
      Alphonſo, Lodovico.

Coz. Contarino!

Contar. My gracious Lord.

Coz. What Entertainment found you
From *Carolo de Charomonte?*

Contar. Free
And bountiful. He's ever like himſelf,
Noble and hoſpitable.

Coz. But did my Nephew
Depart thence willingly?   *Contar.*

Contar. He obey'd your Summons
As did become him.   Yet it was apparent,
But that he durft not crofs your Will, he would
Have fojourn'd longer there, he ever finding
Variety of fweeteft Entertainment.
But there was fomething elfe ; nor can I blame
His Youth, though with fome Trouble he took Leave
Of fuch a fweet Companion.
   Coz. Who was it ?
   Contar. The Daughter, Sir, of Signior *Carolo*,
Fair *Lydia*, a Virgin, at all Parts,
But in her Birth and Fortunes, equal to him.
The rareft Beauties *Italy* can make Boaft of
Are but mere Shadows to her, fhe the Subftance
Of all Perfection.   And, what encreafes
The Wonder, Sir, her Body's matchlefs Form
Is better'd by the Purenefs of her Soul.
Such fweet Difcourfe, fuch ravifhing Behaviour,
Such charming Language, fuch enchanting Manners,
With a Simplicity that fhames all Courtfhip,
Flow hourly from her, that I do believe
Had *Circe*, or *Calypfo* her fweet Graces,
Wand'ring *Ulyffes* never had remember'd
Penelope or *Ithaca*.
   Coz. Be not rap'd fo.   [her,
   Contar. Your Excellence would be fo, had you feen
   Coz. Take up. Take up.—But did your Obfervation
Note any Paffage of Affection
Between her and my Nephew ?
   Contar. How it fhould
Be otherwife between 'em, is beyond
My beft Imagination.   *Cupid*'s Arrows
Were ufelefs there ; for, of Neceffity,
Their Years and Difpofitions do accord fo,
They muft wound one another.
   Coz. Hum ! Thou art
My Secretary, *Contarino*, and more fkill'd
In politick Defigns of State, than in
Thy Judgment of a Beauty ; give me Leave

                                                              In

In this to doubt it.—Here. Go to my Cabinet,
You fhall find there Letters newly receiv'd,
Touching the State of *Urbin*. Pray you, with Care
Perufe them ; leave the Search of this to us.

 Contar. I do obey in all Things.   [*Exit* Contarino.
 Coz. Lydia ! a Diamond fo long conceal'd,
And never worn in Court ? of fuch fweet Feature ?
And he on whom I fix my Dukedom's Hopes,
Made Captive to it !   Hum !—'Tis fomewhat ftrange !
Our Eyes are every where, and we will make
A ftrict Enquiry. *Sanazarro !*

Enter Sanazarro.

 Sanaz. Sir.
 Coz. Is my Nephew at his Reft ?
 Sanaz. I faw him in Bed, Sir.
 Coz. 'Tis well ; and does the Princefs *Fiorinda*
(Nay, do not blufh, fhe is rich *Urbin*'s Heir)
Continue conftant in her Favours to you ?
 Sanaz. Dread Sir, fhe may difpenfe them as fhe pleafes ;
But I look up to her as on a Princefs
I dare not be ambitious of, and hope
Her prodigal Graces fhall not render me
Offended to your Highnefs.
 Coz. Not a Scruple.
He whom I favour, as I do my Friend,
May take all lawful Graces that become him.
But touching this hereafter ; I have now
(And though perhaps it may appear a Trifle)
Serious Employment for thee.
 Sanaz. I ftand ready
For any Act you pleafe.
 Coz. I know it, Friend.
Have you ne'er heard of *Lydia,* the Daughter
Of *Carolo Charomonte ?*
 Sanaz. Him I know, Sir,
For a noble Gentleman, and my worthy Friend ;
But never heard of her.

Coz.

Coz. She is deliver'd,
And feelingly, to us by *Contarino*
For a Mafter-Piece in Nature, I would have you
Ride fuddenly thither to behold this Wonder:
But not as fent by us, that's our firft Caution.
The fecond is, and carefully obferve it,
That, though you are a Bachelor, and endow'd with
All thofe Perfections that may take a Virgin,
On Forfeit of our Favour do not tempt her.
It may be her fair Graces do concern us.'
Pretend what Bufinefs you think fit, to gain
Accefs into her Father's Houfe, and there
Make full Difcovery of her, and return me
A true Relation.—I have fome Ends in it
With which we will acquaint you.

 Sanaz. This is, Sir,
An eafy Tafk.

 Coz. Yet, one that muft exact
Your Secrecy, and Diligence. Let not
Your Stay be long.

 Sanaz. It fhall not, Sir.

 Coz. Farewell,
And be, as you would keep our Favour, careful.

The End of the Firft Act.

A C T II. S C E N E I.

Fiorinda, Calaminta.

Fiorin. **H**OW does this Dreffing fhew?
   Calam. 'Tis of itfelf
Curious and rare; but, borrowing Ornament,
As it does from your Grace that deigns to wear it,
Incomparable.

 Fiorin. Thou flatter'ft me.

Calam.

Calam. I cannot,
Your Excellence is above it.
  Fiorin. Were we lefs perfect,
Yet, being as we are an abfolute Princefs,
We of Neceffity muft be chafte, wife, fair,
By our Prerogative.—Yet all thefe fail
To move where I would have them.   How receiv'd,
Count *Sanazarro* the rich Scarf I fent him
For his laft Vifit ?
  Calam. With much Reverence ;
I dare not fay Affection.   He exprefs'd
More Ceremony in his humble Thanks
Than Feeling of the Favour; and appear'd
Wilfully ignorant, in my Opinion,
Of what it did invite him to.
  Fiorin. No Matter ;
He's blind with too much Light. Have you not heard
Of any private Miftrefs he's engag'd to ?
  Calam. Not any ; and this does amaze me, Madam,
That he, a Soldier, one that drinks rich Wines,
Feeds high, and promifes as much as *Venus*
Could wifh to find from *Mars,* fhould in his Manners
Be fo averfe to Women.
  Fiorin. 'Troth, I know not ;
He's Man enough, and, if he has a Haunt,
He preys far off, like a fubtile Fox.
  Calam. And that Way
I do fufpect him. For I learnt laft Night
(When the Great Duke went to Reft) attended by
One private Follower, he took Horfe ; but whither
He's rid, or to what End, I cannot guefs at,
But I will find it out.
  Fiorin. Do, faithful Servant :

Enter Calandrino.

We would not be abus'd.   Who have we here ?
  Calam. How the Fool ftares !
  Fiorin. And looks as if he were
Conning his Neck-verfe.   *Caland.*

Caland. If I now prove perfect
In my A. B. C. of Courtſhip, *Calandrino*
Is made for ever. I am ſent — let me ſee,
On a How d'ye, as they call't.
   Calam. What would'ſt thou ſay ?'
   Caland. Let me ſee my Notes. Theſe are her Lodg-
         ings.——Well.
   Calam. Art thou an Aſs ?
   Caland. Peace ! thou art a Court-Wagtail
           [Calandrino *ſtill looking on his Inſtructions.*
To interrupt me.
   Fiorin. He has giv'n it you.
   Caland. And then ſay to th' illuſtrious *Fi-o-rin-da.*
—I have it. Which is ſhe ?
   Calam. Why this, Fop-doodle.   [me out,
   Caland. Leave chattering, Bullfinch ; you would put
But 'twill not do.—Then, after you have made
Your three Obeyſances to her, kneel and kiſs
The Skirt of Gown.—I am glad it is no worſe.
   Calam. And why ſo, Sir ?
   Caland. Becauſe I was afraid
That, after the *Italian* Garb, I ſhould
Have kiſs'd her backward.
   Calam. This is Sport unlook'd for.
   Caland. Are you the Princeſs ?
   Fiorin. Yes, Sir.
   Caland. Then ſtand fair
(For I am cholerick) and do not nip
A hopeful Bloſſom.—Out again.—Three low   [*Reads.*
Obeyſances ——
   Fiorin. I am ready.
   Caland. I come on, then.
   Calam. With much Formality.
   Caland. Hum. One, two, three.
               [*Makes antick Curteſies.*
Thus far I am right. Now for the laſt.—O rare !
She is perfum'd all over ! Sure great Women,
Inſtead of little Dogs, are privileg'd
To carry Muſk-Cats.

                                  Fiorin.

Fiorin. Now the Ceremony
Is pafs'd, what is the Subftance ?
　Caland. I'll perufe
My Inftructions, and then tell you.——Her Skirt kifs'd,
Inform her Highnefs, that your Lord ——
　Calam. Who's that ?
　Caland. Prince *Giovanni*, who entreats your Grace,
That he with your good Favour may have Leave
To prefent his Service to you. I think I have nick'd it
For a Courtier of the firft Form.
　Fiorin. To my Wonder.

Enter Giovanni *and a Gentleman.*

Return unto the Prince.——But he prevents
My Anfwer. *Calaminta*, take him off;
And for the neat Delivery of his Meffage
Give him ten Ducats; fuch rare Parts as yours
Are to be cherifh'd.
　Caland. We will fhare : I know
It is the Cuftom of the Court, when ten
Are promis'd, five is fair. Fie! fie! the Princefs
Shall never know it, fo you difpatch me quickly,
And bid me not come To-morrow.
　Calam. Very good, Sir.
　　　　　　　[*Exeunt* Calandrino *and* Calaminta.
　Giov. Pray you, Friend,
Inform the Duke I am putting into Act
What he commanded.
　Gent. I am proud to be employ'd, Sir.
　　　　　　　　　　[*Exit Gentleman.*
　Giov. Madam, that without Warrant I prefume
To 'trench upon your Privacies, may argue
Rudenefs of Manners : But the free Accefs
Your Princely Courtefy vouchfafes to all
That come to pay their Services, gives me Hope
To find a gracious Pardon.
　Fiorin. If you pleafe, not
To make that an Offence in your Conftruction,

<table><tr><td>Vol. III.</td><td>H</td><td>Which</td></tr></table>

Which I receive as a large Favour from you,
There needs not this Apology.

    Giov. You continue,
As you were ever, the greateſt Miſtreſs of
Fair Entertainment.

    Fiorin. You are, Sir, the Maſter,
And in the Country have learnt to out-do
All that in Court is practis'd. But why ſhould we
Talk at ſuch Diſtance? You are welcome, Sir.
We have been more familiar; and ſince
You will impoſe the Province, you ſhould govern,
Of Boldneſs on me, give me Leave to ſay
You are too punctual. Sit, Sir, and diſcourſe
As we were us'd.

    Giov. Your Excellence knows ſo well
How to command, that I can never err
When I obey you.

    Fiorin. Nay, no more of this.
You ſhall o'ercome; no more, I pray you, Sir.
And what Delights, pray you be liberal
In your Relation, hath the Country Life
Afforded you?

    Giov. All Pleaſures, gracious Madam,
But the Happineſs to converſe with your ſweet Virtues.
I had a grave Inſtructor, and my Hours
Deſign'd to ſerious Studies, yielded me
Pleaſure with Profit in the Knowledge of
What before I was ignorant in; the Signior
Carolo de Charomont being ſkilful
To guide me through the Labyrinth of wild Paſſions,
That labour'd to impriſon my free Soul
A Slave to vicious Sloth.

    Fiorin. You ſpeak him well.

    Giov. But ſhort of his Deſerts. Then for the Time
Of Recreation I was allow'd
(Againſt the Form follow'd by jealous Parents
In *Italy*) full Liberty to partake
His Daughter's ſweet Society. She's a Virgin
Happy in all Endowments which a Poet

Could

Could fancy in his Miftrefs; being herfelf
A School of Goodnefs, where chafte Maids may learn
(Without the Aids of foreign Principles)
By the Example of her Life and Purenefs,
To be as fhe is, excellent.   I but give you
A brief Epitome of her Virtues, which,
Dilated on at large, and to their Merit,
Would make an ample Story. .
     Fiorin. Your whole Age,
So fpent with fuch a Father, and a Daughter;
Could not be tedious to you.
     Giov. True, great Princefs:
And now, fince you have pleas'd to grant the Hearing
Of my Time's Expence in the Country, give me Leave
To entreat the Favour, to be made acquainted
What Service, or what Objects in the Court
Have, in your Excellence Acceptance; prov'd
Moft gracious to you?
     Fiorin. I'll meet your Demand,
And make a plain Difcovery.   The Duke's Care
For my Eftate and Perfon holds the firft
And choiceft Place: Then, the Refpect the Courtiers
Pay gladly to me, not to be contemn'd.
But that which rais'd in me the moft Delight
(For I'm a Friend to Valour) was to hear
The noble Actions truly reported
Of the brave Count *Sanazarro.* I profefs,   ·
When it hath been; and fervently, deliver'd,
How boldly in the Horror of a Fight,
Cover'd with Fire and Smoak, and, as if Nature
Had lent him Wings, like Lightning he hath fall'n
Upon the *Turkifh* Gallies, I have heard it
With a Kind of Pleafure, which hath whifper'd to me
This Worthy muft be cherifh'd.
     Giov. 'Twas a Bounty
You never can repent.
     Fiorin. I glory in it.
And when he did return (but ftill with Conqueft)
His Armour off, not young *Antinous*
H 2

A

Appear'd more courtly; all the Graces that
Render a Man's Society dear to Ladies,
Like Pages waiting on him, and it does
Work ſtrangely on me.

    Giov. To divert your Thoughts,
Though they are fix'd upon a noble Subject,
I am a Suitor to you.

    Fiorin. You will aſk,
I do preſume, what I may grant, and then
It muſt not be deny'd.

    Giov. It is a Favour
For which I hope your Excellence will thank me.

    Fiorin. Nay, without Circumſtance.

    Giov. That you would pleaſe
To take Occaſion to move the Duke,
That you, with his Allowance, may command
This matchleſs Virgin *Lydia* (of whom
I cannot ſpeak too much) to wait upon you.
She's ſuch a one, upon the Forfeit of
Your good Opinion of me, that will not
Be a Blemiſh to your Train.

    Fiorin. 'Tis rank! he loves her:
But I will fit him with a Suit. [*Aſide.*] I pauſe not,
As if it bred or Doubt or Scruple in me
To do what you deſire; for I'll effect it,
And make uſe of a fair and fit Occaſion.
Yet, in Return, I aſk a Boon of you,
And hope to find you, in your Grant to me,
As I have been to you.

    Giov. Command me, Madam.

    Fiorin. 'Tis near ally'd to yours. That you would be
A Suitor to the Duke, not to expoſe
(After ſo many Trials of his Faith)
The noble *Sanazarro* to all Dangers,
As if he were a Wall, to ſtand the Fury
Of a perpetual Battery: But now
To grant him, after his long Labours, Reſt
And Liberty to live in Court; his Arms

And

And his victorious Sword and Shield hung up
For Monuments. [4]
    Giov. Hum. I'll embrace, fair Princefs,

Enter Cozimo.

The fooneft Opportunity.   The Duke!
    Coz. Nay, blufh not ; we fmile on your Privacy,
And come not to difturb you.   You are Equals,
And, without Prejudice to eithers Honours,
May make a mutual Change of Love and Courtfhip,
'Till you are made one, and with Holy Rites ;
And we give Suffrage to it.
    Giov. You are gracious.
    Coz. To ourfelf in this.   But now break off: Too
Taken at once of the moft curious Viands   [much
Dulls the fharp Edge of Appetite.   We are now
For other Sports, in which our Pleafure is
That you fhall keep us Company.
    Fiorin. We attend you.   [*Exeunt.*

S C E N E II.

Bernardo, Cauponi, Petruchio.

Bern. Is my Lord ftirring ?
    Caup. No ; he's faft.
    Petru. Let us take, then,
Our Morning Draught.   Such as eat Store of Beef,
Mutton, and Capons, may preferve their Healths
With that thin Compofition call'd Small Beer,
As 'tis faid they do in *England.*   But *Italians,*
That think when they have fupp'd upon an Olive,

---

    [4] *And his victorious Sword and Shield hung up*
       For Monuments.

So in *Shakefpear,*
     Our bruifed Arms hung up for Monuments.
              Richard III. Act 1. Scene 1.

A Root, or bunch of Raiſins, 'tis a Feaſt,
Muſt kill thoſe Crudities, riſing from cold Herbs,
With hot and luſty Wines.
   Caup. A Happineſs
Thoſe Tramontanes ne'er taſted.
   Bern. Have they not
Store of Wine there?
   Caup. Yes, and drink more in two Hours
Then the *Dutchmen* or the *Dane* in four and twenty.
   Petru. But what is't? *French* Traſh, made of rotten
                              [Grapes,
And Dregs and Lees of *Spain*, with *Welch* Metheglin,
A Drench to kill a Horſe, but this pure Nectar
Being proper to our Climate, is too fine
To brook the Roughneſs of the Sea.　The Spirit
Of this begets in us quick Apprehenſions
And active Executions, whereas their
Groſs Feeding makes their Underſtanding like it.
They can fight, and that's their all.⁵　　　[*They drink.*

Enter *Sanazarro,* a Servant.

   Sanaz. Security
Dwells about this Houſe, I think; the Gate's wide open,
And not a Servant ſtirring.　See the Horſes
Set up, and cloth'd.
   Serv. I ſhall, Sir.
   Sanaz. I'll make bold
To preſs a little further.
   Bern. Who is this,
Count *Sanazarro!*
   Petru. Yes, I know him.　Quickly
Remove the Flaggon.
   Sanaz. A good Day to you, Friends!
Nay, do not conceal your Phyſick; I approve it,
And, if you pleaſe, will be a Patient with you.

     ⁵ *They can fight, and that's there all.*
  This tho' a Truth is very conciſe.

                                   Petru.

Petru. My noble Lord.——   [*Drinks.*
Sanaz. A Health to yours.   Well done!
I see you love yourselves.   And I commend you,
'Tis the best Wisdom.
    Petru. May it please your Honour
To walk a Turn in the Gallery, I'll acquaint
My Lord with your being here.   [*Exit* Petruchio.
    Sanaz. Tell him I come
For a Visit only. 'Tis a handsome Pile this.
                              [*Exit* Sanazarro.
    Caup. Why here is a brave Fellow, and a right one;
Nor Wealth nor Greatness makes him proud.
    Bern. There are
Too few of them, for most of our new Courtiers
(Whose Fathers were familiar with the Prices
Of Oil and Corn, with when, and to where to vent 'em,
And left their Heirs rich from their Knowledge that Way)
Like Gourds shot up in a Night, disdain to speak
But to Cloth of Tissue.

Enter Carolo Charomonte *in a Night Gown*, Petruchio
              following.

    Carolo. Stand you prating Knaves,
When such a Guest is under my Roof? See all
The Rooms perfum'd.   This is the Man that carries
The Sway and Swinge of the Court; and I had rather
Preserve him mine with honest Offices, then.——
But I'll make no Comparisons.   Bid my Daughter
Trim herself up to the Height, I know this Courtier
Must have a Smack at her; and, perhaps, by his Place
Expects to wriggle further.   If he does,
I shall deceive his Hopes; for I'll not taint
My Honour for the Dukedom.   Which way went he?
    Caponi. To the Round Gallery.
    Carolo. I will entertain him
As fits his Worth and Quality, but no farther. [*Exeunt.*

H 4   S C E N E

SCENE III.

Sanazarro *alone.*

Sanaz. I cannot apprehend, yet I have argu'd
All Ways I can imagine, for what Reasons
The Great Duke does employ me hither; and,
What does encrease the Miracle, I must render
A strict and true Account, at my Return,
Of *Lydia* this Lord's Daughter, and describe
In what she's excellent, and where defective.
'Tis a hard Task; he that will undergo
To make a Judgment of a Woman's Beauty,
And see through all her Plaisterings and Paintings,
Had need of *Lynceus*'s Eyes, and with more Ease
May look like him through nine Mud-walls, then make
A true Discovery of her.   But th' Intents
And Secrets of my Princes Heart must be
Serv'd and not search'd into.

Enter Carolo Charomonte,

Carolo. Most noble Sir,
Excuse my Age, subject to ease and sloth,
That with no greater Speed I have presented
My Service with your welcome.
   Sanaz. 'Tis more fit
That I should ask your Pardon, for disturbing
Your Rest at this unseasonable Hour.
But my Occasions carrying me so near
Your Hospitable House, my Stay being short too;
Your Goodness, and the Name of Friend, which you
Are pleas'd to grace me with, gave me Assurance
A Visit would not offend.
   Carolo. Offend, my Lord?
I feel myself much younger for the Favour,
How is it with our gracious Master?
   Sanaz. He, Sir,

Holds

Holds ftill his wonted Greatnefs, and confeffes
Himfelf your Debtor, for your Love and Care
To the Prince *Giovanni*, and had fent
Particular Thanks by me, had his Grace known
The quick Difpatch of what I was defign'd to
Would have licenc'd me to fee you.

    Carolo. I am rich
In his Acknowledgment.

    Sanaz. Sir, I have heard
Your Happinefs in a Daughter.

    Carolo. Sits the Wind there ?   [*Afide.*

    Sanaz. Fame gives her out for a rare Mafter-piece.

    Carolo. 'Tis a plain Village Girl, Sir, but obedient;
That's her beft Beauty, Sir.

    Sanaz. Let my Defire
To fee her, find a fair Conftruction from you:
I bring no loofe Thought with me.

    Carolo. You are that Way,
My Lord, free from Sufpicion.   Her own Manners
(Without an Impofition from me)

Enter Lydia *and* Petronella.

I hope, will prompt her to it.   As fhe is,
She come's to make a Tender of that Service
Which fhe ftands bound to pay.

    Sanaz. With your fair Leave,
I make bold to falute you.

    Lydia. Sir, you have it.

    Petro. I am her Gentlewoman, will not he kifs me too?
This is coarfe, 'faith.   [*Afide.*

    Carolo. How he falls off!

    Lydia. My Lord, though Silence beft becomes a Maid,
And to be curious to know but what
Concerns myfelf, and with becoming Diftance,
May argue me of Boldnefs, I muft borrow
So much Modefty as to enquire
Prince *Giovanni*'s Health.

    Sanaz. He cannot want,

What

What you are pleas'd to wish him.

    Lydia. Would 'twere so!
And then there is no Blessing that can make
A hopeful and a noble Prince compleat,
But should fall on him.   O! he was our North-star,
The Light and Pleasure of our Eyes.

    Sanaz. Where am I?
I feel myself another Thing : Can Charms
Be writ on such pure Rubies ? Her Lips melt
As soon as touch'd! not those smooth Gales that glide [6]
O'er happy *Arabia*, or rich *Sabæa*,
Creating in their Passage Gums and Spices,
Can serve for a weak Simile to express
The Sweetness of her Breath.   Such a brave Stature
Homer bestowed on *Pallas*, every Limb
Proportion'd to it.

    Carolo. This is strange, my Lord !

    Sanaz. I crave your Pardon, and yours, matchless Maid,
For such I must report you.

    Petron. There's no Notice
Taken all this while of me.   *[Aside.*

    Sanaz. And I must add
If your Discourse and Reason parallel
The Rareness of your more then human Form,
You are a Wonder.

    Carolo. Pray you, my Lord, make Trial :
She can speak, I can assure you ; and, that my Presence
May not take from her Freedom, I will leave you :
For know, my Lord, my Confidence dares trust her
Where, and with whom, she pleases.   If he be
Taken the right Way with her, I cannot fancy
A better Match; and for false Play I know
The Tricks, and can discern them.   *Petronella!*

    Petron. Yes, my good Lord.

---

    [6] —— *Not those smooth Gales that glide*
    Over happy Arabia, &c.

  In the *New Way to pay Old Debts*, *Massinger* has this beautiful
Simile again.   See Act III. Scene I.

Carolo.

Carolo. I have Employment for you.

                    [*Exeunt* Carolo *and* Petronella.

Lydia. What's your Will, Sir?

Sanaz. Madam, you are so large a Theme to treat of,
And every Grace about you offers to me
Such Copiousness of Language, that I stand
Doubtful which first to touch at.   If I err,
As in my Choice I may, let me entreat you,
Before I do offend, to sign my Pardon,
Let this, the Emblem of your Innocence
Give me Assurance.

    Lydia. My Hand joined to yours,
Without this Superstition, confirms it.
Nor need I fear you will dwell long upon me,
The Barrenness of the Subject yielding nothing
That Rhetorick with all her Tropes and Figures
Can amplify.   Yet, since you are resolved
To prove yourself a Courtier in my Praise,
As I'm a Woman (and you Men affirm
Our Sex loves to be flatter'd) I'll endure it. [Carolo *above.*
Now when you please begin.

    Sanaz. Such *Læda*'s Paps were,   [*Turns from her.*
Down Pillows styl'd by *Jove:* And their pure Whiteness
Shames the Swan's Down, or Snow.   No Heat of Lust
Swells up her Azure Veins.   And yet I feel
That this chaste Ice, but touch'd, fans Fire in me.

    Lydia. You need not, noble Sir, be thus transported,
Or trouble your Invention to express
Your Thought of me: The plainest Phrase and Language
That you can use, will be too high a strain
For such an humble Theme.

    Sanaz. If the great Duke
Made this his End to try my constant Temper,
Though I am vanquish'd, 'tis his Fault, not mine.
For I am Flesh and Blood, and have Affections
Like other Men. Who can behold the Temples,
Or Holy Altars, but the Objects work
Devotion in him? And I may as well
Walk over burning Iron with bare Feet
And be unscorch'd, as look upon this Beauty

                              Without

Without Defire, and that Defire purfu'd too,
'Till it be quench'd with the enjoying thofe
Delights, which to atchieve, Danger is nothing,
And Loyalty but a Word.   [*Afide.*

    Lydia. I ne'er was proud;
Nor can find I'm guilty of a Thought
Deferving this Neglect and Strangenefs from you.
Nor am I amorous.

    Sanaz. Suppofe his Greatnefs
Loves her himfelf, why makes he Choice of me
To be his Agent? It is Tyranny
To call one, pinch'd with Hunger, to a Feaft,
And at that Inftant cruelly deny him
To tafte of what he fees.   Allegiance
Tempted too far, is like the Trial of
A good Sword on an Anvil; as that often
Flies in Pieces without Service to the Owner;
So Truft enforc'd too far proves Treachery,
And is too late repented.   [*Afide.*

    Lydia. Pray you, Sir,
Or licenfe me to leave you, or deliver
The Reafons which invite you to command
My tedious waiting on you.

    Carolo. As I live,
I know not what to think on't.   Is't his Pride,
Or his Simplicity?

    Sanaz. Whither have my Thoughts
Carried me from myfelf? In this my Dulnefs,
I've loft an Opportunity.   [*He turns to her.*

    Lydia. 'Tis true.   *She falls off.*
I was not bred in Court, nor live a Star there;
Nor fhine in rich Embroideries and Pearl,
As they, that are the Miftreffes of great Fortunes,
Are every Day adorn'd with.

    Sanaz. Will you vouchfafe
Your Ear, fweet Lady?

    Lydia. Yet I may be bold
For my Integrity and Fame, to rank
With fuch as are more glorious. Though I never

                                             Did

Did Injury, yet I am senfible
When I'm contemn'd, and fcorn'd.
 Sanaz. Will you pleafe to hear me ?
 Lydia. O the Difference of Natures ! *Giovanni,*
A Prince in Expection, when he liv'd here,
Stole Courtefy from Heav'n, and would not to
The meaneft Servant in my Father's Houfe
Have kept fuch Diftance.
 Sanaz. Pray you, do not think me
Unworthy of your Ear : It was your Beauty
That turn'd me Statue.—I can fpeak, fair Lady.
 Lydia. And I can hear. The Harfhnefs of your Court-
Cannot corrupt my Courtefy   [fhip
 Sanaz. Will you hear me,
If I fpeak of Love ?
 Lydia. Provided you be modeft;
I were uncivil, elfe.
 Carolo. They are come to parley :
I muft obferve this nearer.   [Carolo *defcends.*
 Sanaz. You're a rare one,
And fuch (but that my Hafte commands me hence)
I could converfe with ever. Will you grace me
With Leave to vifit you again ?
 Lydia. So you,
At your Return to Court, do me the Favour
To make a Tender of my humble Service
To the Prince *Giovanni.*
 Sanaz. Ever touching
Upon that String ? And will you give me Hope
Of future Happinefs ?
 Lydia. That, as I fhall find you.
The Fort that's yielded at the firft Affault,
Is hardly worth the taking.

Enter Carolo.

 Carolo. O, they are at it.
 Sanaz. She is a Magazine of all Perfection,
And 'tis Death to part from her, yet I muft —   [*Afide.*
A parting Kifs, fair Maid.   *Lydia.*

Lydia. That Cuftom grants you.

Carolo. A homely Breakfaft does attend your Lord-
Such as the Place affords.   [fhip.

Sanaz. No; I have feafted
Already here.   My Thanks, and fo I leave you:
I will fee you again.   'Till this unhappy Hour
I ne'er was loft; and what to do, or fay,
I have not yet determin'd.   [*Exit* Sanazarro.

Carolo. Gone, fo abruptly?
'Tis very ftrange!

Lydia. Under your Favour, Sir,
His coming hither was to little Purpofe
For any Thing I heard from him.

Carolo. Take heed, *Lydia!*
I do advife you with a Father's Love,
And Tendernefs of your Honour; as I would not
Have you coarfe and harfh in giving Entertainment,
So by no Means be credulous.   For great Men,
'Till they have gain'd their Ends, are Giants in
Their Promifes; but, thofe obtain'd, weak Pigmies
In their Performance.   And it is a Maxim
Allow'd among them, fo they may deceive,
They may fwear any Thing; for the Queen of Love
As they hold conftantly, does never punifh,
But fmile at Lovers' Perjuries.—Yet be wife too;
And when you are fued to in a noble Way,
Be neither nice, nor fcrupulous.

Lydia. All you fpeak, Sir,
I hear as Oracles; nor will digrefs
From your Directions.

Carolo. So fhall you keep
Your Fame untainted.

Lydia. As I would my Life, Sir.   [*Exeunt.*

The End of the Second Act.

A C T

ACT III.　　SCENE I.

Sanazarro, *Servant.*

Sanaz. LEAVE the Horſes with my Grooms; but
　　　　be you careful
With your beſt Diligence and Speed, to find out
The Prince, and humbly in my Name entreat him
I may exchange ſome private Conference with him
Before the Great Duke know of my Arrival.

　Serv. I haſte, my Lord.

　Sanaz. Here I'll attend his coming,
And ſee you keep yourſelf, as much as may be,
Conceal'd from all Men elſe.

　Serv. To ſerve your Lordſhip,
I wiſh I were inviſible.　　　　　　　[*Exit Servant.*

　Sanaz. I am driven
Into a deſperate Streight, and cannot ſteer
A middle Courſe; and of the two Extremes
Which I muſt make Election of, I know not
Which is more full of Horror.　Never Servant
Stood more engag'd to a magnificent Maſter
Than I to *Cozimo.*　And all thoſe Honours
And Glories by his Grace conferr'd upon me,
Or by my proſp'rous Services deſerv'd,
If now I ſhould deceive his Truſt, and make
A Shipwreck of my Loyalty, are ruin'd.
And, on the other Side, if I diſcover
Lydia's divine Perfections, all my Hopes
In her are ſunk, never to be buoy'd up:
For 'tis impoſſible, but as ſoon as ſeen,
She muſt with Adoration be ſu'd to.
A Hermit at his Beads, but looking on her,
Or the cold Cinick, whom *Corinthian Lais,*
Not mov'd with her Luſt's Blandiſhments, call'd a Stone,
At this Object would take Fire.　Nor is the Duke

Such

Such an *Hippolitus*, but that this *Phædra*
But seen, must force him to forsake the Groves
And *Dian*'s Huntmanship, proud to serve under
Venus' soft Ensigns.   No, there is no Way
For me to hope Fruition of my Ends,
But to conceal her Beauties — and how that
May be effected, is as hard a Task
As with a Veil to cover the Sun's Beams,
Or comfortable Light.   Three Years the Prince
Liv'd in her Company, and *Contarino*,
The Secretary, hath possess'd the Duke
What a rare Piece she is.—But he's my Creature,
And may with Ease be frighted to deny
What he hath said.   And, if my long Experience
With some strong Reasons I have thought upon,
Cannot o'er-reach a Youth, my Practice yields me
But little Profit.

Enter Giovanni *and the Servant.*

  Giov. You are well return'd, Sir.
   Sanaz. Leave us. When that your Grace shall know
        the Motives
That forc'd me to invite you to this Trouble,
You will excuse my Manners.   [*Exit Servant,*
   Giov. Sir, there needs not
This Circumstance between us.   You are ever
My noble Friend.
   Sanaz. You shall have further Cause
To assure you of my Faith and Zeal to serve you,
And, when I have committed to your Trust
(Presuming still on your retentive Silence)
A Secret of no less Importance than
My Honour, nay, my Head, it will confirm
What Value you hold with me.
   Giov. Pray you, believe, Sir,
What you deliver to me, shall be lock'd up
In a strong Cabinet, of which you yourself
Shall keep the Key.   For here I pawn my Honour
                         (Which

(Which is the beſt Security I can give yet)
It ſhall not be diſcover'd.

   Sanaz. This Aſſurance
Is more than I with Modeſty could demand
From ſuch a Pay-maſter ; but I muſt be ſudden,
And therefore to the Purpoſe. Can your Excellence
In your Imagination conceive
On what Deſign, or whither the Duke's Will
Commanded me hence laſt Night ?

   Giov. No, I aſſure you ;
And it had been a Rudeneſs to enquire
Of that I was not call'd to.

   Sanaz. Grant me Hearing,
And I will make you truly underſtand
It only did concern you.

   Giov. Me, my Lord ?

   Sanaz. You, in your preſent State, and future Fortunes;
For both lie at the Stake.

   Giov. You much amaze me.
Pray you, reſolve this Riddle.

   Sanaz. You know the Duke,
If he die iſſueleſs· (as yet he is)
Determines you his Heir.

   Giov. It hath pleas'd his Highneſs
Oft to profeſs ſo much.

   Sanaz. But ſay, he ſhould
Be won to prove a ſecond Wife, on whom
He may beget a Son, how in a Moment
Will all thoſe glorious Expectations, which
Render you reverenc'd and remarkable,
Be in a Moment blaſted, howe'er you are
His much-lov'd Siſter's Son ?

   Giov. I muſt bear it
With Patience, and in me it is a Duty
That I was born with ; and 'twere much unfit
For the Receiver of a Benefit
To offer, for his own Ends, to preſcribe
Laws to the Giver's Pleaſure.

Vol. III.   I   *Sanaz.*

Sanaz. Sweetly anfwer'd,
And like your noble Self.   This your rare Temper
So wins upon me, that I would not live
(If that by honeſt Arts I can prevent it)
To fee your Hopes made fruftrate.   And but think
How you fhall be transform'd from what you are,
Should this (as Heav'n avert it) ever happen,
It muſt difturb your Peace.   For whereas now,
Being as you are receiv'd for the Heir apparent,
You are no fooner feen, but wonder'd at ;
The Signiors making it a Bufineſs to
Enquire how you have flept ; and, as you walk
The Streets of *Florence*, the glad Multitude
In Throngs prefs but to fee you, and with Joy
The Father, pointing with his Finger, tells
His Son, This is the Prince, the hopeful Prince,
That muſt hereafter rule, and you obey him.
Great Ladies beg your Picture, and make Love
To that, defpairing to enjoy the Subftance.
And, but the laft Night, when 'twas only rumor'd
That you were come to Court (as if you had
By Sea paft hither from another World)
What general Shouts and Acclamations follow'd,
The Bells rang loud, the Bonfires blaz'd, and fuch
As iov'd not Wine, caroufing to your Health,
Were drunk, and blufh'd not at it.   And is this
A Happineſs to part with ?

 Giov. I allow thefe
As Flourifhes of Fortune, with which Princes
Are often footh'd, but never yet efteem'd 'em
For real Bleffings.

 Sanaz. Yet all thefe were paid
To what you may be, not to what you are ;
For if the Great Duke but fhew to his Servants
A Son of his own, you fhall, like one obfcure,
Pafs unregarded.

 Giov. I confeſs, Command
Is not to be contemn'd, and if my Fate
Appoint me to it, as I may, I'll bear it

With

With willing Shoulders. But, my Lord, as yet,
You've told me of a Danger coming towards me,
But have not nam'd it.

Sanaz. That is foon deliver'd.
Great *Cozimo,* your Uncle, as I more
Than guefs (for 'tis no frivolous Circumftance
That does perfuade my Judgment to believe it)
Purpofes to be married.

Giov. Married, Sir?
With whom, and on what Terms, pray you, inftruct me?

Sanaz. With the fair *Lydia.*

Giov. *Lydia?*

Sanaz. The Daughter
Of Signior *Charomonte:*

Giov. Pardon me
Though I appear incredulous; for on
My Knowledge, he ne'er faw her.

Sanaz. That is granted:
But *Contarino* hath fo fung her Praifes,
And giv'n her out for fuch a Mafter-piece,
That he's tranfported with it, Sir.—And Love
Steals fometimes through the Ear into the Heart
As well as by the Eye. The Duke no fooner
Heard her defcrib'd, but I was fent in Poft
To fee her, and return my Judgment of her.

Giov. And what's your Cenfure?

Sanaz. 'Tis a pretty Creature.

Giov. She's very fair.

Sanaz. Yes, yes, I have feen worfe Faces.

Giov. Her Limbs are neatly form'd.

Sanaz. She hath a Waift
Indeed fiz'd to Love's Wifh.

Giov. A delicate Hand too.

Sanaz. Then for a Leg and Foot;

Giov. And there I leave you,
For I prefum'd no farther.

Sanaz. As fhe is, Sir,
I know fhe wants no gracious Part that may
Allure the Duke; and, if he only fee her,

She

She is his own.   He will not be deny'd,
And then you're loft.   Yet, if you'll fecond me
(As you have Reafon, for it moft concerns you)
I can prevent all yet.

  Giov. I would you could,
A noble Way.

  Sanaz. I will cry down her Beauties;
Efpecially the Beauties of her Mind,
As much as *Contarino* hath advanc'd 'em;
And this, I hope, will breed Forgetfulnefs,
And kill Affection in him.—But you muft
Join with me in my Report, if you be queftion'd.

  Giov. I never told a Lye yet, and I hold it
In fome Degree blafphemous to difpraife
What's worthy Admiration.   Yet, for once,
I will difpraife a little, and not vary
From your Relation.

  Sanaz. Be conftant in it.

Enter Alphonfo.

Alph. My Lord, the Duke hath feen your Man, and
      wonders

Enter Cozimo, Contarino, *and Attendants.*

You come not to him.   See, if his Defire
To have Conference with you hath not brought
Him hither in his own Perfon.

  Coz. They are comely Courfers,
And promife Swiftnefs.

  Contar. They are, of my Knowledge,
Of the beft Race in *Naples.*

  Coz. You are, Nephew,
As I hear, an excellent Horfeman, and we like it.
'Tis a fair Grace in a Prince.   Pray you, make Trial
Of their Strength and Speed, and, if you think them fit
For your Employment, with a liberal Hand

                              Reward

Reward the Gentleman, that did prefent 'em
From the Viceroy of *Naples*.
　Giov. I will ufe
My beft Endeavour, Sir.
　　　　　　　[*Exeunt* Giovanni, Alphonfo, Hippolito.
　Coz. Wait on my Nephew.
Nay, ftay you, *Contarino* ; be within Call ;
It may be we fhall ufe you.　You have rode hard, Sir,
And we thank you for it.　Every Minute feems
Irkfome, and tedious to us, till you have
Made your Difcovery.　Say, Friend, have you feen
This Phœnix of our Age ?
　Sanaz. I have feen a Maid, Sir ;
But, if that I have Judgment, no fuch Wonder
As fhe was deliver'd to you.
　Coz. This is ftrange !
　Sanaz. But certain Truth.　It may be, fhe was look'd
With Admiration in the Country, Sir :　　　　　[on
But, if compar'd with many in your Court,
She would appear but ordinary.
　Coz. Contarino
Reports her otherwife.
　Sanaz. Such as ne'er faw Swans,
May think Crows beautiful.
　Coz. How is her Behaviour ?
　Sanaz. 'Tis like the Place fhe lives in.
　Coz. How her Wit,
Difcourfe, and Entertainment ?
　Sanaz. Very coarfe ;
I would not willingly fay poor, and rude :
But, had fhe all the Beauties of fair Women,
The Dullnefs of her Soul would fright me from her.
　Coz. You are curious, Sir.—I know not what to think
Contarino !　　　　　　　　　　　　　　[on't.
　Contar. Sir.
　Coz. Where was thy Judgment, Man,
T' extol a Virgin, *Sanazarro* tells me
Is nearer to Deformity ?
　　　　　　　　I 3　　　　　　　　　　*Sanaz.*

Sanaz. I faw her,
And curioufly perus'd her; and I wonder
That fhe, that did appear to me, that know
What Beauty is, not worthy the obferving,
Should fo tranfport you.

   Contar. 'Troth, my Lord, I thought then ——
   Coz. Thought? Didft thou not affirm it?
   Contar. I confefs, Sir,
I did believe fo then; but, now I hear
My Lord's Opinion to the contrary,
I am of another Faith; for 'tis not fit
That I fhould contradict him.   I am dim, Sir;
But he's fharp-fighted.

   Sanaz. This is to my Wifh.   [*Afide.*
   Coz. We know not what to think of this; yet would
      not

Enter Giovanni, Hippolita, Lodovico.

Determine rafhly of it.   How do you like
My Nephew's Horfemanfhip?

   Hippol. In my Judgment, Sir,
It is exact and rare.

   Alph. And, to my Fancy,
He did prefent great *Alexander* mounted
On his *Bucephalus.*

   Coz. You are right Courtiers,
And know it is your Duty to cry up
All Actions of a Prince.

   Sanaz. Do not betray
Yourfelf, you're fafe; I've done my Part.
                   [*Afide to* Giovanni.

   Giov. I thank you;
Nor will I fail.

   Coz. What's your Opinion, Nephew,
Of the Horfes?

   Giov. Two of them are, in my Judgment,
The beft I ever back'd : I mean the Roan, Sir,
And the Brown Bay; but for the Chefnut-colour'd,
                       Though

Though he be full of Metal, hot, and fiery,
He treads weak in his Pasterns.

   Coz. So, come nearer ;
This Exercise hath put you into a Sweat ;
Take this and dry it : And now I command you
To tell me truly what's your Censure of
Charomonte's Daughter *Lydia.*

   Giov. I am, Sir,
A Novice in my Judgment of a Lady ;
But, such as it is, your Grace shall have it freely.
I would not speak ill of her, and am sorry,
If I keep myself a Friend to Truth, I cannot
Report her as I would, so much I owe
Her reverend Father : But I'll give you, Sir,
As near as I can, her Character in little.
She's of a goodly Stature, and her Limbs
Not disproportion'd. For her Face, it is
Far from Deformity ; yet they flatter her
That stile it excellent. Her Manners are
Simple and innocent ; but her Discourse
And Wit deserve my Pity, more than Praise.
At the best, my Lord, she is a handsome Picture ;
And, that said, all is spoken.

   Coz. I believe you ;
I ne'er yet found you false.

   Giov. Nor ever shall, Sir.——
——Forgive me, matchless *Lydia !* too much Love,
And jealous Fear to lose thee, do compel me
Against my Will, my Reason, and my Knowledge,
To be a poor Detractor of that Beauty,
Which fluent *Ovid*, if he liv'd again,
Would want Words to express.   [*Aside.*

   Coz. Pray you, make Choice of
The richest of our Furniture for these Horses ;
                   [*To* Sanazarro.
And take my Nephew with you ; we in this
Will follow his Directions.

   Giov. Could I find now
The Princess *Fiorinda*, and persuade her ·

I 4

To

To be silent in the Suit that I mov'd to her,
All were secure.

  Sanaz. In that, my Lord, I'll aid you.

  Coz. We will be private; leave us. All my Studies

          [*Exeunt all but* Cozimo.

And serious Meditations aim no farther
Than this young Man's Good. He was my Sister's Son,
And she was such a Sister, when she liv'd,
I could not prize too much; nor can I better
Make known how dear I hold her Memory,
Than in my cherishing the only Issue
Which she hath left behind her. Who's that?

     Enter Fiorinda.

Fiorin. Sir.

  Coz. My fair Charge, you are welcome to us.

  Fiorin. I have found it, Sir.

  Coz. All Things go well in *Urbin?*

  Fiorin. Your gracious Care to me an Orphan, frees me
From all Suspicion, that my jealous Fears
Can drive into my Fancy.

  Coz. The next Summer
In our own Person, we will bring you thither,
And seat you in your own.

  Fiorin. When you think fit, Sir.
But, in the mean time, with your Highness' Pardon,
I am a Suitor to you.

  Coz. Name it, Madam,
With Confidence to obtain it.

  Fiorin. That you would please
To lay a strict Command on *Charomonte,*
To bring his Daughter *Lydia* to the Court:
And, pray you, think, Sir, that 'tis not my Purpose
T' employ her as a Servant, but to use her
As a most wish'd Companion.

  Coz. Ha! your Reason?   [giv'n her

  Fiorin. The hopeful Prince your Nephew, Sir, hath
To me for such an Abstract of Perfection

              In

In all that can be wifh'd for in a Virgin,
As Beauty, Mufick, ravifhing Difcourfe,
Quicknefs of Apprehenfion, with choice Manners
And Learning too, not ufual with Women;
That I am much ambitious (though I fhall
Appear but as a Foil to fet her off)
To be from her inftructed, and fupply'd
In what I am defective.

   Coz. Did my Nephew
Serioufly deliver this?

   Fiorin. I affure your Grace,
With Zeal and Vehemence; and, even when
With his beft Words he ftriv'd to fet her forth
(Though the rare Subject made him eloquent)
He would complain, all he could fay came fhort
Of her Defervings.

   Coz. Pray you, have Patience.
This was ftrangely carried.—Ha! are we trifled with?
Dare they do this? Is *Cozimo*'s Fury, that
Of late was terrible, grown contemptible?
Well; we will clear our Brows, and undermine
Their fecret Works (tho' they have dig'd like Moles)
And crufh 'em with the Tempeft of my Wrath
When I appear moft calm. He is unfit
To command others, that knows not to ufe it,
And with all Rigour.—Yet my ftern Looks fhall not
Difcover my Intents; for I will ftrike
When I begin to frown. [*Afide.*] You are the Miftrefs
Of that you did demand.

   Fiorin. I thank your Highnefs;
But Speed in the Performance of the Grant
Doubles the Favour, Sir.

   Coz. You fhall poffefs it fooner then you expect;
Only be pleas'd to be ready when my Secretary
Waits upon you, to take the frefh air.—My Nephew!
And my Bofom-friend fo to cheat me? 'tis not fair!
                           [*Afide.*

                                 Enter

Sanaz. Where should this Princess be? Nor in her
      Lodgings,
Nor in the private Walks, her own Retreat,
Which she so much frequented?
  Giov. By my Life,
She's with the Duke; and I much more than fear
Her Forwardness to prefer my Suit, hath ruin'd
What with such Care we built up.
  Coz. Have you furnish'd
Those Coursers, as we will'd you?
  Sanaz. There's no Sign
Of Anger in his Looks.   [*Aside.*
  Giov. They are compleat, Sir.
  Coz. 'Tis well. To your Rest. Soft Sleeps wait on
      you, Madam.
To-morrow, with the Rising of the Sun,
Be ready to ride with us.——They with more Safety
Had trod on fork-tongu'd Adders, than provok'd me.
                 [*Exit* Cozimo.
  Fiorin. I come not to be thank'd, Sir, for the speedy
Performance of my Promise touching *Lydia*;
It is effected.
  Sanaz. We are undone.
  Fiorin. The Duke
No sooner heard me with my best of Language
Describe her Excellencies, as you taught me,
But he confirm'd it.——You look sad, as if
You wish'd it were undone.
  Giov. No, gracious Madam,
I am your Servant for't.
  Fiorin. Be you as careful
For what I mov'd to you. Count *Sanazarro*,
Now I perceive you honour me, in vouchsafing
To wear so slight a Favour.
  Sanaz. 'Tis a Grace
I am unworthy of.

                                 Fiorin.

Fiorin. You merit more,
In prizing fo a Trifle.   Take this Diamond ;
I'll fecond what I have begun : For know
Your Valour hath fo won upon me, that
'Tis not to be refifted.   I have faid, Sir,
And leave you to interpret it.   [*Exit* Fiorinda.
     Sanaz. This to me
Is Wormwood.   'Tis apparent we are taken
In our own Nooze.—What's to be done ?
     Giov. I know not. 7
And 'tis a Punifhment juftly fall'n upon me
For leaving Truth, a conftant Miftrefs, that
Ever protects her Servants, to become
A Slave to Lyes and Falfhood.   What Excufe
Can we make to the Duke ? What Mercy hope for,
Our Packing being laid open ?
     Sanaz. 'Tis not to
Be queftion'd, but his purpos'd Journey is
To fee fair *Lydia.*
     Giov. And to divert him
Impoffible.
     Sanaz. There's now no looking backward.

    7 *I know not.*
    And 'tis a Punifhment juftly fall'n upon me
    For leaving Truth, &c.

Mr. *Mafon,* in his *Elfrida,* has a Paffage that much refembles this.

    ———— As Truth directs,
So only fhall we act.   This Day has fhewn
What dire Effects await its Violation.
Strait is the Road of Truth, and plain,
   And tho' acrofs the facred Way
Ten Thoufand falfe Meanders ftray,
   'Tis our's to walk direct.
        Spoke by the Semichorus, Page 76.

There have been feveral Plays founded on the fame Plot as this before us ; the moft diftinguifhed of which is *Elfrida* by Mr. *Mafon,* written on the Model of the ancient *Greek* Tragedy : The Concurrence of feveral fimilar Paffages in that and in the *Duke of Florence,* makes me think that Mr. *Mafon* had *Maffinger* in his Eye, in the Execution of his Piece.

                         Giov.

Giov. And which Way to go on with Safety, not
To be imagin'd.

Sanaz. Give me Leave.   I have
An Embryon in my Brain, which, I defpair not,
May be brought to Form and Fafhion, provided
You will be open-breafted.

Giov. 'Tis no Time now,
Our Dangers being equal, to conceal
A Thought from you.

Sanaz. What Power hold you o'er *Lydia* ?
Do you think that with fome Hazard of her Life
She would prevent your Ruin ?

Giov. I prefume fo :
If in the Undertaking it, fhe ftray not
From what becomes her Innocence ; and to that
'Tis far from me to prefs her ; I myfelf
Will rather fuffer.

Sanaz. 'Tis enough ; this Night
Write to her by your Servant *Calandrino*,
As I fhall give Directions ; my Man

Enter Calandrino.

Shall bear him Company.   See, Sir, to my Wifh
He does appear, but much transform'd from what
He was when he came hither.

Caland. I confefs
I am not very wife, and yet I find
A Fool, fo he be Parcel Knave, in Court
May flourifh and grow rich.

Giov. Calandrino !

Caland. Peace !
I'm in Contemplation.

Giov. Don't you know me ?

Caland. I tell thee, no ; on Forfeit of my Place,
I muft not know myfelf, much lefs my Father,
But by Petition : That Petition lin'd too
With golden Birds, that fing to the Tune of Profit,
Or I am deaf.

Giov.

Giov. But you've your Senfe of Feeling.
[*Offering to kick him.*

Sanaz. Nay, pray you, forbear.

Caland. I have all that's requifite
To the making up of a Signior.   My fpruce Ruff,
My hooded Cloak, long Stocking, and pain'd Hofe,
My Cafe of Tooth-picks, and my Silver Fork,
To convey an Olive neatly to my Mouth ;
And, what is All in All, my Pockets ring
A golden Peal.   O that the Peafants in the Country
(My quondam Fellows) but faw me as I am,
How they would admire and worfhip me !

Giov. As they fhall ;
For inftantly you muft thither.

Caland. My Grand Signior,
Vouchfafe a *Bezolus Manus*, and a Cringe
Of the laft Edition.

Giov. You muft ride Poft with Letters
This Night to *Lydia*.

Caland. An' it pleafe your Grace,
Shall I ufe my Coach, or foot-cloth Mule ?

Sanaz. You Widgeon,
You are to make all Speed, think not of Pomp.

Giov. Follow for your Inftru&ctions, Sirrah !

Caland. I have one Suit to you,
My good Lord.

Sanaz. What is't ?

Caland. That you would give me
A fubtil Court-Charm, to defend me from
Th' infe&ctious Air of the Country.

Giov. What's the Reafon ?

Caland. Why, as this Court-Air taught me knavifh
By which I am grown rich; if that again   [Wit,
Should turn me Fool and honeft——Vain Hopes, fare-
For I muft die a Beggar.   [wel,

Sanaz. Go to, Sirrah !
You'll be whip'd for this.

Giov. Leave Fooling, and attend us.   [*Exeunt.*
The End of the Third A&ct.

ACT IV. SCENE I.

Carolo Charomonte, Lydia.

Carolo. **D**Aughter, I have obferv'd, fince the Prince
          left us
(Whofe Abfence I mourn with you) and the Vifit
Count *Sannazarro* gave us, you have nourifhed
Sad and retired Thoughts, and parted with
That Freedom and Alacrity of Spirit
With which you us'd to chear me.
   Lydia. For the Count, Sir,
All Thought of him does with his Perfon die;
But, I confefs ingenuoufly, I cannot
So foon forget the Choice, and chafte Delights,
The courteous Converfation of the Prince,
And without Stain, I hope, afforded me
When he made this Houfe a Court.
   Carolo. It is in us
To keep it fo without him. Want we know not,
And all we can complain of (Heav'n be prais'd for't)
Is too much Plenty, and we will make ufe of

Enter Servants.

All lawful Pleafures. How now Fellows, when
Shall we have this lufty Dance?
   Caup. In the Afternoon, Sir.
'Tis a Device, I wis, of my own making,
And fuch a one, as fhall make your Signiorfhip know
I have not been your Butler for nothing, but
I've crotchets in my Head. We'll trip it tightly,
And make my fad young Miftrefs merry again,
Or I'll forfwear the Cellar.
   Bern. If we had
Our fellow *Calandrino* here to dance

His

His Part, we were perfect.

Petru. O! he was a rare Fellow;
But I fear the Court hath spoil'd him.

Caup. When I was young,
I could have cut a Caper on a Pinnacle;
But now I'm old and wife.—Keep your Figure fair,
And follow but the Sample I shall set you,
The Duke himself will send for us, and laugh at us,
And that were Credit.

Lydia. Who have we here?

Enter Calandrino.

Caland. I find   [tender.
What was Brawn in the Country, in the Court grows
The Bots on thefe jolting Jades, I am bruis'd to Jelly.
A Coach for my Money! and that the Courtezans know
Their riding so, makes them laft three Years longer [well
Then such as are hackney'd.

Carolo. Calandrino, 'tis he.   [the Honour

Caland. Now to my Poftures. Let my Hand have
To convey a Kifs from my Lips to the Cover of
Your Foot dear Signior.

Carolo. Fie, you ftoop too low, Sir.

Caland. The Hem of your Veftment, Lady. Your Glove
Nay, I have conn'd my Diftances.   [is for Princes;

Lydia. 'Tis moft Courtly.

Caup. Fellow *Calandrino!*

Caland. Signior *de Cauponi,*
Grand Botelier of the Manfion!

Bern. How is't, Man?   [*Claps him on the Shoulder.*

Caland. Be not fo ruftick in your Salutations,
Signior *Bernardo,* Mafter of the Accounts!
Signior *Petruchio!* May you long continue
Your Function in the Chamber.

Caup. When fhall we learn fuch Gambols in our *Villa?*

Lydia. Sure, he's mad.

Carolo. 'Tis not unlike, for moft of fuch Mufhrooms
What News at Court?   [are fo.

Caland. Bafto! They are Myfteries,

And

And not to be reveal'd. With your Favour, Signior,
I am in private to confer awhile
With this Signiora. But I'll pawn my Honour,
That neither my terse Language, nor my Habit
Howe'er it may convince, nor my new Shrugs,
Shall render her enamour'd.

    Carolo. Take your Pleasure,
A little of these apish Tricks may pass;
Too much is tedious.   [*Exit* Carolo.

    Caland. The Prince in this Paper
Presents his Service.——Nay, it is not Courtly
To see the Seal broke open. So I leave you.
Signiors of the *Villa*, I'll descend to be
Familiar with you.

    Caup. Have you forgot to dance?
    Caland. No, I am better'd.
    Petru. Will you join with us?
    Caland. As I like the Project.
Let me warm my Brains, first, with the richest Grape,
And then I'm for you.

    Caup. We will want no Wine.   [*Exeunt.*

Lydia alone.

    Lydia. That this comes only from the best of Princes,
With a Kind of Adoration does command me
To entertain it, and the sweet Contents [*Kissing the Letter.*
That are inscribed here by his Hand, must be
Much more than musical to me.   All the Service
Of my Life at no Part can deserve this Favour.
O what a Virgin Longing I feel on me
To unrip the Seal, and read it! Yet, to break
What he hath fast'ned, rashly, may appear
A saucy Rudeness in me.——I must do it,
(Nor can I else, learn his Commands, or serve 'em)
But with such Reverence, as I would open
Some Holy Writ, whose grave Instructions beat down
Rebellious Sins, and teach my better Part
How to mount upward.——So, 'tis done, and I
                    [*Opens the Letter. Reads.*
With Eagle's Eyes will curiously peruse it.

                                      Chaste

Chaſte Lydia ! The Favours are ſo great
On me by you conferr'd, that to intreat
The leaſt Addition to 'em, in true Senſe
May argue me of bluſhleſs Impudence.
But, ſuch are my Extremes, if you deny
A farther Grace, I muſt unpittied die.
Haſte cuts off Circumſtance.   As you're admired
For Beauty, the Report of it hath fir'd
The Duke my Uncle, and I fear you'll prove,
Not with a ſacred, but unlawful Love.
If he ſee you, as you are, my hop'd-for Light
Is chang'd into an Everlaſting Night.
How to prevent it, if your Goodneſs find,
You ſave two Lives, and me you ever bind,
    The Honourer of your Virtues, Giovanni.

Were I more deaf then Adders, theſe ſweet Charms
Would through my Ears find Paſſage to my Soul,
And ſoon inchant it.   To ſave ſuch a Prince
Who would not periſh ? Virtue in him muſt ſuffer,
And Piety be forgotten.   The Duke's Luſt
Though it rag'd more then *Tarquin*'s, ſhall not reach me,
All quaint Inventions of chaſte Virgins aid me !
My Prayers are heard—I have't. The Duke ne'er ſaw me ;
Or, if that fail, I am again provided.
    [*This ſpoke as if ſhe ſtudied an Evaſion.*
But for the Servants ! They will take what Form
I pleaſe to put upon them.—*Giovanni,*
Be ſafe, thy Servant *Lydia* aſſures it.
Let Mountains of Afflictions fall on me,
Their Weight is eaſy, ſo I ſet thee free.   [*Exit.*

S C E N E II.

Cozimo, Giovanni, Sanazarro, Carolo, Servants.

Sanaz. Are you not tir'd with Travel, Sir ?
Coz. No, no,
I am Freſh and Luſty.
  Vol. III.   K   *Carolo.*

Carolo. This Day ſhall be ever
A Holy-day to me, that brings my Prince
Under my humble Roof.　　　　　　　　　　*[Weeps.*
　　Giov. See, Sir, my good Tutor
Sheds Tears for Joy.
　　Coz. Dry them up, *Charomonte,*
And all forbear the Room, while we exchange
Some private Words togethe.
　　Giov. O my Lord,
How groſly have we overſhot ourſelves!
　　Sanaz. In what, Sir?
　　Giov. In forgetting to acquaint
My Guardian with our Purpoſe, all that *Lydia*
Can do, avails us nothing—if the Duke
Find out the Truth from him.
　　Sanaz. 'Tis now paſt help,
And we muſt ſtand the Hazard—Hope the beſt, Sir?
　　　　　　　　　　[Exeunt Giovanni and Sanazarro.
　　Carolo. My Loyalty doubted, Sir?
　　Coz. 'Tis more.　Thou haſt
Abus'd our Truſt, and in a high Degree
Committed Treaſon.
　　Carolo. Treaſon? 'Tis a Word
My Innocence underſtands not.　Were my Breaſt
Tranſparent, and my Thoughts to be diſcern'd,
Not one Spot ſhall be found to taint the Candor
Of my Allegeance.　And I muſt be bold
To tell you, Sir (for he that knows no Guilt
Can know no Fear) 'tis Tyranny to o'er-charge
An honeſt Man; and ſuch, till now, I've liv'd,
And ſuch, my Lord, I'll die.
　　Coz. Sir, do not flatter
Yourſelf with Hope, theſe great and glorious Words,
(Which every guilty Wretch, as well as you,
That's arm'd with Impudence, can with Eaſe deliver,
And with as full a Mouth) can work on us?
Nor ſhall gay Flouriſhes of Language clear
What is in Faƈt apparent.
　　Carolo. Faƈt? What Faƈt?

　　　　　　　　　　　　　　　　　　You

You that know only, what it is, inſtruct me,
For I am ignorant.
    Coz. This then, Sir. We gave up
(On our Aſſurance of your Faith and Care)
Our Nephew *Giovanni,* nay, our Heir
In Expectation, to be train'd up by you
As did become a Prince.
    Carolo. And I diſcharg'd it.
Is this the Treaſon?
    Coz. Take us with you, Sir.
And, in reſpect we knew his Youth was prone
To Women, and that living in our Court
He might make ſome unworthy Choice, before
His weaker Judgment was confirm'd, we did
Remove him from it; conſtantly preſuming
You, with your beſt Endeavours, rather would
Have quench'd thoſe Heats in him, then light a Torch,
As you have done to his Looſeneſs.
    Carolo. I? My travail
Is ill-requited, Sir; for, by my Soul,
I was ſo curious that way, that I granted
Acceſs to none could tempt him, nor did ever
One Syllable, or obſcene Accent touch
His Ear that might corrupt him.
    Coz. No? Why, then,
With your Allowance did you give free way
To all familiar Privacy, between
My Nephew and your Daughter? Or why did you
(Had you no other Ends in't but our Service)
Read to 'em, and together (as they had been
Scholars of one Form) Grammar, Rhetorick,
Philoſophy, Hiſtory, and interpret to 'em
The cloſe Temptations of laſcivious Poets?
Or wherefore (for we ſtill had Spies upon you)
Was ſhe ſtill preſent, when by your Advice
He was taught the Uſe of his Weapon, Horſemanſhip,
Wreſtling, nay, Swimming, but to fan in her
A hot Deſire of him? And then, forſooth,
His Exerciſes ended, cover'd with

K 2

A

A fair Pretence of Recreation for him,
When *Lydia* was inſtructed in thoſe Graces
That add to Beauty.   He brought to admire her,
Muſt hear her Sing, while to her Voice, her Hand
Made raviſhing Muſick ; and this applauded, dance
A Light Levalto with her.[8]
   Carolo. Have you ended
All you can charge me with ?
   Coz. Nor ſtop'd you there,
But they muſt unattended walk into
The ſilent Groves, and hear the amorous Birds
Warbling their wanton Notes ; here a ſure Shade
Of barren Sycamores, which the all·ſeeing Sun
Could not pierce through ; near that, an Arbor hung,
With ſpreading Eglantine ; there a bubbling Spring
Wat'ring a Bank of Hyacinths and Lillies,
With all Allurements that could move to Luſt.
And could this, *Charomonte,* (ſhould I grant
They had been Equals both in Birth and Fortune)
Become your Gravity ? Nay, 'tis clear as Air
That your ambitious Hopes to match your Daughter
Into our Family, gave connivence to it.
And this, though not in Act, in the Intent,
I call High Treaſon.
   Carolo. Hear my juſt Defence, Sir,
And, though you are my Prince, it will not take from
Your Greatneſs to acknowledge with a Bluſh,
In this my Accuſation you have been
More ſway'd by Spleen, and jealous Suppoſitions,
Than certain grounds of Reaſon. You had a Father
(Bleſt be his Memory) that made frequent Proofs
Of my Loyalty and Faith, and (would I boaſt
The Dangers I have broke through in his Service)
I could ſay more. Nay, you yourſelf, dread Sir,
Whenever I was put unto the Teſt,
Found me true Gold, and not adulterate Metal ;

----

[8] *A Light* Levalto *with her.*

   What the Dance here alluded to is, I cannot tell, nor can I find an
Explanation of the Word in any Dictionary.

And

And am I doubted now?

    Coz. This is from the Purpose.

    Carolo. I will come to it, Sir, your Grace well knew,
Before the Prince's happy Presence made
My poor House rich, the chiefest Blessings which
I gloried in (though now it prove a Curse)
Was an only Daughter. Nor did you command me,
As a Security to your future Fears,
To cast her off: Which had you done, howe'er
She was the Light of my Eyes, and Comfort of
My feeble Age; so far I priz'd my Duty
Above Affection, she now had been
A Stranger to my Care. But she is fair!
Is that her Fault or mine? Did ever Father
Hold Beauty in his Issue for a Blemish?
" Her Education and her Manners tempt too."
If these offend, they're easily removed:
You may, if you think fit, before my Face,
In Recompence of all my Watchings for you,
With burning Corrosives transform her to
An ugly Leper; and this done to taint
Her Sweetness, prostitute her to a Loathsome Brothel.
This I will rather suffer, Sir, and more,
Then live suspected by you.

    Coz. Let not Passion
Carry you beyond your Reason.

    Carolo. I am calm, Sir;
Yet you must give me leave to grieve, I find
My Actions misinterpreted. Alas! Sir,
Was *Lydia's* Desire to serve the Prince
Call'd an Offence? Or did she practise to
Seduce his Youth, because with her best Zeal
And Fervour she endeavoured to attend him?
'Tis a hard Construction—Though she be my Daughter
I may thus far speak her. From her Infancy
She was ever civil, her Behaviour nearer
Simplicity then Craft; and Malice dares not
Affirm, in one loose Gesture, or light Language,
She gave a Sign she was in Thought unchaste.

K 3

I'll

I'll fetch her to you, Sir, and but look on her
With equal Eyes, you muſt in Juſtice grant
That your Suſpicion wrongs her.

 Coz. It may be;
But I muſt have ſtronger Aſſurance of it
Than paſſionate Words.   And, not to trifle Time,
As we came unexpected to your Houſe,
We will prevent all Means that may prepare her
How t' anſwer that, with which we come to charge her.
And howſoever it may be receiv'd
As a foul Breach to hoſpitable Rites,
On thy Allegeance and boaſted Faith,
Nay, forfeit of thy Head, we do confine thee
Cloſe Priſoner to thy Chamber, till all Doubts
Are clear'd that do concern us.

 Carolo. I obey, Sir,
And wiſh your Grace had followed my Herſe
To my Sepulchre, my Loyalty unſuſpected,
Rather then now? But I am ſilent, Sir.
And let that ſpeak my Duty.　　　　　[*Exit* Carolo.

 Coz. If this Man
Be falſe, diſguiſed Treachery ne'er put on
A Shape ſo near to Truth.   Within there.

Enter Giovanni *and* Sanazarro, *uſhering in* Petronella,
 Calandrino *and others, ſetting forth a Banquet.*

 Sanaz. Sir.
 Coz. Bring *Lydia* forth.
 Giov. She comes, Sir, of herſelf
To preſent her Service to you.
 Coz. Ha! This Perſonage
Cannot invite Affection.
 Sanaz. See you keep State,
 Petro. I warrant you.
 Coz. The Manners of her Mind
Muſt be tranſcendent, if they can defend
Her rougher Out-ſide.   May we with your liking
Salute you, Lady?

Petro.

Petro. Let me wipe my Mouth, Sir,
With my Cambrick-Handkerchief, and then have at you.
   Coz. Can this be poffible ?
   Sanaz. Yes, Sir, you will find her
Such as I gave her to you.
   Petro. Will your Dukefhip
Sit down and eat fome Sugar-plums ? Here's a Caftle
Of March Pane too, and this Quince-Marmalade
Was of my own making.   All fumm'd up together
Did coft the fetting on, and here is Wine too [*Drinks all off.*
As good as e'er was tap'd.   I'll be your Tafter,
For I know the Fafhion—now you muft do me right, Sir,
You fhall, nor will, nor choofe.
   Giov. She's very fimple.
   Coz. Simple, 'tis worfe. Do you drink this often, Lady ?
   Petron. Still when I am thirfty, and eat when I am
                                                              | hungry.
Such Junckets come not every Day. Once more to you,
With a Heart and a half afaith.
   Coz. Pray you, paufe a little ;
If I hold your Cards, I fhall pull down the Side ;
I am not good at the Game.
   Petron. Then I'll drink for you.
   Coz. Nay, pray you ftay. I'll find you out a Pledge
That fhall fupply my Place, what think you of
This compleat Signior ? You are a *Juno,* and in fuch State
Muft feaft this *Jupiter.* What think you of him ?
   Petron. I defire no better.
   Coz. And you will undertake this Service for me ?
You are good at the Sport.
   Caland. Who I ? A Pidler; Sir.
   Coz. Nay, you fhall fit inthron'd, and eat and drink
As you were a Duke.
   Caland. If your Grace will have me,
I'll eat and drink like an Emperor.
   Coz. Take your Place then,
We are amaz'd.
   Giov. This is grofs : Nor can the Impofture

K 4

But

But be difcover'd.

Sanaz. The Duke's too fharp fighted
To be deluded thus.

Caland. Nay, pray you eat fair,
Or devide, and I will choofe. Cannot you ufe
Your Fork as I do? Gape and I will feed you.

[*Feeds her.*

Gape wider yet, this is Court-like.

Petron. To choke Daws with,
I like it not.

Caland. But you like this.   [*They drink.*

Petron. Let it come, Boy.

Coz. What a Sight is this? We could be angry with
How much you did bely her when you told us   [you,
She was only Simple! This is barbarous Rudenefs,
Beyond Belief.

Giov. I would not fpeak her, Sir,
Worfe than fhe was.

Sanaz. And I, my Lord, chofe rather
To deliver her better parted then fhe is,
Then to take from her.

Enter Cauponi.

Caup. Ere I'll lofe my Dance,
I'll fpeak to the Purpofe. I am, Sir, no Prologue;
But in plain Terms muft tell you, we are provided
Of a lufty Hornpipe.

Coz. 'Prithee, let us have it,
For we grow dull.

Caup. But, to make up the Medley,
For it is of feveral Colours, we muft borrow
Your Grace's Ghoft here.

Caland. Pray you, Sir, depofe me,
It will not do elfe. I am, Sir, the Engine
                    [*Rifes and refigns his Chair.*
By which it moves.

Petron. I will dance with my Duke too,
I will not out.

                                        Coz.

Coz. Begin then. There's more in this   [*Dance.*
Then yet I have difcovered,   Some *Oedipus*
Refolve this Riddle.
    Petron. Did I not foot it roundly ?   [*Falls down.*
    Coz. As I live, ftark drunk. Away with her.   We'll
                                                [reward you,
When you have cool'd yourfelves in the Cellar.
    Caup. Heaven preferve you.   [*Exeunt Dancers.*
    Coz. We pity *Charomonte*'s wretched Fortune
In a Daughter, nay, a Monfter.   Good old Man !
The Place grows tedious : Our Remove fhall be
With Speed. We'll only in a Word or two
Take leave and comfort him.
    Sanaz. 'Twill rather, Sir,
Encreafe his Sorrow, that you know his Shame,
Your Grace may do it by Letter.
    Coz. Who fign'd you
A Patent to direct us ? Wait our coming
In the Garden.
    Giov. All will out.
    Sanaz. I more then fear it. [*Exeunt* Giov. *and* Sanaz.
    Coz. Thefe are ftrange *Chimeras* to us ! What to judge
Is paft our Apprehenfion ! One Command   [of it
Charomonte to attend us. Can it be,   [*Exit* Servant.
That *Contarino* could be fo befotted
As to admire this Prodigy ? Or her Father
To dote upon it ? Or does fhe perfonate,
For fome Ends unknown to us, this rude Behaviour,
Within the Scene prefented, would appear
Ridiculous and impoffible. O you are welcome.

Enter Carolo.

We now acknowledge the much Wrong we did you
In our unjuft Sufpicion. We have feen
The Wonder, Sir, your Daughter.
    Carolo. And have found her
Such as I did report her. What fhe wanted
In Courtfhip, was, I hope, fupplied in civil
                                                And

And modeſt Entertainment.
   Coz. Pray you, tell us,
And truly we command you, Did you never
Obſerve ſhe was given to drink ?
   Carolo. To drink, Sir ?
   Coz. Yes.   Nay, more, to be drunk.
   Carolo. I had rather ſee her buried.
   Coz. Dare you truſt your own Eyes, if you find her now
More then diſtemper'd ?
   Carolo. I will pull them out, Sir,
If your Grace can make this good.   And if you pleaſe
To grant me Liberty, as ſhe is, I'll fetch her,
And in a Moment.
   Coz. Look you do, and fail not,
On the Peril of your Head.
   Carolo. Drunk ?—She diſdains it.   [*Exit* Carolo.
   Coz. Such Contrarieties were never read of.
Charomonte is no Fool, nor can I think
His Confidence built on Sand. We are abuſed,
'Tis too apparent.

Enter Carolo *and* Lydia.

   Lydia. I am indiſpoſed, Sir,
And that Life, you tender'd once, much indanger'd
In forcing me from my Chamber.
   Carolo. Here ſhe is, Sir,
Suddenly Sick, I grant ; but, ſure, not drunk,
Speak to my Lord the Duke.
   Lydia. All is diſcover'd,   [*Kneels.*
   Coz. Is this your only Daughter ?
   Carolo. And my Heir, Sir,
Nor keep I any Woman in Houſe
(Unleſs for ſordid Offices) but one,
I do maintain trimm'd up in her caſt Habits,
To make her Sport. And ſhe, indeed, loves Wine,
And will take too much of it. And perhaps, for Mirth,
She was preſented to you.
   Coz. It ſhall yield

No

No Sport to the Contrivers,—'Tis too plain now.
Her Prefence does confirm what *Contarino*
Deliver'd of her; nor can Sicknefs dim
The Splendor of her Beauties ; being herfelf, then,
She muft exceed his Praife.
　　Lydia. Will your Grace hear me ?
I'm faint and can fay little.
　　Coz. Here are Accents,
Whofe every Syllable is mufical !
Pray you let me raife you, and a-while reft here,
Falfe *Sanazarro*, treacherous *Giovanni !*
But ftand we talking ?
　　Carolo. Here's a Storm foon raifed.
　　Coz. As thou art our Subjeft, *Charomonte*, fwear
To aft what we Command.
　　Carolo. That is an Oath
I long fince took.
　　Coz. Then, by that Oath we charge thee,
Without Excufe, Denial or Delay
To apprehend, and fuddenly, *Sanazzaro*,
And our ingrateful Nephew.—We have faid it.
Do it without Reply, or we pronounce thee,
Like them, a Traytor to us. See them guarded
In feveral Lodgings, and forbid Accefs
To all, but when we warrant. Is our Will
Heard, fooner then obey'd ?
　　Carolo. Thefe are ftrange Turns;
But I muft not difpute 'em.　　　　　　　[*Exit* Carolo.
　　Coz. Be fevere in't.
O my abufed Lenity ! From what Height
Is my Power fall'n ?
　　Lydia. O me moft miferable !
That, being innocent, make others guilty :
Moft gracious Prince !—
　　Coz. Pray you rife, and then fpeak to me.
　　Lydia. My Knees fhall firft be rooted in this Earth,
And *Myrrha* like, I'll grow up to a Tree,
Dropping perpetual Tears of Sorrow, which,
Harden'd by the rough Wind, and turn'd to Amber,
　　　　　　　　　　　　　　　Unfortunate

Unfortunate Virgins like myfelf fhall wear,
Before I'll make Petition to your Greatnefs
But with fuch Reverence, my Hands held up thus,
As I would do to Heav'n.   You Princes are
As Gods on Earth to us, and to be fu'd to
With fuch Humility, as his Deputies
May challenge from their Vaffals.

   Coz. Here's that Form
Of Language I expected; pray you, fpeak,
What is your Suit?

   Lydia. That you would look upon me
As an humble Thing, that Millions of Degrees
Is plac'd beneath you.   For what am I? dread Sir?
Or what can fall in the whole Courfe of my Life,
That may be worth your Care, much lefs your Trouble?
As the lowly Shrub is to the lofty Cedar,
Or a Mole-hill to *Olympus*, if compar'd,
I am to you. Sir.   Or, fuppofe the Prince,
(Which cannot find Belief in me) forgetting
The Greatnefs of his Birth and Hopes, hath thrown
An Eye of Favour on me, in me punifh
(That am the Caufe) the Rafhnefs of his Youth.
Shall the Queen of the Inhabitants of the Air,
The Eagle, that bears Thunder on her Wings,
In her angry Mood, deftroy her hopeful Young,
For fuffering a Wren to perch too near 'em?
Such is our Difproportion.

   Coz. With what Fervour
She pleads againft herfelf!

   Lydia. For me, poor Maid,
I know the Prince to be fo far above me,
That my Wifhes cannot reach him.   Yet I am
So much his Creature, that, to fix him in
Your wonted Grace and Favour, I'll abjure
His Sight for ever, and betake myfelf
To a religious Life (where in my Prayers
I may remember him) and ne'er fee Man more
But my ghoftly Father.   Will you truft me, Sir?
In Truth I'll keep my Word; or, if this fail,

A

A little more of Fear what may befall him,
Will ſtop my Breath for ever.
   Coz. Had you thus argu'd   [*Raiſes her.*
As you were yourſelf, and brought as Advocates
Your Health and Beauty, to make way for you,
No Crime of his could put on ſuch a Shape,
But I ſhould look with th' Eyes of Mercy on it.
What would I give to ſee this Diamond
In her perfect Luſtre, as ſhe was before
The Clouds of Sickneſs dim'd it.   Yet, take Comfort,
And, as you would obtain Remiſſion for
His Treachery to me, cheer your drooping Spirits,
And call the Blood again into your Cheeks,
And then plead for him.   And in ſuch a Habit
As in your higheſt Hopes you would put on,
If we were to receive you for our Bride.
   Lydia. I'll do my beſt, Sir.
   Coz. And that Beſt will be
A Crown of all Felicity to me.   [*Exeunt.*

The End of the Fourth Act.

ACT V. SCENE I.

Sanazarro *above.*

Sanaz. 'TIS prov'd in me, the Curſe of human
                    Frailty,
(Adding to our Afflictions) makes us know
What's good; and yet our violent Paſſions force us
To follow what is ill.   Reaſon aſſur'd me
It was not ſafe to ſhave a Lion's Skin;
And that to trifle with a Sovereign, was
To play with Lightning: Yet imperious Beauty,
Treading upon the Neck of Underſtanding,
Compell'd me to put off my natural Shape
Of loyal Duty, to diſguiſe myſelf

                                 In

In the adulterate and cobweb Mafque
Of difobedient Treachery.   Where is now
My borrow'd Greatnefs ? or the promis'd Lives
Of following Courtiers echoing my Will ?
In a Moment vanifh'd.   Power, that ftands not on
Its proper Bafe, which is peculiar only
To abfolute Princes, falls or rifes, with
Their Frown or Favour. The Great Duke, my Mafter
(Who almoft chang'd me to his other Self)
No fooner takes his Beams of Comfort from me,
But I, as one unknown, or unregarded,
Unpity'd fuffer ! Who makes Interceffion
To his Mercy for me, now ? Who does remember
The Service I have done him ? Not a Man ;
And fuch as fpake no Language, but my Lord,
The Favourite of *Tufcany*'s Grand Duke,

        [*Looks backwards.*

Deride my Madnefs.—Ha ! What Noife of Horfes ?
A goodly Troop ! This back-part of my Prifon
Allows me Liberty to fee and know them.
Contarino ! Yes, 'tis he ; and *Lodovico* ;
And the Dutchefs *Fiorinda*, *Urbin*'s Heir,
A Princefs I have flighted ; yet I wear
Her Favours.   And, to teach me what I am,
She whom I fcorn'd can only meditate for me.
This Way fhe makes, yet fpeak to her I dare not ;
And how to make Suit to her, is a Tafk
Of as much Difficulty.—Yes, thou bleffed Pledge

  [*Takes off the Ring, and writes on a Pane of Glafs.*

Of her Affection, aid me.   This fupplies
The Want of Pen and Ink, and this of Paper.
It muft be fo ; and I in my Petition
Concife and pithy.

Enter Contarino, *leading in* Fiorinda, Alphonfo, Lodovico, Hieronimo, Calaminta.

 Fiorin. 'Tis a goodly Pile, this.
 Hieron. But better by the Owner.

           Alph.

Alph. But moſt rich
In the great States it covers.
   Fiorin. The Duke's Pleaſure
Commands us hither.
   Contar. Which was laid on us
To attend you to it.
   Lodov. Signior *Charomonte,*
To ſee your Excellence his Gueſt, will think
Himſelf moſt happy.
   Fiorin. Tye my Shoe.——What's that?
                               [*The Pane thrown down.*
A Pane thrown from the Window, no Wind ſtirring?
   Calam. And at your Feet too fall'n; there's ſomething
                writ on't.
   Contar. Some Courtier, belike, would have it known
He wore a Diamond.
   Calam. Ha! it is directed
To the Princeſs *Fiorinda.*
   Fiorin. We will read it.

The Inſcription.

He, whom you pleas'd to favour, is caſt down ;
Paſt hope of riſing, by the Great Duke's Frown,
If by your gracious Means, he cannot have
A Pardon.——And, that got, he lives your Slave.

The Subſcription.

Of Men the moſt diſtreſſed,
                        S A N A Z A R R O.

Of me the moſt belov'd, and I will ſave thee,
Or periſh with thee. Sure, thy Fault muſt be
Of ſome prodigious Shape, if that my Prayers
And humble Interceſſion to the Duke

Enter Cozimo *and* Carolo.

Prevail not with him.——Here he comes; Delay
Shall not make leſs my Benefit.
                                  Coz.

 Coz. What we purpose
Shall know no Change, and therefore move me not.
We were made as Properties, and what we shall
Determine of 'em, cannot be call'd Rigour,
But noble Juftice. When they prov'd difloyal,
They were cruel to themfelves. The Prince, that pardons
The firft Affront offer'd to Majefty,
Invites a fecond, rend'ring that Power
Subjects fhould tremble at, contemptible.
Ingratitude is a Monfter, *Carolo*,
To be ftrangl'd in the Birth, not to be cherifh'd.
Madam, you're happily met with.
 Fiorin. Sir, I am
An humble Suitor to you ; and the rather
Am confident of a Grant, in that your Grace,
When I made Choice to be at your Devotion,
Vow'd to deny me nothing.
 Coz. To this Minute
We have confirm'd it. What's your Boon ?
 Fiorin. It is, Sir,
That you, in being gracious to your Servant,
The ne'er fufficiently prais'd *Sanazarro*,
(That now under your heavy Difpleafure fuffers)
Would be good unto yourfelf. His Services,
So many, and fo great, (your Storm of Fury
Calm'd by your better Judgment) muft inform you,
Some little Slip (for fure it is no more)
From his loyal Duty, with your Juftice cannot
Make foul his fair Defervings. Great Sir, therefore,
Look backward on his former Worth, and, turning
Your Eye from his Offence (what 'tis I know not)
And, I am confident, you will receive him
Once more into your Favour.
 Coz. You fay well,
You're ignorant in the Nature of his Fault,
Which when you underftand (as we'll inftruct you)
Your Pity will appear a Charity
(It being confer'd on an unthankful Man)
To be repented. He's a Traytor, Madam,

To

To you, to us, to Gratitude ; and in that
All Crimes are comprehended.
      Fiorin. If his Offence
Aim'd at me only, whatfoe'er it is,
'Tis freely pardon'd.
      Coz. This Compaffion in you
Muft make the Colour of his Guilt more ugly.
The Honours we have hourly heap'd upon him,
The Titles, the Rewards, to th' Envy of
The old Nobility, as the common People,
We now forbear to touch at, and will only
Infift on his grofs Wrongs to you. You were pleas'd,
Forgetting both yourfelf and proper Greatnefs,
To favour him, nay, to court him to embrace
A Happinefs, which on his Knees with Joy
He fhould have fu'd for. Who repin'd not at
The Grace you did him ? Yet in Recompence
Of your large Bounties, the difloyal Wretch
Makes you a Stale ; and what he might be by you
Scorn'd and derided, gives himfelf up wholly
To the Service of another. If you can
Bear this with Patience, we muft fay you have not
The Bitternefs of Spleen, or ireful Paffions
Familiar to Women. Paufe upon it,
And when you ferioufly have weigh'd his Carriage,
Move us again, if your Reafon will allow it,
His Treachery known. And then, if you continue
An Advocate for him, we, perhaps, becaufe
We would deny you nothing, may awake
Our fleeping Mercy. *Carolo !*
      Carolo. My Lord.   [*They whifper.*
      Fiorin. To endure a Rival, that were equal to me,
Cannot but fpeak my Poverty of Spirit ;
But an Inferior, more : Yet true Love muft not
Know, or Degrees, or Diftances. *Lydia* may be
As far above me in her Form, as fhe
Is in her Birth beneath me ; and what I
In *Sanazarro* lik'd, he loves in her.
But, if I free him now, the Benefit

Vol. III.LBeing

Being done ſo timely, and confirming too
My Strength and Power, my Soul's beſt Faculties being
Bent wholly to preſerve him muſt ſupply me
With all I am defective in, and bind him
My Creature ever.   It muſt needs be ſo,
Nor will I give it o'er thus.

   Coz. Does our Nephew
Bear his Reſtraint ſo conſtantly, as you
Deliver it to us ?

   Carolo. In my Judgment, Sir,
He ſuffers more for his Offence to you,
Than in his Fear of what can follow it.
For he is ſo collected and prepar'd
To welcome that you ſhall determine of him,
As if his Doubts and Fears were equal to him.
And ſure he's not acquainted with much Guilt,
That more laments the telling one Untruth,
Under your Pardon ſtill (for 'twas a Fault, Sir)
Than others, that pretend to Conſcience, do
Their crying ſecret Sins.

   Coz. No more ; this Gloſs
Defends not the Corruption of the Text,
Urge it no more.   [Carolo *and the others whiſper.*

   Fiorin. I once more muſt make bold, Sir,
To trench upon your Patience.   I have
Conſider'd my Wrongs duly : Yet that cannot
Divert my Interceſſion for a Man
Your Grace, like me, once favour'd.   I am ſtill
A Suppliant to you, that you would vouchſafe
The Hearing his Defence, and that I may
With your Allowance ſee, and comfort him.
Then, having heard all that he can allege
In his Excuſe, for being falſe to you,
Cenſure him as you pleaſe.

   Coz. You will o'ercome ;
There's no contending with you.   Pray you, enjoy
What you deſire, and tell him, he ſhall have
A ſpeedy Trial, in which we'll forbear
To ſit a Judge, becauſe our Purpoſe is
To riſe up his Accuſer.   *Fiorin.*

Fiorin. All Increase
Of Happiness wait on *Cozimo.*

     [*Exeunt* Fiorinda *and* Calaminta.

 Alph. Was it no more ?

 Carolo. My Honour's pawn'd for it.

 Contar. I'll second you.

 Lodov. Since it is for the Service and the Safety
O' th' hopeful Prince, fall what can fall, I'll run
The desp'rate Hazard.

 Hieron. He's no Friend to Virtue
That does decline it.

They all kneel.

 Coz. Ha ! what sue you for ?
Shall we be ever troubled ? Do not tempt
That Anger may consume you.

 Carolo. Let it, Sir :
The Loss is less, though Innocents we perish,
Than that your Sister's Son should fall unheard
Under your Fury.   Shall we fear t' entreat
That Grace for him, that are your faithful Servants,
Which you vouchsafe the Count, like us a Subject ?

 Coz. Did not we vow, till Sickness had forsook
Thy Daughter *Lydia,* and she appear'd
In her perfect Health and Beauty to plead for him,
We were deaf to all Persuasion ?

 Carolo. And that Hope, Sir,
Hath wrought a Miracle.   She is recover'd,
And, if you please to warrant her, will bring
The penitent Prince before you.

 Coz. To enjoy
Such Happiness, what would we not dispense with ?

 Alph. Ludov. Hieron. We all kneel for the Prince.

 Contar. Nor can it stand
With your Mercy, that are gracious to Strangers,
To be cruel to your own.

 Coz. But art thou certain
I shall behold her at the best ?

L 2

Carolo.

Carolo. If ever
She was handfome, as it fits not me to fay fo,
She is now much better'd.

Coz. Rife ; thou art but dead
If this prove otherwife. *Lydia*, appear,
And feaft an Appetite almoft pin'd to Death
With longing Expectation to behold
Thy Excellencies : Thou, as Beauty's Queen,
Shalt cenfure the Detractors.   Let my Nephew
Be led in Triumph under her Command ;
We'll have it fo ; and *Sanazarro* tremble
To think whom he hath flander'd.   We'll retire
Ourfelves a little, and prepare to meet
A Bleffing, which Imagination tells us
We are not worthy of, and then come forth ;
But with fuch Reverence, as if I were
(Myfelf the Prieft, the Sacrifice my Heart)
To offer at the Altar of that Goodnefs
That muft or kill or fave me.   [*Exit* Cozimo.

Carolo. Are not thefe
Strange Gambols in the Duke ?

Alph. Great Princes have,
Like meaner Men, their Weaknefs.

Lodov. And may ufe it
Without Controul or Check.

Contar. 'Tis fit they fhould ;
Their Privilege were lefs, elfe, than their Subjects.

Hieron. Let them have their Humours ; there's no
crolling 'em.

S C E N E II.

Fiorinda, Sanazarro, Calaminta.

Sanaz. And can it be your Bounties fhould fall down
In Showers on my Ingratitude ? Or the Wrongs
Your Greatnefs fhould revenge, teach you to pity ?
What Retribution can I make ? what Service
Pay to your Goodnefs, that, in fome Proportion,

May

May to the World expreſs, I would be thankful ?
Since my Engagements are ſo great, that all
My beſt Endeavours to appear your Creature
Can but proclaim my Wants, and what I owe
To your Magnificence.

Fiorin. All Debts are diſcharg'd
In this Acknowledgment : Yet, ſince you pleaſe
I ſhall impoſe ſome Terms of Satisfaction
For that which you profeſs yourſelf oblig'd for,
They ſhall be gentle ones, and ſuch as will not,
I hope, afflict you.

Sanaz. Make me underſtand,
Great Princeſs, what they are, and my Obedience
Shall, with all cheerful Willingneſs, ſubſcribe
To what you ſhall command.

Fiorin. I will bind you to
Make good your Promiſe. Firſt, I then injoin you
To love a Lady, that a Noble Way
Truly affects you, and that you would take
To your Protection and Care the Dukedom
Of *Urbin,* which no more is mine, but yours.
And that, when you have full Poſſeſſion of
My Perſon, as my Fortunes, you would uſe me
Not as a Princeſs, but inſtruct me in
The Duties of an humble Wife, for ſuch
(The Privilege of my Birth no more remember'd)
I will be to you. This conſented to,
All Injuries forgotten, on your Lips
I thus ſign your *Quietus.*

Sanaz. I am wretched,
In having but one Life to be imploy'd
As you pleaſe to diſpoſe it : And, believe it,
If it be not already forfeited
To the Fury of my Prince, as 'tis your Gift,
With all the Faculties of my Soul, I'll ſtudy,
In what I may, to ſerve you.

Fiorin. I am happy.

Enter

Enter Giovanni and Lydia.

In this Affurance.——What
Sweet Lady's this?

   Sanaz. 'Tis *Lydia* Madam, fhe——

   Fiorin. I underftand you.
Nay, blufh not; by my Life fhe is a rare one!
And, if I were your Judge, I would not blame you,
To like and love her.——But, Sir, you are mine now.
And I prefume fo on your Conftancy,
That I dare not be jealous.

   Sanaz. All Thoughts of her
Are in your Goodnefs buried.

   Lydia. Pray you, Sir,
Be comforted; your Innocence fhould not know
What 'tis to fear, and if you but look on
The Guards that you have in yourfelf, you cannot.
The Duke's your Uncle, Sir, and though a little
Incens'd againft you, when he fees your Sorrow
He muft be reconcil'd. What rugged *Tartar*,
Or *Canibal*, though bath'd in Human Gore,
But, looking on your Sweetnefs, would forget
His cruel Nature, and let fall his Weapon,
Though then aim'd at your Throat?

   Giov. O *Lydia*,
Of Maids the Honour, and your Sexes Glory!
It is not Fear to die, but to lofe you
That brings this Fever on me. I will now
Difcover to you, that which, till this Minute,
I durft not truft the Air with. Ere you knew
What Power the Magick of your Beauty had,
I was inchanted by it, lik'd, and lov'd it,
My Fondnefs ftill encreafing with my Years.
And, flatter'd by falfe Hopes, I did attend
Some blefied Opportunity to move
The Duke, with his Confent to make you mine.
But now, fuch is my Star-crofs'd Deftiny,
When he beholds you as you are, he cannot

Deny

Deny himſelf the Happineſs to enjoy you.
And I as well in Reaſon may entreat him
To give away his Crown, as to part from
A Jewel of more Value, ſuch you are:
Yet, howſoever, when you are his Dutcheſs,
And I am turn'd into forgotten Duſt,
Pray you, love my Memory.—I ſhould ſay more,
But I'm cut off.

Enter Cozimo, Carolo, Contarino, *and others.*

Sanaz. The Duke? That Countenance, once,
When it was cloth'd in Smiles, ſhew'd like an Angel's,
But, now 'tis folded up in Clouds of Fury,
'Tis terrible to look on.   [*The Duke admiring* Lydia.
   Lydia. Sir.
   Coz. A while
Silence your muſical Tongue, and let me feaſt
My Eyes with the moſt raviſhing Object that
They ever gaz'd on. There's no Miniature
In her fair Face, but is a copious Theme
Which would (diſcours'd at large of) make a Volume.
What clear arch'd Brows? What ſparkling Eyes? The
Contending with the Roſes in her Cheeks,   [Lillies
Who ſhall moſt ſet them off? What ruby Lips?
Or unto what can I compare her Neck,
But to a Rock of Chryſtal? Every Limb
Proportion'd to Love's Wiſh, and in their Neatneſs
Add Luſtre to the Riches of her Habit,
Not borrow from it.
   Lydia. You are pleas'd to ſhew, Sir,
The Fluency of your Language, in advancing
A Subject much unworthy.
   Coz. How unworthy?
By all the Vows which Lovers offer at
The *Cyprian* Goddeſs' Altars, Eloquence
Itſelf preſuming, as you are, to ſpeak you,   [then?
Would be ſtruck dumb.—And what have you deſerv'd,
(Wretches, you kneel to late) that have endeavour'd

L 4

To

To fpout the Poifon of your black Detraction
On this immaculate Whitenefs? Was it Malice
To her Perfections ? Or——

   Fiorin. Your Highnefs promis'd
A gracious Hearing to the Count.

   Lydia. And Prince too;
Do not make void fo juft a Grant.

   Coz. We will not;
Yet, fince their Accufation muft be urg'd,
And ftrongly, ere their weak Defence have Hearing,
                            [*Seats the Ladies.*
We feat you here, as Judges, to determine
Of your grofs Wrongs and ours. And now, rememb'ring
Whofe Deputies you are, be neither fway'd,
Or with particular Spleen, or foolifh Pity;
For neither can become you.

   Carolo. There's fome hope, yet,
Since they have fuch gentle Judges.

   Coz. Rife, and ftand forth, then,
And hear with horror to your guilty Souls
What we will prove againft you.   Could this Princefs
(Thou Enemy to thyfelf!) ftoop her high Flight
Of tow'ring Greatnefs to invite thy Lownefs
To look up to it, and with nimble Wings
Of Gratitude, couldft thou forbear to meet it ?
Were her Favours boundlefs in a noble Way,
And warranted by our Allowance, yet
In thy Acceptation there appear'd no Sign
Of a modeft Thankfulnefs ?

   Fiorin. Pray you, forbear
To prefs that farther; 'tis a Fault we have
Already heard, and pardon'd.

   Coz. We will then
Pafs over it, and briefly touch at that
Which does concern ourfelf; in which both being
Equal Offenders, what we fhall fpeak, points
Indifferently at either.   How we rais'd thee,
Forgetful *Sanazarro* of our Grace,
To a full Poffeffion of Power and Honours,

It

It being too well known, we'll not remember.
And what thou wert (rash Youth) in Expectation
(And from which headlong thou hast thrown thyself)
Not *Florence*, but all *Tuscany* can witness
With Admiration.   To assure thy Hopes,
We did keep constant to a widowed Bed,
And did deny ourself those lawful Pleasures,
Our absolute Power and Height of Blood allow'd us.
Made both, the Keys that open'd our Heart's Secrets,
And what you spake, believ'd as Oracles.
But you, in Recompence of this, to him
That gave you all, to whom you ow'd your Being,
With treach'rous Lies endeavour'd to conceal
This Jewel from our Knowledge, which ourself
Could only lay just Claim too.
 Giov. 'Tis most true, Sir.
 Sanaz. We both confess a guilty Cause.
 Coz. Look on her ;
Is this a Beauty fit to be embrac'd
By any Subject's Arms ? Can any Tire
Become that Forehead, but a Diadem ?
Or, should we grant your being false to us
Could be excus'd, your Treachery to her
In seeking to deprive her of that Greatness
(Her matchless Form consider'd) she was born too,
Must ne'er find Pardon ? We have spoken, Ladies,
Like a rough Orator, that brings more Truth
Then Rhetorick to make good his Accusation,
And now expect your Sentence.
      [*The Ladies descend from the State.*
 Lydia. In your Birth, Sir,
You were mark'd out the Judge of Life and Death,
And we, that are your Subjects to attend
With trembling Fear your Doom.
 Fiorin. We do resign
This Chair as only proper to yourself
 Giov. And, since in Justice we are lost, we fly
Unto your saving Mercy.   [*All kneeling.*
 Sanaz. Which sets off

A

A Prince much more then Rigour.
    Carolo. And becomes him
When 'tis exprefs'd to fuch as fell by Weaknefs
(That being a twin-born Brother to Affection)
Better then Wreaths of Conqueft.
    Hieron. Lodov. Contar. Alph. We all fpeak
Their Language, mighty Sir.
    Coz. You know our Temper,
And therefore with more Boldnefs venture on it :
And, would not our Confent to your Demands
Deprive us of a Happinefs hereafter
Ever to be defpair'd of, we, perhaps,
Might hearken nearer to you, and could wifh
With fome Qualification or Excufe
You might make lefs the Mountains of your Crimes,
And fo invite our Clemency to feaft with you.
But you that knew with what Impatience
Of Grief we parted from the fair *Clarinda,*
Our Dutchefs (let her Memory ftill be facred !)
And with what Imprecations on ourfelf
We vow'd, not hoping e'er to fee her equal,
Ne'er to make trial of a fecond Choice,
If Nature fram'd not one that did excel her,
(As this Maid's Beauty prompts us that fhe does)
And yet, with Oaths then mix'd with Tears, upon
Her Monument we fwore our Eye fhould never
Again be tempted, 'tis true, and thofe Vows
Are regifter'd above, fomething here tells me.
Carolo, thou heardft us fwear.
    Carolo. And fwear fo deeply,
That if all Women's Beauties were in this
(As fhe's not to be nam'd with the dead Dutchefs)
Nay, all their Virtues bound up in one Story
(Of which mine is fcarce an Epitome)
If you fhould take her as a Wife, the Weight
Of your Perjuries would fink you. If I durft,
I had told you this before.
    Coz. 'Tis ftrong Truth, *Carolo* :
And yet, what was Neceffity in us

Cannot

Cannot free them from Treafon.

Carolo. There's your Error.
The Prince, in Care to have you keep your Vows
Made unto Heav'n, vouchfafed to love my Daughter.

Lydia. He told me fo, indeed, Sir.

Fiorin. And the Count
Aver'd as much to me.

Coz. You all confpire
To force our Mercy from us.

Carolo. Which giv'n up
To after-times, preferves you unforfworn,
An Honour, which will live upon your Tomb,
When your Greatnefs is forgotten.

Coz. Though we know
All this is Practice, and that both are falfe,
Such Reverence we will pay to dead *Clarinda*,
And to our ferious Oaths, that we are pleas'd
With our own Hand to blind our Eyes, and not
Know what we underftand. Here, *Giovanni*,
We pardon thee, and take from us in this,
More then our Dukedom: love her. As I part
With her, all Thoughts of Women fly faft from us.
Sanazarro, we forgive you: In your Service
To this Princefs merit it. Yet, let not others
That are in Truft and Grace, as you have been,
By the Example of our Lenity,
Prefume upon their Sovereign's Clemency.   [*A Shout.*

Enter Calandrino, Petronella.

All. Long live great *Cozimo!*

Caland. Sure the Duke is
In the giving Vein they are fo loud. Come on, Spoufe,
We have heard all, and we will have our Boon too.

Coz. What is't?

Caland. That your Grace, in Remembrance of
My Share in a Dance, and that I play'd your Part
When you fhould have drunk hard, would get this Sig-
To give this Damfel to me in the Church, [nior's grant
                                                                    For

For we are contracted.—In it you shall do
Your Dukedom Pleasure.
    Coz. How ?
    Caland. Why the whole Race
Of such as can act naturally Fools Parts,
Are quite worn out, and they that do survive,
Do only zanie us ; and we will bring you,
If we die not without Issue, of both Sexes
Such chopping Mirth-makers, as shall preserve
Perpetual Cause of Sport, both to your Grace
And your Posterity, that sad Melancholly
Shall never approach you.
    Coz. We are pleas'd in it,
And will pay her Portion.   May the Passage prove
Of what's presented, worthy of your Love,
And Favour, as was aim'd ; and we have all
That can in compass of our Wishes fall.

The E N D.

THE
UNNATURAL COMBAT.

A
TRAGEDY,

As it was prefented by the King's Majefty's Servants,
at the *Globe*.   1639.

WRITTEN
By PHILIP MASSINGER.

To my much Honoured Friend,

ANTHONY SENTLIGER,

Of *Oakham* in KENT, Efq;

SIR,

*T*HAT the Patronage of Trifles, in this Kind, hath long fince render'd Dedications, and Infcriptions obfolete, and out of Fafhion, I perfectly underftand, and cannot but ingenuoufly confefs, that I walking in the fame Path, may be truly argued by you of Weaknefs, or wilful Error: But the Reafons and Defences, for the Tender of my Service this Way to you, are fo juft, that I cannot (in my Thankfulnefs for fo many Favours received) but be ambitious to publifh them. Your noble Father, Sir Warham Sentliger (whofe remarkable Virtues muft be ever remembred) being, while he lived, a Mafter, for his Pleafure, in Poetry, feared not to hold converfe with divers, whofe neceffitous Fortunes made it their Profeffion, among which, by the Clemency of his Judgment, I was not in the laft Place admitted. You (the Heir of his Honour and Eftate) inherited his good Inclinations to Men of my poor Quality, of which I cannot give any ampler Teftimony, than by my free and glad Profeffion of it to the World. Befides, (and it was not the leaft Encouragement to me) many of Eminence, and the beft of fuch, who difdained not to take Notice of me, have not thought themfelves difparaged, I dare not fay honoured, to be celebrated the Patrons of my humble Studies. In the firft File of which, I am confident, you fhall have no Caufe to blufh, to find your Name written. I prefent you with this old Tragedy, without Prologue cr Epilogue, it being compofed in a Time (and that too, peradventure, as knowing as this) when fuch by Ornaments, were not advanced above the Fabrick of the whole Work. Accept it I befeech you, as it is, and continue your Favour to the Author.

Your Servant,

PHILIP MASSINGER.

Dramatis

Dramatis Personæ.

BEAUFORT Senior, Governor of *Marseilles*.
BEAUFORT Junior, his Son.
MALEFORT Senior, Admiral of *Marseilles*.
MALEFORT Junior, his Son.
CHAMONT,
MONTAIGN, }Affiftants to the Governor.
LANOUR,
MONTREVILE, a pretended Friend to *Malefort* Senior.
BELGARD, a poor Captain.
Three Sea Captains of the Navy of *Malefort* Junior.
Servants.
Soldiers.

THEOCRINE, Daughter to *Malefort* Senior.
Two Waiting-Women.
Ufher.
Bawd.
Page.
Two Wenches.

The S C E N E M A R S E I L L E S.

THE
UNNATURAL COMBAT.
A
TRAGEDY.

ACT I. SCENE I.

Enter Montrevile, Theocrine, *Uſher, Page, Waiting Women.*

Montrevile.

NOW to be modeſt, Madam, when you are
A Suitor for your Father, would appear
Coarſer than Boldneſs ; you awhile muſt part
With ſoft Silence, and the Bluſhings of a Vir-
gin.
Though I muſt grant, did not this Cauſe command it,
They are rich Jewels you have ever worn
To all Men's Admiration, in this Age.
If by our own forc'd Importunity,
Or others purchas'd Interceſſion, or
Corrupting Bribes, we can make our Approaches
To Juſtice, guarded, from us by ſtern Power,
We bleſs the Means and Induſtry.
  Uſher. Here's Muſick
In this Bag ſhall wake her, tho' ſhe had drunk Opium,
Or eaten Mandrakes.   Let Commanders talk
Of Cannons to make Breaches, give but Fire

To this Petard, it shall blow open, Madam,
Th' Iron Doors of a Judge, and make you Entrance;
When they (let them do what they can) with all
Their Mines, their Culverins, and Basilisco's,
Shall cool their Feet without, this being the Picklock
That never fails.

  Mont. 'Tis true, Gold can do much,
But Beauty more.   Were I the Governor,
Though the Admiral, your Father, stood convicted
Of what he's only doubted, half a Dozen
Of sweet close Kisses from these Cherry Lips,
With some short active Conference in private,
Should sign his general Pardon.

    Theoc. These light Words, Sir,
Do ill become the Weight of my sad Fortune;
And I much wonder you, that do profess
Yourself to be my Father's bosom Friend,
Can raise Mirth from his Misery.

    Mont. You mistake me;
I share in his Calamity, and only
Deliver my Thoughts freely, what I should do
For such a rare Petitioner; and if
You'll follow the Directions I prescribe
With my best Judgment, I'll mark out the Way
For his Enlargement.

    Theoc. With all real Joy
I shall put what you counsel into Act,
Provided it be honest.

    Mont. Honesty
In a fair She Client (trust to my Experience)
Seldom or never prospers; the World's wicked:
We are Men, not Saints, sweet Lady; you must practice
The Manners of the Time, if you intend
To have Favour from it.   Do not deceive yourself
By building too much on the false Foundations
Of Chastity and Virtue. Bid your Waiters
Stand farther off, and I'll come nearer to you.

    1 *Wom.* Some wicked Counsel, on my Life.

    2 *Wom.* Ne'er doubt it,
If it proceed from him.   *Usher.*

Page. I wonder that
My Lord fo much affects him.

Ufher. Thou art a Child, and doft not underftand
on what ftrong Bafis this Friendfhip's rais'd, between
this *Montrevile* and our Lord Monfieur *Malefort*, but
I'll teach thee : From thy Years they have been joint
Purchafers, in Furs, and Water-Works, and truck'd
together.

Page. In Fire and Water-works ?

Ufher. Commodities, Boy,
Which you may know hereafter.

Page. And deal in 'em
When the Trade has given you over, as appears
By the Increafe of your high Forehead.

Ufher. Here's a Crack !
I think they fuck this Knowledge in their Milk.

Page. I had an ignorant Nurfe elfe.   I have ty'd, Sir,
My Lady's Garter, and can guefs.

Ufher. Peace, Infant;   [Theocrine *falls off.*
Tales out o' School, take heed, you will be breech'd elfe.

1 *Wom.* My Lady's Colour changes.

2 *Wom.* She falls off too.

Theoc. You are a naughty Man, indeed you are;
And I will fooner perifh with my Father,
Than at this Price redeem him.

Mont. Take your own Way,
Your modeft legal Way ; 'tis not your Veil,
Nor Mourning Habit, nor thefe Creatures taught
To howl, and cry, when you begin to whimper;
Nor following my Lord's Coach in the Dirt,
Nor that which you rely upon, a Bribe,
Will do it, when there's fomething he likes better.
Thefe Courfes in an old Crone of Threefcore,
That had feven Years together tir'd the Court
With tedious Petitions and Clamours,
For the Recovery of a ftrangling Hufband,
To pay, forfooth, the Duties of one to her;
But for a Lady of your tempting Beauties,
Your Youth, and ravifhing Features, to hope only

In such a Suit as this is, to gain Favour
Without Exchange of Courtesy, you conceive me,

Enter Beaufort *jun. and* Belgard.

Were Madness at the Height. Here's brave young
    Beaufort,
The Meteor of *Marseilles*; one that holds
The Governor his Father's Will and Power
In more Awe than his own.   Come, come, advance,
Present your Bag cram'd with Crowns of the Sun,
Do you think he cares for Money ? He loves Pleasure.
Burn your Petition; burn it : He doats on you,
Upon my Knowledge : To his Cabinet, do.
And he will point you out a certain Course,
Be the Cause right or wrong, to have your Father
Releas'd with much Facility.   [*Exit* Montrevile.
   Theoc. Do you hear ?
Take a Pander with you.
   Beauf. jun, I tell thee there is neither
Employment yet, nor Money.
   Belg. I have commanded
And spent my own Means in my Country's Service,
In Hopes to raise a Fortune.
   Beauf. jun. Many have hop'd so,
But Hopes prove seldom Certainties with Soldiers.
   Belg. If no Preferment, let me but receive
My Pay that is behind, to set me up
A Tavern, or a Vaulting House; while Men love
Or Drunkenness, or Lechery, they'll ne'er fail me :
Shall I have that ?
   Beauf. jun. As our Prizes are brought in.
Till then you must be patient.
   Belg. In the mean Time,
How shall I do for Cloaths ?
   Beauf. jun. As most Captains do,
Philosopher like, carry all you have about you.
   Belg. But how shall I do to satisfy *Calon,* Monsieur ?
There lies the Doubt.

                                              Beauf.

Beauf. jun. That's eafily decided ;
My Father's Table's free for any Man
That hath borne Arms.
    Belg. And there's good Store of Meat ?
    Beauf. jun. Never fear that.
    Belg. I'll feek no other Ordinary then,
But be his daily Gueft without Invitement :
And if my Stomach hold, I'll feed fo heartily
As he fhall pay me fuddenly to be quit of me.
    Beauf. jun. 'Tis fhe.
    Belg. And further ———
    Beauf. jun. Away, you are troublefome,
Defigns of more Weight.
    Belg. Ha ! fair *Theocrine !*
Nay, if a Velvet Petticoat move in the Front,
Buff Jerkins muft to the Rear : I know my Manners ;
This is indeed great Bufinefs, mine a Gewgaw.
I may dance Attendance, this muft be difpatch'd,
And fuddenly, or all will go to Wreck.
Charge her home in the Flank, my Lord : Nay, I am
        gone, Sir.   [*Exit* Belgard.
    Beauf. jun. Nay, pray you, Madam, rife, or I'll kneel
        with you.   [man.
    Page. I would bring you on your Knees, were I a Wo-
    Beauf. jun. What is it can deferve fo poor a Name,
As a Suit to me ? This more than mortal Form
Was fafhion'd to command, and not intreat :
Your Will but known is ferv'd.
    Theoc. Great Sir ! my Father,
My brave deferving Father ; but that Sorrow
Forbids the Ufe of Speech.
    Beauf. jun. I underftand you,
Without the Aids of thofe Interpreters
That fall from your fair Eyes : I know you labour
The Liberty of your Father ; at the leaft,
An equal Hearing to acquit himfelf :
And, 'tis not to endear my Service to you,
Tho' I muft add, and pray you with Patience hear it,
'Tis hard to be effected, in Refpect

M 3

The

The State's incens'd againſt him : All preſuming
The World of Outrages his impious Son,
Turn'd worſe than Pirate in his Cruelties
Exprefs'd to this poor Country, could not be
With ſuch Eaſe put in Execution, if
Your Father (of late our great Admiral)
Held not or Correſpondence, or conniv'd
At his Proceedings.
   Theoc. And muſt he then ſuffer,
His Cauſe unheard ?
   Beauf. jun. As yet it is reſolv'd ſo,
In their Determination. But ſuppoſe,
For I would nouriſh Hope, not kill it in you,
I ſhould divert the Torrent of their Purpoſe,
And render them that are implacable,
Impartial Judges, and not ſway'd with Speen :
Will you, I dare not ſay in Recompence,
For that includes a Debt you cannot owe me,
But in your liberal Bounty, in my Suit
To you, be gracious ?
   Theoc. You entreat of me, Sir,
What I ſhould offer to you, with Confeſſion
That you much undervalue your own Worth,
Should you receive me. Since there come with you
Not luſtful Fires, but fair and lawful Flames.
But I muſt be excus'd, 'tis now no Time
For me to think of Hymenæal Joys.
Can he (and pray you, Sir, conſider it)
That gave me Life, and Faculties to Love,
Be, as he is now ready to be devour'd
By ravenous Wolves, and at that Inſtant, I
But entertain a Thought of thoſe Delights,
In which perhaps my Ardour meets with yours ?
Duty and Piety forbid it, Sir.
   Beauf. jun. But this effected, and your Father free,
What is your Anſwer ?
   Theoc. Every Minute to me
Will be a tedious Age till our Embraces
Are warrantable to the World.

Beauf.

Beauf. jun. I urge no more:
Confirm it with a Kiss.
  Theoc. I doubly seal it.
  Usher. This would do better a-bed, the Business ended;
They 'ere the loving'st Couple——

Enter Beaufort, *sen. the Governor.* Montaigne,
Chamont, Lanour.

  Beauf. jun. Here comes my Father
With the Council of War: Deliver your Petition,
And leave the rest to me.
  Beauf. sen. I am sorry, Lady,
Your Father's Guilt compels your Innocence
To ask what I in Justice must deny.
  Beauf. jun. For my Sake, Sir, pray you receive,
        and read it.
  Beauf. sen. Thou foolish Boy, I can deny thee nothing.
  Beauf. jun. Thus far we are happy. Madam, quit the
You shall hear how we succeed.   [Place,
  Theoc. Goodness reward you.
             [*Exeunt* Theocrine, *Usher,* Page, *Women.*
  Mont. It is apparent, and we stay too long
To censure *Malefort* as he deserves.
  Cham. There is no Colour of Reason that makes for
Had he discharg'd the Trust committed to him,   [him:
With that Experience and Fidelity
He practis'd heretofore, it could not be
Our Navy should be block'd up, and in our Sight
Our Goods made Prize, our Sailors sold for Slaves,
By his prodigious Issue.
  Lan. I much grieve,
After so many brave and high Atchievements,
He should in one Ill forfeit all the Good
He ever did his Country.
  Beauf. sen. Well, 'tis granted.
  Beauf. jun. I humbly thank you, Sir.
  Beauf. sen. He shall have Hearing,
M 4

His

His Irons too ſtruck off, bring him before us,
But ſeek no farther Favour.

    Beauf. jun. Sir, I dare not.   [*Exit* Beauf. *jun.*

    Beauf. ſen. Monſieur *Chamont, Montaigne, Lanour,*
        Aſſiſtants

By a Commiſſion from the moſt Chriſtian King
In puniſhing, or freeing *Malefort,*
Our late great Admiral : Tho' I know you need not
Inſtructions from me, how to diſpoſe of
Yourſelves in this Man's Trial (that exacts
Your cleareſt Judgments) give me Leave with Favour
To offer my Opinion : We are to hear him,
A little looking back on his fair Actions,
Loyal, and true Demeanour ; not as now
By the general Voice, already he's condemn'd.
But if we find, as moſt believe, he hath held
Intelligence with his accurſed Son,
Fall'n off from all Allegiance, and turn'd
(But for what Cauſe we know not) the moſt bloody
And fatal Enemy, this Country ever
Repented to have brought forth ; all Compaſſion
Of what he was, or may be, if now pardon'd,
We ſit engag'd to cenſure him with all
Extremity and Rigour.

    Cham. Your Lordſhip ſhews us
A Path which we will tread in.

    Lan. He that leaves
To follow, as you lead, will loſe himſelf.

    Monta. I'll not be ſingular.

Enter Beaufort *jun.* Montreville, Malefort *ſen.* Bel-
        gard, *Officers.*

    Beauf. ſen. He comes, but with
A ſtrange diſtracted Look.

    Malef. ſen. Live I once more
To ſee theſe Hands and Arms free, theſe, that often
In the moſt dreadful Horror of a Fight,
Have been as Sea-marks to teach ſuch as were

Seconds

Seconds in my Attempts, to fteer between
The Rocks of too much daring, and pale Fear,
'To reach the Port of Victory ? When my Sword,
Advanc'd thus, to my Enemies appear'd
A hairy Comet, threat'ning Death and Ruin
To fuch as durft behold it.   Thefe the Legs,
That when our Ships were grappl'd, carried me
With fuch fwift Motion from Deck to Deck,
As they that faw it, with Amazement cry'd,
He does not run, but flies.
    Monta. He ftill retains
The Greatnefs of his Spirit.
    Malef. fen. Now crampt with Irons,
Hunger and Cold, they hardly do fupport me.
But I forget myfelf.   O my good Lords,
That fit there as Judges to determine
The Life and Death of *Malefort*, where are now
Thofe Shouts, thofe chearful Looks, thofe loud Applaufes
With which, when I return'd loaden with Spoil,
You entertain'd your Admiral ? All's forgotten,
And I ftand here to give Account for that
Of which I am as free and innocent
As he that never faw the Eye of him
For whom I ftand fufpected.
    Beauf. fen. Monfieur *Malefort*,
Let not your Paffion fo far tranfport you,
As to believe from any private Malice,
Or Envy to your Perfon, you are queftion'd;
Nor do the Suppofitions want Weight,
That do invite us to a ftrong Affurance.——
Your Son.——
    Malef. fen. My Shame.
    Beauf. fen. Pray you hear with Patience.—Never
Without Affiftance or fure Aids from you,
Could, with the Pirates of *Algiers* and *Tunis*,
E'en thofe that you had almoft twice defeated,
Acquire fuch Credit, as with them to be
Made Abfolute Commander ? (pray you obferve me)
If there had not fome Contract pafs'd between you,

That

That when Occafion ferv'd you, would join with 'em
To the Ruin of *Marfeilles?*
   Monta. More, what urg'd
Your Son to turn Apoftate?
   Cham. Had he from
The State, or Governor, the leaft Neglect
Which Envy could interpret for a Wrong?
   Lan. Or, if you fiept not in your Charge, how could
So many Ships as do infeft our Coaft
And have in our own Harbour fhut our Navy,
Come in unfought with?
   Beauf. jun. They put him hardly to it.
   Malef. fen. My Lords, with as much Brevity as I can,
I'll anfwer each particular Objection
With which you charge me. The main Ground, on which
You raife the Building of your Accufation,
Hath Reference to my Son: Should I now curfe him,
Or wifh, in th' Agony of my troubled Soul,
Light'ning had found him in his Mother's Womb,
You'll fay, 'tis from the Purpofe; and I therefore
Betake him to the Devil, and fo leave him.
Did never loyal Father but myfelf
Beget a treacherous Iffue? Was't in me
With as much Eafe to fafhion up his Mind,
As in his Generation to form
The Organs of his Body, muft it follow,
Becaufe that he is impious, I am falfe?
I would not boaft my Actions, yet 'tis lawfull
To upbraid my Benefits to unthankful Men.
Who funk the *Turkifh* Gallies in the Streights,
But *Malefort?* Who refcu'd the *French* Merchants,
When they were boarded, and ftowed under Hatches
By the Pirates of *Algiers,* when every Minute
They did expect to be chain'd to the Oar,
But your now doubted Admiral? Then you fill'd
The Air with fhouts of Joy, and did proclaim
When Hope had left them, and Grim-look'd Defpair
Hover'd with fail-ftretch'd Wings over their Heads,
To me, as to the *Neptune* of the Sea,

They

They ow'd the Reftitution of their Goods,
Their Lives, their Liberties.   O can it then
Be probable, my Lords, that he that never
Became the Mafter of a Pirate's Ship,
But at the Main-yard hung the Captain up,
And caufed the Reft to be thrown over-board,
Should after all thefe Proofs of deadly Hate,
So oft expreffed againft 'em, entertain
A Thought of Quarter with 'em, but much lefs
(To the Perpetual Ruin of my Glories)
To join with them to lift a wicked Arm
Againft my Mother Country, this *Marfeilles*,
Which with my Prodigal Expence of Blood
I have fo oft protected.

 Beauf. fen. What you have done
Is granted and applauded ; but yet know
This glorious Relation of your Actions
Muft not fo blind our Judgments, as to fuffer
This moft unnatural Crime you ftand accus'd of,
To pafs unqueftion'd.

 Cham. No, you muft produce
Reafons of more Validity and Weight,
To plead in your Defence, or we fhall hardly
Conclude you Innocent.

 Monta. The large Volume of
Your former worthy Deeds, with your Experience,
Both what, and when to do, but makes againft you.

 Lan. For had your Care and Courage been the fame
As heretofore, the Dangers we are plung'd in
Had been with Eafe prevented.

 Malef. fen. What have I
Omitted in the Power of Flefh and Blood,
Even in the Birth to ftrangle the Defigns
Of this Hell-bred Wolf my Son ? Alas ! my Lords,
I am no God, nor like him could forefee
His cruel Thoughts, and curfed Purpofes ;
Nor would the Sun at my Command forbear
To make his Progrefs to the other World,
Affording to us one continued Light.

Nor

Nor could my Breath disperse those foggy Mists
Covered with which, and Darkness of the Night,
Their Navy undiscern'd, without Resistance
Beset our Harbour. Make not that my Fault,
Which you in Justice must ascribe to Fortune.
But if that nor my former Acts, nor what
I have deliver'd, can prevail with you
To make good my Integrity and Truth;
Rip up this Bosom, and pluck out the Heart
That hath been ever Loyal.   [*A Trumpet within.*

   Beauf. sen. How! a Trumpet!   [*Montrevile goes off.*
Enquire the Cause.

   Malef. sen. Thou Searcher of Men's Hearts,
And sure Defender of the Innocent,
(My other crying Sins—awhile not look'd on)
If I in this am Guilty, strike me Dead,
Or by some unexpected Means confirm,
I am accus'd unjustly.

     Enter Montrevile *and a Sea Captain.*

   Beauf. sen. Speak the Motives
That brings thee hither.

   Capt. From our Admiral thus :
He does salute you fairly, and desires
It may be understood no publick Hate,
Hath brought him to *Marseilles* ; nor seeks he
The Ruin of his Country, but aims only
To wreak a private Wrong; and if from you
He may have Leave and Liberty to decide it
In a single Combat, he'll give up good Pledges :
If he fall in the Trial of his Right,
We shall weigh Anchor and no more molest
This Town with hostile Arms.

   Beauf. sen. Speak to the Man,
(If in this Presence he appear to you)
To whom you bring this Challenge.

   Capt. 'Tis to you.

   Beauf. sen. His Father!

Mont.

Mont. Can it be!

Beauf. jun. Strange and Prodigious.   [Thunder,

Malef. sen. Thou seest I stand unmov'd; were thy Voice
It should not shake me; say what would the Viper?

Capt. The Reverence a Father's Name may Challenge,
And Duty of a Son, no more remember'd
He does defy thee to the Death.

Malef. sen. Go on.

Capt. And with his Sword well prove it on thy Head,
Thou art a Murderer, an Atheist,
And that all Attributes of Men turn'd Furies
Cannot express thee; this he will make good
If thou dar'st give him Meeting.

Malef. sen. Dare I live,
Dare I, when Mountains of my Sin o'erwhelm me,
At my last Gasp ask for Mercy? How I bless
Thy coming, Captain, never Man to me
Arriv'd so opportunely; and thy Message,
However it may seem to threaten Death,
Does yield to me a second Life in curing
My wounded Honour.   Stand I yet suspected
As a Confederate with this Enemy,
Whom of all Men, against all Ties of Nature
He marks out for Destruction? You are Just
Immortal Powers, and in this Merciful,
And it takes from my Sorrow, and my Shame
For being the Father to so bad a Son,
In that you are pleased to offer up the Monster
To my Correction. Blush and Repent
As you are bound my Honourable Lords
Your ill Opinions of me.   Not great *Brutus*
The Father of the *Roman* Liberty,
With more assured Constancy beheld
His traitor Sons, for labouring to call home
The banish'd *Tarquins*, scourg'd with Rods to Death,
Then I will shew, when I take back the Life
This Prodigy of Mankind received from me.

Beauf. sen. We are sorry Monsieur *Malefort* for our
And are much taken with your Resolution;   [Error,

But

But the Difparity of Years and Strength,
Between you, and your Son duly confidered
We would not fo expofe you.
 Malef. fen. Then you kill me
Under pretence to fave me. O my Lords
As you love Honour, and a wrong'd Man's Fame,
Deny me not this fair and noble Means
To make me right again to all the World.
Should any other but myfelf be chofen
To punifh this Apoftate Son with Death,
You rob a wretched Father of a Juftice
That to all after Times will be Recorded.
I wifh his Strength were Centuple, his Skill equal
To my Experience, that in his Fall
He may not fhame my Victory. I feel
The Powers and Spirits of Twenty ftrong Men in me.
Were he with Wild Fire circl'd, I undaunted
Would make Way to him. As you do affect, Sir,
My Daughter *Theocrine*, as you are
My true and ancient Friend, as thou art Valiant,
And as all love a Soldier, fecond me
       [*They all fue to the Governor.*
In this my juft Petition. In your Looks
I fee a grant my Lord.
 Beauf. fen. You fhall o'erbear me,
And fince you are fo confident in your Caufe,
Prepare you for the Combat.
 Malef. fen. With more Joy
Then yet I ever tafted; by the next Sun,
The difobedient Rebell fhall hear from me
And fo return in Safety, my good Lords,
To all my Service. I will Die or Purchafe
Reft to *Marfeilles*, nor can I make doubt,
But his Impiety is a potent Charm,
To Edge my Sword and add Strength to my Arm.
         [*Exeunt.*

The End of the Firft Act.

ACT II. SCENE I.

Enter Three Sea Captains.

2 Capt. HE did accept the Challenge then?
    1. *Capt.* Nay more,
Was overjoy'd in it; and as it had been
A fair Invitement to a folemn Feaft,
And not a Combat to conclude with Death,
He chearfully embraced it.
    3. *Capt.* Are the Articles
Sign'd too on both Parts?
    1 *Capt.* At the Father's Suit,
With much Unwillingnefs the Governor
Confented to 'em.
    2 *Capt.* You are inward with
Our Admiral; could you yet never learn
What the Nature of the Quarrel is, that renders
The Son, more then incenfed, implacable
Againft the Father?
    1 *Capt.* Never; yet I have
As far as Manners would give Warrant to it,
With my beft Curioufnefs of Care obferv'd him.
I have fat with him in his Cabbin a Day together,[1]
Yet not a Syllable exchang'd between us.
Sigh he did often, as if inward Grief
And Melancholy at that Inftant would
Choke up his vital Spirits, and now and then
A Tear or two, as in Derifion of
The Toughnefs of his Rugged Temper would
Fall on his hallow Cheeks, which but once felt,
A fudden Flafh of Fury did dry up,
And laying then his Hand upon his Sword,

[1] *I have fat with him in his Cabbin,* &c.

This beautiful Paffage expreffing concealed Refentment, deferves
to be remarked by every Reader of Tafte and Judgment.

He

He would Murmur, but yet so as I oft heard him,
" We shall meet, cruel Father, yes, we shall,
" When I'll exact for every Womanish Drop
" Of Sorrow from these Eyes, a strict Accompt
" Of much more from thy Heart."
   2 *Capt.* 'Tis wond'rous Strange.
   3 *Capt.* And past my Apprehension.
   1 *Capt.* Yet what makes
The Miracle greater, when from the Main-Top
A Sail's descry'd, all Thoughts that do concern
Himself laid by, no Lion pinch'd with Hunger,
Rouzes himself more fiercely from his Den,
Than he comes on the Deck, and there how wisely
He gives Directions, and how stout he is
In his Executions, we to Admiration,
Have been Eye-witnesses ; yet he never minds
The Booty when 'tis made ours, but as if
The Danger, in the Purchase of the Prey
Delighted him much more then the Reward,
His Will made known, he does retire himself
To his private Contemplation, no Joy
Exprefs'd by him for Victory.

Enter Malefort *Junior.*

   2 *Capt.* Here he comes
But with more chearful Looks then ever yet
I saw him wear.
   Malef. jun. It was long since resolv'd on
Nor must I stagger now. May the Caufe
That forces me to this unnatural Act,
Be buried in Everlafting Silence,
And I find Reft in Death, or my Revenge ;
To either I stand equal. Pray you, Gentlemen,
Be Charitable in your Cenfures of me,
And do not entertain a falfe Belief
That I am Mad, for undertaking that
Which muft be, when Effected, still repented.
It adds to my Calamity that I have

Difcourfe

Difcourfe and Reafon, and but too well know
I can nor live, nor end a wretched Life,
But both Ways I am impious.   Do not therefore
Afcribe the Perturbation of my Soul
To a fervile Fear of Death : I oft have view'd
All Kinds of his inevitable Darts,
Nor are they terrible.   Were I condemn'd to leap
From the cloud-cover'd Brows of a fteep Rock
Into the Deep; or, *Curtius* like, to fill up,
For my Country's Safety, and an After-Name,
A bottomlefs Abyfs, or charge through Fire,
It could not fo much fhake me, as th' Encounter
Of this Day's fingle Enemy.
   1 *Capt.* If you pleafe, Sir,
You may fhun it, or defer it.
   Malef. jun. Not for the World :
Yet two Things I entreat you; the firft is,
You'll not enquire the Difference between
Myfelf and him, which as a Father once
I honour'd, now my deadlieft Enemy.
The laft is, if I fall, to bear my Body
Far from this Place, and where you pleafe interr it.
I fhould fay more, but by his fudden coming
I am cut off.

Enter Beaufort *jun. and* Montrevile *leading in* Malefort
       fen. Belgard *following with others.*

   Beauf. jun. Let me, Sir, have the Honour
To be your Second.
   Mont. With your Pardon, Sir,
I muft put in for that, fince our tried Friendfhip
Hath lafted from our Infancy.
   Belg. I have ferv'd
Under your Command, and you have feen me fight,
And handfomely, though I fay it; and if now
At this downright Game, I may but hold your Cards,
I'll not pull down the Side.
   VOL. III.   N   *Malef.*

Malef. fen. I reft much bound
To your fo noble Offers, and I hope
Shall find your Pardon, though I now refufe 'em,
For which I'll yield ftrong Reafons, but as briefly
As the Time will give me Leave. For me to borrow
(That am fuppos'd the Weaker) any Aid
From the Affiftance of my Second's Sword,
Might write me down in the black Lift of thofe
That have nor Fire, nor Spirit of their own ;
But dare, and do, as they derive their Courage
From his Example, on whofe Help and Valour
They wholly do depend. Let this fuffice
In my Excufe for that. Now, if you pleafe
On both Parts to retire to yonder Mount,
Where you, as in a *Roman* Theatre,
May fee the bloody Difference determin'd,
Your Favours meet my Wifhes.

Malef. jun. 'Tis approv'd of
By me, and I command you lead the Way,
And leave me to my Fortune.

Beauf. jun. I would gladly
Be a Spectator (fince I am deny'd
To be an Actor) of each Blow, and Thruft,
And punctually obferve 'em.

Malef. jun. You fhall have
All you defire ; for in a Word or two
I muft make bold to entertain the Time,
If he give Suffrage to it.

Malef. fen. Yes, I will ;
I'll hear thee, and then kill thee: Nay, farewel.

Malef. jun. Embrace with Love on both Sides, and
Leave deadly Hate and Fury. [with us

Malef. fen. From this Place
You ne'er fhall fee both living.

They embrace on both Sides, and take Leave
feverally of the Father and Son.

Belg. What's paft Help, is
Beyond Prevention.

Malef.

Malef. sen. Now we are alone, Sir,
And thou haft Liberty to unload the Burthen
Which thou groan'ft under.   Speak thy Griefs.
      Malef. jun. I fhall, Sir ;
But in a perplex'd Form and Method, which
You only can interpret ; would you had not
A guilty Knowledge in your Bofom of
The Language which you force me to deliver,
So I were nothing.   As you are my Father,
I bend my Knee, and uncompell'd profefs
My Life, and all that's mine, to be your Gift ;
And that in a Son's Duty I ftand bound
To lay this Head beneath your Feet, and run
All defp'rate Hazards for your Eafe and Safety.
But this confeft on my Part, I rife up,
And not as with a Father, (all Refpect,
Love, Fear, and Reverence caft off,) but as
A wicked Man I thus expoftulate with you.
Why have you done that which I dare not fpeak ?
And in the Action chang'd the humble Shape
Of my Obedience, to rebellious Rage
And infolent Pride ? and with fhut Eyes conftrain'd me
To run my Bark of Honour on a Shelf
I muft not fee, nor if I faw it, fhun it ?
In my Wrongs Nature fuffers, and looks backward,
And Mankind trembles to fee me purfue
What Beafts would fly from.   For when I advance
This Sword, as I muft do againft your Head,
Piety will weep, and filial Duty mourn,
To fee their Altars which you built up in me,
In a Moment raz'd and ruin'd.   That you could
(From my griev'd Soul I wifh it) but produce
To qualify, not excufe your Deed of Horror,
One feeming Reafon that I might fix here,
And move no farther.
      Malef. fen. Have I fo far loft
A Father's Power, that I muft give Account
Of my Actions to my Son ? or muft I plead
As a fearful Prifoner at the Bar, while he

N 2

That

That owes his Being to me fits a Judge
To cenfure that, which only by myfelf
Ought to be queftion'd? Mountains fooner fall [2]
Beneath their Vallies, and the lofty Pine
Pay Homage to the Bramble, or what elfe is
Prepofterous in Nature, ere my Tongue
In one fhort Syllable yields Satisfaction
To any Doubt of thine; nay, though it were
A Certainty difdaining Argument.
Since, tho' my Deeds wore Hell's black Livery,
To thee they fhould appear triumphal Robes,
Set off with glorious Honour, thou being bound
To fee with my Eyes, and to hold that Reafon,
That takes or Birth or Fafhion from my Will.
    Malef. jun. This Sword divides that flavifh Knot.
    Malef. fen. It cannot:
It cannot, Wretch; and if thou but remember   [it.
From whom thou hadft this Spirit, thou dar'ft not hope
Who train'd thee up in Arms but I? Who taught thee
Men were Men only when they durft look down
With Scorn on Death and Danger, and contemn'd
All Oppofition, till plum'd Victory [3]

[2] ——————— *Mountains fooner fall*
    Beneath their Vallies, &c.

    I have before obferved, that *Maffinger* makes frequent Ufe of
Scripture Expreffions; how beautiful they are when happily introduced, and the Majefty they throw over Works of this Nature would
be needlefs to remark, being obvious to all. — For the above Allu-
fions, fee *Ifaiah*, Chap. xl. ver. 3, 4.

[3] ———— *Till plum'd Victory*
    Had made her conftant Stand upon their Helmets.

    This noble Image feems to have been copied by *Milton*, who de-
fcribing *Satan*, fays.
      —His Stature reach'd the Skies, and on his Creft
      Sat Horror plum'd!

    And in another Place, thus:
      —At his Right Hand, Victory
      Sat, Eagle wing'd.

    The whole Speech of *Maffinger*'s here noticed is truly fublime,
and above all Commendation.

Had

Had made her conftant Stand upon their Helmets?
Under my Shield thou haft fought as fecurely
As the young Eglet, cover'd with the Wings
Of her fierce Dam, learns how and where to prey.
All that is manly in thee, I call mine;
But what is weak and womanifh, thine own.
And what I gave, fince thou art proud, ungrateful,
Prefuming to contend with him, to whom
Submiffion is due, I will take from thee.
Look therefore for Extremities, and expect not
I will correct thee as a Son, but kill thee
As a Serpent fwoln with Poifon; who furviving
A little longer, with infectious Breath,
Would render all Things near him, like itfelf,
Contagious.   Nay, now my Anger's up,
Ten Thoufand Virgins kneeling at my Feet,
And with one general Cry howling for Mercy,
Shall not redeem thee.
    Malef. jun. Thou incenfed Power,
A while forbear thy Thunder: Let me have
No Aid in my Revenge, if from the Grave
My Mother ——
    Malef. fen. Thou fhalt never name her more.

Above Beaufort *jun.* Montrevile, Belgard, *the three*
                Sea Captains.

    Beauf. jun. They are at it.
    2 *Capt.* That Thruft was put ftrongly home.
    Mont. But with more Strength avoided.
    Belg. Well come in;
He has drawn Blood of him yet: Well done, old Cock.
    1 *Capt.* That was a ftrange Mifs.
    Beauf. jun. That a certain Hit.
    Belg. He's fall'n, the Day is ours.
                        [*Young* Malefort *flain.*
    2 *Capt.* The Admiral's flain.
    Mont. The Father is victorious!
            N 3   *Belg.*

Belg. Let us hafte
To gratulate his Conqueft.
  1 *Capt.* We to mourn
The Fortune of the Son.
  Beauf. jun. With utmoft Speed
Acquaint the Governor with the good Succefs,
That he may entertain, to his full Merit,
The Father of his Country's Peace and Safety.
                                    [*They defcend.*

  Malef. fen. Were a new Life hid in each mangled
        Limb,
I would fearch, and find it.   And howe'er to fome
I may feem cruel, thus to tyrannize
Upon this fenfelefs Flefh, I glory in it.
That I have Power to be unnatural,
Is my Security ; die all my Fears,
And waking Jealoufies, which have fo long
Been my Tormentors ; there's now no Sufpicion :
A Fact, which I alone am confcious of,
Can never be difcover'd, or the Caufe
That call'd this Duel on.   I being above
All Perturbations, nor is it in
The Power of Fate, again to make me wretched.

  Enter Beaufort *jun.* Montrevile, Belgard, *the three
        Sea Captains.*

  Beauf. jun. All Honour to the Conqueror. Who
My Friend of Treachery now ?   [dares tax
  Belg. I am very glad, Sir,
You have fped fo well.   But I muft tell you thus much,
To put you in Mind that a low Ebb muft follow
Your high fwoln Tide of Happinefs. You have purchas'd
This Honour at a high Price.
  Malef. 'Tis, *Belgard,*
Above all Eftimation, and a little
To be exalted with it cannot favour   .
Of Arrogance : That to this Arm and Sword
Marfeilles owes the Freedom of her Fears,

                                        Or

Or that my Loyalty, not long fince eclips'd,
Shines now more bright than ever, are not Things
To be lamented.   Though indeed they may
Appear too dearly bought, my falling Glories
Being made up again, and cemented
With a Son's Blood.   'Tis true, he was my Son,
While he was worthy ; but when he fhook off
His Duty to me, (which my fond Indulgence
Upon Submiffion, might perhaps have pardon'd)
And grew his Country's Enemy, I look'd on him
As a Stranger to my Family, and a Traytor
Juftly profcrib'd, and he to be rewarded
That could bring in his Head.   I know in this
That I am cenfur'd Rugged, and Auftere,
That will vouchfafe not one fad Sigh or Tear
Upon his flaughter'd Body.   But I reft
Well fatisfy'd in myfelf, being affur'd
That extraordinary Virtues, when they foar
Too high a Pitch for common Sights to judge of,
Lofing their proper Splendor, are condemn'd
For moft remarkable Vices.
      Beauf. jun. 'Tis too true, Sir,
In the Opinion of the Multitude :
But for myfelf, that would be held your Friend,
And hope to know you by a nearer Name,
They are as they deferve, receiv'd.
      Malef. My Daughter
Shall thank you for the Favour.
      Beauf. jun. I can wifh
No Happinefs beyond it.
      1 *Capt.* Shall we have Leave
To bear the Corps of our dead Admiral,
As he enjoin'd us, from this Coaft ?
      Malef. Provided
The Articles agreed on, be obferv'd,
And you depart hence with it, making Oath
Never hereafter but as Friends to touch
Upon this Shore.
      1 *Capt.* We'll faithfully perform it.

Malef.

Malef. Then as you pleaſe diſpoſe of it. 'Tis an Object
That I could wiſh remov'd.   His Sins die with him :
So far he has my Charity.
    1 *Capt.* He ſhall have
A Soldier's Funeral.   [*The Sea Captains bear the*
    Malef. Farewel.   *Body off with ſad Muſick,*
    Beauf. jun. Theſe Rites
Paid to the Dead, the Conqueror that ſurvives
Muſt reap the Harveſt of his bloody Labour.
Sound all loud Inſtruments of Joy and Triumph,
And with all Circumſtance, and Ceremony,
Wait on the Patron of our Liberty,
Which he at all Parts merits.
    Malef. I am honour'd
Beyond my Hopes.
    Beauf. jun. 'Tis ſhort of your Deſerts.
Lead on : Oh, Sir, you muſt : You are too modeſt.
                        [*Exeunt with loud Muſick,*

S C E N E II.

Theocrine, *Page, Woman.*

Theoc. Talk not of Comfort. I am both Ways wretch-
And ſo diſtracted with my Doubts and Fears,   led,
I know not where to fix my Hopes.   My Loſs
Is certain in a Father, or a Brother,
Or both ; ſuch is the Cruelty of my Fate,
And not to be avoided.
    1 *Wom.* You muſt bear it
With Patience, Madam.
    2 *Wom.* And what's not in you
To be prevented, ſhould not cauſe a Sorrow
Which cannot help it.
    Page. Fear not my brave Lord
Your noble Father ; Fighting is to him
Familiar as Eating.   He can teach
Our modern Duelliſts how to cleave a Button,

                                              And

And in a new Way, never yet found out
By old *Caranza*. [4]

    1 *Wom.* May he be victorious,
And punish Disobedience in his Son,
Whose Death, in Reason, should at no Part move you,
He being but half your Brother, and the Nearness,
Which that might challenge from you, forfeited
By his impious Purpose to kill him, from whom
He receiv'd Life.   [*A Shout within.*

    2 *Wom.* A general Shout.

    1 *Wom.* Of Joy.

    Page. Look up, dear Lady; sad News never came
Usher'd with loud Applause.

    Theoc. I stand prepar'd
To endure the Shock of it.

Enter Usher.

    Usher. I am out of Breath
With running to deliver first.

    Theoc. What?

    Usher. We are all made.
My Lord has won the Day; your Brother's slain;
The Pirates gone; and by the Governor,
And States, and all the Men of War he is
Brought home in Triumph.——Nay, no Musing, pay me
For my good News hereafter.

    Theoc. Heaven is just!

    Usher. Give Thanks at Leisure; make all Haste to
            meet him.
I could wish I were a Horse, that I might bear you
To him upon my Back.

    Page. Thou art an Ass,
And this is a sweet Burthen.

    Usher. Peace, you Crack-rope.   [*Exeunt.*

----

    [4] *By old* Caranza.
  See the 5th Note on the *Guardian*, Vol. IV. Page 44.

S C E N E

S C E N E III.

Loud Musick. Montreville, Belgard, Beaufort *Senior,*
   Beaufort *Junior;* Malefort, *followed by* Montaigne,
   Chamont, Lanour.

   Beauf. sen. All Honours we can give you, and Re-
Tho' all that's rich, or precious in *Marseilles*   [wards,
Were laid down at your Feet; can hold no Weight
With your Deservings. Let me glory in
Your Action as if it were mine own;
And have the Honour, with the Arms of Love,
To embrace the great Performer of a Deed
Transcending all this Country ere could boast of.
   Mont. Imagine, noble Sir, in what we may
Express our Thankfulness, and rest assur'd
It shall be freely granted.
   Cham. He's an Enemy
To Goodness and to Virtue, that dares think
There's any other Thing within our Power to give,
Which you in Justice may not boldly challenge.
   Lan. And as your own, for we will ever be
At your Devotion.
   Malef. Much honour'd Sir,
And you my noble Lords, I can say only,
The Greatness of your Favours overwhelm me,
And like too large a Sail, for the small Bark
Of my poor Merits, sinks me. That I stand
Upright in your Opinions, is an Honour
Exceeding my Deserts, I having done
Nothing but what in Duty I stood bound to:
And to expect a Recompence were base,
Good Deeds being ever in themselves rewarded.
Yet since your liberal Bounties tell me that
I may, with your Allowance be a Suitor,
To you, my Lord, I am an humble one,
And must ask that, which known, I fear you will
Censure me over-bold.

Beauf.

Beauf. fen. It muſt be ſomething
Of a ſtrange Nature, if it find from me
Denial or Delay.
     Malef. Thus then, my Lord,
Since you encourage me :   You are happy in
A worthy Son, and all the Comfort that
Fortune has left me is one Daughter ; now
If it may not appear too much Preſumption,
To ſeek to match my Lowneſs with your Height,
I ſhould deſire (and if I may obtain it,
I write *Nil ultra* to my largeſt Hopes)
She may in your Opinion be thought worthy
To be receiv'd into your Family,
And married to your Son :   Their Years are equal,
And their Deſires I think too ; ſhe is not
Ignoble, nor my State contemptible,
And if you think me worthy your Alliance,
'Tis all I do aſpire to.
     Beauf. jun. You demand
That which with all the Service of my Life
I ſhould have labour'd to obtain from you.
O Sir, why are you flow to meet ſo fair
And noble an Offer ? Can *France* ſhew a Virgin
That may be paralell'd with her ? Is ſhe not
The Phœnix of the Time ? the faireſt Star
In the bright Sphere of Women ?
     Beauf. fen. Be not rap'd ſo :
Tho' I diſlike not what is motion'd, yet
In what ſo near concerns me, it is fit
I ſhould proceed with Judgment.

          Enter Uſher, Theocrine, *Page, Women.*

     Beauf. jun. Here ſhe comes :
Look on her with impartial Eyes, and then
Let Envy, if it can, name one grac'd Feature
In which ſhe is defective.
                                             Malef.

Malef. Welcome, Girl :
My Joy, my Comfort, my Delight, my All, [5]
Why doft thou come to greet my Victory
In fuch a Sable Habit ? This fhew'd well
When thy Father was a Prifoner, and fufpected ;
But now his Faith and Loyalty are admir'd,
Rather than doubted, in your outward Garments
You are to exprefs the Joy you feel within ;
Nor fhould you with more Curioufnefs and Care
Pace to the Temple to be made a Bride,
Than now, when all Mens Eyes are fixt upon you ;
You fhould appear to entertain the Honour,
From me defcending to you, and in which
You have an equal Share.

Theoc. Heaven has my Thanks
With all Humility paid for your fair Fortune,
And fo far Duty binds me ; yet a little
To mourn a Brother's Lofs, however wicked,
The Tendernefs familiar to our Sex,
May, if you pleafe, excufe.

Malef. Thou art deceiv'd.
He living was a Blemifh to thy Beauties,
But in his Death gives Ornament and Luftre
To thy Perfections, but that they are
So exquifitely rare, that they admit not
The leaft Addition. Ha ! here's yet a Print
Of a fad Tear on thy Cheek ; How it takes from
Our prefent Happinefs ! with a Father's Lips,
A loving Father's Lips, I'll kifs it off,
The Caufe no more remember'd.

Theoc. You forget, Sir,
The Prefence we are in.

Malef. 'Tis well confider'd ;
And yet who is the Owner of a Treafure,

---

[5] *My Joy, my Comfort, my Delight, my All.*
And thus in the *Duke of Milan,*
    My Pride, my Glory, in a Word my All.
        See the Note on the fame, Act I. Scene 3.

Above

Above all Value, but without Offence,
May glory in the glad Poſſeſſion of it.
Nor let it in you Excellence beget Wonder,
Or any here that looking on the Daughter,
I feaſt myſelf in the Imagination
Of thoſe ſweet Pleaſures, and allow'd Delights,
I taſted from the Mother, who ſtill lives
In this her perfect Model ; for ſhe had
Such ſmooth and high arch'd Brows, ſuch ſparkling Eyes,
Whoſe every Glance ſtor'd *Cupid*'s emptied Quiver ;
Such ruby Lips, and ſuch a lovely Brown,
Diſdaining all adulterate Aids of Art,
Kept a perpetual Spring upon her Face,
As Death himſelf lamented, being forc'd
To blaſt it with his Paleneſs ; and if now,
Her Brightneſs dim'd Sorrow, take and pleaſe you,
Think, think, young Lord, when ſhe appears herſelf
(This Veil remov'd) in her own natural Pureneſs,
How far ſhe will tranſport you.
    Beauf. jun. Did ſhe need it,
The Praiſe which you (and well deſerv'd) give to her,
Muſt of Neceſſity raiſe new Deſires
In one indebted more to Years ; to me
Your Words are but as Oil pour'd on a Fire,
That flames already at the Height.
    Malef. No more ;
I do believe you, and let me from you
Find ſo much Credit. When I make her yours,
I do poſſeſs you of a Gift, which I
With much Unwillingneſs part from. My good Lords,
Forbear your further Trouble ; give me Leave,
For on the ſudden I am indiſpos'd,
To retire to my own Houſe, and Reſt. To-morrow,
As you command me, I will be your Gueſt,
And having deck'd my Daughter like herſelf,
You ſhall have farther Conference.
    Beauf. ſen. You are Maſter
Of your own Will ; but fail not, I'll expect you.
Malef.

Malef. Nay, I will be excus'd; I muſt part with you.
      [*To young* Beaufort *and the reſt.*
My deareſt *Theocrine*, give me thy Hand,
I will ſupport thee.

 Theoc. You gripe it too hard, Sir.

 Malef. Indeed I do, but have no farther End in it
But Love and Tenderneſs, ſuch as I may challenge,
And you muſt grant. Thou art a ſweet one ; yes,
And to be cheriſhed.

 Theoc. May I ſtill deſerve it.
       [*They go off ſeveral Ways.*

The End of the Second Act.

ACT III.　SCENE I.

Enter Beaufort *Senior, Servant.*

Beauf. ſen. HAVE you been careful ?
 Serv. With my beſt Endeavours.
Let them bring Stomachs, there's no Want of Meat, Sir.
Portly and curious Viands are prepar'd,
To pleaſe all Kinds of Appetites.

 Beauf. ſen. 'Tis well.
I love a Table furniſh'd with full Plenty,
And Store of Friends to eat it : but with this Caution,
I would not have my Houſe a common Inn,
For ſome Men that come rather to devour me,
Than to preſent their Service. At this Time too,
It being a ſerious and ſolemn Meeting,
I muſt not have my Board peſter'd with Shadows,
That under other Mens Protection break in
Without Invitement.

 Serv. With your Favour, then,
You muſt double your Guard, my Lord, for on my
   Knowledge,

           There

There are fome fo fharp fet, not to be kept out
By a File of Mufketeers.   And 'tis lefs Danger,
I'll undertake, to ftand at Pufh of Pike
With an Enemy in a Breach, that undermin'd too,
And the Cannon playing on it, than to ftop
One Harpy, your perpetual Gueft, from Entrance,
When the Dreffer, the Cook's Drum, thunders come on,
The Service will be loft elfe.
    Beauf. fen. What is he?
    Serv. As tall a Trencher-man, that is moft certain,
As e'er demolifh'd Pye-Fortification
As foon as batter'd; and if the Rim of his Belly
Were not made up of a much tougher Stuff
Than his Buff Jerkin, there were no Defence
Againft the Charge of his Guts : You needs muft know
He's Eminent for his Eating.   [him,
    Beauf. fen. O! *Belgard!*
    Serv. The fame, one of the Admiral's caft Captains,
Who fwears, there being no War, nor hope of any,
The only drilling is to Eat devoutly,
And to be ever Drinking (that's allow'd of)
But they know not where to get it, there's the Spite on't.
    Beauf. fen. The more their Mifery, yet if you can
For this Day put him off.——
    Serv. It is beyond the Invention of Man.
    Beauf. fen. No :—Say this only,   [*Whifpers to him.*
And as from me; you apprehend me?
    Serv. Yes, Sir.
    Beauf. fen. But it muft be done gravely.
    Serv. Never doubt me, Sir.   [Mufick
    Beauf. fen. We'll dine in the great Room, but let the
And Banquet be prepar'd here.   [*Exit Beauf. fen.*
    Serv. This will make him
Lofe his Dinner at the leaft, and that will vex him.
As for the Sweet Meats, when they are trod under Foot,
Let him take his Share with the Pages and Lacqueys
Or fcramble in the Rufhes.

Enter

Enter Belgard.

 Belg. 'Tis near Twelve,
I keep a Watch within me never misses.
—Save thee, Master Steward.
 Serv. You are most welcome, Sir.
 Belg. Has thy Lord slept well To-night? I come to
   enquire.
I had a foolish Dream, that, against my Will,
Carried me from my Lodging, to learn only
How he is dispos'd.
 Serv. He's in most perfect Health, Sir.
 Belg. Let me but see him feed heartily at Dinner,
And I'll believe so too, for from that ever
I make a certain Judgment.
 Serv. It holds surely
In your own Constitution.
 Belg. And in all Mens
'Tis the best Symptom: Let us lose no Time,
Delay is dangerous.
 Serv. Troth, Sir, if I might,
Without Offence, deliver what my Lord has
Committed to my Trust, I shall receive it
As a special Favour.
 Belg. We'll see't, and discourse,
As the Proverb says, for Health Sake after Dinner,
Or rather after Supper, willingly then
I'll walk a Mile to hear thee.
 Serv. Nay, good Sir,
I will be brief and pithy.
 Belg. Pr'ythee be so.
 Serv. He bid me say, of all his Guests, that he
Stands most affected to you, for the Freedom
And Plainness of your Manners. He ne'er observ'd you
To twirl a Dish about you did not like of,
All being pleasing to you; or to take
A Say of Venison, or stale Fowl, by your Nose,
(Which is a Solecism at another's Table)

But

But by ſtrong eating of 'em did confirm
They never were delicious to your Palate,
But when they were mortify'd, as the *Hugonot* ſays,
And ſo your Part grows greater; nor do you
Find Fault with the Sauce, keen Hunger being the beſt,
Which ever, to your much Praiſe, you bring with you;
Nor will you with impertinent Relations,
Which is a Maſter-piece, when Meat's before you,
Forget your Teeth, to uſe your nimble Tongue,
But do the Feat you come for.

   Belg. Be advis'd,
And end your Jeering; for if you proceed
You'll feel, as I can eat I can be angry,
And Beating may enſue.

   Serv. I'll take your Counſel,
And roundly come to the Point: My Lord much won-
That you, that are a Courtier as a Soldier,   [ders
In all Things elſe, and every Day can vary
Your Actions and Diſcourſe, continue conſtant
To this one Suit?

   Belg. To one! 'tis well I have one,
Unpawn'd, in theſe Days; every caſt Commander
Is not bleſt with the Fortune, I aſſure you.
But why this Queſtion? Does this offend him?

   Serv. Not much; but he believes it is the Reaſon
You ne'er preſume to ſit above the Salt, [6]
And therefore this Day (our great Admiral
With other States being invited Gueſts)
He does intreat you to appear among 'em,
In ſome freſh Habit.

   Belg. This Staff ſhall not ſerve

---

   6 You ne'er preſume to ſit above the Salt.

   This refers to the Manner in which our Anceſtors were uſually
ſeated at their Meals. The Tables being long, the *Salt* was com-
monly placed about the Middle, and ſerved as a Kind of Boundary
to the different Quality of the Gueſts invited. Thoſe of Diſtinction
were ranked above; the Space below was aſſigned to the Depend-
ents, or inferior Relations of the Maſter of the Houſe. See Mr.
Whalley's Edition of *Ben Johnſon*, Vol. I. Page 327, &c.

To beat the Dog off; thefe are Soldier's Garments,
And fo by Confequence grow contemptible.
    Serv. It has ftung him.
    Belg. I would I were acquainted with the Players,
In Charity they might furnifh me; but there is
No Faith in Brokers; and for believing Taylors,
They are only to be read of, but not feen,
And fure they are confin'd to their own Hells,
And there they live invifible. [*Afide.*] Well, I muft not
Be fobb'd off thus.   Pray you report my Service
To the Lord Governor.   I will obey him,
And though my Wardrobe's poor, rather than lofe
His Company at this Feaft, I will put on
The richeft Suit I have, and fill the Chair
That makes me worthy of ——   [*Exit* Belgard.
    Serv. We are fhut of him.
He will be feen no more here.   How my Fellows
Will blefs me for his Abfence! he had ftarv'd 'em
Had he ftay'd a little longer; would he could,
For his own Sake, fhift a Shirt, and that's the utmoft
Of his Ambition: Adieu, good Captain —   [*Exit.*

Enter Beaufort *Senior,* and Beaufort *Junior.*

Beauf. fen. 'Tis a ftrange Fondnefs.
Beauf. jun. 'Tis beyond Example.
His Refolution to part with his Eftate,
To make her Dower the weightier is nothing;
But to obferve how curious he is
In his own Perfon to add Ornament
To his Daughter's ravifhing Features, is the Wonder.
I fent a Page of mine in the Way of Courtfhip
This Morning to her, to prefent my Service,
From whom I underftand all: There he found him
Sollicitous in what Shape fhe fhould appear:
This gown was rich, but the Fafhion ftale; the other
Was quaint, and neat, but the Stuff not rich enough;
Then does he curfe the Taylor, and in Rage
Falls on her Shoemaker, for wanting Art,

                                        To

To exprefs in every Circumftance, the Form
Of her moft delicate Foot; then fits in Council
With much Deliberation to find out
What Tire would beft adorn her; and one chofen,
Varying in his Opinion, he tears off,
And ftamps it under Foot; then tries a fecond,
A third, and fourth; and fatisfy'd at length
With much ado in that, he grows again
Perplex'd and troubled where to place her Jewels
To be moft mark'd, and whether fhe fhould wear
This Diamond on her Forehead, or between
Her milk-white Paps, difputing on it both Ways;
Then taking in this Hand a Rope of Pearl,
(The beft of *France*) he ferioufly confiders
Whither he fhould difpofe it, on her Arm,
Or on her Neck; with twenty other Trifles,
Too tedious to deliver.

    Beauf. fen. I have known him from
His firft Youth, but never yet obferv'd,
In all the Paffages of his Life, and Fortunes,
Virtues fo mix'd with Vices: Valiant the World fpeaks
But with that Bloody; liberal in his Gifts too;   [him,
But to maintain his prodigal Expence,
A fierce Extortioner; an impotent Lover
Of Women for a Flafh, but, his Fires quench'd,]
Hating as deadly.   The Truth is, I am not
Ambitious of this Match; nor will I crofs
You in your Affections.

    Beauf. jun. I have ever found you
(And 'tis my Happinefs) a loving Father.

                          [*Loud Mufick.*
And careful of my Good:——By the loud Mufick,
As you gave Order for his Entertainment,
He's come into the Houfe.   Two long Hours fince,
The Colonels, Commiffioners and Captains,
To pay him all the Rites his Worth can challenge,
Went to wait on him hither.

Enter Malefort, Montaign, Chamont, Lanour, Montrevile, Theocrine, *Ufher, Page, Women.*

Beauf. fen. You are moft welcome,
And what I fpeak to you, does from my Heart
Difperfe itfelf to all.
   Malef. You meet, my Lord, your Trouble.
   Beauf. fen. Rather, Sir, Increafe of Honour,
When you are pleas'd to grace my Houfe.
   Beauf. jun. The Favour is doubled on my Part,
       moft worthy Sir,
Since your fair Daughter, my incomparable Miftrefs,
Deigns us her Prefence.
   Malef. View her well, brave *Beaufort,*
But yet at Diftance; you hereafter may
Make your Approaches nearer, when the Prieft
Hath made it lawful; and were not fhe mine,
I durft aloud proclaim it. *Hymen* never
Put on his Saffron colour'd Robe to change
A barren Virgin Name with more good Omens
Than at her Nuptials. Look on her again,
Then tell me if fhe now appear the fame,
That fhe was Yefterday.
   Beauf. fen. Being herfelf,
She cannot but be excellent. Thefe rich
And curious Dreffings, which in others might
Cover Deformities, from her take Luftre,
Nor can add to her.
   Malef. You conceive her right,
And in your Admiration of her Sweetnefs,
You only can deferve her. Blufh not, Girl;
Thou art above his Praife, or mine; nor can
Obfequious Flattery, though fhe fhould ufe
Her thoufand oil'd Tongues to advance thy Worth,
Give aught (for that's impoffible) but take from
Thy more than Human Graces; and even then,
When fhe hath fpent herfelf with her beft Strength,
The Wrong fhe has done thee fhall be fo apparent,
                    That

That, lofing her own fervile Shape and Name,
She will be thought Detraction.   But I
Forget myfelf; and fomething whifpers to me,
I have faid too much.
   Monta. I know not what to think on't,
But there's fome Myftery in it, which I fear
Will be too foon difcover'd.   [*Afide.*
   Malef. I much wrong
Your Patience, noble Sir, by too much hugging
My proper Iffue, and like the foolifh Crow
Believe my black Brood Swans.
   Beauf. fen. There needs not, Sir,
The leaft Excufe for this; nay, I muft have
Your Arm, you being the Mafter of the Feaft,
And this the Miftrefs.
   Theoc. I am any Thing
That you fhall pleafe to make me.
   Beauf. jun. Nay, 'tis yours,
Without more Compliment.   [*Loud Mufick.*
   Mont. Your Will's a Law, Sir.
      [*Exeunt* Beaufort *fen.* Malefort, Theocrine, Beau-
         fort *jun.* Montaign, Chamont, Lanour, Montrev.
   Ufher. Would I had been born a Lord.
   1 *Wom.* Or I a Lady.
   Page. It may be you were both begot in Court,
Though bred up in the City; for your Mothers,
As I have heard, lov'd the Lobby, and there nightly
Are feen ftrange Apparitions, and who knows
But that fome noble Fawn, heated with Wine,
And cloy'd with Partridge, had a Kind of Longing
To trade in Sprats? This needs no Expofition,
But can you yield a Reafon for your Wifhes?
   Ufher. Why, had I been born a Lord, I had been
            no Servant.
   1 *Wom.* And whereas now Neceffity makes us Waiters,
We had been attended on.
   2 *Wom.* And might have flept then
As long as we pleafe, and fed when we had Stomachs,
                    O 3   And

And worn new Cloaths, nor liv'd as now in Hope
Of a caſt Gown, or Petticoat.

   Page. You are Fools,
And ignorant of your Happineſs.   Ere I was
Sworn to the Pantofle, I have heard my Tutor
Prove it by Logick, that a Servant's Life
Was better than his Maſter's ; and by that
I learn from him, if that my Memory fail not,
I'll make it good.

   Uſher. Proceed, my little Wit,
In decimo ſexto.

   Page. Thus then : From the King
To the Beggar, by Gradation, all are Servants ;
And you muſt grant, the Slavery is leſs
To ſtudy to pleaſe one, than many.

   Uſher. True.

   Page. Well then ; and firſt to you, Sir : You complain
You ſerve one Lord, but your Lord ſerves a Thouſand,
Beſides his Paſſions (that are his worſt Maſters)
You muſt humour him, and he is bound to ſooth
Every grim Sir above him [7] : If he frown,
For the leaſt Neglect you fear to loſe your Place ;
But if, and with all ſlaviſh Obſervation,
From the Minion's ſelf, to the Groom of his Cloſe-ſtool,
He hourly ſeeks not Favour, he is ſure
To be eas'd of his Office, tho' perhaps he bought it.
Nay, more ; that high Diſpoſer of all ſuch
That are ſubordinate to him, ſerves and fears
The Fury of the many-headed Monſter,
The giddy Multitude. And as a Horſe
Is ſtill a Horſe, for all his golden Trappings,
So your Men of purchas'd Titles, at their beſt, are
But Serving-Men in rich Liveries.

   Uſher. Moſt rare Infant,
Where learnd'ſt thou this Morality ?

---

    7 *Every grim Sir above him.*

  Mr. *Dodſley* reads *trim*, which tho' it ſeems to be a juſt Alteration,
I have followed the Text of the old Copies.

Page.

Page. Why, thou dull Pate,
As I told thee, of my Tutor.
  2 *Wom.* Now for us, Boy.
  Page. I am cut off.——The Governor.

Enter Beaufort *Senior,* Beaufort *Junior, Servants setting
    forth a Banquet.*

  Beauf. sen. Quick, quick, Sirs.
See all Things perfect.
  Serv. Let the Blame be ours elfe.
  Beauf. sen. And as I faid, when we are at the Banquet,
And high in our Cups, for 'tis no Feaft without it,
Efpecially among Soldiers ; *Theocrine*
Being retir'd, as that's no Place for her,
Take you Occafion to rife from the Table,
And lofe no Opportunity.
  Beauf. jun. 'Tis my Purpofe,
And if I can win her to give her Heart,
I have a Holy Man in Readinefs
To join our Hands ; for the Admiral, her Father,
Repents him of his Grant to me, and
So far tranfported with a ftrange Opinion
Of her fair Features, that, fhould we defer it,
I think ere long he will believe, and ftrongly,
The Dauphin is not worthy of her.   I
Am much amaz'd with't.
  Beauf. sen. Nay, Difpatch there, Fellows.
                    [*Exeunt* Beauf. *sen.* Beauf. *jun.*
  Serv. We are ready when you pleafe. Sweet Forms,
        your Pardon.
It has been fuch a bufy Time I could not
Tender that ceremonious Refpect
Which you deferve ; but now the great Work ended,
I will attend the lefs, and with all Care
Obferve, and ferve you.
  Page. This is a penn'd Speech,
            O 4   And

And ferves as a perpetual Preface to
A Dinner made of Fragments.
   Ufher. We wait on you.   *[Loud Mufick.*

S C E N E II.

Beaufort *Senior,* Malefort, Montaign, Chamont, Lanour,
       Beaufort *Junior,* Montrevile, *Servants.*

   Beauf. fen. You are not merry, Sir.
   Malef. Yes, my good Lord,
You have given us ample Means to drown all Cares——
And yet I nourifh ftrange Thoughts, which I would
Moft willingly deftroy.   *[Afide,*
   Beauf. fen. Pray you take your Place.
   Beauf. jun. And drink a Health ; and let it be, if
       you pleafe,
To the Worthieft of Women.——Now obferve him.
   Malef. Give me the Bowl ; fince you do me the Ho-
I will begin it,   *[nour,*
   Cham. May we know her Name, Sir ?
   Malef. You fhall ; I will not chufe a foreign Queen's,
Nor yet our own, for that would relifh of
Tame Flattery ; nor do their Height of Title,
Or abfolute Power, confirm their Worth and Goodnefs,
Thefe being Heav'ns Gifts, and frequently confer'd
On fuch as are beneath 'em ; nor will I
Name the King's Miftrefs, howfoe'er fhe
In his Efteem may carry it ; but if I,
As Wine gives Liberty, may ufe my Freedom ;
Not fway'd this Way, or that with Confidence,
(And I will make it good on any Equal)
If it muft be to her, whofe outward Form
Is better'd by the Beauty of her Mind,
She lives not that with Juftice can pretend
An Intereft to this fo facred Health,
But my fair Daughter. He that only doubts it,
I do pronounce a Villain : This to her then. *[Drinks.*
   Mont. What may we think of this ?   *[Loud Mufick.*
                              Beauf.

Beauf. fen. It matters not.

Lan. For my Part, I will footh him, rather than
Draw on a Quarrel, *Chamont.*

Mont. 'Tis the fafeft Courfe; and one I mean to follow.

Beauf. jun. It has gone round, Sir.

       [*Exit* Beaufort *jun.*

Malef. Now you have done her Right; if there be any
Worthy to fecond this, propofe it boldly,
I am your Pledge.

Beauf. fen. Let's Paufe here, if you pleafe,
And entertain the Time with fomething elfe.
Mufick there, in fome lofty Strain; the Song too
That I gave Order for; the new one, call'd
The Soldier's Delight.

 The Song ended, Enter Belgard *in Armour, a Cafe of*
    Carbines by his Side.

Belg. Who ftops me now?
Or who dares only fay that I appear not
In the moft rich and glorious Habit that
Renders a Man compleat? What Court fo fet off
With State and ceremonious Pomp, but thus
Accoutred I may enter? Or what Feaft,
Tho' all the Elements at once were ranfack'd
To ftore it with Variety tranfcending
The Curioufnefs and Coft on *Trajan's* Birth-day,
Where Princes only and confederate Kings
Did fit as Guefts, ferv'd and attended on
By the Senators of *Rome*, fat with a Soldier
In this his natural and proper Shape,
Might not, and boldly, fill a Seat, and by
His Prefence make the great Solemnity
More honour'd and remarkable?

Beauf. fen. 'Tis acknowledg'd,
And this a Grace done to me unexpected.

Mont. But why in Armour?

Malef. What's the Myftery?
Pray you, reveal that.

           Belg.

Belg. Soldiers out of Action,
That very rare, but like unbidden Guests
Bring their Stools with 'em, for their own Defence,
At Court should feed in Gauntlets, they may have
Their Fingers cut else: There your Carpet Knights,
That never charg'd beyond a Mistress' Lips,
Are still most keen, and valiant.   But to you,
Whom it does most concern, my Lord, I will
Address my Speech, and with a Soldier's Freedom
In my Reproof, return the bitter Scoff
You threw upon my Poverty: You contemn'd
My coarser Outside, and from that concluded,
(As by your Groom you made me understand)
I was unworthy to sit at your Table
Among these Tissues and Embroideries,
Unless I chang'd my Habit.   I have done it,
And shew myself in that which I have worn
In the Heat and Fervor of a bloody Fight;
And then it was in Fashion, not as now
Ridiculous and despis'd: This hath past through
A Wood of Pikes, and every one aim'd at it,
Yet scorn'd to take Impression from their Fury:
With this, as still you see it fresh and new,   [bles,
I have charg'd thro' Fire that would have sing'd your Sa-
Black Fox, and Ermins, and chang'd the proud Colour
Of Scarlet, though of the right Tyrian Dye:
But now, as if the Trappings made the Man,
Such only are admir'd that come adorn'd
With what's no Part of them.   This is mine own,
My richest Suit, a Suit I must not part from,
But not regarded now; and yet remember
'Tis we that bring you in the Means of Feasts,
Banquets and Revels, which, when you possess,
With barbarous Ingratitude you deny us
To be made Sharers in the Harvest, which
Our Sweat and Industry reap'd, and sow'd for you.
The Silks you wear, we with our Blood spin for you;
This massy Plate, that with the ponderous Weight
Does make your Cupboards crack, we (unaffrighted
                                                  With

With Tempefts, or the long and tedious Way,
Or dreadful Monfters of the Deep, that wait
With open Jaws ftill ready to devour us)
Fetch from the other World.   Let it not then
In after Ages to your Shame be fpoken,
That you with no relenting Eyes look on
Our Wants that feed your Plenty; or confume
In prodigal and wanton Gifts on Drones
The Kingdom's Treafure, yet detain from us
The Debt that with the Hazard of our Lives,
We have made you ftand engag'd for; or force us,
Againft all civil Government, in Armour
To require that, which with all Willingnefs
Should be tender'd, ere demanded.
     Beauf. fen. I commend
This wholefome Sharpnefs in you, and prefer it
Before obfequious Tamenefs; it fhews lovely:
Nor fhall the Rain of your good Counfel fall
Upon the barren Sands, but fpring up Fruit,
Such as you long have wifh'd for.   And the reft
Of your Profeffion, like you, difcontented
For want of Means, fhall in their prefent Payment
Be bound to praife your Boldnefs: And hereafter
I will take Order you fhall have no Caufe,
For want of Change to put your Armour on
But in the Face of an Enemy; not as now
Among your Friends.   To that which is due to you,
To furnifh you like yourfelf, of mine own Bounty
I'll add five hundred Crowns.
     Cham. I to my Power
Will follow the Example.
     Mont. Take this, Captain;
'Tis all my prefent Store; but, when you pleafe,
Command me farther.
     Lan. I could wifh it more.
     Belg. This is the luckieft Jeft ever came from me.
Let a Soldier ufe no other Scribe to draw
The Form of his Petition.   This will fpeed
When your thrice humble Supplications,

With

With Prayers for Increafe of Health and Honours
To their grave Lordfhips, fhall, as foon as read,
Be pocketed up, the Caufe no more remember'd.
When this dumb Rhetorick —— Well, I have a Life,
Which I in Thankfulnefs for your great Favours,
My noble Lords, when you pleafe to command it,
Muft never think mine own.   Broker, be happy,
Thefe golden Birds fly to thee.   [*Exit* Belgard.

    Beauf. fen. You are dull, Sir,
And feem not to be taken with the Paffage
You faw prefented.

    Malef. Paffage? I obferv'd none,
My Thoughts were elfewhere bufied.—Ha! fhe is
In Danger to be loft, to be loft for ever,
If fpeedily I come not to her Refcue,
For fo my Genius tells me.   [*Afide.*

    Mont. What Chimeras
Work on your Phantafy?

    Malef. Phantafies? They are Truths,
Where is my *Theocrine?* You have plotted
To rob me of my Daughter: Bring me to her,
Or I'll call down the Saints to witnefs for me,
You are inhofpitable.

    Beauf. fen. You amaze me.
Your Daughter's fafe, and now exchanging Courtfhip
With my Son her Servant. Why do you hear this
With fuch diftracted Looks, fince to that End
You brought her hither?

    Malef. 'Tis confefs'd I did.
But now pray you pardon me; and, if you pleafe,
Ere fhe deliver up her Virgin Fort,
I would obferve what is the Art he ufes
In planting his Artillery againft it.
She is my only Care, nor muft fhe yield
But upon noble Terms.

    Beauf. fen. 'Tis fo determin'd.

    Malef. Yet I am jealous.

    Mont. Overmuch, I fear.
What Paffions are thefe?

Beauf.

Beauf. fen. Come, I will bring you
Where you, with thefe, if they fo pleafe, may fee
The Love Scene acted.
  Mont. There is fomething more
Than fatherly Love in this.
  Monta. We wait upon you.   [*Exeunt omnes.*

S C E N E IV.

Beaufort *jun. and* Theocrine.

  Beauf. jun. Since then you meet my Flames with
            equal Ardour,
As you profefs, it is your Bounty, Miftrefs,
Nor muft I call it Debt; yet 'tis your Glory,
That your Excefs fupplies my Want, and makes me,
Strong in my Weaknefs, which could never be,
But in your good Opinion.
  Theoc. You teach me, Sir,
What I fhould fay; fince from your Sun of Favour,
I, like dim *Phœbe*, in herfelf obfcure,
Borrow that Light I have.
  Beauf. jun. Which you return
With large Increafe (fince that you will o'ercome,
And I dare not contend) were you but pleas'd
To make what's yet divided one.
  Theoc. I have
Already in my Wifhes, Modefty
Forbids me to fpeak more.
  Beauf. jun. But what Affurance
(But ftill without Offence) may I demand
That may fecure me that your Heart and Tongue
Join to make up this Harmony.
  Theoc. Choofe any,
Suiting your Love, diftinguifhed from Luft,
To afk, and mine to grant.

                                      Enter

Enter (as unseen) Beaufort *sen.* Malefort, Montrevile,
and the rest.

   Beauf. sen. Yonder they are.
   Malef. At Diftance too! 'tis yet well.
   Beauf. jun. I may take then
This Hand, and with a Thoufand burning Kiffes,
Swear 'tis the Anchor to my Hopes?
   Theoc. You may, Sir.
   Malef. This is fomewhat too much.
   Beauf. jun. And this done, view myfelf
In thefe true Mirrors.
   Theoc. Ever true to you, Sir.
And may they lofe th' Ability of Sight,
When they feek other Object.
   Malef. This is more
Than I can give Confent to.
   Beauf. jun. And a Kifs
Thus printed on your Lips will not diftafte you?
   Malef. Her Lips!
   Montr. Why, where fhould hekifs? are you diftracted?
   Beauf. jun. Then, when this Holy Man hath made it
        lawful ——   [*brings in a Prieft.*
   Malef. A Prieft fo ready too? I muft break in.
   Beauf. jun. And what's fpoke here is regifter'd above.
I muft engrofs thofe Favours to myfelf
Which are not to be nam'd.
   Theoc. All I can give,
But what they are I know not.
   Beauf. jun. I'll inftruct you.
   Malef. O how my Blood boils!
   Mont. Pray you, contain yourfelf:
Methinks this Courtfhip's modeft.
   Beauf. jun. Then being mine,
And wholly mine, the River of your Love
To Kinfmen and Allies; nay, to your Father,
(Howe'er out of his Tendernefs he admires you)
Muft in the Ocean of your Affection

To

To me be fwallow'd up, and want a Name
Compar'd with what you owe me.
   Theoc. 'Tis moft fit, Sir.
The ftronger Bond that binds me to you, muft
Diffolve the weaker.
   Malef. I am ruin'd, if
I come not fairly off.
   Beauf. fen. There's nothing wanting
But your Confent.
   Malef. Some ftrange Invention aid me.
This! yes, it muft be fo.   [*Afide.*
   Montr. Why do you ftagger,
When what you feem'd fo much to wifh is offer'd ?
Both Parties being agreed to.
   Beauf. fen. I'll not court
A Grant from you, nor do I wrong your Daughter,
Though I fay my Son deferves her.
   Malef. 'Tis far from
My humble Thoughts to undervalue him
I cannot prize too high.   For howfoever
From my own fond Indulgence I have fung
Her Praifes with too prodigal a Tongue,
That Tendernefs laid by, I ftand confirm'd
All that I fancied excellent in her
Ballanc'd, with what is really his own,
Holds Weight in no Proportion.
   Montr. New Turnings !
   Beauf. fen. Whither tends this ?
   Malef. Had you obferv'd, my Lord,
With what a fweet Gradation he woo'd,
As I did punctually, you cannot blame her,
Though fhe did liften with a greedy Care
To his fair modeft Offers : But fo great
A good as then flow'd to her, fhould have been
With more deliberation entertain'd,
And not with fuch hafte fwallow'd ; fhe fhall firft
Confider ferioufly what the Bleffing is,
And in what ample Manner to give thanks for't,
And then receive it.   And though I fhall think

Short

Short Minutes years till it be perfected,
I will defer that which I moſt deſire,
And ſo muſt ſhe, till longing Expectation,
That heightens Pleaſure, makes her truly know
Her Happineſs, and with what out-ſtretch'd Arms
She muſt embrace it.

   Beauf. jun. This is curiouſneſs
Beyond Example.

   Malef. Let it then begin
From me; in what's mine own I'll uſe my Will,
And yield no further Reaſon. I lay claim to
The Liberty of a Subject. Fall not off,
But be obedient, or by the Hair
I'll drag thee Home. Cenſure me as you pleaſe,
I'll take my own Way.—O the inward Fires
That, wanting vent, conſume me! [*Exit with* Theocrine.

   Montr. 'Tis moſt certain
He's Mad, or worſe.

   Beauf. How, worſe?

   Montr. Nay, there I leave you,
My Thoughts are free.

   Beauf. jun. This I foreſaw.

   Beauf. ſen. Take Comfort,
He ſhall walk in Clouds, but I'll diſcover him:
And he ſhall find and feel, if he excuſe not,
And with ſtrong Reaſons this groſs Injury,
I can make uſe of my Authority.   [*Exeunt omnes.*

The End of the Third Act.

ACT IV.   SCENE I.

Malefort *folus.*

WHAT Flames are thefe my wild Defires fan in me?
The Torch that feeds them, was not lighted at
Thy Altars, *Cupid:* Vindicate thyfelf,
And do not own it: And confirm it rather,
That this infernal Brand that turns me Cinders,
Was by the Snake-hair'd Sifters thrown into
My guilty Bofom.   O that I was ever
Accurs'd in having Iffue! my Son's Blood,
(That like the poifon'd Shirt of *Hercules*
Grows to each part about me) which my Hate
Forc'd from him with much willingnefs, may admit
Some weak Defence ; but my moft Impious Love
To my fair Daughter *Theocrine,* none.
Since my Affection (rather wicked Luft)
That does purfue her, is a greater Crime
Than any Deteftation, with which
I fhould afflict her Innocence. With what Cunning
I have betray'd myfelf, and did not feel
The fcorching Heat that now with Fury rages.
Why was I tender of her ? Cover'd with
That fond Difguife, this Mifchief ftole upon me.
I thought it no Offence to kifs her often,
Or twine mine Arms about her fofter Neck,
And by falfe Shadows of a Father's Kindnefs
I long deceiv'd myfelf : But now the Effect
Is too apparent. How I ftrove to be
In her Opinion held the worthieft Man
In Courtfhip, Form and Feature! Envying him
That was preferr'd before me, and yet then
My Wifhes to myfelf were not difcover'd.
But ftill my Fires increas'd, and with Delight

I would call her Miſtreſs, wilfully forgetting
The Name of Daughter, chooſing rather ſhe
Should ſtile me Servant, then with Reverence Father,
Yet mocking. I ne'er cheriſh'd obſcene Hopes,
But in my troubled Slumbers often thought
She was too near to me, and then ſleeping bluſh'd
At my Imagination which paſs'd
My Eyes being open, not condemning it,
I was Raviſh'd with the Pleaſure of the Dream.
Yet ſpight of theſe Temptations I have Reaſon
That pleads againſt 'em, and commands me to
Extinguiſh theſe abominable Fires,
And I will do it ; I will ſend her back
To him that Loves her Lawfully. Within there.

Enter Theocrine.

   Theo. Sir, did you call ?
   Malef. I look no ſooner on her,
But all my boaſted Power of Reaſon leaves me, [wait me ?
And Paſſion again uſurps her Empire, does none elſe
    Theo. I am wretch'd, Sir, ſhould any owe more Duty.
    Malef. This is worſe then Diſobedience, leave me.
    Theo. On my Knees, Sir, as I have ever ſquar'd my
                           [Will by yours.
And lik'd, and loath'd with your Eyes I beſeech you
To teach me what the Nature of my Fault is,
That hath incens'd you, (ſure 'tis one of Weakneſs
And not of Malice) which your gentler Temper
On my Submiſſion I hope will Pardon ;
Which granted by your Piety, if that I
Out of the leaſt Neglect of mine hereafter,
Make you remember it, may I ſink ever
Under your dread Command.
   Malef. O my Stars ! who can but dote on this Humility
That Sweetens; lovely in her Tears ? The Fetters
That ſeem'd to leſſen in their Weight ; but now
By this grow Heavier on me.
   Theoc. Dear, Sir.—

Malef.

Malef. Peace, I muft not hear thee.

Theoc. Nor look on me.

Malef. No, thy Looks and Words are Charms.

Theoc. May they have Power then
To calm the Tempeft of your Wrath.   Alas, Sir,
Did I but know in what I give Offence
In my Repentance I would fhew my Sorrow,
For what is paft, and in my Care hereafter
Kill the Occafion or ceafe to be ;
Since Life without your Favour is to me
A Load I would caft off.

Malef. O that my Heart
Were rent in funder, that I might expire,
The Caufe in my Death buried : Yet I know not
With fuch prevailing Oratory 'tis beg'd from me
That to deny thee would convince me to
Have fuck'd the Milk of Tigers, rife, and I
But in a perplex'd, and myfterious Method,
Will make Relation : That which all the World
Admires and cries up in thee for Perfections,
Are to unhappy me foul Blemifhes,
And mulcts in Nature.   If thou hadft been born '
Deform'd and Crook'd in the Features of
Thy Body, as the Manners of thy Mind,
Moor Lip'd, flat Nos'd, dim Ey'd, and beetle Brow'd
With a dwarf's Stature to a giant Wafte,
Sower Breath'd, with Claws for Fingers on thy Hands,
Splay Footed, gouty Leg'd, and over all
A loathfome Leprofy had fpread itfelf,
And made thee fhun'd of Human Fellowfhips :
I had been bleft.

   , *If thou hadft been born.*

Thus in King *John*, the Mother fpeaking of her Son, fays,
   If thou, that bid'ft me be con ent, were grim,
   Ugly, and fland'rous to thy Mother's Womb,
   Full of unpleafing Blots, and flightlefs Stains,
   Lame. Foolifh, Crooked, Swart, Prodigious,
   Patch'd with foul Moles, and eye offending Marks :
   I would not care, I then would be content :
   For then I fhould not love thee.   *Act.* III.

Theoc. Why would you wish a Monster, -
For such a one or worse you have describ'd,
To call you Father.
    Malef. Rather then as now,
Tho' I had drown'd thee for it in the Sea
Appearing as thou dost a new Pandora,
With *Juno*'s fair Cow Eyes,[10] *Minerva*'s Brow,
Aurora's blushing Cheeks, *Hebe*'s fresh Youth,
Venus's soft Paps, with *Thetis*'s silver Feet.
    Theoc. Sir, you have lik'd and lov'd them, and oft forc'd
(With your Hyperboles of Praise pour'd on them)
My Modesty to a defensive Red,
Strow'd over that Paleness, which you then were pleased
To stile the purest White.
    Malef. And in that Cup
I drank the Poison I now feel dispersed
Through every Vein and Artery, wherefore art thou
So cruel to me ? This thy outward Shape
Brought a fierce War against me, not to be
By Flesh and Blood resisted : But to leave me
No hope of Freedom from the Magazine
Of thy Mind's Forces, treacherously thou drew'st up
Auxiliary Helps to strengthen that
Which was already in itself too potent.
Thy Beauty gave the first Charge, but thy Duty
Seconded with thy Care, and watchful Studies
To please, and serve my Will in all that might
Raise up Content in me, like Thunder brake through
All Opposition, and my Ranks of Reason
Disbanded, my victorious Passions fell
To bloody Execution, and compell'd me
With willing Hands to tie on my own Chains,
And with a Kind of flatt'ring Joy to glory

    [10] *With* Juno's *fair Cow Eyes,* &c.

    These Lines of *Massinger* are an immediate Translation from a pretty *Greek* Epigram, the Author of which compares his Mistress's Eyes to *Juno*'s, her Paps to *Venus*, &c.

    Ομματ' ιχεις Ηρης, Μιλιτη, τας χειρας Αθηνης,
      Τας μαζυς Παφιης, τα σφυρα της Θετιδος, &c.

In

In my Captivity.

Theoc. I, in this you fpeak, Sir,
Am Ignorance itfelf.

Malef. And fo continue,
For Knowledge of the Arms thou bear'ft againft me
Would make thee curfe thyfelf, but yield no Aids
For thee to help me, and 'twere Cruelty
In me to wound that fpotlefs Innocency
How 'ere it make me guilty.   In a Word "
The Plurify of Goodnefs is thy Ill,
Thy Virtues Vices, and thy humble Lownefs
Far worfe than ftubborn Sullennefs and Pride,
Thy Looks that ravifh all Beholders elfe
As killing as the Bafilifks : Thy Tears
Exprefs'd in Sorrow for the much I fuffer,
A glorious Infultation, and no fign
Of pity in thee ; and to hear thee fpeak
In thy Defence, though but in filent Action,
Would make the Hurt already deeply fefter'd
Incurable ; and therefore as thou wouldft not
By thy Prefence raife frefh Furies to torment me,
I do conjure thee by a Father's Power,
(And 'tis my Curfe I dare not think it lawful
To fue unto thee in a nearer Name)
Without Reply to leave me.

Theoc. My Obedience
Never learn'd yet to queftion your Commands,
But willingly to ferve 'em ; yet I muft
Since that your Will forbids the Knowledge of
My Fault, lament my Fortune.   [*Exit.*

Malef. O that
I have Reafon to difcern the better Way
And yet purfue the worfe.   When I look on her

" ————————— In a Word
The Plurify of Goodnefs, &c.

   Plurify of Goodnefs—Not the Diftemper that would have been
Nonfenfe, but a Word coined from the *Latin.* Thy Plurify of Good-
nefs, *i. e.* Thy Goodnefs more than common—Thy extraordinary
Share of it, which tempted me to think this Vice was thy Ill.

P 3   I

I burn with Heat, and in her Abſence freeze
With the cold Blaſts of Jealouſy, that another
Should e'er taſte thoſe Delights that are deny'd me,
And which of their Afflictions bring leſs Torture,
I hardly can diſtinguiſh ; is there then
No Mean ? No, ſo my Underſtanding tells me,
And that by my croſs Fates it is determin'd
That I am both Ways wretched.

Enter Uſher and Montrevile.

Uſher. Yonder he walks, Sir,
In much Vexation : He hath ſent my Lady
His Daughter weeping in ; but what the Cauſe is
Reſts yet in Suppoſition.
  Montr. I gueſs at it,
But muſt be further ſatisfy'd ; I will ſift him
In private, therefore quit the Room.
  Uſher. I am gone, Sir.   [*Exit.*
  Malef. Ha ! who diſturbs me ? *Montrevile ?* Your
         Pardon.   [ſpeak it
  Montr. Would you could grant one to yourſelf. (I
With the Aſſurance of a Friend) and yet
Before it be too late, make Reparation
Of the groſs Wrong your Indiſcretion offer'd
To the Governor and his Son ; nay, to yourſelf,
For there begins my Sorrow.
  Malef. Would I had
No greater Cauſe to mourn than their Diſpleaſure.
For I dare juſtify ——
  Montr. We muſt not do all that we dare.
We're private Friend.   I obſerv'd your Alterations
With a ſtricter Eye perhaps than others;
And to loſe no Time in Repetition,
Your ſtrange Demeanour to your ſweet Daughter ——
  Malef. Would you could find ſome other Theme to
         treat of.
  Montr. None but this ; and this I'll dwell on,
How ridiculous and ſubject to Conſtruction.——
                                          Malef.

Malef. No more !

Montr. You made yourfelf, amazes me, and if
The frequent Trials interchang'd between us
Of Love and Friendfhip, be to their Defert
Efteem'd by you, as they hold Weight with me,
No inward Trouble fhould be of a Shape
So horrid to yourfelf, but that to me
You ftand bound to difcover it, and unlock
Your fecret Thoughts; tho' the moft innocent were
Loud crying Sins.

Malef. And fo perhaps they are;
And therefore be not curious to learn that
Which known muft make you hate me.

Montr. Think not fo.
I am yours in Right and Wrong; nor fhall you find
A verbal Friendfhip in me, but an active;
And here I vow, I fhall no fooner know
What the Difeafe is, but if you give Leave
I will apply a Remedy.   Is it Madnefs ?
I am familiarly acquainted with a deep-read Man
That can with Charms and Herbs
Reftore you to your Reafon; or fuppofe
You are bewitch'd, he with more potent Spells
And magical Rites fhall cure you. Is't Heav'ns Anger ?
With Penitence and Sacrifice appeafe it :
Beyond this, there is nothing that I can
Imagine dreadful.   In your Fame and Fortunes
You are fecure; your impious Son remov'd too,
That render'd you fufpected to the State,
And your fair Daughter———

Malef. Oh ! prefs me no farther.

Montr. Are you wrung there ? Why, what of her ?
          Hath fhe
Made Shipwreck of her Honour, or confpir'd
Againft your Life ? or feal'd a Contract with
The Devil of Hell, for the Recovery of
Her young Inamorato ?

Malef. None of thefe;
And yet what muft increafe the Wonder in you,

Being innocent in herſelf, ſhe hath wounded me,
But where enquire not. Yet, I know not how
I am perſuaded from my Confidence
Of your vow'd Love to me, to truſt you with
My deareſt Secret, pray you chide me for it,
But with a Kind of Pity, not inſulting
On my Calamity.

   Montr. Forward.

   Malef. This ſame Daughter——

   Montr. What is her Fault?

   Malef. She is too fair to me.

   Montr. Ha! how is this?

   Malef. And I have look'd upon her
More than a Father ſhould, and languiſh to
Enjoy her as a Huſband.

   Montr. Heaven forbid it.

   Malef. And this is all the Comfort you can give me?
Where are your promis'd Aids, your Charms, your Herbs?
Your deep-read Scholar, Spells, and magic Rites?
Can all theſe diſenchant me? No, I muſt be
My own Phyſician, and upon myſelf
Practice a deſperate Cure.

   Montr. Do not contemn me.
Enjoin me what you pleaſe with any Hazard,
I'll undertake it. What Means have you practic'd
To quench this helliſh Fire?

   Malef. All I could think on,
But to no Purpoſe; and yet ſometimes Abſence
Does yield a Kind of Intermiſſion to
The Fury of the Fit.

   Montr. See her no more then.

   Malef. 'Tis my laſt Refuge, and 'twas my Intent
And ſtill 'tis, to deſire your Help.

   Montr. Command it.

   Malef. Thus then, you have a Fort of which you are
The abſolute Lord, whither I pray you bear her:
And that the Sight of her may not again
Nouriſh thoſe Flames, which I feel ſomething leſſen'd,
By all the Ties of Friendſhip I conjure you,

And

And by a folemn Oath you muſt confirm it,
That tho' my now calm'd Paſſions ſhould rage higher
Than ever heretofore, and ſo compel me
Once more to wiſh to ſee her ; tho' I uſe
Perſuaſions mix'd with Threatnings ; nay, add to it,
That I, this failing, ſhould with Hands held up thus
Kneel at your Feet, and bathe them with my Tears,
Prayers or Curſes, Vows or Imprecations,
Only to look upon her, though at Diſtance,
You ſtill muſt be obdurate,
　　Montr. If it be
Your Pleaſure, Sir, that I ſhall be unmov'd,
I will endeavour.
　　Malef. You muſt ſwear to be
Inexorable, as you would prevent
The greateſt Miſchief to your Friend, that Fate
Could throw upon him.
　　Montr. Well, I will obey you.
But how the Governor will be anſwer'd, yet,
And 'tis material, is not conſider'd.
　　Malef. Leave that to me.　I'll preſently give Order
How you ſhall ſurprize her ; be not frighted with
Her Exclamations.
　　Montr. Be you conſtant to
Your Reſolution, I will not fail
In what concerns my Part.
　　Malef. Be ever bleſſed for't.　　　　　　*[Exeunt.*

S C E N E II.

Enter Beaufort *jun.* Chamont, Lanour.

Cham. Not to be ſpoke with, ſay you ?
Beauf. jun. No.
Lan. Nor you
Admitted to have Conference with her ?
　　Beauf. jun. Neither.
His Doors are faſt lock'd up, and Solitude
Dwells round about 'em, no Acceſs allow'd
To Friend or Enemy, but ——　　　　　　　*Cham.*

Cham. Nay, be not mov'd, Sir ;
Let his Paffion work, and like a hot rein'd Horfe [2]
'Twill quickly tire itfelf.

Beauf. jun. Or in his Death
Which for her Sake 'till now I have forborne,
I will revenge the Injury he hath done
To my true lawful Love.

Lan. How does your Father,
The Governor, relifh it ?

Beauf. jun. Troth, he never had
Affection to the Match ; yet in his Pity
To me, he's gone in Perfon to his Houfe,
Nor will he be deny'd ; and if he find not
Strong and fair Reafons, *Malefort* will hear from him
In a Kind he does not look for.

Cham. In the mean Time,
Pray you put on cheerful Looks.

Beauf. jun. Mine fuit my Fortune.

Enter Montaign.

Lan. O here's *Montaign.*
Monta. I never could have met you
More opportunely.   I'll not ftale the Jeft
By my Relation ; but if you will look on
The Malecontent *Belgard*, newly rigg'd up
With the Train that follows him, 'twill be an Object
Worthy of your noting.

Beauf. jun. Look you the Comedy,
Make good the Prologue, or the Scorn will dwell
Upon yourfelf.

Monta. I'll hazard that, obferve now.

[2] ————— *And like a hot rein'd Horfe,*
    'Twill quickly tire itfelf.

This is directly copied from *Shakefpear*, who fays,

————— *Anger is like*
A full hot Horfe, who being allow'd his Way,
Self-mettle tires him.

Henry VIIIth. Act I. Scene 2.

Enter

Enter Belgard *in a gallant Habit; ſtays at the Door with
his Sword drawn; ſeveral Voices within.*

   Wenches. Nay, Captain! glorious Captain!
   Belg. Fall back, Raſcals;
Do you make an Owl of me? this Day I will
Receive no more Petitions.
Here are Bills of all Occaſions, and all Sizes!
If this be the Pleaſure of a rich Suit, would I were
Again in my Buff Jerkin, or my Armour,
Then I walk'd ſecurely by my Creditors Noſes,
And not a Dog mark'd me; every Officer ſhun'd me,
And not one louzy Priſon would receive me:
But now, as the Ballad ſays, I am turn'd Gallant,
There does not live that Thing I owe a Souſe to
But does torment me.   A faithful Cobler told me,
With his Awl in his Hand, I was behind-hand with him
For ſetting me upright, and bade me look to myſelf.
A Sempſtreſs too, that traded but in Socks,
Swore ſhe would ſet a Serjeant on my Back
For a borrow'd Shirt: My Pay, and the Benevolence
The Governor and the States beſtow'd upon me,
The City Cormorants, my Money-Mongers,
Have ſwallow'd down already; they were Sums,
I grant, but that I ſhould be ſuch a Fool
Againſt my Oath, being a caſhier'd Captain,
To pay Debts, though grown up to one and twenty,
Deſerves more Reprehenſion, in my Judgment,
Than a Shop-keeper, or a Lawyer that lends Money,
In a long dead Vacation.
   Monta. How do you like
His Meditation?
   Cham. Peace! let him proceed.
   Belg. I cannot now go on the Score for Shame,
And where I ſhall begin to pawn: Ay, marry,
That is conſider'd timely; I paid for
This Train of yours, Dame *Eſtridge*, fourteen Crowns,
And yet it is ſo light, 'twill hardly paſs

For

For a Tavern Reck'ning, unlefs it be
To fave the Charge of Painting, nail'd on a Poft
For the Sign of the Feathers. Pox upon the Fafhion,
That a Captain cannot think himfelf a Captain,
If he wear not this like a Fore-Horfe ; yet it is not
Staple Commodity ; thefe are perfum'd too
Of the *Roman* Wafh, and yet a ftale Red Herring
Would fill the Belly better, and hurt the Head lefs :
And this is *Venice* Gold, would I had it again
In *French* Crowns in my Pocket.   O you Commanders
That, like me, have no dead Pays, nor can couzen
The Commiffary at a Mufter, let me ftand
For an Example to you, as you would
Enjoy your Privileges : *videlicet*,
To pay your Debts, and take your Lechery gratis ;
To have your Iffue warm'd by others Fires ;
To be often drunk, and fwear, yet pay no Forfeit
To the Poor, but when you fhare with one another,
With all your other choice Immunities :
Only of this I ferioufly advife you,
Let Courtiers trip like Courtiers,
And your Lords of Dirt and Dunghills mete
Their Woods and Acres, in Velvets, Sattins, Tiffues,
But keep you conftant to Cloth and Shamois.
   Monta. Have you heard of fuch a penitent Homily ?
   Belg. I am ftudying now
Where I fhall hide myfelf till the Rumour of
My Wealth and Bravery vanifh : Let me fee,
There is a kind of a Vaulting Houfe not far off,
Where I us'd to fpend my Afternoons, among
Suburb She-Gamefters ; and yet, now I think on't,
I have crack'd a Ring or two there, which they made
Others to folder. No——

Enter a Bawd and two Wenches, with two Children.

   1 *Wench.* O! have we fpy'd you !
   Bawd. Upon him without Ceremony, now's the Time
While he is in the paying Vein.
2 *Wench.*

2 *Wench.* Save you, brave Captain.

Beauf· jun. 'Slight! how he ſtares!
They are worſe than She-Wolves to him.   [you.
　Belg. Shame me not in the Streets. I was coming to
　1 *Wench.* O Sir, you may in Publick pay for the Fid-
You had in Private.   [ling
　2 *Wench.* We hear you are full of Crowns, Sir.
　1 *Wench.* And therefore knowing you are open-handed,
Before all be deſtroy'd, I'll put you in Mind, Sir,
Of your young Heir here.
　2 *Wench.* Here's a ſecond, Sir,
That looks for a Child's Portion.
　Bawd. There are Reckonings
For Muſkadine and Eggs too, muſt be thought on.
　1 *Wench.* We have not been haſty, Sir.
　Bawd. But ſtay'd your Leiſure;
But now you are ripe, and loaden with Fruit.
　2 *Wench.* 'Tis fit you ſhould be pull'd; here's a Boy,
Pray you kiſs him, 'tis your own, Sir.   [Sir,
　1 *Wench.* Nay, buſs this firſt,
It hath juſt your Eyes, and ſuch a promiſing Noſe,
That if the Sign deceive me not, in Time
'Twill prove a notable Striker, like his Father.
　Belg. And yet you laid it to another.
　1 *Wench.* True,
While you were poor, and it was Policy,
But ſhe that has Variety of Fathers,
And makes not Choice of him that can maintain it,
Ne'er ſtudied *Ariſtotle*'s Problems.
　Lan. A ſmart Quean.
　Belg. Why, Brachs, will you worry me?
　2 *Wench.* No, but eaſe you
Of your golden Burthen; the heavy Carriage may
Bring you to a Sweating Sickneſs.
　Belg. Very likely,
I foam all o'er already.
　1 *Wench.* Will you come off, Sir?
　Belg. Would I had ne'er come on: Hear me with Pa-
Or I will anger you. Go to, you know me   [tience,
                                                And

And do not vex me farther : By my Sins
And your Difeafes, which are certain Truths,
Whate'er you think, I am not Mafter, at
This Inftant, of a Livre.

  2 Wench. What, and in
Such a glorious Suit?

  Belg. The liker, wretched Things,
To have no Money.

  Bawd. You may pawn your Cloaths, Sir.

  1 Wench. Will you fee your Iffue ftarve ?

  2 Wench. Or the Mothers beg?

  Belg. Why, you unconfcionable Strumpets, would you
          have me
Transform my Hat to Double Clouts and Biggins ?
My Corflet to a Cradle ? or my Belt
To Swaddlebands ? or turn my Cloak to Blankets?
Or to fell my Sword and Spurs for Soap and Candles ?
Have you no Mercy ? What a chargeable Devil
We carry in our Breeches!

  Beauf. jun. Now 'tis Time
To fetch him off.

          Enter Beaufort *fen.*

  Monta. Your Father does it for us.

  Bawd. The Governor !

  Beauf. fen. What are thefe ?

  1 Wench. And it like your Lordfhip,
Very poor Spinfters.

  Bawd. I am his Nurfe and Laundrefs.

  Belg. You have nurs'd and lander'd me, Hell take
Vanifh.   [you for it.

  Cham. Do, do, and talk with him hereafter.

  1 Wench. 'Tis our beft Courfe.

  2 Wench. We'll find a Time to fit him.
                    [*Exit Bawd and Whores.*

  Beauf. fen. Why in this Heat, *Belgard?*

  Belg. You are the Caufe of 't.

  Beauf. fen. Who, I ?

                                        Belg.

Belg. Yes, your pied Livery, and your Gold
Draw thefe Vexations on me, pray you ftrip me
And let me be as I was: I will not lofe
The Pleafures and the Freedom which I had
In my certain Poverty ; for all the Wealth
Fair *France* is proud of?
   Beauf. fen. We at better leifure
Will learn the Caufe of this.
   Beauf. jun. What Anfwer, Sir,
From the Admiral ?
   Beauf. fen. None, his Daughter is remov'd
To the Fort of *Montrevile,* and he himfelf
In Perfon fled, but where is not difcover'd ;
I could tell you Wonders, but the Time denies me
Fit Liberty.   In a Word, let it fuffice
The Power of our great Mafter is contemn'd,
The facred Laws of God and Man prophan'd,
And if I fit down with this Injury,
I am unworthy of my Place, and thou
Of my Acknowledgment : Draw up all the Troops,
As I go, I will inftruct you to what purpofe.
Such as have Power to punifh, and yet fpare
From Fear or from Connivance, others ill
Though not in Act affift them in their Will.

The End of the Fourth Act.

ACT V. SCENE I.

Montrevile, Theocrine, *Servants.*

Montr. **B**IND them, and gag their Mouths fure, I alone
      Will be your Convoy.
  1 *Wom.* Madam,
  2 *Wom.* Deareft Lady,
  Page. Let me fight, for my Miftrefs.

Exce.

Serv. 'Tis in vain,
Little Cockerell of the Kind.
   Montr. Away with them,
And do as I command you,
                     [*Exeunt Servants,* Page, Women.
   Theoc. Montrevile
You are my Father's Friend, nay, more a Soldier,
And if a right one, as I hope to find you,
Though in a lawful War you had furpriz'd
A City, that bow'd humbly to your Pleafure,
In Honour you ftand bound to guard a Virgin
From Violence; but in a free Eftate
Of which you are a Limb, to do a Wrong
Which noble Enemies never confent to
Is fuch an Infolence.
   Montr. How her Heart beats!
Much like a Partridge in a Sparhawk's Foot,
That with a panting Silence does lament
The Fate fhe cannot fly from! Sweet, take Comfort,
You are fafe, and nothing is intended to you
But Love and Service.
   Theoc. They came never cloth'd
In Force and Outrage. Upon what Affurance
(Rememb'ring only that my Father lives
Who will not tamely fuffer the Difgrace.)
Have you prefum'd to hurry me from his Houfe,
And as I were not worth the waiting on,
To fnatch me from the Duty and Attendance
Of my poor Servants.
   Montr. Let not that afflict you,
You fhall not want Obfervance, I will be
Your Page, your Woman, Parafite or Fool,
Or any other Property, provided
You anfwer my Affection.
   Theoc. In what Kind?
   Montr. As you had done young *Beaufort's.*
   Theoc. How?
   Montr. So, Lady,
Or, if the Name of Wife appear a Yoke

Too

Too heavy for your tender Neck, so I
Enjoy you as a private Friend or Mistress,
'Twill be sufficient.
  Theoc. Blessed Angels guard me
What frontless Impudence is this? What Devil
Hath to thy certain Ruin tempted thee
To offer me this Motion? By my Hopes
Of after Joys, Submission, nor Repentance
Shall expiate this foul Intent.
  Montr. Intent?
'Tis more, I'll make it Act.
  Theoc. Ribald, thou darest not,
And if (and with a Feaver to thy Soul)
Thou but consider that I have a Father
And such a Father, as when this arrives at
His Knowledge, as it shall, the Terror of
His Vengeance, which as sure as Fate must follow,
Will make thee curse the Hour in which Lust taught thee
To nourish these base Hopes, and 'tis my Wonder
Thou darest forget how tender he is of me
And that each Shadow of Wrong done to me,
Will raise in him a Tempest not to be
But with thy Heart-blood calm'd: This when I see him—
  Montr. As thou shalt never.
  Theoc. Wilt thou Murther me?
  Montr. No, no, 'tis otherwise determin'd, Fool.
The Master which in Passion kills his Slave
That may be useful to him, does himself
The Injury: Know thou most wretched Creature,
That Father thou presum'st upon, that Father,
That when I sought thee in a noble Way,
Deny'd thee to me, fancying in his Hope
A higher Match from his excess of Dotage,
Hath in his Bowels kindled such a Flame
Of Impious most unnatural Lust,
That now he fears his furious Desires,
May force him to do that, he shakes to think on.
  Theoc. O me most Wretched.
  Montr. Never hope again

VoL. III.   Q   To

To blaſt him with thoſe Eyes, their Golden Beams
Are unto him Arrows of Death and Hell,
But unto me Divine Artillery.
And therefore ſince what I ſo long in vain
Purſued is offer'd to me, and by him
Given up to my Poſſeſſion : Do not flatter
Thyſelf with an Imaginary Hope,
But that I'll take Occaſion by the Forelock,
And make uſe of my Fortune ; as we walk
I'll tell thee more.

   Theoc. I will not ſtir.
   Montr. I'll force thee :
   Theoc. Help, help.
   Montr. In vain.
   Theoc. In me my Brother's Blood
Is puniſh'd at the Height.
   Montr. The Coach there.
   Theoc. Dear, Sir,
   Montr. Tears, Curſes, Prayers, are alike to me ;
I can, and muſt enjoy my preſent Pleaſure,
And ſhall take Time to mourn for it at Leiſure. [*Exeunt.*

S C E N E II.

Enter Malefort *ſolus.*

   Malef. I have play'd the Fool, the groſs Fool to believe
The Boſom of a Friend will hold a Secret ;
Mine own could not contain ; and my Induſtry
In taking Liberty from my innocent Daughter,
Out of falſe Hopes of Freedom to myſelf,
Is in the little Help it yields me, puniſh'd.
She's abſent, but I have her Figure here,
And every Grace and Rarity about her,
Are by the Pencil of my Memory
In living Colours painted on my Heart.
My Fires too a ſhort Interim cloſed up,
Break out with greater Fury.   Why was I
Since 'twas my Fate, and not to be declin'd

In

In this ſo tender conſcienc'd? Say I had
Injoy'd what I deſir'd, what had it been
But Inceſt? and there's ſomething here that tells me
I ſtand accomptable for greater Sins,
I never check'd at: Neither had the Crime
Wanted a Preſident.   I have read in Story
Thoſe firſt great Hero's that for their brave Deeds
Were in the Worlds firſt Infancy ſtil'd Gods,
Freely enjoy'd what I deny'd myſelf.
Old *Saturn* in the golden Age embraced
His Siſter *Ops* and in the ſame Degree
The Thunderer *Juno*, *Neptune*, *Thetis*, and
By their Example after the firſt Deluge
Deucalion Pirrhæ.   Univerſal Nature
As every Day 'tis evident, allows it
To Creatures of all Kinds.   The gallant Horſe
Covers the Mare to which he was the Sire;
The Bird with fertile Seed gives new encreaſe
To her that hatch'd him. Why ſhould envious Man then
Brand that cloſe Act which adds Proximity
To what's moſt near him, with the abhorred Title
Of Inceſt? Or our later Laws forbid
What by the firſt was granted? Let old Men
That are not capable of theſe Delights
And ſolemn ſuperſtious Fools preſcribe
Rules to themſelves, I will not curb my Freedom,
But conſtantly go on, with this Aſſurance,
I but walk in a Path which greater Men
Have trod before me.   Ha! this is the Fort,
Open the Gate.   Within there.

Enter two Soldiers with Muſkets.

 1 *Sold.* With your Pardon
We muſt forbid your Entrance.
 Malef. Do you know me?
 2 *Sold.* Perfectly my Lord.
 Malef. I am this Captain's Friend.
 1 *Sold.* It may be ſo, but till we know his Pleaſure
Q 2

You

You muſt excuſe us.

  2 Sold. We'll acquaint him with
Your waiting here.

  Malef. Waiting Slave, he was ever
By me Commanded.

  1 Sold. As we are by him.

  Malef. So punctual, pray you then in my Name intreat
His Preſence.

  2 Sold. That we ſhall do.   [*Exeunt Soldiers.*

  Malef. I muſt uſe
Some ſtrange Perſuaſions to work him to
Deliver her, and to forget her Vows,
And horrid Oaths I in my Madneſs made him.
Take to the Contrary, and may I get her
Once more in my Poſſeſſion, I will bear her
Into ſome cloſe Cave or Deſert, where we'll end
Our Luſts and Lives together.

Enter Montrevile *and Soldiers.*

  Montr. Fail not, on
The Forfeit of your Lives to execute
What I commanded.

  Malef. Montrevile, how is't Friend ?

  Montr. I am glad to ſee you wear ſuch chearful Looks,
The World's well altered.

  Malef. Yes, I thank my Stars.
But me thinks thou art troubled.

  Montr. Some light croſs,
But of no Moment.

  Malef. So I hope, beware
Of ſad and impious Thoughts, you know how far
They wrought on me.

  Montr. No ſuch come near me, Sir.
I have like you no Daughter, and much wiſh
You never had been curs'd with one.

  Malef. Who I ?
Thou art deceiv'd, I am moſt happy in her.

Mont.

Montr. I am glad to hear it.

Malef. My inceftuous Fires
Towards her are quite burnt out; I love her now
As a Father, and no further.

Montr. Fix there then
Your conftant Peace, and do not try a fecond
Temptation from her.

Malef. Yes, Friend, though fhe were
By Millions of Degrees more excellent
In her Perfections : Nay, tho' fhe could borrow
A Form Angelical to take my Frailty,
It would not do ; and therefore, *Montrevile,*
(My chief Delight next her) I come to tell thee
The Governor and I are reconcil'd,
And I confirm'd, and with all poffible Speed
To make large Satisfaction to young *Beaufort,*
And her whom I have fo much wrong'd, and for
Thy Trouble in her Cuftody, of which
I'll now difcharge thee, there is nothing in
My Nerves or Fortunes, but fhall ever be
At thy Devotion.

Montr. You promife faintly,
Nor doubt I the Performance ; yet I would not
Hereafter be reported to have been
The principal Occafion of your falling
Into a Relapfe ; or but fuppofe out of
The Eafinefs of my Nature, and Affurance
You are firm, and can hold out, I could confent :
You needs muft know there are fo many Lets
That make againft it, that it is my Wonder
You offer me the Motion, having bound me
With Oaths and Imprecations on no Terms,
Reafons, or Arguments, you could propofe,
I ever fhould admit you to her Sight,
Much lefs reftore her to you.

Malef. Are we Soldiers, and ftand on Oaths ?

Montr. 'Tis beyond my Knowledge
In what we are more worthy, than in keeping
Our Words, much more our Vows.

Q 3

Malef.

Malef. Heaven pardon all.
How many Thousands in our Heat of Wine,
Quarrels and Play, and in our younger Days
(In Private, I may say) between ourselves
In Points of Love, have we to answer for,
Should we be scrupulous that Way.

Montr. You say well,
And very aptly call to Memory
Two Oaths against all Ties and Rites of Friendship
Broken by you to me.

Malef. No more of that.

Montr. Yes, 'tis material, and to the Purpose:
The first (and think upon't) was, when I brought you
As a Visitant to my Mistress, then, the Mother
Of this same Daughter, whom, with dreadful Words,
Too hideous to remember, you swore deeply
For my Sake never to attempt; yet then,
Then, when you had a sweet Wife of your own,
I know not with what Arts, Philtres, and Charms,
(Unless in Wealth and Fame you were above me)
You won her from me, and her Grant obtain'd,
A Marriage with the Second waited on,
The Burial of the First (that to the World
Brought your dead Son   this I sat tamely down by,
Wanting, indeed, Occasion and Power
To be at the Height revenged.

Malef. Yet this you seem'd
Freely to pardon,

Montr. As perhaps I did.
Your Daughter *Theocrine* growing ripe,
(Her Mother too deceas'd) and fit for Marriage,
I was a Suitor for her, had your Word
Upon your Honour, and our Friendship made
Authentical, and ratified with an Oath,
She should be mine: But Vows with you being like
To your Religion, a Nose of Wax
To be turn'd every Way, that very Day
The Governor's Son but making his Approaches
Of Courtship to her, the Wind of your Ambition

For

For her Advancement, fcatter'd the thin Sand
In which you wrote your full Confent to me,
And drew you to his Party.   What hath pafs'd fince
You bear a Regifter in your own Bofom,
That can at large inform you.
   Malef. Montrevile,
I do confefs all that you charge me with
To be ftrong Truth, and that I bring a Caufe
Moft miferably guilty, and acknowledge
That tho' your Goodnefs made me mine own Judge,
I fhould not fhew the leaft Compaffion
Or Mercy to myfelf.   O, let not yet
My Foulnefs taint your Purenefs, or my Falfhood
Divert the Torrent of your loyal Faith.
My Ills, if not return'd by you, will add
Luftre to your much Good, and to o'ercome
With noble Suff'rance will exprefs your Strength,
And triumph o'er my Weaknefs.   If you pleafe too,
My black Deeds being only known to you,
And in furrend'ring up my Daughter buried :
You not alone make me your Slave (for I
At no Part do deferve the Name of Friend)
But in your own Breaft raife a Monument
Of Pity to a Wretch on whom with Juftice
You may exprefs all Cruelty.
   Montr. You much move me.
   Malef. O that I could but hope it, to revenge
An Injury is proper to the Wifhes
Of feeble Women, that want Strength to act it :
But to have Power to punifh, and yet pardon,
Peculiar to Princes, fee thefe Knees,
That have been ever ftiff to bend to Heaven,
To you are fupple.   Is there ought beyond this
That may fpeak my Submiffion ? Or can Pride
(Though I well know it is a Stranger to you)
Defire a Feaft of more Humility
To kill her growing Appetite ?
   Montr. I requir'd not
To be fought in this poor Way ; yet 'tis fo far

Q 4

A

A Kind of Satisfaction, that I will
Difpenfe a little with thofe ferious Oaths
You made me take : Your Daughter fhall come to you,
I will not fay as you deliver'd her,
But as fhe is, you may difpofe of her
As you fhall think moft requifite.   [*Exit* Montrevile.
  Malef. His laft Words
Are Riddles to me.   Here the Lion's Force
Would have prov'd ufelefs, and againft my Nature
Compell'd me from the Crocodile, to borrow   [ward,
Her counterfeit Tears :   There's now no turning back-
May I but quench thefe Fires that rage within me,
And fall what can fall, I am arm'd to bear it.
            [*The Soldiers thruft forth* Theocrine; *her Garments
                  loofe, her Hair difhevell'd.*
  2 *Sold.* You muft be packing.
  Theoc. Hath he robb'd me of
Mine Honour, and denies me now a Room
To hide my Shame ?
  2 *Sold.* My Lord the Admiral
Attends your Ladyfhip.
  1 *Sold.* Clofe the Port, and leave 'em.
                              [*Exeunt Soldiers.*
  Malef. Ha! who is this ? how alter'd ! how deform'd !
It cannot be.   And yet this Creature has
A Kind of a Refemblance to my Daughter,
My *Theocrine !* but as different
From that fhe was, as Bodies dead are in
Their beft Perfections, from what they were
When they had Life and Motion.
  Theoc. 'Tis moft true, Sir ;
I am dead indeed to all but Mifery.
O come not near me, Sir, I am infectious ;
To look on me at Diftance is as dangerous
As from a Pinacle's Cloud-kiffing Spire,
With giddy Eyes to view the fteep Defcent ;
But to acknowledge me, a certain Ruin.
O, Sir !
  Malef. Speak, *Theocrine* ; force me not

                                          To

To farther Queſtion; my Fears already
Have choak'd my vital Spirits.
   Theoc. Pray you turn away
Your Face, and hear me, and with my laſt Breath
Give me Leave to accuſe you.   What Offence
From my firſt Infancy did I commit
That for a Puniſhment you ſhould give up
My Virgin Chaſtity to the treacherous Guard
Of Goatiſh *Montrevile?*
   Malef. What hath he done?
   Theoc. Abus'd me, Sir, by Violence; and this told,
I cannot live to ſpeak more : May the Cauſe
In you find Pardon, but the ſpeeding Curſe
Of a raviſh'd Maid fall heavy, heavy on him :
Beaufort, my lawful Love, farewel for ever.   [*She dies.*
   Malef. Take not thy Flight ſo ſoon, immaculate Spi-
'Tis fled already.   How the Innocent,   [rit.
As in a gentle Slumber, paſs away !
But to cut off the knotty Thread of Life,
In guilty Men, muſt force ſtern *Atropos*
To uſe her ſharp Knife often.   I would help
The Edge of her's with the ſharp Point of mine,
But that I dare not die, 'till I have rent
This Dog's Heart Piecemeal.   O, that I had Wings
To ſcale theſe Walls, or that my Hands were Cannons
To bore their flinty Sides, that I might bring
The Villain in the Reach of my good Sword,
The *Turkiſh* Empire offer'd for his Ranſom
Should not redeem his Life.   O that my Voice
Were loud as Thunder, and with horrid Sounds
Might force a dreadful Paſſage to his Ears,
And through them reach his Soul, libidinous Monſter,
Foul Raviſher, as thou durſt do a Deed
Which forc'd the Sun to hide his glorious Face
Behind a ſable Maſque of Clouds, appear,
And as a Man defend it, or like me
Shew ſome Compunction for it.
       [*Montrevile above, the Curtain ſuddenly drawn.*
   Montr. Ha, ha, ha !
                        Malef.

Malef. Is this an Object to raife Mirth?

Montr. Yes, yes.

Malef. My Daughter's dead.

Montr. Thou hadſt beſt follow her;
Or if thou art the Thing thou art reported,
Thou ſhould'ſt have led the Way.   Do tear thy Hair,
Like a Village Nurſe, and mourn while I laugh at thee.
Be but a juſt Examiner of thyſelf,
And in an equal Balance poize the Nothing,
Or little Miſchief I have done, compar'd
With the pond'rous Weight of thine, and how canſt thou
Accuſe or argue with me? Mine was a Rape,
And ſhe being in a Kind contracted to me,
The Fact may challenge ſome Qualification:
But thy Intent made Nature's Self run backward,
And done, had caus'd an Earthquake.

Enter Soldiers above.

1 *Sold.* Captain.

Montr. Ha!

2 *Sold.* Our Outworks are ſurpriz'd, the Centinel ſlain,
The Corps de Guard defeated too.

Montr. By whom?

1 *Sold.* The ſudden Storm and Darkneſs of the Night
Forbids the Knowledge; make up ſpeedily,
Or all is loſt.

Montr. In the Devil's Name, whence comes this?

[*They deſcend.*

Malef. Do, do; rage on; rend open, *Æolus,* [13]

---

[13] ———— *Do, do, rage on,* &c.

This Deſcription of the Horrors of a guilty Mind is inimitable:—
Shakeſpear has a Paſſage in the *Tempeſt*, to the ſame Purpoſe, which I
ſhall here ſet down.

O, it is monſtrous! monſtrous!————
Methought the Billows ſpoke, and told me of it;
The Winds did ſing it to me; and the Thunder,
That deep and dreadful Organpipe, pronounc'd
The Name of *Proſper.*   Act III. Scene 4.

Thy

Thy brazen Prifon, and let loofe at once   [*A Storm.*
Thy ftormy Iffue, bluftring *Boreas,*
Aided with all the Gales, the Pilot numbers
Upon his Compafs, cannot raife a Tempeft
Through the vaft Region of the Air, like that
I feel within me: for I am poffefs'd
With Whirl-winds, and each guilty Thought to me is
A dreadful Hurricane; though this Centre
Labour to bring forth Earthquakes, and Hell open
Her wide-ftretch'd Jaws, and let out all her Furies,
They cannot add an Atom to the Mountain
Of Fears and Terrors that each Minute threaten
To fall on my accurfed Head.   Ha! is't Fancy?

Enter the Ghoft of young Malefort, *naked from the Waift,*
   full of Wounds, leading in the Shadow of a Lady, her
   Face leprous. [14]

Or hath Hell heard me, and makes Proof if I
Dare ftand the Trial?   Yes, I do, and now
I view thefe Apparitions, I feel
I once did know the Subftances.   For what come you?
Are your aerial Forms depriv'd of Language,
And fo deny'd to tell me? that by Signs
             [*The Ghofts ufe feveral Geftures.*
You bid me afk here of myfelf? 'Tis fo,
And there is fomething here makes Anfwer for you.
You come to launce my fear'd-up Confcience? Yes,
And to inftruct me, that thofe Thunderbolts,
That hurl'd me headlong from the Height of Glory,

[14] This is the only Play in which *Maffinger* has introduced Ghofts; and I may venture to fay that he has done it with Propriety, and Juftnefs: For though Ghofts are very frequent in *Englifh* Tragedies; Ghofts, as well as Fairies, feem to be the peculiar Province of *Shakefpear.* In fuch Circles, none but he could move with Dignity. That in *Hamlet* is introduced with the utmoft Solemnity, awful throughout, and majeftic. At the Appearance of *Banquo* in *Macbeth,* Act III. Scene 5. the Images are fet off in the ftrongeft Expreffion, and ftrike the Imagination with high Degrees of Horror, which is fupported with furprizing Art through the whole Scene."

Wealth,

Wealth, Honours, worldly Happiness, were forg'd
Upon the Anvil of my impious Wrongs
And Cruelty to you.   I do confefs it;
And that my Luft compelling me to make Way
For a fecond Wife, I poifon'd thee, and that
The Caufe (which to the World is undifcover'd)
That forc'd thee to fhake off thy Filial Duty
To me thy Father, had its Spring and Source
From thy Impatience to know thy Mother,
That with all Duty and Obedience ferv'd me,
(For now with Horror I acknowledge it)
                        [*Anfwer'd ftill by Signs.*
Remov'd unjuftly: Yet thou being my Son,
Wert not a competent Judge mark'd out by Heaven
For her Revenger, which thy falling by
My weaker Hand confirm'd. 'Tis granted by thee.
Can any Penance expiate my Guilt?
Or can Repentance fave me? They are vanifh'd.
                         [*Exeunt Ghofts.*
What's left to do then? I'll accufe my Fate
That did not fafhion me for nobler Ufes:
Or if thofe Stars, crofs to me in my Birth,
Had not deny'd their profperous Influence to it
With Peace of Confcience like to innocent Men,
I might have ceas'd to be; and not as now,
To curfe my Caufe of Being.
          [*He's kill'd with a Flafh of Lightning.*

Enter Belgard *with Soldiers.*

  Belg. Here is a Night
To feafon my Silks. Buff-jerkin, now I mifs thee,
Thou haft endur'd many foul Nights, but never
One like to this: How fine my Feather looks now!
Juft like a Capon's Tail ftoln out of the Pen,
And hid in the Sink; and yet 't had been Difhonour
To have charg'd me without it. — Wilt thou never
      ceafe?

Is the Petarde, as I gave Directions, faften'd
On the Portcullis?
 Another Sold. It hath been attempted
By divers, but in vain.
 Belg. Thefe are your Gallants,
That at a Feaft take the firft Place; poor I,
Hardly allow'd to follow. Marry, in
Thefe foolifh Bufineffes they are content
That I fhall have Precedence. I much thank
Their Manners, or their Fear. Second me, Soldiers,
They have had no Time to undermine, or if
They have, 'tis but blowing up, and fetching
A Caper or two in the Air, and I will do it,
Rather than blow my Nails here.
 Sold. O brave Captain !   *[Exeunt.*

An Alarum, Noife and Cries within.   A Flourifh.

Enter Beaufort *fen.* Beaufort *jun.* Montaign, Chamont,
  Lanour, Belgard, Montrevile, *Soldiers.*

 Montr. Racks cannot force more from me than I have
Already told you.   I expect no Favour.
I have caft up my Accompt.
 Beauf. fen. Take you the Charge
Of the Fort, *Belgard*; your Dangers have deferv'd it.
 Belg. I thank your Excellence; this will keep me
   fafe yet
From being pull'd by the Sleeve, a nd bid remember
The Thing I wot of.
 Beauf. jun. All that have Eyes to weep,
Spare one Tear with me. *Theocrine*'s dead.
 Mont. Her Father too lies breathlefs here, I think,
Struck dead with Thunder.
 Cham. 'Tis apparant : How
His Carcafe fmells !
 Lan. His Face is alter'd to
Another Colour.
         Beauf.

Beauf. jun. But here's one retains
Her native Innocence, that never yet
Call'd down Heaven's Anger.

    Beauf. fen. 'Tis in vain to mourn
For what's paft Help. We will refer, Bad Man,
Your Sentence to the King: May we make ufe of
This great Example, and learn from it, that
There cannot be a Want of Power above
To punifh Murther, and unlawful Love.

[Exeunt omnes.

The   E N D.

THE
BASHFUL LOVER.

A

TRAGI-COMEDY.

As it hath been often acted at the Private-House in *Black-Friers*, by his late Majesty's Servants, with great Applause. 1655.

WRITTEN

By PHILIP MASSINGER.

PROLOGUE.

THIS from our Author, far from all Offence,
 To abler Writers, or the Audience
Met here to judge his Poem. He, by me,
Prefents his Service, with fuch Modefty
As well becomes his Weaknefs. 'Tis no Crime,
He hopes, as we do in this curious Time,
To be a little diffident, when we are
To pleafe fo many with one Bill of Fare.
Let others, building on their Merit, fay
Y'are in the wrong, if you move not that Way
Which they prefcribe you; as you were bound to learn
Their Maxims, but uncapable to difcern
'Twixt Truth and Falfhood. Ours had rather be
Cenfur'd by fome, for too much Obfequy,
Than tax'd of Self-Opinion. If he hear
That his Endeavours thriv'd, and did appear
Worthy your View (tho' made fo by your Grace,
With fome Defert) he in another Place
Will thankfully report, one Leaf of Bays
Truly confer'd upon this Work, will raife
More Pleafure in him, you the Givers free,
Than Garlands ravifh'd from the Virgin-Tree.

Dramatis Personæ.

GONZAGA, Duke of *Mantua*.
LORENZO, Duke of *Tuscany*.
UBERTI, Prince of *Parma*.
FARNEZE, Cousin to *Gonzaga*.
ALONZO, Nephew to *Lorenzo*.
MANFROY, a Lord of *Mantua*.
OCTAVIO, General, once, to *Gonzaga*; now exil'd.
GOTHRIO, his Servant.
ASCANIO, a Page.
GALEAZZO, a Nobleman disguised.
JULIO, his Man,
PISANO, a *Tuscan* Lord.
MARTINIO, a Captain.
Two Captains more.
Ambassadors.
Soldiers.

MATILDA, Daughter to *Gonzaga*.
BEATRICE, her Waiting-Gentlewoman.
MARIA, Daughter to *Octavio*, disguis'd as a Page.
Two Women.

T H E

THE

BASHFUL LOVER.

ACT I. SCENE I.

Enter Galeazzo *and* Julio.

Julio.

Dare not crofs you, Sir, but I would gladly
(Provided you allow it) render you
My perfonal Attendance.
    Gal. You fhall better difcharge the Duty of
      an honeft Servant,
In following my Inftructions, which you have
Receiv'd already, than in queftioning
What my Intents are, or upon what Motives
My Stay's refolv'd in *Mantua:* Believe me,
That Servant overdoes, that's too officious;
And, in prefuming to direct your Mafter,
You argue him of Weaknefs, and yourfelf
Of Arrogance and Impertinence.
   Jul. I have done, Sir;
But what my Ends are ——
   Gal. Honeft ones, I know it:
I have my Bills of Exchange, and all Provifions
Entrufted to you; you have fhewn yourfelf
Juft and difcreet, what would you more? and yet,
To fatisfy in fome Part your curious Care,
Hear this, and leave me: I defire to be
Obfcur'd; and, as I have demean'd myfelf

R 2

Thefe

These six Months past in *Mantua*, I'll continue
Unnoted and unknown, and, at the best,
Appear no more than a Gentleman, and a Stranger
That travels for his Pleasure.

   Jul. With your Pardon,
This hardly will hold Weight, tho' I should swear it,
With your noble Friends and Brother.

   Gal. You may tell 'em,
Since you will be my Tutor, there's a Rumour
(Almost cry'd up into a Certainty)
Of Wars with *Florence*, and that I am determin'd
To see the Service: Whate'er I went forth,
(Heav'n prosp'ring my Intents) I would come home
A Soldier, and a good one.

   Jul. Should you get
A Captain's Place, nay, Colonel's, 'twould add little
To what you are; few of your Rank will follow
That dangerous Profession.

   Gal. 'Tis the noblest,
And Monarchs honour'd in it: But no more,
On my Displeasure.

   Jul. Saints and Angels guard you.   [*Exit.*

   Gal. A War indeed is threaten'd, nay, expected
From *Florence*; but it is 'gainst me already
Proclaim'd in *Mantua*: I find it, here, [a]
No foreign, but intestine War: I have
Defy'd myself, in giving up my Reason
A Slave to Passion, and am led Captive
Before the Battle's fought: I fainted, when
I only saw mine Enemy, and yielded,
Before that I was charg'd; and, tho' defeated,
I dare not sue for Mercy. Like *Ixion*,

---

    [a] ———— *I find it here.*

  Shakespear, in *Troilus and Cressida*, has a Passage something similar
to this.

     Call here my Varlet; I'll unarm again.
     Why should I war without the Walls of *Troy*,
     That find such cruel Battle here within?
               Act I. Scene 1.

I look

I look on *Juno*, feel my Heart turn Cinders
With an invisible Fire: And yet, should she
Deign to appear cloath'd in a various Cloud,
The Majesty of the Substance is so sacred,
I durst not clasp the Shadow.   I behold her
With Adoration; feast my Eye, while all
My other Senses starve; and, oft frequenting
The Place which she makes happy with her Presence,
I never yet had Power with Tongue or Pen
To move her to Compassion, or make known
What 'tis I languish for; yet I must gaze still,
Though it increase my Flame.—However, I
Much more than fear I am observ'd, and censur'd
For bold Intrusion.   [*Walks sadly.*

Enter Beatrice *and* Afcanio.

Beat. Know you, Boy, that Gentleman?
Afc. Who, Monsieur *Melancholy?* hath not your Ho-
Mark'd him before?   [nour

Beat. I have seen him often wait
About the Princess' Lodgings, but ne'er guess'd
What his Designs were.
Afc. No? what a Sigh he breath'd now!
Many such will blow up the Roof.—On my small Credit
There's Gunpowder in 'em.
Beat. How, Crack! Gunpowder?
He's Flesh and Blood, and Devils only carry
Such roaring Stuff about 'em.   You cannot prove
He is or Spirit, or Conjurer.
Afc. That I grant:
But he's a Lover, and that's as bad; their Sighs
Are like Petards, and blow all up.
Beat. A Lover!
I've been in Love myself: but ne'er found yet
That it could work such strange Effects.
Afc. True, Madam,
In Women it cannot; for when they miss th' enjoying
Of their full Wishes, all their Sighs and Heigh-hoes,

R 3   At

At the worst, breed Tympanies, and these are cur'd too
With a Kiss or two of their Saint, when he appears
Between a Pair of Sheets : but with us Men
The Case is otherwise.

  Beat. You will be breech'd, Boy,
For your physical Maxims—But how are you assur'd
He is a Lover?

  Asc. Who, I? I know with whom too;
—But that is to be whisper'd.   [*Whispers.*

  Beat. How? the Princess? th' unparallel'd *Matilda?*
Some Proof of it; I'll pay for my Intelligence.
                                        [*Gives him Gold.*

  Asc. Let me kiss
Your Honour's Hand; 'twas ever fair, but now
Beyond Comparison.

  Beat. I guess the Reason;
A giving Hand is still fair to the Receiver.

  Asc. Your Ladyship's in the right : But to the Purpose.
He is my Client, and pays his Fees as duly
As ever Usurer did in a bad Cause
To his Man of Law; and yet I get, and take 'em
Both easily and honestly : All the Service
I do him, is, to give him Notice when
And where the Princess will appear; and that
I hope's no Treason.   If you miss him, when
She goes to the Vesper or the Mattins, hang me;
Or when she takes the Air, be sure to find him
Near her Coach, at her going forth, or coming back :
But, if she walk, he's ravish'd. I have seen him smell out
Her Footing like a Lime-Hound, and knows it
From all the rest of her Train.

  Beat. Yet I ne'er saw him
Present her a Petition.

  Asc. Nor e'er shall :
He only sees her, sighs, and sacrifices
A Tear or two—then vanishes.

  Beat. 'Tis most strange!
What a sad Aspect he wears! but I'll make use of't.
The Princess is much troubled with the Threats
                                        That

That come from *Florence*; I will bring her to him,
The Novelty may afford her Sport, and help
To purge deep melancholy.   Boy, can you stay
Your Client here for the third Part of an Hour?
I have some Ends in't.

  Asc. Stay him, Madam? fear not:
The present Receipt of a round Sum of Crowns,
And that will draw most Gallants from their Prayers,
Cannot drag him from me.

  Beat. See you do.

  Asc. Ne'er doubt me,   [*Exit* Beatrice.
I'll put him out of his Dream.—Good Morrow, Signior!

  Gal. My little Friend, good Morrow!   Hath the
Slept well To-night?   [Princess

  Asc. I hear not from her Women
One Murmur to the contrary.

  Gal. Heav'n be prais'd for't:
Does she go to Church this Morning?

  Asc. 'Troth, I know not;
I keep no Key of her Devotion, Signior.

  Gal. Goes she abroad? Pray tell me.

  Asc. 'Tis thought rather
She is resolv'd to keep her Chamber.

  Gal. Ah me!

  Asc. Why do you sigh? If that you have a Business
To be dispatch'd in Court, shew ready Money,
You shall find those that will prefer it for you.

  Gal. Business! can any Man have Business, but
To see her, than admire her, and pray for her,
She being compos'd of Goodness? For myself,
I find it a Degree of Happiness
But to be near her; and I think I pay
A strict religious Vow, when I behold her,
And that's all my Ambition.

  Asc. I believe you:
Yet, she being absent, you may spend some Hours
With Profit and Delight too.   After Dinner,
The Duke gives Audience to a rough Ambassador,
Whom yet I never saw, nor heard his Title,

R 4

Employ'd

Employ'd from *Florence* : I'll help you to a Place
Where you shall see and hear all.
  Gal. 'Tis not worth
My Observation.
  Asc. What think you of
An excellent Comedy to be presented
For his Entertainment ? He that penn'd it, is
The Poet of the Time ; and all the Ladies
(I mean the amorous and learned ones)
Except the Princess, will be there to grace it.
  Gal. What's that to me ? Without her all is nothing;
The Light that shines in Court, *Cimmerian* Darkness;
-I will to Bed again, and there contemplate
On her Perfections.

     Enter Matilda, Beatrice, *and two Women.*

  Asc. Stay, Sir ! see the Princess,
Beyond our Hopes.
  Gal. Take that. [*Gives him Money.*]   As *Moors* salute
The rising Sun with joyful Superstition,
I could fall down and worship.——O my Heart !
Like *Phœbe* breaking through an envious Cloud,
Or something which no Simile can express,
She shews to me ; a reverend Fear, but blended
With Wonder and Amazement, does possess me.
Now glut thyself, my famish'd eye !   [*Aside.*
  Beat. That's he,
An't please your Excellence
  1 *Wom.* Observe his Posture,
But with a Quarter-Look.
  2 *Wom.* Your Eye fix'd on him
Will breed Astonishment.
  Matil. A comely Gentleman !
I would not question your Relation, Lady,
Yet faintly can believe it.—How he eyes me !
Will he not speak ?
  Beat. Your Excellence hath depriv'd him
Of Speech and Motion.

Matil,

Matil. 'Tis moſt ſtrange!

Aſc. Theſe Fits are uſual with him.

Matil. Is it not, *Aſcanio*,
A perſonated Folly ? or is he a Statue ?
If it be, it is a Maſter-piece; for Man
I cannot think him.

Beat. For your Sport, vouchſafe him
A little Conference.

Matil. In Compaſſion rather :
For ſhould he love me as you ſay (though hopeleſs)
It ſhould not be return'd with Scorn; that were
An Inhumanity, which my Birth nor Honour
Could privilege, were they greater.   Now I perceive
He has Life and Motion in him; to whom, Lady,
Pays he that Duty ?

          [Galeazzo, *bowing, offers to go off.*

Beat. Sans doubt, to yourſelf.

Matil. And whither goes he now ?

Aſc. To his private Lodging;
But to what End I know not : This is all
I ever noted in him.

Matil. Call him back :
In Pity I ſtand bound to counſel him,
Howe'er I am denied, though I were willing
To eaſe his Sufferings.

Aſc. Signior, the Princeſs
Commands you to attend her.

Gal. How! the Princeſs ?
Am I betray'd ?

Aſc. What a Lump of Fleſh is this !
You are betray'd, Sir, to a better Fortune
Than you durſt ever hope for.—What a *Tantalus*
Do you make yourſelf! The flying Fruit ſtays for you,
And the Water, that you long'd for, riſing up
Above your Lip, do you refuſe to taſte it ?
Move faſter, ſluggiſh Camel, or I will thruſt
This Goad in your Breech. Had I ſuch a promiſing
I ſhould need the Reins, not Spurs.   [Beard,

Matil. You may come nearer.

                          Why

Why do you fhake, Sir ? If I flatter not
Myfelf, there's no Deformity about me,
Nor any Part fo monftrous to beget
An Ague in you.
    Gal. It proceeds not, Madam,
From Guilt, but Reverence.
    Matil. I believe you, Sir ;
Have you a Suit to me ?
    Gal. Your Excellence
Is wondrous fair.
    Matil. I thank your good Opinion,
    Gal. And I befeech you that I may have Licence
To kneel to you.
    Matil. A Suit I cannot crofs.
    Gal. I humbly thank your Excellence.
    Matil. But what
As you are proftrate on your Knee before me,
Is your Petition ?
    Gal. I have none, great Princefs.
    Matil. Do you kneel for nothing ?
    Gal. Yes, I have a Suit ;
But fuch a one, as, if denied, will kill me.
    Matil. Take Comfort ; it muft be of fome ftrange
Unfitting you to afk, or me to grant,   [Nature,
If I refufe it.
    Gal. It is, Madam, ——
    Matil. Out with 't.
    Gal. That I may not offend you, this is all,
When I prefume to look on you.
    Afc. A flat Eunuch !
To look on her ? I fhould defire myfelf
To move a little farther.   [*Afide.*
    Matil. Only that ?
    Gal. And I befeech you, Madam, to believe
I never did yet with a wanton Eye,
Or cherifh one lafcivious Wifh beyond it.
    Beat. You'll never make good Courtier, or be
In Grace with Ladies.
    1 *Wom.* Or us Waiting-women,

                                                  If

If that be your *Nil Ultra*.

    2 Wom. He's no Gentleman,
On my Virginity, it is apparent :
My Taylor has more Boldnefs ; nay, my Shoe-maker
Will fumble a little farther, he could not have
The Length of my Foot elfe.

    Matil. Only to look on me ?
Ends your Ambition there ?

    Gal. It does, great Lady ;
And that confin'd too, and at fitting Diftance :
The Fly that plays too near the Flame, burns in it.
A I behold the Sun, the Stars, the Temples,
I look upon you, and wifh 'twere no Sin,
Should I adore you.

    Matil. Come, there's fomething more in't ;
And fince that you will make a Goddefs of me,
As fuch a one, I'll tell you, I defire not
The meaneft Altar rais'd up to mine Honour
To be pull'd down.　I can accept from you
(Be your Condition ne'er fo far beneath me)
One Grain of Incenfe with Devotion offer'd,
Beyond all Perfumes, or *Sabæan* Spices,
By one that proudly thinks he merits in it.
I know you love me.

    Gal. Next to Heaven, Madam,
And with as pure a Zeal.　That, we behold
With th' Eyes of Contemplation, but can
Arrive no nearer to it in this Life ;
But when that is divorc'd, my Soul fhall ferve yours,
And witnefs my Affection.

    Matil. Pray you, rife ;
But wait my further Pleafure.

Enter Farneze *and* Uberti.

    Farn. I'll prefent you,
And give you Proof I am your Friend, a true one ;
And in my Pleading for you, teach the Age,
That calls erroneoufly Friendfhip but a Name,

It

It is a Subftance.——Madam, I am bold
To trench fo far upon your Privacy,
As to defire my Friend (let not that wrong him,
For he's a worthy one) may have the Honour
To kifs your Hand.
　Matil. His own Worth challengeth
A greater Favour.
　Farn. Your Acknowledgment
Confirms it, Madam.　If you look on him
As he's built up a Man, without Addition
Of Fortune's liberal Favours, Wealth or Titles,
He doth deferve no ufual Entertainment :
But, as he is a Prince, and for your Service
Hath left fair *Parma* (that acknowledges
No other Lord) and uncompel'd expofes
His Perfon to the Dangers of War,
Ready to break in Storms upon our Heads ;
In noble Thankfulnefs you may vouchfafe him
Nearer Refpect, and fuch Grace as may nourifh,
Not kill, his amorous Hopes.
　Matil. Coufin, you know
I am not the Difpofer of myfelf,
The Duke my Father challengeth that Power :
Yet thus much I dare promife ; Prince *Uberti*
Shall find the Seed of Service that he fows
Falls not on barren Ground.
　Uber. For this high Favour
I am your Creature, and profefs I owe you
Whatever I call mine.　　　　　　　　*[They walk.*
　Gal. This great Lord is
A Suitor to the Princefs ?
　Afc. True, he is fo.
　Gal. Fame gives him out too for a brave Commander.
　Afc. And in it does him but deferved Right ;
The Duke hath made him General of his Horfe
On that Affurance.
　Gal. And the Lord *Farneze*
Pleads for him, as it feems.
　Afc. 'Tis too apparent :

　　　　　　　　　　　　　　　　　　And,

And, this confider'd, give me Leave to afk
What Hope have you, Sir?
  Gal. I may ftill look on her,
Howe'er he wear the Garland.
  Afc. A thin Diet,
And will not feed you fat, Sir.
  Uber. I rejoice,
Rare Princefs, that you are not to be won
By Carpet-Courtfhip, but the Sword: With this
Steel Pen I'll write on *Florence* Helm, how much
I can, and dare do for you.
  Matil. 'Tis not queftion'd.
Some private Bufinefs of mine own difpos'd of,
I'll meet you in the Prefence.
  Uber. Ever your Servant.
                    [*Exit* Uberti *and* Farneze.
  Matil. Now, Sir, to you. You have obferv'd, I doubt
(For Lovers are fharp-fighted) to what Purpofe [not,
This Prince follicits me; and yet I am not
So taken with his Worth, but that I can
Vouchfafe you further Parley.   The firft Command
That I'll impofe upon you, is to hear
And follow my good Counfel.   I am not
Offended that you love me: perfift in it;
But love me virtuoufly; fuch Love may fpur you
To noble Undertakings, which atchiev'd
Will raife you into Name, Preferment, Honour:
For all which, though you ne'er enjoy my Perfon,
(For that's impoffible) you are indebted
To your high Aims.   Vifit me when you pleafe;
I do allow it, nor will blufh to own you,
(So you confine yourfelf to what you promife)
As my virtuous Servant.
  Beat. Farewel, Sir! You have
An unexpected Cordial.
  Afc. May it work well!
                    [*Exeunt all but* Galeazzo.
  Gal. Your Love—yes, fo fhe faid, may fpur you to
Brave Undertakings: Adding this, you may
                                        Vifit

Viſit me when you pleaſe.   Is this allow'd me,
And any Act within the Power of Man
Impoſſible to be effected ? No:
I will break through all Oppoſitions that
May ſtop me in my full Career to Honour;
And, borrowing Strength to do, from her high Favour,
Add, ſomething to *Alcides*' greateſt Labour.   [*Exit.*

SCENE II.

Enter Gonzaga, Uberti, Farneze, Manfroy, *Attendants.*

Gonz. This is your Place; and, were it in our Power,
You ſhould have greater Honour, Prince of *Parma.*
The reſt know theirs.—Let ſome attend with Care
On the Ambaſſador, and let my Daughter
Be preſent at his Audience.   Reach a Chair,
We'll do all fit Reſpects; and, pray you, put on
Your milder Looks; you're in a Place where Frowns
Are no prevailing Agents.

Enter (at one Door) Alonzo *and Attendants :* Matilda,
   Beatrice, Aſcanio, Galeazzo, *and Waiting - Women*
   (at the other.)

Aſc. I have ſeen
More than a Wolf, a *Gorgon !*   [*Swoons.*
   Gonz. What's the Matter ?
   Matil. A Page of mine is fall'n into a Swoon :
Look to him carefully.
   Gonz. Now, when you pleaſe,
The Cauſe that brought you hither.
   Alon. The Protraction
Of my Diſpatch forgotten, from *Lorenzo*
The *Tuſcan* Duke, thus much to you, *Gonzaga,*
The Duke of *Mantua.* By me, his Nephew,
He does ſalute you fairly, and entreats
(A Word not ſuitable to his Power and Greatneſs)
                                             You

You would confent to tender that, which he
Unwillingly muft force, if contradicted.
Ambition, in a private Man a Vice,
Is in a Prince a Virtue.

   Gonz. To the Purpofe;
Thefe Ambages are impertinent.

   Alon. He demands
The fair *Matilda* (for I dare not take
From her Perfections) in a noble Way;
And in creating her the Confort of
His Royal Bed, to raife her to a Height
Her flatt'ring Hopes could not afpire to, where fhe
With Wonder fhall be gaz'd upon, and live
The Envy of her Sex.

   Gonz. Suppofe this granted?

   Uber. Or, if denied, what follows?

   Alon. Prefent War,
With all Extremities the Conqueror can
Inflict upon the Vanquifh'd.

   Uber. Grant me Licence
To anfwer this Defiance. What Intelligence
Holds your proud Mafter with the Will of Heaven,
That, ere th' uncertain Dye of War be thrown,
He dares affure himfelf the Victory?
Are his unjuft, invading Arms of Fire?
Or thofe we put on, in Defence of Right,
Like Chaff to be confum'd in the Encounter?
I look on your Dimenfions, and find not
Mine own of leffer Size; the Blood that fills
My Veins, as hot as yours; my Sword as fharp,
My Nerves of equal Strength, my Heart as good;
And, confident we have the better Caufe,
Why fhould we fear the Trial?

   Farn. You prefume
You are fuperior in Numbers; we
Lay hold upon the fureft Anchor, Virtue;
Which, when Tempeft of the War roars loudeft,
Muft prove a ftrong Protection.

   Gonz. Two main Reafons

Seconding

(Seconding thofe you have already heard)
Gives us Encouragement : The Duty that
I owe my Mother Country, and the Love
Defcending to my Daughter.   For the firft,
Should I betray her Liberty, I deferv'd
To have my Name with Infamy raz'd from
The Catalogue of good Princes ; and I fhould
Unnaturally forget I am a Father,
If, like a *Tartar*, or for Fear or Profit,
I fhould confign her as a Bond-woman
To be difpos'd of at another's Pleafure,
Her own Confent or Favour never fu'd for,
And mine by Force exacted.   No, *Alonzo*,
She is my only Child, my Heir ; and, if
A Father's Eyes deceive me not, the Hand
Of prodigal Nature hath given fo much to her,
As, in the former Ages, Kings would rife up
In her Defence, and make her Caufe their Quarrel :
Nor can fhe, if that any Spark remain
To kindle a Defire to be poffefs'd
Of fuch a Beauty, in our Time want Swords
To guard it fafe from Violence.
　　Gal. I muft fpeak,
Or I fhall burft ; now to be filent, were
A Kind of Blafphemy.   If fuch Purity,
Such Innocence, an Abftract of Perfection,
The Soul of Beauty, Virtue, in a Word,
A Temple of Things facred, fhould groan under
The Burthen of Oppreffion, we might
Accufe the Saints, and tax the Powers above us
Of Negligence or Injuftice. [*Afide.*] — Pardon, Sir,
A Stranger's Boldnefs, and in your Mercy call it
True Zeal, not Rudenefs.   In a Caufe like this,
The Hufbandman would change his Ploughing-Irons
To Weapons of Defence, and leave the Earth
Untill'd, although a general Dearth fhould follow :
The Student would forfwear his Book ; the Lawyer
Put of his thriving Gown, and without Pay
Conclude this Caufe is to be fought, not pleaded.

The

The Women will turn *Amazons*, as their Sex
In her were wrong'd; and Boys write down their Names
I' th' Muster-book for Soldiers.

   Gonz. Take my Hand——
Whate'er you are, I thank you.   How are you call'd?

   Gal. Hortensio, a *Milanese.*

   Gonz. I wish *Mantua*
Had many such.   My Lord Ambassador,
Some Privacy, if you please.   *Manfroy,* you may
Partake it, and advise us.   [*They go aside.*

   Uber. Do you know, Friend,
What this Man is, or of what Country?

   Farn. Neither.

   Uber. I'll question him myself.—What are you, Sir?

   Gal. A Gentleman.

   Uber. But if there be Gradation
In Gentry, as the Heralds say, you have
Been over-bold i' th' Presence of your Betters.

   Gal. My Betters, Sir?

   Uber. Your Betters! As I take it,
You are no Prince.

   Gal. 'Tis Fortune's Gift you were born one:
I have not heard that glorious Title crowns you
As a Reward of Virtue: It may be
The first of your House deserv'd it; yet his Merits
You can but faintly call your own.

   Matil. Well answer'd.

   Uber. You come up to me.

   Gal. I would not turn my Back
If you were the Duke of *Florence,* tho' you charg'd me
I' th' Head of your Troops.

   Uber. Tell me in gentler Language,
(Your passionate Speech induces me to think so)
Do you love the Princess?

   Gal. Were you mine Enemy,
Your Foot upon my Breast, Sword at my Throat,
E'en then I would profess it.   The Ascent
To th' Height of Honour, is by Arts or Arms:
And if such an unequal'd Prize might fall

VOL. III.   S   On

On him that did deferve beft in Defence
Of this rare Princefs, in the Day of Battle,
I fhould lead you a Way would make your Greatnefs
Sweat Drops of Blood to follow.

   Uber. Can your Excellence
Hear this without Rebuke from one unknown?
Is he a Rival for a Prince?

   Matil. My Lord,
You take that Liberty I never gave you.
In Juftice you fhould give Encouragement
To him, or any Man, that freely offers
His Life to do me Service, not deter him;
I give no Suffrage to it. Grant he loves me,
As he profeffes, how are you wrong'd in it?
Would you have all Men hate me but yourfelf?
No more of this, I pray you: If this Gentleman
Fight for my Freedom, in a fit Proportion
To his Defert and Quality, I can
And will reward him; yet give you no Caufe
Of Jealoufy or Envy.

   Gal. Heavenly Lady!

   Gonz. No Peace, but on fuch poor and bafe Condi-
We will not buy it at that Rate.—Return   [tions?
This Anfwer to your Mafter: Though we wifh'd
To hold fair Quarter with him, on fuch Terms
As Honour would give Way to, we are not
So Thunder-ftruck with the loud Voice of War,
As to acknowledge him our Lord before
His Sword hath made us Vaffals. We long fince
Have had Intelligence of the unjuft Gripe
He purpos'd to lay on us; neither are we
So unprovided as you think, my Lord,
He fhall not need to feek us, we will meet him
And prove the Fortune of a Day.—Perhaps,
Sooner than he expects.

   Alon. And find Repentance,
When 'tis too late. Farewel!   [*Exit with* Farneze,

   Gonz. No, my *Matilda*,
We muft not part fo. Beafts and Birds of Prey

To

To their laft Gafp defend their Brood; and *Florence*
Over thy Father's Breaft fhall march up to thee,
Before he force Affection.   The Arms
That thou muft put on for us and thyfelf,
Are Pray'rs and pure Devotion, which will
Be heard, *Matilda*.   *Manfroy*, to your Truft
We do give up the City, and my Daughter;
On both keep a ftrong Guard.—No Tears, they are omi-
O my *Octavio*, my try'd *Octavio*,   [nous.
In all my Dangers! now I want thy Service,
In Paffion recompenc'd with Banifhment.
Error of Princes, who hate Virtue when
She's prefent with us, and in vain admire her
When fhe is abfent!—'Tis too late to think on't.
The wifh'd-for Time is come, Princely *Uberti*,
To fhew your Valour.   Friends being to do, not talk.
All Rhetorick is fruitlefs; only this,
Fate cannot rob you of deferv'd Applaufe,
Whether you win, or lofe, in fuch a Caufe.   [*Exeunt.*
            The End of the Firft Act.

ACT II. SCENE I.

Enter Matilda Beatrice, *and two Women.*

Matil. **N**O Matter for the Ring I afk'd you for :—
            The Boy not to be found?
Beat. Nor heard of, Madam.
  1 *Wom.* He hath been fought and fearch'd for, Houfe
            by Houfe,
Nay, every Nook of the City, but to no Purpofe.
  2 *Wom.* And how he fhould efcape hence, the Lord
Being fo vigilant o'er the Guards, appears   [*Manfroy*
A Thing impoffible.
    Matil. I never faw him
Since he fwoon'd in the Prefence, when my Father
Gave Audience to th' Ambaffador: But I feel
            S 2   A

A fad mifs of him; on any flight Occafion
He would find out fuch pretty Arguments
To make me Sport, and with fuch witty Sweetnefs
Deliver his Opinion, that I muft
Ingenuoufly confefs his harmlefs Mirth,
When I was moft opprefs'd with Care, wrought more
In the removing of it, than Mufick on me.

    Beat. An't pleafe your Excellence, I have obferv'd him
Waggifhly witty; yet, fometimes, on the fudden,
He would be very penfive, and then talk
So feelingly of Love, as if he had
Tafted the Bitter-Sweets of't.

    1 *Wom.* He would tell too
A pretty Tale of a Sifter, that had been
Deceiv'd by her Sweetheart; and then, weeping, fwear
He wonder'd how Men could be falfe.

    2 *Wom.* And that,
When he was a Knight, he'd be the Ladies Champion,
And travel o'er the World to kill fuch Lovers
As durft play falfe with their Miftreffes.

    Matil. I'm fure
I want his Company.

Enter Manfroy *with a Letter.*

    Manf. There are Letters, Madam,
In Poft come from the Duke; but I am charg'd
By the careful Bringer, not to open them
But in your Prefence.

    Matil. Heav'n preferve my Father!
Good News, an't be thy Will!

    Manf. Patience muft arm you
Againft what's ill.

    Matil. I'll hear 'em in my Cabinet.   [*Exeunt.*

SCENE

SCENE II.

Enter Galeazzo *and* Afcanio *(with a Ring.)*

Gal. Why have you left the Safety of the City
And Service of the Princefs, to partake
The Dangers of the Camp? and at a Time too
When the Armies are in View, and every Minute
The dreadful Charge expected.

Afc. You appear
So far beyond yourfelf, as you are now
Arm'd like a Soldier, (though I grant your Prefence
Was ever gracious) that I grow enamour'd
Of the Profeffion ; in the Horror of it
There is a Kind of Majefty.

Gal. But too heavy
To fit on thy foft Shoulders, Youth ; retire
To the Duke's Tent that's guarded.

Afc. Sir, I come
To ferve you : Knight-Adventurers are allow'd
Their Pages ; and I bring a Will that fhall
Supply my Want of Power.

Gal. To ferve me, Boy !
I wifh (believe it) that 'twere in my Nerves
To do thee any Service ; and thou fhalt,
If I furvive the Fortune of this Day,
Be fatisfy'd I am ferious.

Afc. I am not
To be put off fo, Sir : Since you neglect
My offer'd Duty, I muft ufe the Power
I bring along with me, that may command you :
You've feen this Ring?

Gal. Made rich by being worn
Upon the Princefs' Finger.

Afc. 'Tis a Favour
To you, by me fent from her.—View it better ;
But why coy to receive it ?

Gal. I am unworthy

Of

Of fuch a Bleffing. I have done nothing yet
That may deferve it ; no Commander's Blood
Of th' adverfe Party hath yet dy'd my Sword
Drawn out in her Defence.—I muft not take it.
This were a Triumph for me when I had
Made *Florence* Duke my Prifoner, and compell'd him
To kneel for Mercy at her Feet.

 Afc. 'Twas fent, Sir,
To put you in Mind whofe Caufe it is you fight for ;
And, as I am her Creature, to revenge
A Wrong to me done.

 Gal. By what Man ?

 Afc. Alonzo.

 Gal. Th' Ambaffador ?

 Afc. The fame.

 Gal. Let it fuffice.
I know him by his Armour and his Horfe ;
And if we meet——I am cut off, the Alarm
Commands me hence : Sweet Youth, fall off.

 Afc. I muft not ;
You are too noble to receive a Wound
Upon your Back ; and, following clofe behind you,
I am fecure, though I could wifh my Bofom
Were your Defence.

 Gal. Thy Kindnefs will undo thee.   [*Exeunt.*

SCENE III.

Enter Lorenzo, Alonzo, Pifano, Martinio.

 Lor. We'll charge the main Battalia, fall you
Upon the Van, preferve your Troops entire
To force the Rear : He dies that breaks his Ranks,
'Till all be ours and fure.

 Pifa. 'Tis fo proclaim'd.   [*Exeunt.*

Alarm.

Enter Galeazzo, Afcanio, *and* Alonzo.

 Gal. 'Tis he, *Afcanio :* Stand !

Alon.

Alon. I never ſhun'd
A ſingle Oppoſition ; but tell me
Why in the Battle, of all Men, thou haſt
Made Choice of me ?

Gal. Look on this Youth ; his Cauſe
Sits on my Sword.

Alon. I know him not.

Gal. I'll help
Your Memory.   [*Fight.*

Aſc. What have I done ? I am doubtful
To whom to wiſh the Victory ; for, ſtill
My Reſolution wav'ring, I ſo love
The Enemy that wrong'd me, that I cannot
Without Repentance wiſh Succeſs to him
That ſeeks to do me Right.—Alas ! he's fall'n !
                                   [Alonzo *falls.*

As you are gentle, hold, Sir ! or, if I want
Pow'r to perſuade ſo far, I conjure you
By her lov'd Name I'm ſent from.

Gal. 'Tis a Charm
Too ſtrong to be reſiſted.—He is yours.
Yet, why ſhould you make Suit to ſave that Life
Which you ſo late deſir'd ſhould be cut off
For Injuries receiv'd, begets my Wonder.

Aſc. Alas ! we fooliſh ſpleenful Boys would have
We know not what : I have ſome private Reaſons ;
But now not to be told.

Gal. Shall I take him Priſoner ?

Aſc. By no Means, Sir ; I will not ſave his Life
To rob him of his Honour : When you give,
Give not by Halves.—One ſhort Word, and I follow.
                                   [*Exit* Galeazzo.

My Lord *Alonzo*, if you have receiv'd
A Benefit, and would know to whom you owe it,
Remember what your Entertainment was
At old *Octavio*'s Houſe, one you call'd Friend,
And how you did return it.   [*Exit.*

Alon. I remember
I did not well ; but it is now no Time
S 4   To

To think upon't; my wounded Honour calls
For Reparation, I muſt quench my Fury
For this Diſgrace in Blood, and ſome ſhall ſmart for't.

[*Exit.*

SCENE IV.

Enter Uberti, Farneze *(wounded)*

Farn. O Prince *Uberti*, Valour cannot ſave us;
The Body of our Army's pierc'd and broken,
The Wings are routed, and our ſcatter'd Troops
Not to be rallied up.

Uber. 'Tis, yet, ſome Comfort,
The Enemy muſt ſay we were not wanting
In Courage or Direction; and we may
Accuſe the Powers above us partial, when
A good Cauſe, well defended too, muſt ſuffer
For want of Fortune.

Farn. All is loſt; the Duke
Too far engag'd, I fear, to be brought off:
Three Times I did attempt his Reſcue, but
With Odds was beaten back: Only the Stranger
(I ſpeak it to my Shame) ſtill follow'd him,
Cutting his Way; but 'tis beyond my Hopes
That either ſhould return.

Uber. That noble Stranger,
Whom I in my proud Vanity of Greatneſs
As one unknown contemn'd, when I was thrown
Out of my Saddle by the great Duke's Lance,
Hors'd me again, in ſpight of all that made
Reſiſtance; and then whiſper'd in mine Ear,
Fight bravely, Prince *Uberti*; there's no Way, elſe,
To the fair *Matilda*'s Favour.

Farn. 'Twas done nobly.

Uber. In you, my Boſom-friend, I had call'd it noble:
But ſuch a Courteſie from a Rival, merits
The higheſt Attribute.

Enter

Enter Galeazzo *and* Gonzaga.

Farn. Stand on your Guard,
We are purfu'd.
   Uber. Preferv'd! Wonder on Wonder.
   Farn. The Duke in Safety?
   Gonz. Pay your Thanks, *Farneze,*
To this brave Man, if I may call him fo,
Whofe Acts were more than human.   If thou art
My better Angel, from my Infancy
Defign'd to guard me, like thyfelf appear;
For fure thou'rt more than mortal.
   Gal. No, great Sir;
A weak and finful Man; though I have done you
Some profp'rous Service that hath found your Favour,
I'm loft unto myfelf; but lofe not you
The offer'd Opportunity to delude
The hot purfuing Enemy: Thefe Woods,
Nor the dark Veil of Night, cannot conceal you,
If you dwell long here.—You may rife again,
But I am fall'n for ever.
   Farn. Rather borne up
To the fupreme Sphere of Honour.
   Uber. I confefs
My Life your Gift.
   Gonz. I my Liberty: You've fnatch'd
The Wreath of Conqueft from the Victor's Head,
And do alone, in Scorn of *Lorenzo*'s Fortune,
Though we are flav'd, by true heroic Valour
Deferve a Triumph.   From whence then proceeds
This poor Dejection?
   Gal. In one Suit I'll tell you,
Which I befeech you grant,—I lov'd your Daughter;
But how? as Beggars in their wounded Fancy
Hope to be Monarchs: I long languifh'd for her;
But did receive no Cordial, but what
Defpair, my rough Phyfician, prefcrib'd me.
At length her Goodnefs and Compaffion found it:
And,

And, whereas I expected, and with Reason,
The Diftance and Difparity confider'd
Between her Birth and mine, fhe would contemn me,
The Princefs gave me Comfort.

    Gonz. In what Meafure ?

    Gal. She did admit me for her Knight and Servant,
And fpur'd me to do fomething in this Battle
Fought for her Liberty, that might not blemifh
So fair a Favour.

    Gonz. This you have perform'd
To th' Height of Admiration.

    Uber. I fubfcribe to't,
That am your Rival.

    Gal. You are charitable :
But how fhort of my Hopes, nay, the Affurance
Of thofe Atchievements which my Love and Youth
Already held accomplifh'd, this Day's Fortune
Muft fadly anfwer.   What I did, fhe gave me
The Strength to do; her Piety preferv'd
Her Father; and her Gratitude for the Dangers
You threw yourfelf into for her Defence,
Protected you, by me her Inftrument :
But when I came to ftrike in mine own Caufe,
And to do fomething fo remarkable,
That fhould at my Return command her Thanks
And gracious Entertainment, then, alas !
I fainted like a Coward.   I made a Vow too
(And it is regifter'd) ne'er to prefume
To come into her Prefence, if I brought not
Her Fears and Dangers bound in Fetters to her,
Which now's impoffible.——Hark ! the Enemy
Makes his Approaches: Save yourfelves !—This only
Deliver to her Sweetnefs ; I have done
My poor Endeavours, and pray her not repent
Her Goodnefs to me.   May you live to ferve her,
This Lofs recover'd, with a happier Fate,
And make Ufe of this Sword.   Arms I abjure,
And Converfation of Men : I'll feek out
Some unfrequented Cave, and die Love's Martyr. [*Exit.*
                                         Gonz.

Gonz. Follow him.

Uber. 'Tis in vain ; his nimble Feet
Have borne him from my Sight.

Gonz. I suffer for him.

Farn. We share in it ; but must not, Sir, forget
Your Means of Safety.

Uber. In the War I've serv'd you,
And to the Death will follow you.

Gonz. 'Tis not fit :
We must divide ourselves. My Daughter, if I retain not
A Sov'reign's Power o'er thee, or Friends with you,
Do, and dispute not ; by my Example change
Your Habits : As I thus put off my Purple,
Ambition dies ; this Garment of a Shepherd
Left here by Chance will serve ; in Lieu of it
I leave this to the Owner. Raise new Forces,
And meet me at St. *Leo*'s Fort ; my Daughter,
As I commanded *Manfroy*, there will meet us.
The City cannot hold out, we must part.
Farewell ; thy Hand ——

Farn. You still shall have my Heart.   [*Exeunt.*

S C E N E V.

Enter Lorenzo, Alonzo, Pisano, Martino, *Captains,*
Soldiers.

Loren. The Day is ours, tho' it cost dear ; yet 'tis not
Enough to get a Victory, if we lose
The true Use of it. We have hitherto
Held back your forward Swords, and in our Fear
Of Ambushes, defer'd the wish'd Reward
Due to your bloody Toil : But now give Freedom,
Nay, Licence to your Fury and Revenge.
Now glut yourselves with Prey. Let not the Night,
Nor these thick Woods, give Sanctuary to
The fear-struck Hares our Enemies : Fire these Trees,
And force the Wretches to forsake their Holes,
And offer their scorch'd Bodies to your Swords,

Or

Or burn 'em as a Sacrifice to your Angers.
Who brings *Gonzaga*'s Head, or takes him Prisoner,
(Which I incline to rather, that he may
Be sensible of those Tortures, which I vow
T' inflict upon him, for denial of
His Daughter to our Bed) shall have a Blank,
With our Hand and Signet made authentical,
In which he may write down himself, what Wealth
Or Honours he desires.
　　Alon. The great Duke's Will
Shall be obey'd.
　　Pisan. Put it in Execution.
　　Mart. Begirt the Wood, and fire it.
　　Sold. Follow, follow!　　　　　　　　　*[Exeunt.*

SCENE VI.

Enter Farneze *(with a* Florentine *Soldier's Coat.)*

　　Farn. Uberti! Prince *Uberti!* O my Friend,
Dearer than Life! I've lost thee! Cruel Fortune,
Unsatisfy'd with our Sufferings! We no sooner
Were parted from the Duke, and e'en then ready
To take a mutual Farewel, when a Troop
Of th' Enemy's Horse fell on us: We were forc'd
To take the Woods again, but in our Flight
Their hot Pursuit divided us. We had been happy
If we had dy'd together; to survive him
To me is worse than Death, and therefore should not
Embrace the Means of my Escape, though offer'd.
When Nature gave us Life, she gave a Burthen;
But at our Pleasure not to be cast off,
Though weary of it; and my Reason prompts me,
This Habit of a *Florentine*, which I took
From a dying Soldier, may keep me unknown,
'Till Opportunity mark me out a Way
For Flight, and with Security.

Enter

Enter Uberti.

Uber. Was there ever
Such a Night of Horror?   [*Afide.*
   Farn. My Friend's Voice? I now
In Part forgive thee, Fortune.
   Uber. The Wood flames,
The Bloody Sword devours all that it meets,
And Death in feveral Shapes rides here in Triumph.
I'm like a Stag, clos'd in a Toil, my Life,
As foon as found, the cruel Huntfman's Prey:
Why fly'ft thou, then, what is inevitable?
Better to fall with manly Wounds before
Thy cruel Enemy, than furvive thine Honour:
And yet to charge him, and die unreveng'd,
Mere Defperation.
   Farn. Heroic Spirit!   [*Afide.*
   Uber. Mine own Life I contemn, and would not fave
But for the future Service of the Duke,   [it
And Safety of his Daughter; having Means,
If I efcape, to raife a fecond Army,
And what is neareft to me, to enjoy
My Friend *Farneze.*
   Farn. I am ftill his Care.   [*Afide.*
   Uber. What fhall I do? If I call loud, the Foe
That hath begirt the Wood, will hear the Sound.
Shall I return by the fame Path? I cannot;
The Darknefs of the Night conceals it from me:
Something I muft refolve.
   Farn. Let Friendfhip rouze
Thy fleeping Soul, *Farneze:* Wilt thou fuffer
Thy Friend, a Prince, nay, one that may fet free
Thy captiv'd Country, perifh, when 'tis in
Thy Power with this Difguife to fave his Life?
Thou haft liv'd too long, therefore refolve to die;
Thou haft feen thy Country ruin'd, and thy Mafter
Compell'd to fhameful Flight; the Fields and Woods
Strew'd o'er with Carcafes of thy Fellow-Soldiers:
The

Thefe Miferies thou art fall'n in, and before
Thy Eyes the Horror of this Place, and thoufand
Calamities to come ; and after all thefe
Can any Hope remain ? Shake off Delays,
Doft thou doubt yet ?   To fave a Citizen,
The conqu'ring *Roman,* in a General,
Efteem'd the higheft Honour ; can it be then
Inglorious to preferve a Prince ? thy Friend ?
Uberti, Prince *Uberti,* ufe this Means
Of thy Efcape ; conceal'd in this thou may'ft
Pafs through the Enemy's Guards.—The Time denies
Longer Difcourfe : Thou haft a noble End ;
Live, therefore, mindful of thy dying Friend.   [*Exit.*

   Uber. Farneze, ftay thy hafty Steps : *Farneze !*
Thy Friend *Uberti* calls thee.—'Tis in vain ;
He's gone to Death an Innocent, and makes Life,
The Benefit he confers on me, my Guilt.
Thou art too covetous of another's Safety ;
Too prodigal and carelefs of thine own.
'Tis a Deceit in Friendfhip to enjoin me
To put this Garment on, and live, that he
May have alone the Honour to die nobly.
O cruel Pity, in our equal Danger
To rob thyfelf of that thou giv'ft thy Friend !
It muft not be.—I will reftore his Gift
And die before him.—How ? where fhall I find him ?
Thou art o'ercome in Friendfhip.   Yield, *Uberti,*
To the Extremity of the Time, and live :
A heavy Ranfom ! but it muft be paid.
I will put on this Habit : Pitying Heaven,
As it loves Goodnefs, may protect my Friend,
And give me Means to fatisfy the Debt
I ftand engag'd for ; if not, pale Defpair,
I dare thy Worft ; thou canft but bid me die,
And fo much I'll force from an Enemy.   [*Exit.*

SCENE

S C E N E VII.

Enter Alonzo, Pifano, Farneze *(bound)* Soldiers *(with
Torches)* Farneze's *Sword in one of the Soldiers Hands.*

 Alon. I know him, he's a Man of Ranfom.
 Pifan. True.
But if he live, 'tis to be paid to me.
 Alon. I forc'd him to the Woods.
 Pifan. But my Art found him;
Nor will I brook a Partner in the Prey
My Fortune gave me.
 Alon. Render him, or expect
The Point of this.
 Pifan. Wer't Lightning, I would meet it
Rather than be out-brav'd.
 Alon. I thus decide the Difference.
 Pifan. My Sword fhall plead my Title. [*They fight.*

Enter Lorenzo, Martinio, *two Captains.*

 Lor. Ha! where learn'd you this Difcipline? My
   Commanders
Oppos'd 'gainft one another? What blind Fury
Brings forth this Brawl? *Alonzo* and *Pifano*
At bloody Difference!——Hold! or I tilt
At both as Enemies.——Now fpeak, how grew
This ftrange Divifion?
 Pifan. Againft all Right;
By Force *Alonzo* ftrives to reap the Harveft
Sown by my Labour.
 Alon. Sir, this is my Prifoner,
The Purchafe of my Sword, which proud *Pifano*,
That hath no Intereft in him, would take from me.
 Pifan. Did not the Prefence of the Duke forbid me,
I would fay——
 Alon. What?
 Pifan. 'Tis falfe.

[*Lor.*

Lor. Before my Face? ——
Keep 'em afunder.   And was this the Caufe
Of fuch a mortal Quarrel? This the Bafe
To raife your Fury on? The Ties of Blood,
Of Fellowfhip in Arms, Refpect, Obedience
To me your Prince and General, no more
Prevailing on you? This a Price for which
You would betray our Victory, or wound
Your Reputation with Mutinies,
Forgetful of yourfelves, Allegiance, Honour?
This is a Courfe to throw us headlong down
From that proud Height of Empire, upon which
We were fecurely feated.   Shall Divifion
O'erturn what Concord built? If you defire
To bathe your Swords in Blood, the Enemy
Still flies before you : Would you have Spoil, the Coun-
Lies open to you.   O unheard-of Madnefs !   [try
What greater Mifchief could *Gonzaga* wifh us,
Than you pluck on our Heads?—No, my brave Leaders,
Let Unity dwell in our Tents, and Difcord
Be banifh'd to our Enemies.
    Alon. Take the Prifoner,
I do give up my Title.
    Pifan. I defire
Your Friendfhip, and will buy it.   He is yours.
                              [*They embrace.*
    Alon. No Man's a faithful Judge in his own Caufe :
Let the Duke determine of him ; we are Friends, Sir.
    Lor. Shew it in Emulation to o'ertake
The flying Foe : This curfed Wretch difpos'd of,
With our whole Strength we'll follow.
                    [*Exeunt* Alonzo *and* Pifano *embracing.*
    Farn. Death at length
Will fet a Period to Calamity.

        Enter Uberti *like a Soldier, and fhuffles in among 'em.*

I fee it in this Tyrant's Frowns hafte to me.
                                                Lor.

Lor. Thou Machine of this Mifchief, look to feel
Whate'er the Wrath of an incenfed Prince
Can pour upon thee : With thy Blood I'll quench
(But drawn forth flowly) the invifible Flames
Of Difcord;—by thy Charms firft fetch'd from Hell,
Then forc'd into the Breafts of my Commanders.
——Bring forth the Tortures.

   Uber. Hear, victorious Duke,
The Story of my miferable Fortune,
Of which this Villain (by your facred Tongue
Condemn'd to die) was the immediate Caufe :
And, if my humble Suit have Juftice in it,
Vouchfafe to grant it.

    Lor. Soldier, be brief ;
Our Anger cannot brook a long Delay.

    Uber. I am the laft
Of three Sons, by one Father got, and train'd up
With his beft Care for Service in your Wars :
My Father dy'd under his fatal Hand,
And two of my poor Brothers.   Now I hear,
(Or Fancy, wounded by my Grief, deludes me)
Their pale and mangled Ghofts, crying for Vengeance
On Perjury and Murther.—Thus the Cafe ftood.——
My Father (on whofe Face he durft not look
In equal Mart) by his Fraud circumvented,
Became his Captive.   We his Sons, lamenting
Our old Sire's hard Condition, freely offer'd
Our utmoft for his Ranfom.   That refus'd,
The fubtle Tyrant, for his cruel Ends,
(Conceiving that our Piety might enfnare us)
Propos'd my Father's Head to be redeem'd,
If two of us would yield ourfelves his Slaves.
We, upon any Terms refolv'd to fave him,
Though with the Lofs of Life which he gave to us ;
With an undaunted Conftancy drew Lots
(For each of us contended to be one)
Who fhould preferve our Father.   I was exempted ;
But, to my more Affliction, my Brothers
Deliver'd up.   The perjur'd Homicide

Laughing in Scorn, and by his hoary Locks
Pulling my wretched Father on his Knees,
Said thus : " Receive the Father you have ranfom'd ;"
And inftantly ftruck off his Head.

   Lor. Moft barbarous !

   Farn. I never faw this Man.

   Lor. One Murmur more,
I'll have thy Tongue pull'd out.—Proceed.

   Uber. Conceive, Sir,
How thunderftruck we ftood, being made Spectators
Of fuch an unexpected Tragedy :
Yet this was a Beginning, not an End
To his intended Cruelty ; for, purfuing
Such a Revenge as no *Hyrcanian* Tygrefs,
Robb'd of her Whelps, durft aim at, in a Moment
Treading upon my Father's Trunk, he cut off
My pious Brothers Heads, and threw 'em at me.
Oh, what a Spectacle was this ! What Mountain
Of Sorrow overwhelm'd me ! My poor Heart-ftrings,
As tenter'd by his Tyranny, crack'd ; my Knees
Beating 'gainft one another, Groans and Tears
Blended together follow'd ; not one Paffion
Calamity ever yet exprefs'd, forgotten.
Now, mighty Sir, (bathing your Feet with Tears)
Your Suppliant's Suit is, that he may have Leave,
With any Cruelty Revenge can fancy,
To facrifice this Monfter, to appeafe
My Father's Ghoft and Brothers.

   Lor. Thou haft obtain'd it :
Choofe any Torture ; let the Memory
Of what thy Father and thy Brothers fuffer'd
Make thee ingenious in it ; fuch a one
As *Phalaris* would wifh to be call'd his.
Martinio, guarded with your Soldiers, fee
The Execution done ; but bring his Head,
On Forfeiture of your own, to us : Our Prefence
Long fince was elfewhere look'd for.

                    [*Exit, with Attendants.*

                         Mart.

Mart. Soldier, to work ;
Take any Way thou wilt, for thy Revenge,
Provided that he die.   His Body's thine ;
But I muſt have his Head.

    Uber. I have already
Concluded of the Manner.—O juſt Heaven,
The Inſtrument I wiſh'd for offer'd me !

    Mart. Why art thou rap'd thus ?

    Uber. In this Soldier's Hand
I ſee the Murtherer's own Sword ; I know it ;
Yes, this is it by which my Father and
My Brothers were beheaded : Noble Captain,
Command it to my Hand.—Stand forth and tremble :
This Weapon, of late drunk with innocent Blood,
Shall now carouſe thine own.   Pray, if thou canſt ;
For, though the World ſhall not redeem thy Body,
I would not kill thy Soul.

    Farn. Canſt thou believe
There is a Heav'n, or Hell, or Soul ? Thou haſt none,
In Death to rob me of my Fame, my Honour,
With ſuch a forged Lye ? Tell me, thou Hangman,
Where did I ever ſee thy Face ? or when
Murder'd thy Sire or Brothers ? Look on me,
And make it good : Thou dar'ſt not.

    Uber. Yes I will   [*Unbinds his Arms.*
In one ſhort Whiſper ; and, that told, thou art dead.
I am *Uberti*.—Take thy Sword, fight bravely ;
We'll live or die together.

    Mart. We are betray'd.
            [*Martinio ſtruck down, the Soldiers run away.*
    Farn. And have I Leave once more, brave Prince,
My Head on thy true Boſom ?   [*to eaſe*

    Uber. I glory more
To be thy Friend, than in the Name of Prince,
Or any higher Title.

    Farn. My Preſerver !

    Uber. The Life you gave to me, I but return ;
And pardon, deareſt Friend, the bitter Language
Neceſſity made me uſe.

T 2

Farn.

Farn. O Sir, I am
Outdone in all ; but comforted, that none
But you can wear the Laurel.
    Uber. Here's no Place
Or Time to argue this ; let us fly hence.
    Farn. I follow.   [*Exeunt.*
    Mart. A thousand Furies keep you Company !
I was at the Gate of ——— but now I feel
My Wound's not mortal ; I was but astonish'd,
And, coming to myself, I find I am
Reserv'd for th' Gallows.   There's no looking on
Th' enraged Duke, Excuses will not serve ;
I must do something that may get my Pardon ;
If not, I know the worst, a Halter ends all.   [*Exit.*

The End of the Second Act.

ACT III.   SCENE I.

Enter Octavio (a Book in his Hand.)

Oct. 'TIS true, by Proof I find it, Human Reason
            Views with such dim Eyes what's good or
That, if the great Disposer of our Being   [ill,
Should offer to our Choice all worldly Blessings,
We know not what to take.—When I was young,
Ambition of Court-Preferment fir'd me :
And, as there were no Happiness beyond it,
I labour'd for't and got it : No Man stood
In greater Favour with his Prince ; I had
Honours and Offices ; Wealth flow'd unto me ;
And, for my Service both in Peace and War,
The general Voice gave out I did deserve 'em.
But, O vain Confidence in subordinate Greatness !
When I was most secure it was not in
The Power of Fortune to remove me from

                                                    The

The Flat I firmly ſtood on, in a Moment
My Virtues were made Crimes, and popular Favour
(To new-rais'd Men ſtill fatal) bred Suſpicion
That I was dangerous ; which no ſooner enter'd
Gonzaga's Breaſt, but ſtrait my Ruin follow'd ;
My Offices were taken from me, my 'State ſeiz'd on ;
And, had I not prevented it by Flight,
The Jealouſy of the Duke had been remov'd
With the Forfeiture of my Head.

Galeazzo within.

Gal. Or ſhew Compaſſion,
Or I will force it.
    Oct. Ha ! is not Poverty ſafe ?
I thought proud War, that aim'd at Kingdoms Ruins,
The Sack of Palaces and Cities, ſcorn'd
To look on a poor Cottage.

Enter Galeazzo, with Aſcanio in his Arms, Gothrio
following.

Goth. What would you have ?　The Devil ſleeps in
my Pocket; I have no Croſs to drive him from it.　Be
you or Thief or Soldier, or ſuch a Beggar as will not
be denied, My Scrip, my Tar-Box, Hook and Coat
will prove but a thin Purchaſe ; if you turn my Inſide
Outwards, you'll find it true.
    Gal. Not any Food ?　　　　　　*[Searches his Scrip.*
    Goth. Alas ! Sir, I am no Glutton. but an Under-
Shepherd ; the very Picture of Famine ; judge by my
Cheeks, elſe : I have my Pittance by Ounces, and ſtarve
myſelf, when I pay a Penſioner I have, an ancient Mouſe,
a Crum a-meal.
    Gal. No Drop left ?　　　　　　*[Takes the Bottle.*
Drunkard ! haſt thou ſwill'd up all ?
    Goth. How ! Drunkard, Sir ? I am a poor Man :
You miſtake me, Sir : Alas ! Drunkard's a Title for
the Rich, my Betters ; a Calling in Repute.——Some

T 3

fell

fell their Lands for't, and roar Wine's better than
Money. Our poor Beverage of Buttermilk or Whey,
allay'd with Water, ne'er raife our Thoughts fo high.
Drunk? I had never the Credit to be fo yet.

  Gal. *Afcanio*,
Look up, dear Youth, *Afcanio*, did thy Sweetnefs
Command the greedy Enemy to forbear
To prey upon it? And I thank my Fortune
For fuff'ring me to live, that in fome Part
I might return thy Courtefies: And now,
To heighten my Afflictions, muft I be
Inforc'd, no pitying Angel near to help us,
Heav'n deaf to my Complaints too, to behold thee
Die in my Arms for Hunger?——No Means left
To lengthen Life a little? I will open
A Vein, and pour my Blood, not yet corrupted
With any finful Act, but pure as he is,
Into his famifh'd Mouth.

  Oct. Young Man, forbear
Thy favage Pity; I have better Means
To call back flying Life
[They apply themfelves to Afcanio.

  Goth. You may believe him; it is his Sucking-Bot-
tle, and confirms, An Old Man's twice a Child; his
Nurfe's Milk was ne'er fo chargeable: Should you put
it too for Soap and Candles, tho' he fell his Flock for't,
the Baby muft have this Dug: He fwears 'tis ill for
my Complexion, but wond'rous comfortable for an old
Man that would never die.

  Oct. Hope well, Sir:
A temperate Heat begins to thaw his Numbnefs;
The Blood too by Degrees takes frefh Poffeffion
On his pale Cheeks; his Pulfe beats high.——Stand off,
Give him more Air, he ftirs.
[Gothrio fteals the Bottle.

  Goth. And have I got thee,
Thou Bottle of Immortality!

  Afc. Where am I?
What cruel Hand hath forc'd back wretched Life?

Is

Is Reſt in Death deny'd me ?

Goth. O ſweet Liquor !
Were here enough to make me drunk, I might
Write myſelf Gentleman, and never buy
A Coat of th' Heralds.

Oct. How now, Slave ?

Goth. I was fainting,
A clown-like Qualm ſeiz'd on me ; but I am
Recover'd, Thanks to your Bottle, and begin
To feel new Stirrings, gallant Thoughts.—One Draught
Will make me a perfect Signior.   [*more*

Oct. A tough Cudgel
Will take this gentle Itch off : Home to my Cottage,
See all Things handſome.

Goth. Good Sir, let me have
The Bottle along to ſmell to :—O rare Perfume ! [*Ex.*

Gal. Speak once more, dear *Aſcanio !* How he eyes
     you,
Then turns away his Face ! Look up, ſweet Youth !
The Object cannot hurt you ; this good Man,
Next Heav'n, is your Preſerver.

Aſc. Would I had periſh'd
Without Relief, rather than live to break
His good old Heart with Sorrow. O my Shame !
My Shame ! my never-dying Shame !

Oct. I have been
Acquainted with this Voice, and know the Face too :
—'Tis ſhe, 'tis too apparent ; O my Daughter !
I mourn'd long for thy Loſs ; but thus to find thee,
Is more to be lamented.

Gal. How ? your Daughter ?

Oct. My only Child : I murmur'd againſt Heaven
Becauſe I had no more ; but now I find
This one too many. Is *Alonzo* glutted

                              [*Aſcanio weeps.*

With thy Embraces ?

Gal. At his Name a Shower
Of Tears falls from her Eyes.—She faints again.
Grave Sir, over-rule your Paſſion, and defer

T 4   The

The Story of your Fortune. On my Life
She is a worthy one: Her Innocence
Might be abus'd; but Mifchief's Self wants Power
To make her guilty. Shew yourfelf a Father
In her Recovery; then as a Judge,
When fhe hath Strength to fpeak in her own Caufe,
You may determine of her.

   Oct. I much thank you
For your wife Counfel: You direct, Sir,
As one indebted more to Years, and I
As a Pupil will obey you. Not far hence
I have a homely Dwelling; if you pleafe there
To make fome fhort Repofe, your Entertainment,
Tho' coarfe, fhall relifh of a Gratitude;
And that's all I can pay you. Look up, Girl,
Thou'rt in thy Father's Arms.

   Gal. She's weak and faint ftill:——
O fpare your Age! I'm young and ftrong, and this Way
To ferve her is a Pleafure, not a Burthen:
Pray you, lead the Way.

   Oct. The Saints reward your Goodnefs.   [*Exeunt.*

S C E N E II.

Enter Manfroy, *and* Matilda *(difguis'd)*

   Matil. No Hope of Safety left?
   Manf. We are defcry'd.
   Matil. I thought that, cover'd in this poor Difguife,
I might have pafs'd unknown.
   Manf. A Diamond,
Though fet in Horn, is ftill a Diamond,
And fparkles as in pureft Gold. We're follow'd:
Out of the Troops that fcour'd the Plains, I faw
Two gallant Horfemen break forth (who by their
Brave Furniture and Habiliments for the War
Seem'd to command the reft) fpurring hard towards us.
See with what winged Speed they climb the Hill,
Like Falcons on the Stretch to feize the Prey:

                                   Now

Now they difmount, and on their Hands and Knees
'O'ercome the fteep Afcent that guards us from them.
Your Beauty hath betray'd you ; for it can
No more be Night when bright *Apollo* fhines
In our Meridian, than that be conceal'd.

    Matil. It is my Curfe, not Blefﬁug; fatal to
My Country, Father, and myfelf.——Why did you
Forfake the City ?

    Manf. 'Twas the Duke's Command ——
No Time to argue that; we muft defcend ;
If undifcover'd your foft Feet (unus'd
To fuch rough Travail; can but carry you
Half a League hence, I know a Cave which will
Yield us Protection.

    Matil. I wifh I could lend you
Part of my Speed ; for me, I can outftrip
Daphne or *Atalanta.*

    Manf. Some good Angel
Defend us, and ftrike blind our hot Purfuers !   [*Exeunt.*

       Enter Alonzo *and* Pifano.

    Alon. She cannot be far off.——How glorioufly
She fhew'd to us in the Valley !

    Pifan. In my Thought,
Like to a blazing Comet.

    Alon. Brighter far :
Her Beams of Beauty made the Hill all Fire ;
From whence remov'd, 'tis cover'd with thick Clouds.
But we lofe Time ; I'll take that Way.

    Pifan. I this.   [*Exeunt.*

S C E N E III.

    Enter Galeazzo, *drefs'd as a Shepherd.*

    Gal. 'Tis a Degree of Comfort in my Sorrow,
I have done one good Work in reconciling
Maria, long hid in *Afcanio's* Habit,

                      To

To griev'd *Octavio*.   What a Sympathy
I found in their Affections! She with Tears
Making a free Confession of her Weakness,
In yielding up her Honour to *Alonzo*,
Upon his Vows to marry her: *Octavio*
Prepar'd to credit her Excuses, nay,
T' extenuate her Guilt ; she the Delinquent,
And Judge, as 'twere, agreeing.—But to me,
The moft forlorn of Men, no Beam of Comfort
Deigns to appear ; nor can I in my Fancy
Fashion a Means to get it : To my Country
I'm loft for ever, and 'twere Impudence
To think of a Return.—Yet this I could
Endure with Patience : But to be divorc'd
From all my Joy on Earth, the Happiness
To look upon the Excellence of Nature,
That is Perfection in herself, and needs not
Addition or Epithet, Rare *Matilda*
Would make a Saint blafpheme.   Here, *Galeazzo*,
In this obfcure Abode 'tis fit thou fhould'ft
Confume thy Youth, and grow old in lamenting
Thy Star-crofs'd Fortune, in this Shepherd's Habit ;
This Hook thy beft Defence ; fince thou could'ft ufe
(When thou didft fight in fuch a Princefs' Caufe)
Thy Sword no better.   [*Lies down.*

Enter Alonzo, Pifano, Matilda.

Matil. Are you Men, or Monfters ?
Whither will you drag me ? Can the open Ear
Of Heav'n be deaf, when an unfpotted Maid
Cries out for Succour!
   Pifan. 'Tis in vain ; caft Lots
Who fhall enjoy her firft.
   Alon. Flames rage within me,
And fuch a Spring of Nectar near to quench 'em !
My Appetite fhall be cloy'd firft.—Here I ftand
Thy Friend, or Enemy ; let me have Precedence,
I write a Friend's Name in my Heart ; deny it,
As an Enemy I defy thee.   *Pifan.*

Pifan. Friend or Foe
In this alike I value; I difdain
To yield Priority.——Draw thy Sword.
    Alon. To fheath it
In thy ambitious Heart.
    Matil. O curb this Fury,
And hear a wretched Maid firft fpeak.
    Gal. I'm Marble.
    Matil. Where fhall I feek out Words, or how reftrain
My Enemy's Rage, or Lovers'?——Oh the latter
Is far more odious! [*Afide.*] Did not your Luft
Provoke you, for that is its proper Name,
My Chaftity were fafe; and yet I tremble more
To think what dire Effects Luft may bring forth,
Than what, as Enemies, you can inflict,
And lefs I fear it. Be Friends to yourfelves,
And Enemies to me : Better I fall
A Sacrifice to your Attonement, than
Or one, or both, fhould perifh. I'm the Caufe
Of your Divifion; remove it, Lords,
And Concord will fpring up : Poifon this Face
That hath bewitch'd you; this Grove cannot want
Afpicks or Toads, Creatures, though juftly call'd
For their Deformity the Scorn of Nature,
More happy than myfelf with this falfe Beauty
(The Seed and Fruit of Mifchief) you admire fo.
I thus embrace your Knees, and yours a Suppliant,
If Tigers did not nurfe you, or you fuck
The Milk of a fierce Lionefs, fhew Compaffion
Unto yourfelves in being reconciled,
And Pity to poor me, my Honour fafe,
In taking loath'd Life from me.
    Pifan. What fhall we do ?
Or end our Difference in killing her,
Or fight it out ?
    Alon. To the laft Gafp. I feel
The moift Tears on my Cheeks, and blufh to find
A Virgin's Plaints can move fo.
    Pifan. To prevent

Her

Her Flight while we contend, let's bind her faft
To this Cyprefs-Tree.

   Alon. Agreed.

   Matil. It does prefage
My Funeral Rites.

   Gal. I fhall turn Atheift,
If Heaven fee and fuffer this.   Why did I
Abandon my good Sword ? with unarm'd Hands
I cannot refcue her.   Some Angel pluck me
From the Apoftacy I'm falling to,
And by a Miracle lend me a Weapon
To underprop falling Honour.

   Pifan. She is faft,
Refume your Arms.

   Alon. Honour, Revenge, the Maid too
Lie at the Stake.

   Pifan. Which thus I draw ——   [*They fight,*
   Alon. All's mine.   Pifano *falls.*
But bought with fome Blood of mine own. *Pifano,*
Thou wert a noble Enemy ; wear that Laurel
In Death to comfort thee ; for the Reward,
'Tis mine now without Rival.

           [Galeazzo *fnatches up* Pifano's *Sword.*
   Gal. Thou art deceiv'd ;
Men will grow up, like to the Dragon's Teeth
From *Cadmus'* Helm fown in the Field of *Mars,*
To guard pure Chaftity from Luft and Rape.
Libidinous Monfter, Satyr, Fawn, or what
Does better fpeak thee Slave to Appetite
And fenfual Bafenefs; if thy profane Hand
But touch this Virgin Temple, thou art dead.

   Matil. I fee the Aid of Heav'n, tho' flow, is fure.

   Alon. A ruftic Swain dare to retard my Pleafure?

   Gal. No Swain, *Alonzo,* but her Knight and Servant,
To whom the World fhould owe and pay Obedience ;
One that thou haft encounter'd, and fhrunk under
His Arm, that fpar'd thy Life in the late Battle
At th' Interceffion of the Princefs' Page.
Look on me better.

                              Matil.

Matil. 'Tis my virtuous Lover:
Under his Guard 'twere Sin to doubt my Safety.

Alon. I know thee, and with Courage will redeem
What Fortune then took from me.

Gal. Rather keep   [*Fight.* Alonzo *falls.*
Thy Compeer Company in Death.—Lie by him,
A prey for Crows and Vultures: Thefe fair Arms,
                              [*He unbinds* Matilda.

Unfit for Bonds, fhould have been Chains to make
A Bridegroom happy, though a Prince, and proud
Of fuch Captivity.   Whatfoe'er you are,
I glory in the Service I have done you ;
But I intreat you pay your Vows and Prayers
For Prefervation of your Life and Honour,
To the moft virtuous Princefs, chafte *Matilda.*
I am her Creature, and what Good I do
You truly may call hers ; what's Ill, mine own.

Matil. You never did do Ill, my virtuous Servant :
Nor is it in the Pow'r of poor *Matilda*
To cancel fuch an Obligation as
With humble Willingnefs fhe muft fubfcribe to.

Gal. The Princefs ? Ha !

Matil. Give me a fitter Name,
Your manumis'd Bondwoman, but even now
In the Poffeffion of Luft, from which
Your more than brave heroic Valour bought me :
And can I then, for Freedom unexpected,
But kneel to you, my Patron ?

Gal. Kneel to me !
For Heav'n's fake rife ; I kifs the Ground you tread on,
My Eyes fix'd on the Earth ; for I confefs
I am a Thing not worthy to look on you,
'Till you have fign'd my Pardon.

Matil. Do you interpret
The much Good you have done me, an Offence ?

Gal. The not performing your Injunctions to me,
Is more than capital : Your Allowance of
My Love and Service to you, with Admiffion
To each Place you made Paradife with your Prefence,
                                        S[h]ould

Should have enabled me to bring home Conqueſt:
Then, as a Sacrifice, to offer it
At the Altar of your Favour.   Had my Love
Anſwer'd your Bounty or my Hopes, an Army
Had been as Duſt before me; whereas I
Like a Coward turn'd my Back, and durſt not ſtand
The Fury of th' Enemy.

Matil. Had you done nothing
In the Battle, this laſt Act deſerves more
Than I, the Duke my Father joining with me,
Can ever recompence.   But take your Pleaſure;
Suppoſe you have offended, in not graſping
Your boundleſs Hopes, I thus ſeal on your Lips
A full Remiſſion.

Gal. Let mine touch your Foot,
Your Hand's too high a Favour.

Matil. Will you force me
To raviſh a Kiſs from you?

Gal. I'm intranc'd.

—*Matil.* So much Deſert and Baſhfulneſs ſhould not
            march   [me
In the ſame File. Take Comfort; when you've brought
To ſome Place of Security, you ſhall find
You have a Seat here, a Heart that hath
Already ſtudy'd, and vow'd to be thankful.

Gal. Heav'n make me ſo! Oh, I am overwhelm'd
With an Exceſs of Joy! Be not too prodigal,
Divineſt Lady, of your Grace and Bounties
At once; if you are pleas'd, I ſhall enjoy 'em.
Not taſte 'em, and expire.

Matil. I'll be more ſparing..   [*Exeunt.*

Enter Octavio, Gothrio, *and* Maria.

Oct. What Noiſe of claſhing Swords, like Armour
            faſhion'd
Upon an Anvil, pierc'd mine Ears? The Echo
Redoubling the loud Sound through all the Vallies,
This Way the Wind aſſures me that it came.

Goth.

Goth. Then, with your Pardon, I'll take this.

Oct. Why, Sirrah?

Goth. Becaufe, Sir, I will truft my Heels before
All Winds that blow in the Sky : We are wifer far
Than our Grandfires were, and in this I'll prove it;
They faid, " Hafte to the Beginning of a Feaft,
(There I am with 'em) " but to the End of a Fray,"
That is apocryphal; 'tis more canonical
Not to come there at all.——After a Storm
There are ftill fome Drops behind.

Mar. Pure Fear hath made
The Fool a Philofopher.

Oct. See, *Maria*, fee!
I did not err; here lie two brave Men welt'ring
In their own Gore.

Mar. A pitiful Object.

Goth. I am in a Swoon to look on't.

Oct. They are ftiff already.

Goth. But are you fure they're dead?

Oct. Too fure, I fear.

Goth. But are they ftark dead?

Oct. Leave prating!

Goth. Then I am valiant, and dare come nearer to 'em.
This Fellow without a Sword fhall be my Patient.

Oct. Whate'er they are, Humanity commands us
To do our beft Endeavour.——Run, *Maria*,
To th' neighbour Spring for Water; you'll find there
A wooden Difh, the Beggar's Plate, to bring it in.

[Exit Maria.

Why doft not, dull Drone, bend his Body, and feel
If any Life remain?

Goth. By your Leave
He fhall die firft, and then I'll be his Surgeon.

Oct. Tear ope his Doublet,
And prove if his Wounds be mortal.

Goth. Fear not me, Sir:
Here's a large Wound —— How it is fwoln and im-
   pofthum'd!——   [*His Pocket.*

This

This muſt be cunningly drawn out; ſhould it break,
[*Pulls out his Purſe.*

'Twould ſtrangle him: What a deal of foul Matter's
here! ——   [*His little Pocket.*
This hath been long a gathering: Here's a Gaſh too
On the Rim of his Belly, it may have Matter in it.
He was a cholerick Man, ſure: What comes from him
[*Gold.*

Is yellow as Gold: How! troubled with the Stone too?
[*A Diamond Ring.*

I'll cut you for this.

 Piſan. Oh, oh!   [*Starts up and quakes.*
 Goth. He roars before I touch him.
 Piſan. Robb'd of my Life?
 Goth. No, Sir; nor of your Money
Nor Jewel; I keep 'em for you.—If I had been
A perfect Mountebank, he had not liv'd
To call for his Fees again.
 Oct. Give me Leave —There's Hope of his Recovery.
 Goth. I had rather bury him quick   [not.
Than part with my Purchaſe; let his Ghoſt walk, I care

Enter Maria *(with a Diſh of Water.)*

 Oct. Well done, *Maria,* lend thy helping Hand:
He hath a deep Wound in his Head, waſh off
The clotted Blood.—He comes to himſelf.
 Alon. My Luſt!
The Fruit that grows upon the Tree of Luſt!
With Horror now I taſte it.
 Oct. Do you not know him?
 Mar. Too ſoon.—*Alonzo!* Ah me! though diſloyal,
Still dear to thy *Maria.*
 Goth. So they know not
My Patient, all's cock-ſure: I do not like
The Romaniſh Reſtitution.
 Oct. Riſe and leave him.
Applaud Heav'n's Juſtice.

Mar.

Mar. 'Twill become me better
T' implore its faving Mercy.
   Oct. Haft thou no Gall?
No Feeling of thy Wrongs?
   Mar. Turtles have none;
Nor can there be fuch Poifon in her Breaft
That truly loves, and lawfully.
   Oct. True, if that Love
Be plac'd on a worthy Subject.   What he is,
In thy Difgrace is publifh'd; Heav'n hath mark'd him
For Punifhment, and 'twere rebellious Madnefs
In thee t' attempt to alter it : Revenge,
A fovereign Balm for Injuries, is more proper
To thy. robb'd Honour.   Join with me, and thou
Shalt be thyfelf the Goddefs of Revenge,
This Wretch the Vaffal of thy Wrath : I'll make him,
While yet he lives, partake thofe Torments which
For perjur'd Lovers are prepar'd in Hell,
Before his curs'd Ghoft enter it.   This Oil,
Extracted and fublim'd from all the Simples
The Earth when fwoln with Venom e'er brought forth,
Pour'd in his Wounds, fhall force fuch Anguifh as
The Furies' Whips but imitate [2]; and when
Extremity of Pain fhall haften Death,
Here is another that fhall keep in Life,
And make him feel a Perpetuity
Of ling'ring Tortures.

---

[2] *The Furies' Whips but imitate.*

Many of the Images in this Play are very noble, and fhew great
Strength of Imagination; but to remark every Beauty of an Author
would be difpleafing : Readers love to judge for themfelves; how-
ever, I fhall here fet down the following from the Play before us,
Act II. Scene the laft, fpoken by *Uberti* in behalf of his .Friend
Farneze, whom he delivers by Stratagem,

    Oh what a Spectacle was this ! What Mountain
    Of Sorrow overwhelm'd me ! My poor Heartftrings,
    As tenter'd by his Tyranny, crack'd ; my Knees
    Beat againft one another ; Groans and Tears
    Blended together follow'd ; not one Paffion
    Calamity ever yet exprefs'd forgotten.

Goth. Knock 'em both o' th' Head, I fay,
And it be but for their Skins ; they are embroider'd,
And will fell well i' th' Market.
   Mar. Ill-look'd Devil,
Tie up thy bloody Tongue !—O Sir ! I was flow
In beating down thofe Propofitions which
You urge for my Revenge ; my Reafons being
So many, and fo forcible, that make
Againft yours, that, until I had collected
My fcatter'd Powers, I waver'd in my Choice
Which I fhould firft deliver.   Fate hath brought
My Enemy (I can faintly call him fo)
Proftrate before my Feet : Shall I abufe
The Bounty of my Fate, by trampling on him ?
He alone ruin'd me, nor can any Hand
But his rebuild my late demolifh'd Honour.
If you deny me Means of Reparation,
To fatisfy your Spleen, you are more cruel
Than ever yet *Alonzo* was ; you ftamp
The Name of Strumpet on my Forehead, which
Heav'n's Mercy would take off ; you fan the Fire
E'en ready to go out ; forgetting that
'Tis truly noble, having Power to punifh,
Nay, King-like, to forbear it.   I would purchafe
My Hufband by fuch Benefits, as fhould make him
Confefs himfelf my Equal, and difclaim
Superiority.
   Oct. My Bleffing on thee !
What I urg'd, was a Trial ; and my Grant
To thy Defires fhall now appear, if Art
Or long Experience can do him Service ;
Nor fhall my Charity to this be wanting,
Howe'er unknown.   Help me, *Maria.*   You, Sir,
Do your beft to raife him.—So.
   Goth. He's wond'rous heavy.————
But the Porter's paid, there's the Comfort.
   Oct. 'Tis but a Trance,
And 'twill forfake both.

Mar.

Mar. If I live, I fear not
He will redeem all, and in Thankfulnefs
Confirm he owes you for a fecond Life,
And pays the Debt in making me his Wife.   [*Exeunt.*

The End of the Third Act.

ACT IV.   SCENE I.

Enter Lorenzo, *and Captains.*

Lor. MANTUA is ours; place a ftrong Garrifon
         in it
To keep it fo; and as a due Reward
To your brave Service, be our Governor in it.
   1 *Capt.* I humbly thank your Excellence.   [*Exit.*
   Lor. Gonzaga
Is yet out of our Gripe; but his ftrong Fort
St. *Leo*, which he holds impregnable
By th' Aids of Art, as Nature, fhall not long
Retard our abfolute Conqueft.   The Efcape
Of fair *Matilda*, my fuppofed Miftrefs,
(For whofe defir'd Poffeffion 'twas given out
I made this War) I value not.   Alas!
Cupid's too feeble-ey'd to hit my Heart;
Or, could he fee, his Arrows are too blunt
To pierce it; his imagin'd Torch is quench'd
With the more glorious Fire of my Ambition
T' enlarge my Empire.   Soft and filken Amours,
With Carpet-courtfhip, which weak Princes ftile
The happy Iffue of a flourifhing Peace,
My Toughnefs fcorns.   Were there an Abftract made
Of all the eminent and canoniz'd Beauties
By Truth recorded, or by Poets feign'd,
I could unmov'd behold it; as a Picture,
Commend the Workmanfhip, and think no more on't;

U 2

I have

I have more noble Ends.—Have you not heard, yet,
Of *Alonzo*, or *Pifano?*

2 *Capt.* My Lord, of neither.

Lor. Two turbulent Spirits, unfit for Difcipline,
Much lefs Command in War; if they were loft,
I fhall not pine with Mourning.

Enter Martinio, Matilda, Galeazzo, *and Guard.*

Mart. Bring 'em forward;
This will make my Peace, tho' I had kill'd his Father;
Befides the Reward that follows.

Lor. Ha! *Martinio?*
Where is *Farneze*'s Head?—Doft thou ftare? and where
The Soldier that defir'd the Torture of him?

Mart. An't pleafe your Excellence——

Lor. It doth not pleafe us.
Are our Commands obey'd?

Mart. Farneze's Head, Sir,
Is a Thing not worth your Thought; the Soldier's lefs,
I have brought your Highnefs fuch a Head! a Head
So well fet on too! a fine Head——

Lor. Take that   '[*Strikes him.*
For thy Impertinence: What Head, ye Rafcal?

Mart. My Lord, if they that bring fuch Prefents to
Are thus rewarded, there are few will ftrive   [you
To be near your Grace's Pleafures: But I know
You will repent your Choler. Here's the Head;
And, now I draw the Curtain, it hath a Face too,
And fuch a Face——

Lor. Ha!

Mart. View her all o'er, my Lord;
My Company on't, fhe's found of Wind and Limb,
And will do her Labour tightly, a *Bona Roba*:
And for her Face, as I faid, there are Five Hundred
City-dub'd Madams in the Dukedom, that would part
          with   [Head, Maid.
Their Jointures to have fuch another.—Hold up your

Lor. Of what Age is the Day?

Mart.

Mart. Sir, since Sun-rising
About two Hours.

Lor. Thou ly'st; the Sun of Beauty,
In modest Blushes on her Cheeks, but now
Appear'd to me, and in her Tears breaks forth
As through a Show'r in *April*; every Drop
An Orient Pearl, which, as it falls, congeal'd,
Were Ear-rings for the Catholick King,
Worn on his Birth-day.

Mart. Here's a sudden Change.

Lor. Incensed *Cupid*, whom e'en now I scorn'd, *
Hath took his Stand, and by Reflexion shines
(As if he had two Bodies, or indeed
A Brother-twin whom Sight cannot distinguish)
In her fair Eyes.—See how they head their Arrows
With her bright Beams; now frown, as if my Heart,
Rebellious to their Edicts, were unworthy,
Should I rip up my Bosom, to receive
A Wound from such Divine Artillery.

Mart. I am made for ever.

Matil. We are lost, dear Servant.   [*Aside.*

Gal. Virtue's but a Word;
Fortune rules all.

—*Matil.* We are her Tennis-Balls.

Lor. Allow her fair, her Symmetry and Features
So well proportion'd, as the heavenly Object
With Admiration would strike *Ovid* dumb,
Nay, force him to forget his Faculty
In Verse, and celebrate her Praise in Prose,
What's this to me? I that have pass'd my Youth
Unscorch'd with wanton Fires, my sole Delight
In glitt'ring Arms, my conq'ring Sword my Mistress;
Neighing of barbed Horse, the Cries and Groans
Of vanquish'd Foes suing for Life, my Musick:

* 'Tis dangerous to contemn the Pow'r of Love,
　　He rules o'er all Things, and is King above.
　　　　　　　　　　　　　　　　　OTWAY.

U 3

And

And fhall I in the Autumn of my Age,[3]
Now when I wear the Livery of Time
Upon my Head and Beard, fuffer myfelf
To be transform'd, and like a puling Lover,
With Arms thus folded up, echo *Ay me's!*
And write myfelf a Bondman to my Vaffal?
It muft not, nay, it fhall not be: Remove
The Object, and th' Effect dies.—Nearer, *Martinio.*

　Mart. I fhall have a Regiment.—Colonel *Martinio,*
I cannot go lefs.　　　　　　　　　　　　　[*Afide.*

　Lor. What Thing is this thou haft brought me?

　Mart. What Thing? Heaven blefs me! are you a
　　　　Florentine?
Nay, the Great Duke of *Florentines,* and having had her
So long in your Power, do you now afk what fhe is?
Take her afide and learn; I have brought you that
I look to be dearly paid for.

　Lor. I am a Soldier;
And Ufe of Women will, *Martinio,* rob
My Nerves of Strength.

　Mart. All Armour, and no Smock?
Abominable! A little of the one with the other
Is excellent: I ne'er knew General yet,
Nor Prince that did deferve to be a Worthy,
But he defir'd to have his Sweat wafh'd off
By a juicy Bedfellow.

　Lor. But fay fhe be unwilling
To do that Office?

　Mart. Wreftle with her, I will wager
Ten to one on your Grace's Side.

　Lor. Slave, haft thou brought me
Temptation in a Beauty not to be
With Pray'rs refifted; and in Place of Counfel

----

[3] *And fhall I in the Autumn of my Age.*

Thus *Shakefpear* in *Macbeth,*

————— My Way of Life
Is fall'n into the Sear, the yellow Leaf.
　　　　　　　　　　　Act V. Scene 3.

To mafter my Affections, and to guard
My Honour now befieg'd by Luft, with the Arms
Of fober Temperance, mark me out a Way
To be a Ravifher? Would thou had'ft fhewn me
Some Monfter, though in a more ugly Form
Than *Nile* or *Africk* ever bred.   The Bafilifk
(Whofe envious Eye yet never brook'd a Neighbour)
Kills but the Body.   Her more potent Eye
Buries alive mine Honour: Shall I yield thus?
And all brave Thoughts of Victory and Triumphs,
The Spoils of Nations, the loud Applaufes
Of happy Subjects made fo by my Conquefts;
And, what's the Crown of all, a glorious Name
Infculp'd on Pyramids to Pofterity,
Be drench'd in *Lethe*, and no Object take me
But a weak Woman, rich in Colours only,
Too delicate to touch, and fome rare Features
Which Age or fudden Sicknefs will take from her;
And where's then the Reward of all my Service?
Love-foothing Paffions, nay Idolatry
I muft pay to her.   Hence, and with thee take
This fecond, but more dangerous *Pandora*,
Whofe fatal Box, if open'd, will pour on me
All Mifchiefs that Mankind is fubject to.
To the Defarts with this *Circe*, this *Calypfo*,
This fair Enchantrefs; let her Spells and Charms
Work upon Beafts and thee, than whom wife Nature
Ne'er made a viler Creature.
   Matil. Happy Exile!
   Gal. Some Spark of Hope remains yet.
   Mart. Come, you're mine now;
I will remove her where your Highnefs fhall not
Or fee or hear more of her.—What a Sum,
Will fhe yield for the *Turk*'s Seraglio!
   Lor. Stay, I feel
A fudden Alteration.
   Mart. Here are fine Whimfies.
   Lor. Why fhould I part with her? Can any Foulnefs
Inhabit fuch a clean and gorgeous Palace?

U 4

The

The Fifh, the Fowl, the Beafts may fafer leave
The Elements they were nourifh'd in, and live,
Than I endure her Abfence.——Yet her Prefence
Is a Torment to me: Why do I call it fo?
My Sire enjoy'd a Woman, I had not been, elfe;
He was a complete Prince, and fhal! I blufh
To follow his Example? Oh! but my Choice,
Though fhe gave Suffrage to it, is beneath me:
But even now in my proud Thoughts I fcorn'd
A Princefs, fair *Matilda*; and is't decreed
For Punifhment, I ftraight muft doat on one,
What, or from whence, I know not? Grant fhe be
Obfcure, without a Coat or Family,
Thofe I can give.——And yet, if fhe were noble,
My Fondnefs were more pardonable.——*Martinio*, ·
Doft thou know thy Prifoner?

    Mart. Do I know myfelf?
I kept that for the Lenvoy; 'tis the Daughter
Of your Enemy, Duke *Gonzaga*.

    Lor. Fair *Matilda!*
I now call to my Memory her Picture,
And find this is the Subftance; but her Painter
Did her much Wrong, I fee it.

    Mart. I am fure
I tugg'd hard for her; here are Wounds can witnefs,
Ere I could call her mine.

    Lor. No Matter how:
Make thine own Ranfom, I will pay it for her.

    Mart. I knew 'twould come at laft.

    Matil. We're loft again.

    Gal. Variety of Afflictions!

    Lor. That his Knee,
That never yet bow'd to Mortality,   *[Kneels.*
Kiffes the Earth, happy to bear your Weight,
I know, begets your Wonder: Hear the Reafon,
And caft it off.——Your Beauty does command it.
'Till now, I never faw you; Fame hath been
Too fparing in Report of your Perfections,
Which now with Admiration I gaze on.

                                        Be

Be not afraid, fair Virgin ; had you been
Employ'd to mediate your Father's Caufe,
My Drums had been unbrac'd, my Trumpets hung up ;
Nor had the Terror of the War e'er frighted
His peaceful Confines ; your Demands had been,
As foon as fpoke, agreed to.   But you'll anfwer,
And may with Reafon, Words make no Satisfaction
For what's in Fact committed.   Yet, take Comfort,
Something my pious Love commands me do,
Which may call down your Pardon.
    Matil. This Expreffion
Of Reverence to your Perfon, better fuits
[*Takes him up and kneels.*
With my low Fortune.   That you deign to love me,
My Weaknefs would perfuade me to believe
(Though confcious of mine own Unworthinefs)
You being as the liberal Eye of Heaven
Which may fhine where it pleafes.   Let your Beams
Of Favour warm and comfort, not confume me !
For, fhould your Love grow to Excefs, I dare not
Deliver what I fear.
    Lor. Dry your fair Eyes ;
I apprehend your Doubts, and could be angry
If humble Love could warrant it, you fhould
Nourifh fuch bafe Thoughts of me. Heav'n bear Witnefs,
And, if I break my Vow, dart Thunder at me,
You are, and fhall be, in my Tent as free
From Fear of Violence, as a cloyfter'd Nun
Kneeling before the Altar.   What I purpofe
Is yet an Embrion ; but, grown into Form,
I'll give you Power to be the fweet Difpofer
Of Bleffings unexpected ; that your Father,
Your Country, People, Children yet unborn too,
In holy Hymns on Feftivals fhall fing
The Triumph of your Beauty.   On your Hand
Once more I fwear it.—O imperious Love !
Look down, and, as I truly do repent,
Profper the good Ends of thy Penitent.   [*Exeunt.*

S C E N E

SCENE II.

Enter Octavio and Maria.

Oct. You muſt not be too ſudden, my *Maria*,
In being known.—I'm, in this Friar's Habit,
As yet conceal'd.——Though his Recovery
Be almoſt certain, I muſt work him to
Repentance by Degrees.   When I would have you
Appear in your true Shape of Sorrow to
Move his Compaſſion, I will ſtamp thus —— Then
You know to act your Part.
   Mar. I ſhall be careful.   [*Exit Mar.*
   Oct. If I can cure the Ulcers of his Mind,
As I deſpair not of his Body's Wounds,
Felicity crowns my Labour.   *Gothrio !*

Enter Gothrio.

Goth. Here, Sir.
   Oct. Deſire my Patients to leave their Chamber,
And take freſh Air here.   How have they ſlept ?
   Goth. Very well, Sir.
I would we were ſoon rid of 'em.
   Oct. Why ?
   Goth. I fear one hath the Art of Memory, and will
Remember his Gold and Jewels : Could you not miniſter
A Potion of Forgetfulneſs ? What would Gallants
That are in Debt, give me for ſuch a Receipt
To pour in their Creditors Drink ?
   Oct. You ſhall reſtore all :
Believ't you ſhall.—Will you pleaſe to walk ?
   Goth. Will you pleaſe to put off
Your holy Habit, and ſpic'd Conſcience ? One
I think infects the other.   [*Exit.*
   Oct. I have obſerv'd
Compunction in *Alonzo* ; he ſpeaks little,
But full of retir'd Thoughts : The other is

Jocund

Jocund and merry, no doubt, becaufe he hath
The lefs Accompt to make here.

Enter Alonzo.

Alon. Reverend Sir,
I come to wait your Pleafure ; but, my Friend,
(Your Creature I fhould fay, being fo myfelf)
Willing to take further Repofe, entreats
Your Patience a few Minutes.
Oct. At his Pleafure :
Pray you fit down ; you are faint ftill.
Alon. Growing to Strength,
I thank your Goodnefs : But my Mind is troubled,
Very much troubled, Sir ; and I defire,
Your pious Habit giving me Affurance
Of your Skill and Power that Way, that you would pleafe
To be my Mind's Phyfician.
Oct. Sir, to that
My Order binds me, if you pleafe to unload
The Burthen of your Confcience, I will minifter
Such heavenly Cordials as I can, and fet you
In a Path that leads to Comfort.
Alon. I will open
My Bofom-fecrets to you.—That I am
A Man of Blood, being brought up in the Wars,
And cruel Executions my Profeffion,
Admits not to be queftion'd : But in that,
Being a Subject, and bound to obey
Whate'er my Prince commanded, I have left
Some Shadow of Excufe : With other Crimes,
As Pride, Luft, Gluttony (it muft be told)
I am befmear'd all over.
Oct. On Repentance
Mercy will wafh it off.
Alon. O Sir, I grant
Thefe Sins are deadly ones ; yet their Frequency
With wicked Men, make them lefs dreadful to us.
But I am confcious of one Crime, with which

All

All Ills I have committed from my Youth
Put in the Scale weigh nothing : Such a Crime,
So odious to Heaven and Man, and to
My fear'd-up Confcience fo full of Horror,
As Penance cannot expiate.
  Oct. Defpair not,
'Tis impious in Man to prefcribe Limits
To the Divine Compaffion.—Out with it.
  Alon. Hear then, good Man ; and when that I have
           given you
The Character of it, and confefs'd myfelf
The Wretch that acted it, you muft repent
The Charity you have extended towards me.
  Not long before thefe Wars began, I had
Acquaintance ('tis not fit I ftile it Friendfhip,
That being a Virtue, and not to be blended
With vicious Breach of Faith) with th' Lord *Octavio,*
The Minion of his Prince and Court, fet off
With all the Pomp and Circumftance of Greatnefs :
To this, then happy, Man I offer'd Service,
And with Infinuation wrought myfelf
Into his Knowledge, grew familiar with him,
Ever a welcome Gueft.   This noble Gentleman
Was blefs'd with one fair Daughter, (fo he thought
And boldly might believe fo, for fhe was
In all Things excellent without a Rival)
'Till I (her Father's Mafs of Wealth before
My greedy Eyes, but hood-wink'd to mine Honour)
With far more fubtle Arts than perjur'd *Paris*
Ere practis'd on poor credulous *Oenone,*
Befieg'd her Virgin-Fort, in a Word, took it ;
No Vows or Imprecation forgotten
With Speed to marry her.
  Oct. Perhaps fhe gave you
Juft Caufe to break thofe Vows.
  Alon. She Caufe ? alas !
Her Innocence knew no Guilt, but too much Favour
To me unworthy of it : 'Twas my Bafenefs,
My foul Ingratitude.—What fhall I fay more ?
                         The

The good *Octavio* no sooner fell
In the Displeasure of his Prince, his 'State
Confiscated, and he forc'd to leave the Court,
And she expos'd to Want, but all my Oaths
And Protestation of Service to her,
Like seeming Flames rais'd by Enchantment, vanish'd ;
This, this sits heavy here.

   Oct. He speaks as if
He were acquainted with my Plot. [*Aside.*] You have
      Reason
To feel Compunction, for 'twas most inhuman
So to betray a Maid.

   Alon. Most barbarous.

   Oct. But does your Sorrow for the Fact beget
An Aptness in you to make Satisfaction
For th' Wrong you did her ?

   Alon. Gracious Heaven ! an Aptness ?
It is my only Study : Since I tasted
Of your Compassion, these Eyes ne'er were clos'd ;
But fearful Dreams cut off my little Sleep,
And, being awake in my Imagination,
Her Apparition haunted me.

   Oct. 'Twas mere Fancy.   [*He stamps.*

   Alon. 'Twas more, grave Sir—Nay, 'tis——Now it
      appears.

Enter Maria.

   Oct. Where ?

   Alon. Do you not see there the gliding Shadow
Of a fair Virgin ? That is she, and wears
The very Garments that adorn'd her when
She yielded to my Crocodile Tears : A Cloud
Of Fears and Diffidence then so chac'd away
Her purer White and Red, as it foretold
That I should-be disloyal.   Blessed Shadow !
For 'twere a Sin, far, far exceeding all
I have committed, to hope only that
Thou art a Substance : Look on my true Sorrow,
Nay, Soul's Contrition ; hear again those Vows
My Perjury cancell'd, stamp'd in Brass, and never
To be worn out——   *Enter*

Enter Gothrio.

Mar. I can endure no more;
Action, not Oaths, muſt make me Reparation:
I am *Maria.*
 Alon. Can this be?
 Oct. It is,
And I *Octavio.*
 Alon. Wonder on Wonder!
How ſhall I look on you? or with what Forehead
Deſire your Pardon?
 Mar. You truly ſhall deſerve it
In being conſtant.
 Oct. If you fall not off,
But look on her in Poverty with thoſe Eyes
As when ſhe was my Heir in Expectation,
You thought her beautiful.
 Alon. She's in herſelf
Both *Indies* to me.
 Goth. Stay, ſhe ſhall not come
A Beggar to you, my ſweet young Miſtreſs! no,
She ſhall not want a Dower: Here's White and Red
Will aſk a Jointure; but how you ſhould make her one,
Being a Captain, would beget ſome Doubt,
If you ſhould deal with a Lawyer.
 Alon. I have ſeen this Purſe.
 Goth. How the World's given—I dare not ſay to Ly-
ing, becauſe you are a Soldier; you may ſay as well,
this Gold is mark'd too: you, being to receive it, ſhould
ne'er aſk how I got it. I'll run for a Prieſt to diſpatch
the Matter; you ſhall not want a Ring, I have one for
the Purpoſe. Now, Sir, I think I'm honeſt.   [*Exit.*
 Alon. This Ring was *Piſano's.*
 Oct. I'll diſſolve this Riddle at better Leiſure:
The Wound given to my Daughter, which in your Ho-
You're bound to cure, exacts our preſent Care.   [nour
 Alon. I am all yours, Sir.   [*Exeunt.*

S C E N E

S C E N E III.

Enter Gonzaga, Uberti, Manfroy.

Gonz. Thou haſt told too much to give Aſſurance that
Her Honour was too far engag'd to be
By human Help redeem'd : If thou hadſt given
Thy ſad Narration this full Period,
She's dead; I had been happy.   [*Weeps.*
     Uber. Sir, theſe Tears
Do well become a Father; and my Eyes
Would keep you Company as a forlorn Lover,
But that the burning Fire of my Revenge
Dries up thoſe Drops of Sorrow.   We once more,
Our broken Forces rallied up, and with
Full Numbers ſtrengthen'd, ſtand prepar'd t'endure
A ſecond Trial ; nor let it diſmay us
That we are once again to affront the Fury
Of a victorious Army ; their Abuſe
Of Conqueſt hath diſarm'd themſelves, and call'd down
The Pow'rs above to aid us.   I have read
Some Piece of Story, yet ne'er found but that
The General, that gave Way to Cruelty,
The Profanation of Things Sacred, Rapes
Of Virgins, Butchery of Infants, and
The Maſſacre in Cold Blood of reverend Age,
Againſt the Diſcipline and Law of Arms,
Did feel the Hand of Heav'n lie heavy on him,
When moſt ſecure.—We have had a late Example ;
And let us not deſpair but that, in *Lorenzo*,
It will be ſeconded.
     Gonz. You argue well,
And 'twere a Sin in me to contradict you :
Yet we muſt not neglect the Means that's lent us
To be the Miniſters of Juſtice.
     Uber. No, Sir :
One Day giv'n to refreſh our weary'd Troops,
Tir'd with a tedious March, we'll be no longer
Coop'd

Coop'd up, but charge the Enemy in his Trenches,
And force him to a Battle.   [*Shouts within.*
    Gonz. Ha! how's this?
In such a general Time of Mourning, Shouts
And Acclamations of Joy?
           Within they cry,
Long live the Princess! Long live *Matilda!*
    Uber. *Matilda!*
The Princess' Name!
          Matilda, oft re-echo'd.

         Enter Farneze.

    Gonz. What speaks thy Haste?
    Farn. More Joy and Happiness
Than weak Words can deliver, or strong Faith
Almost give Credit to: The Princess lives.——
I saw her, kiss'd her Hand.
    Gonz. By whom deliver'd?
    Farn. That is not to be 'stall'd by my Report,
This only must be told.——As I rode forth
With some choice Troops to make Discovery
Where th' Enemy lay, and how intrench'd, a Leader
Of th' adverse Party, but unarm'd, and in
His Hand an Olive-branch, encounter'd me.
He shew'd the Great Duke's Seal that gave him Power
To parley with me: His Desires were, that
Assurance for his Safety might be granted
To his Royal Master, who came as a Friend,
And not as an Enemy, to offer to you
Conditions of Peace: I yielded to it.
This being return'd, the Duke's *Prætorium* open'd;
When suddenly, in a triumphant Chariot
Drawn by such Soldiers of his own as were
For Insolence after Victory condemn'd
Unto this slavish Office, the fair Princess
Appear'd, a Wreath of Laurel on her Head,
Her Robes majestical, their Richness far
Above all Value, as if the present Age

                      Con-

Contended that a Woman's Pomp should dim
The glitt'ring Triumphs of the *Roman Cæsars.*
—I am cut off; no Cannon's Throat now thunders,
Nor Fife nor Drum beat up a Charge; choice Musick
Ushers the Parent of Security,
Long-absent Peace.

    Manf. I know not what to think on't.
    Uber. May it poise the Expectation!

Enter Soldiers (unarm'd, with Olive Branches) Captains,
    Lorenzo, Galeazzo, Martino, Matilda, *(a Wreath*
    of Laurel on her Head, in her Chariot drawn through
    them.)

    Gonz. Thus to meet you,
Great Duke of *Tuscany,* throws Amazement on me:
But to behold my Daughter, long since mourn'd for,
And lost even to my Hopes, thus honour'd by you,
With an Excess of Comfort overwhelms me:
And yet I cannot truly call myself
Happy in this Solemnity, 'till your Highness
Vouchsafe to make me understand the Motives
That in this peaceful Way hath brought you to us.

    Lor. I must crave Licence first; for know, *Gonzaga,*
I'm subject to another's Will, and can
Nor speak nor do without Permission from her.
My curled Forehead, of late terrible
                    [*While* Lorenzo *speaks,* Uberti *and the rest*
                        present themselves to Matilda.
To those that did acknowledge me their Lord,
Is now as smooth as Rivers when no Wind stirs:
My Frowns or Smiles, that kill'd or sav'd, have lost
Their potent Awe, and Sweetness: I am transform'd
(But do not scorn the Metamorphosis)
From that fierce Thing Men held me; I am captiv'd,
And by the unresistable Force of Beauty
Led hither as a Prisoner. Is't your Pleasure that
I shall deliver those Injunctions which
Your absolute Command impos'd upon me,

Or deign yourself to speak 'em?

   Matil. Sir, I am
Your Property, you may use me as you please;
But what is in your Power and Breast to do,
No Orator can dilate so well.

   Lor. I obey you.
That I came hither as an Enemy,
With hostile Arms, to th' utter Ruin of
Your Country, what I have done makes apparent:
That Fortune seconded my Will, the late
Defeature will make good : That I resolv'd
To force the Scepter from your Hand, and make
Your Dukedom tributary, my Surprizal
Of *Mantua* your Metropolis can well witness :
And that I cannot fear the Change of Fate,
My Army, flesh'd in Blood, Spoil, Glory, Conquest,
Stand ready to maintain : Yet, I must tell you
By whom I am subdu'd, and what's the Ransom
I am commanded to lay down.

   Gonz. My Lord,
You humble yourself too much ; 'tis fitter you
Should first propose, and we consent.

   Lor. Forbear,
The Articles are here subscrib'd and sign'd
By my obedient Hand : All Prisoners
Without a Ransom set at Liberty ;
Mantua to be deliver'd up ; the Rampiers
Ruin'd in the Assault, to be repair'd ;
The Loss the Husbandman receiv'd, his Crop
Burnt up by wanton Licence of the Soldier
To be made good — with whatsoever else
You could impose on me, if you had been
The Conqu'ror, I your Captive.

   Gonz. Such a Change
Wants an Example : I must owe this Favour
To th' Clemency of the old heroic Valour,
That spar'd when it had Power to kill ; a Virtue
Buried long since, but rais'd out of the Grave
By you to grace this latter Age.

   Lor. Mistake not

The

The Caufe that did produce this good Effect,
If as fuch you receive it: 'Twas her Beauty
Wrought firft on my rough Nature; but the Virtues
Of her fair Soul, dilated in her Converfe,
That did confirm it.

   Matil. Mighty Sir, no more:
You honour her too much, that is not worthy
To be your Servant.

   Lor. I have done; and now
Would gladly underftand that you allow of
The Articles propounded.

   Gonz. Do not wrong
Your Benefits with fuch a Doubt; they are
So great and high, and with fuch Reverence
To be receiv'd, that, if I fhould profefs
I hold my Dukedom from you as your Vaffal,
Or offer'd up my Daughter as you pleafe
To be difpos'd of, in the Point of Honour
And a becoming Gratitude, 'twould not cancel
The Bond I ftand engag'd for.—But accept
Of that which I can pay: My All is yours, Sir;
Nor is there any here (though I muft grant
Some have deferv'd much from me, for fo far
I dare prefume) but will furrender up
Their Intereft to that your Highnefs fhall
Deign to pretend a Title.

   Uber. I fubfcribe not
To this Condition.

   Farn. The Services this Prince
Hath done your Grace in your moft Danger,
Are not to be fo flighted.

   Gal. 'Tis far from me
To urge my Merits; yet, I muft maintain
Howe'er my Power is lefs, my Love is more:
Nor will the gracious Princefs fcorn t'acknowledge
I've been her humble Servant.

   Lor. Smooth your Brows:
I'll not incroach upon your Right, for that were
Once more to force Affection (a Crime

X 2

With

With which should I the second Time be tainted,
I did deserve no Favour); neither will I
Make use of what is offer'd by the Duke,
Howe'er I thank his Goodness.   I'll lay by
My Power; and though I should not brook a Rival,
(What we are, well consider'd) I'll descend
To be a third Competitor.   He that can
With Love and Service best deserve the Garland,
With your Consent let him wear it; I despair not
The Trial of my Fortune.
    Gonz. Bravely offer'd,
And like yourself, great Prince.
    Uber. I must profess
I am so taken with it, that I know not
Which Way t' express my Service.
    Gal. Did I not build
Upon the Princess' Grace, I could sit down,
And hold it no Dishonour.
    Matil. How I feel
My Soul divided! All have deserv'd so well,
I know not where to fix my Choice.
    Gonz. You have
Time to consider.   Will you please to take
Possession of the Fort? Then, having tasted
The Fruits of Peace, you may at Leisure prove
Whose Plea will prosper in the Court of Love.
                                    [*Exeunt.*

The End of the Fourth Act.

ACT V. SCENE I.

Enter Alonzo, Octavio, Pisano, Maria *(with a Purse)*
Gothrio.

Alon. YOU need not doubt, Sir, were not Peace
                      proclaim'd,
And celebrated with a general Joy,   The

The high Difpleafure of the *Mantuan* Duke,
Rais'd on juft Grounds, not jealous Suppofitions.
The faving of our Lives (which, next to Heaven,
To you alone is proper) would force Mercy
For an Offence, though capital.

 Pifan. When the Conqueror
Ufes Entreaties, they are arm'd Commands
The Vanquifh'd muft not check at.

 Mar. My Piety pay the Forfeit,
If Danger come but near you! I have heard
My gracious Miftrefs often mention you,
(When I ferv'd her as a Page) and feelingly
Relate how much the Duke her Sire repented
His hafty Doom of Banifhment, in his Rage
Pronounc'd againft you.

 Oct. In a private Difference,
I grant that Innocence is a Wall of Brafs,
And fcorns the hotteft Battery : But, when
The Caufe depends between the Prince and Subject,
'Tis an unequal Competition; Juftice
Muft lay her Balance by, and ufe her Sword
For his Ends that protect it. I was banifh'd,
And, 'till revok'd from Exile, to tread on
My Sovereign's Territories with forbidden Feet,
The fevere Letter of the Law calls Death ;
Which I am fubject to in coming fo near
His Court and Perfon. But my only Child
Being provided for, her Honour falv'd too,
(I thank your noble Change) I fhall endure
Whate'er can fall, with Patience.

 Alon. You have us'd
That Medicine too long ; prepare yourfelf
For Honour in your Age, and reft fecure of't.

 Mar. Of what is your Wifdom mufing?

 Goth. I am gazing on this gorgeous Houfe; our
Cot's a Difhclout to it : It has no Sign.—What do you
call't ?

X 3

Mar.

Mar. The Court;
I've liv'd in't a Page.
　Goth. Page! very pretty :
May I not be a Page ? I am old enough,
Well-timber'd too, and I've a Beard to carry it :
Pray you, let me be your Page ; I can swear already
Upon your Pantoffle.
　Mar. What ?
　Goth. That I'll be true
Unto your Smock.
　Mar. How, Rascal ?
　Oct. Hence, and pimp
To your Rams and Ewes ; such foul Pollution is
To be whipp'd from Court. I've now no more Use of
Return to you Trough.　　　　　　　　　　[you ;
　Goth. Must I feed on Husks,
Before I have play'd the Prodigal ?
　Oct. No, I'll reward
Your Service ; live in your own Element
Like an honest Man ; all that is mine in the Cottage
I freely give you.
　Goth. Your Bottles too, that I carry
For your own Tooth ?
　Oct. Full as they are.
　Mar. And Gold,
That will replenish 'em.
　Goth. I'm made for ever.
This was done i' th' Nick.
　Oct. Why in the Nick ?
　Goth. O Sir ! 'twas well for me that you did reward
　　　　　my Service
Before you enter'd the Court ; for 'tis reported
There is a Drink of Forgetfulness, which once tasted,
Few Masters think of their Servants, who, grown old,
Are turn'd off like lame Hounds and Hunting Horses,
To starve on the Commons.
　Alon. Bitter Knave !

Enter

Enter Martinio.

There's Craft i' the clouted Shoe.[4]   Captain !
   Mart. I am glad to kifs
Your valiant Hand, and yours : But pray you, take No-
My Title's chang'd, I am a Colonel.   [tice
   Pifan. A Colonel ! where's your Regiment ?
   Mart. Not rais'd yet ;
All the old ones are cafhier'd, and we are now
To have a new Militia.   All is Peace here,
Yet I hold my Title ftill, as many do
That never faw an Enemy.
   Alon. You are pleafant,
And it becomes you.   Is the Duke ftirring ?
   Mart. Long fince,
Four Hours at leaft ; but yet not ready.
   Pifan. How ?
   Mart. Even fo ; you make a Wonder of't, but leave
Alas, he is not now (Sir) in the Camp,   [it:
To be up and arm'd upon the leaft Alarm ;
There's fomething elfe to be thought on.
Here he comes, with his Officers, new-rigg'd.

Enter Lorenzo, *Doctor, Gent. Page (employed about him
as from his Chamber.)*

   Alon. A Looking-glafs !
Upon my Head, he faw not his own Face
Thefe feven Years paft, but by Reflexion
From a bright Armour.
   Mart. Be filent, and obferve.
   Lor. So, have you done yet ?
Is your Building perfect ?
   Doct. If your Highnefs pleafe,
Here is a Water.

<hr>

4 *There's Craft i' the clouted Shoe.*

   Thus *Hamlet,* fpeaking of the Clown, fays, " That the Toe of
" the Peafant comes fo near the Heel of the Courtier, he galls his
" Kibe."   *Lar.*

X 4

Lor. To what Ufe ? my Barber
Hath wafh'd my Face already.

Doct. But this Water
Hath a ftrange Virtue in't, beyond his Art ;
It is a facred Relique, Part of that
Moft powerful Juice, which with *Medæa* made
Old *Æfon* young.

Lor. A Fable.——But fuppofe
I fhould give Credit to it, will it work
The fame Effect on me ?

Doct. I'll undertake
This will reftore the honour'd Hair that grows
Upon your Highnefs' Head and Chin, a little
Inclining unto Grey.

Lor. Inclining, Doctor ?

Doct. Pardon me, mighty Sir, I went too far ;
Not Grey at all.—I dare not flatter you,
'Tis fomething chang'd ; but this apply'd will help it
To the firft Amber-Colour, every Hair
As frefh as when, your Manhood in the Prime,
Your Grace arriv'd at Thirty.

Lor. Very well.

Doct. Then here's a precious Oil (to which the Maker
Hath not yet given a Name) will foon fill up
Thefe Dimples in your Face and Front.   I grant
They are terrible to your Enemies, and fet off
Your Frowns with Majefty : But you may pleafe
To know (as fure you do) a fmooth Afpect,
Softnefs and Sweetnefs, in the Court of Love,
Though dumb, are the prevailing Orators.

Lor. Will he new create me ?

Doct. If you deign to tafte too
Of this Confection.

Lor. I'm in Health, and need
No Phyfick.

Doct. Phyfick, Sir ! An Emprefs
(If that an Emprefs' Lungs, Sir, may be tainted
With Putrefaction) would tafte of it
That Night on which fhe were to print a Kifs

Upon

Upon the Lips of her long-abfent Lord
Returning home with Conqueft.

   Lor. 'Tis predominant
Over a ftinking Breath, is it not, Doctor?

   Doct. Cloath the Infirmity with fweeter Language;
'Tis a Prefervative that Way.

   Lor. You are then
Admitted to the Cabinets of great Ladies,
And have the Government of the borrow'd Beauties
Of fuch as write near Forty.

   Doctor. True, my good Lord,
And my Attempts have profper'd.

   Lor. Did you never
Minifter to the Princefs?

   Doct. Sir, not yet;
She's in the *April* of her Youth, and needs not
The Aids of Art, my gracious Lord: But in
The Autumn of her Age I may be ufeful,
And fworn her Highnefs' Doctor, and your Grace
Partake of the Delight.

   Lor. Slave! Witch! Impoftor!   [*Kicks him.*
Mountebank! Cheater! Traitor to great Nature!
In thy Prefumption to repair what fhe
In her immutable Decrees defign'd
For fome few Years to grow up, and then wither.
Or is't not Crime enough thus to betray
The Secrets of the weaker Sex, thy Patients,
But thou muft make the Honour of this Age,
And Envy of the Time to come, *Matilda,*
(Whofe facred Name I bow to) guilty of
A future Sin in thy ill-boding Thoughts,
Which for a Perpetuity of Youth
And Pleafure fhe difdains to act, fuch is
Her Purity and Innocence?
               [*His Foot on the Doctor's Breaft.*

   Alon. Long fince
I look'd for this Lenvoy.

   Mart. Would I were well off!
He's dang'rous in thefe Humours.

                                      Oct.

Oct. Stand conceal'd.

Doct. O Sir, have Mercy! in my Thought I never
Offended you.

Lor. Me ? moſt of all, thou Monſter!
What a Mock-man Property in thy Intent
Would'ſt thou have made me ? a meer Pathick to
Thy Deviliſh Art, had I given Suffrage to it.
Are my Grey Hairs, the Ornament of Age,
And held a Bleſſing by the wiſeſt Men,
And for ſuch warranted by Holy Writ,[s]
To be conceal'd, as if they were my Shame ?
Or plaiſter up theſe Furrows in my Face,
As if I were a painted Bawd or Whore?
By ſuch baſe Means if that I could aſcend
To the Height of all my Hopes, their full Fruition
Would not wipe off the Scandal. No, thou Wretch!
Thy coz'ning Water and adult'rate Oil
I thus pour in thine Eyes, and tread to Duſt
Thy loath'd Confection, with thy Trumperies :
Vaniſh for ever !

Mart. You've your Fee, as I take it,
Dear *Domine Doctor !* I'll be no Sharer with you.

[*Exit Doctor.*

Lor. I'll court her like myſelf ; theſe rich Adornments
And Jewels, worn by me an Abſolute Prince ;
My Order too, of which I am the Sovereign,
Can meet no ill Conſtruction : Yet 'tis far
From my Imagination to believe
She can be taken with ſublimed Clay,
The Silk-worm's Spoils, or rich Embroideries :
Nor muſt I borrow Helps from Power or Greatneſs ;
But as a loyal Lover plead my Cauſe,
If I can feelingly expreſs my Ardour,
And make her ſenſible of the much I ſuffer

-----

[s] ————*Warranted by Holy Writ.*
This alludes to the *Proverbs* of *Solomon,* who ſays,

" The Hoary Head is a Crown of Glory, if it be found in the
Way of Righteouſneſs.   Chap. xvi. ver. 31.

In

In Hopes and Fears, and she vouchsafe to take
Compassion on me.—Ha! Compassion?
The Word sticks in my Throat: What's here that tells
I do descend too low? Rebellious Spirit,   [me
I conjure thee to leave me: There is now
No Contradiction or Declining left,
I must and will go on.
    Mart. The Tempest's laid;
You may present yourselves.
    Alon. My gracious Lord!
    Pisan. Your humble Vassal.
    Lor. Ha! both living?
    Alon. Sir,
We owe our Lives to this good Lord, and make it
Our humble Suit ———
    Lor. Plead for yourselves: We stand
Yet unresolv'd whether your Knees or Prayers
Can save the Forfeiture of your own Heads:
Though we have put our Armour off.—Your Pardon
For leaving the Camp without our Licence
Is not yet sign'd.   At some more fit Time wait us.
                    [*Exit* Lor. *and Attendants.*
    Alon. How's this?
    Mart. 'Tis well it is no worse; I met with
A rougher Entertainment, yet I had
Good Cards to shew. He's parcel mad, you'll find him
Every Hour in a several Mood, this foolish Love
Is such a Shuttlecock; but all will be well
When a better Fit comes on him, never doubt it.
                              [*Exeunt.*

S C E N E II.

Enter Gonzaga, Uberti, Farneze, Manfroy.

    Gonz. How do you find her?
    Uber. Thankful for my Service,
And yet she gives me little Hope; my Rival
Is too great for me.
    Gonz. The Great Duke, you mean?
                                   Uber.

Uber. Who elfe ? the *Millanois,* although he be
A compleat Gentleman, I am fure defpairs
More than myfelf.

· *Farn.* A high Eftate, with Women,
Takes Place of all Defert.

Uber. I muft ftand my Fortune.

Enter Lorenzo *and Attendants.*

Manf. The Duke of *Florence,* Sir !

Gonz. Your Highnefs' Prefence
Anfwers my Wifh. Your private Ear :—I have us'd
My beft Perfuafion with a Father's Power
To work my Daughter to your Ends ; yet fhe,
Like a fmall Bark on a tempeftuous Sea,
Tofs'd here and there by oppofite Winds, refolves not
At which Port to put in, this Prince's merits ;
Your Grace and Favour ; nor is fhe unmindful
Of· the brave Acts (under your Pardon, Sir,
I· needs muft call them fo) *Hortenfio*
Hath done to gain her good Opinion of him :
'All thefe together tumbling in her Fancy,
Do much diftract her.   I have Spies upon her,
And am affur'd this inftant Hour fhe gives
Hortenfio private Audience ; I will bring you
Where we will fee and hear all.

Lor. You oblige me.

Uber. I do not like this Whifpering.

Gonz. Fear no foul Play.   [*Exeunt.*

SCENE III.

Enter Galeazzo, Beatrice, *and two Waiting-Women.*

1 *Wom.* The Princefs, Sir, long fince expected you ;
And, would I beg a Thanks, I could tell you that
I've often mov'd her for you.

Gal. I'm your Servant.

                                        Enter

Enter Matilda.

Beat. She's come; there are others I muſt place to hear
The Conference.   [*Exit.*

   1 *Wom.* Is't your Excellency's Pleaſure
That we attend you?

   Matil. No; wait me in the Gallery.

   1 *Wom.* Would each of us, Wench, had a Sweetheart
To paſs away the Time!   [too,

   2 *Wom.* There I join with you.
                     [*Exit Waiting-Women.*

   Matil. I fear this is the laſt Time we ſhall meet.

   Gal. Heaven forbid!

Enter (above) Beatrice, Lorenzo, Gonzaga, Uberti,
Farneze.

   Matil. O my *Hortenſio!*
In me behold the Miſery of Greatneſs,
And that which you call Beauty.   Had I been
Of a more low Condition, I might
Have call'd my Will and Faculties mine own,
Not ſeeing that which was to be belov'd
With other's Eyes: But now, ay me! moſt wretched
And miſerable Princeſs! in my Fortune
To be too much engag'd for Service done me,
It being impoſſible to make Satisfaction
To my ſo many Creditors; all deſerving,
I can keep Touch with none.

   Lor. A ſad *Exordium!*

   Matil. You lov'd me long, and without Hope, (alas,
I die to think on't!) *Parma*'s Prince, invited
With a too partial Report of what
I was, and might be to him, left his Country
To fight in my Defence.   Your brave Atchievements
I' the War, and what you did for me, unſpoken,
(Becauſe I would not force the Sweetneſs of

                           Your

Your Modesty to a Blush) are written here :
And, that there might be nothing wanting to
Sum up my numerous Engagements (never
In my Hopes to be cancell'd) the Great Duke,
Our mortal Enemy, when my Father's Country
Lay open to his Fury, and the Spoil
Of the victorious Army, and I brought
Into his Power, hath shewn himself so noble,
So full of strictest Honour, Temperance,
And all Virtues that can set off a Prince,
That, though I cannot render him that Respect
I would, I'm bound in Thankfulness t' admire him.
   Gal. 'Tis acknowledg'd, and on your Part
To be return'd.
   Matil. But oh! how can I,
Without the Brand of foul Ingratitude
To you, and Prince *Uberti ?*
   Gal. Hear me, Madam,
And what your Servant shall with Zeal deliver,
As a *Dædalean* Clew may guide you out of
This Labyrinth of Destruction.   He that loves
His Mistress truly, should prefer her Honour
And Peace of Mind, above the glutting of
His rav'nous Appetite : He should affect
But with a fit Restraint, and not take from her
To give himself : He should make it the Height
Of his Ambition, if it lie in
His stretch'd-out Nerves t' effect it, though she fly in
An eminent Place, to add Strength to her Wings,
And mount her higher, though he fall himself
Into the bottomless Abyss ; or else
The Services he offers are not real,
But counterfeit.
   Matil. What can *Hortensio*
Infer from this ?
   Gal. That I stand bound in Duty
(Though in the Act I take my last Farewel
Of Comfort in this Life) to sit down willingly,
And move my Suit no farther.   I confess,

While

While you were in Danger, and Heav'n's Mercy made
      me
Its Inftrument to preferve you, (which your Goodnefs
Priz'd far above the Merit) I was bold
To feed my ftarv'd Affection with falfe Hopes
I might be worthy of you : For know, Madam,
How mean foever I appear'd in *Mantua*,
I had in Expectation a Fortune,
Though not poffefs'd of 't, that encourag'd me
With Confidence to prefer my Suit, and not
To fear the Prince *Uberti* as my Rival.
    Gonz. I ever thought him more than what he feem'd.
    Lor. Pray you, forbear.
    Gal. But when the Duke of *Florence*
Put in his Plea, in my Confideration
Weighing well what he is, as you muft grant him,
A *Mars* of Men in Arms ; and, thofe put off,
The great Example for a Kingly Courtier
To imitate : Annex to thefe his Wealth,
Of fuch a large Extent, as other Monarchs
Call him the King of Coin ; and, what's above all,
His lawful Love, with all the Happinefs
This Life can fancy, from him flowing to you ;
The true Affection which I have ever borne you,
Does not alone command me to defift,
But, as a faithful Counfellor, to advife you
To meet and welcome that Felicity
Which haftes to crown your Virtues.
    Lor. We muft break off this Parley.
Something I have to fay.   [*Exeunt above.*
    Matil. In Tears I thank
Your Care of my Advancement ; but I dare not
Follow your Counfel.   Shall fuch Piety
Pafs unrewarded ? Such a pure Affection,
For any Ends of mine, be undervalu'd ?
Avert it, Heaven ! I will be thy *Matilda*,
Or ceafe to be : No other Heat but what
Glows from thy pureft Flames, fhall warm this Bofom,
                                                    Nor

Nor *Florence*, nor all Monarchs of the Earth
Shall keep thee from me.

Enter Lorenzo, Gonzaga, Uberti, Farneze, Manfroy,
two Waiting-Women.

   Gal. I fear, gracious Lady,
Our Conference hath been o'erheard.
   Matil. The better :
Your Part is acted ; give me Leave at Diftance
To zany it. —— Sir, on my Knees thus proftrate
Before your Feet.   [*To* Lorenzo.
   Lor. This muft not be : I fhall
Both wrong myfelf and you in fuff'ring it.
   Matil. I will grow here, and weeping thus turn Mar-
Unlefs you hear and grant the firft Petition   [ble,
A Virgin, and a Princefs, ever tendred :
Nor doth the Suit concern poor me alone,
It hath a ftronger Reference to you
And to your Honour ; and, if you deny it,
Both Ways you fuffer.   Remember, Sir, you were not
Born only for yourfelf ; Heav'n's liberal Hand
Defign'd you to command a potent Nation,
Gave you heroic Valour, which you have
Abus'd in making unjuft War upon
A Neighbour-Prince, a Chriftian ; while the *Turk*,
Whofe Scourge and Terror you fhould be, fecurely
Waftes the *Italian* Confines : 'Tis in you
To force him to pull in his horned Crefcents,
And 'tis expected from you.
   Lor. I have been in
A Dream, and now begin to wake.
   Matil. And will you
Forbear to reap the Harveft of fuch Glories,
Now ripe, and at full Growth, for the Embraces
Of a flight Woman ? or exchange your Triumphs
For Chamber-pleafures ? melt your able Nerves
(That fhould with your victorious Sword make Way
Through th'Armies of your Enemies) in loofe

And

And wanton Dalliance?   Be yourfelf, great Sir,
The Thunderbolt of War, and fcorn to fever
Two Hearts long fince united : Your Example
May teach the Prince *Uberti* to fubfcribe
To that which you allow of.
    Lor. The fame Tongue
That charm'd my Sword out of my Hand, and threw
A frozen Numbnefs on my active Spirit,
Hath difenchanted me.   Rife, faireft Princefs !
And, that it may appear I do receive
Your Counfel as infpir'd from Heav'n, I will
Obey and follow it : I am your Debtor,
And muft confefs you've lent my weaken'd Reafon
New Strengths once more to hold a full command
Over my Paffions.   Here to the World
I freely do profefs that I difclaim
All Intereft in you, and give up my Title,
Such as it is, to you, Sir; and, as far
As I have Power, thus join your Hands.
    Gonz. To yours
I add my full Confent.
    Uber. I am loft, *Farneze.*
    Farn. Much nearer to the Port than you fuppofe :
In me our Laws fpeak, and forbid this Contract.
    Matil. Ay me ! new Stops ?
    Gal. Shall we be ever crofs'd thus ?
    Farn. There is an Act upon Record, confirm'd
By your wife Predeceffors, that no Heir
Of *Mantua* (as queftionlefs the Princefs
Is the undoubted one) muft be join'd in Marriage,
But where the Match may ftrengthen the Eftate
And Safety of the Dukedom.   Now this Gentleman,
However I muft ftile him Honourable,
And of a high Defert, having no Power
To make this good in his Alliance, ftands
Excluded by our Laws ; whereas this Prince,
Of equal Merit, brings to *Mantua*
The Power and Principality of *Parma :*
And therefore, fince the Great Duke hath let fall

His Plea, there lives no Prince that juftlier can
Challenge the Princefs' Favour.
    Lor. Is this true, Sir ?
    Gonz. I cannot contradict it.

Enter Manfroy.

    Manf. There's an Ambaffador
From *Milan*, that defires a prefent Audience ;
His Bufinefs is of higheft Confequence,
As he affirms : I know him for a Man
Of the beft Rank and Quality.
    ·*Gal.* From *Milan ?*
    Gonz. Admit him.

Enter Ambaffador and Julio *with a Letter, which he pre-*
fents on his Knee to Galeazzo.

—How ? fo low !
    Amb. I am forry, Sir,
To be the Bringer of this heavy News :
But fince it muft be known ————
    Gal. Peace reft with him !
I fhall find fitter Time to mourn his Lofs.
My faithful Servant too, *Julio !*
    Jul. I am o'erjoy'd,
To fee your Highnefs fafe.
    Gal. Pray you perufe this,
And there you'll find that the Objection
The Lord *Farneze* made, is fully anfwer'd.
    Gonz. The great *John Galeas* dead ?
    Lor. And this his Brother,
The abfolute Lord of *Milan.*
    Matil. I'm reviv'd.
    Uber. There's no contending againft Deftiny,
I wifh both Happinefs.

Enter

Lor. Marry'd, *Alonzo?*
I will falute your Lady, fhe's a fair one,
And feal your Pardon on her Lips.
Gonz. Octavio,
Welcome e'en to my Heart! Rife, I fhould kneel
To thee for Mercy.
Oct. The poor Remainder of
My Age fhall truly ferve you.
Matil. You refemble a Page I had, *Afcanio.*
Mar. I am your Highnefs' Servant ftill.
Lor. All ftand amaz'd
At this unlook'd-for Meeting: But defer
Your feveral Stories. Fortune here hath fhewn
Her various Power; but Virtue in the End
Is crown'd with Laurel: Love hath done his Parts too;
And mutual Friendfhip, after bloody Jars,
Will cure the Wounds received in our Wars.
[*Exeunt omnes.*

EPILOGUE.

E P I L O G U E.

PRAY you, Gentlemen, keep your Seats; some-
          thing I would
Deliver to gain Favour, if I could,
To us, and the ſtill doubtful Author.   He,
When I deſir'd an Epilogue, anſwer'd me,
" 'Twas to no Purpoſe : He muſt ſtand his Fate,
" Since all Intreaties now would come too late ;
" You being long ſince reſolv'd what you would ſay
" Of him, or us, as ye riſe, or of the Play."
A ſtrange old Fellow ! yet this ſullen Mood
Would quickly leave him, might it be underſtood
You part not hence diſpleas'd.   I am deſign'd
To give him certain Notice : If you find
Things worth your Liking, ſhew it.   Hope and Fear,
Though different Paſſions, have the ſelf-ſame Ear.

E N D of V O L. III.